P9-DHJ-898

KIDNAPPED

"I hope you make it back home," Susannah said.

He stared at her a moment, his dark gaze moving over her face. She shivered, wondering if it was caused by the cold wind stirring the dust, or by the sudden desire that blazed in the Indian's black eyes.

She swallowed hard, knowing she would never see him again, wondering why the thought filled her with such sadness. She didn't really know him, after all.

"Su-san-nah." He closed the distance between them. Slowly, he lifted his hand and caressed her cheek. She had not realized how tall he was. The top of her head barely reached his shoulder. Oh, Lord, she thought, he's going to kiss me. She swayed toward him, then gasped as he caught her around the waist and thrust her onto the stallion's back.

Before she could think or cry out, he was up behind her, his heels drumming into the horse's sides. The stallion bolted forward.

LEISURE BOOKS **NEW YORK CITY**

To Anthony Amodeo
Computer whiz extraordinaire
Who keeps my computer running
at peak efficiency.
Thanks Anthony!

A LEISURE BOOK®

March 1997

Published by

Dorchester Publishing Co., Inc.
276 Fifth Avenue
New York, NY 10001

Printed in the United States of America.

Prologue

The Black Hills
Fall 1864

Tate Sapa stood alone at the foot of his mother's burial scaffold, his arms extended over his head, reaching upward in supplication as he pleaded with the Great Spirit for guidance. The eagle feather he wore on a rawhide loop around his wrist fluttered in the faint breeze that whispered over the holy mountain.

Tate Sapa lifted his voice to the heavens in mighty prayer, pleading for the welfare of his people. The old ones had lost hope, the women were discouraged and tired, the children were hungry and afraid. And the young men . . .

As always, the young men were eager for war, anxious to prove their bravery in battle, to count coup on the enemy. The blood of their parents, their wives, and their children watered the ground, crying out for vengeance against the Blue Coats. The hearts of the young men were filled with anger, with the need to fight, to seek vengeance for the wrongs inflicted upon the people by the *wasichu*.

Tate Sapa understood their anger. His blood burned as hotly as theirs with the need for revenge. He, too, had lost loved ones. His gentle mother, his young sister, both had fallen before the soldier coats. And yet, as much as he yearned to lead the warriors into battle, to ease his anger by shedding the blood of his enemies, Tate Sapa knew war was not the answer. The time to fight had passed. The Lakota were brave warriors, fearless in battle, but their numbers grew smaller each year, while the *wasichu* seemed to be as numerous as the blades of grass that covered the prairie in summer. The Lakota did not have an endless supply of weapons and ammunition and young men.

The fate of his people rested heavily on his shoulders. "Help me, *Wakan Tanka*, show me what I must do."

He stared into the sun, oblivious to the chill in the air, to the cold wind that sent shivers down his spine. He had been three days without food and water. Hunger gnawed at his belly, his tongue felt thick in his mouth, his throat dry as a buffalo wallow in summer.

Weak with hunger, burdened by despair, he dropped to his knees and bowed his head.

"Help me, *Wakan Tanka*," he cried softly. "Help me lest I perish."

Hands resting on his thighs, Tate Sapa stared into the distance, listening to the wail of the winter wind as it howled across the mountaintop. His home was here, in the heart of the *Paha Sapa*. Indeed, this land was the heart of his people. Stretching away from the sacred hills lay a land as empty as the sky, patchy with buffalo grass, sharp green cactus, and sage. But the hills themselves abounded with life—deer, elk, porcupines, beaver, badgers, squirrels. The wolf and the bear made their home in the sacred hills. Once, *pte* had roamed the prairies, the great buffalo herds causing the very earth to shake as they passed by. But the *wasichu* had hunted the shaggy beasts relentlessly until there were only hundreds where there had once been countless thousands.

It was one more reason why he hated the whites. They killed the buffalo indiscriminately, taking the hides, sometimes the tongue and the tail, leaving the meat to rot in the sun.

He shivered as the day turned suddenly dark. Looking up, he saw black clouds racing across the sky. Thunder shook the earth beneath him; lightning crackled overhead.

And there, between one lightning burst and the next, he saw a vision of a white woman, saw her as close and as clearly as if she had been standing before him. She had dark brown eyes, a generous mouth, a fine straight nose, and lips redder than any he had ever seen. Curly brown hair fell to her shoulders. The shirt she wore was white, with long full sleeves; the pants were snug blue denim that emphasized every feminine curve. In her hands she held a piece of paper, and on the paper he saw his own likeness, clearly drawn.

He stared at her, at his image, in astonishment, wondering how a white woman had captured his likeness. What did it mean? What cruel trick were the gods playing on him, to send him a vision of a white woman when he had come seeking their help?

A bolt of lightning sizzled across the sky, the brightness blinding him, and in those few seconds when his sight was gone, a kaleidoscope of disjointed images flashed through his mind—Blue Coats plundering a Lakota village, an iron-barred house, a noose swinging in the wind, bodies lying broken and bloody in a green valley, and over all, the face of the white woman, her dark brown eyes filled with tears. . . .

In the blink of an eye, the images were gone, the sky was clear, and the sun was shining as before.

Rising to his feet, Tate Sapa fastened the eagle feather to the scaffold that held his mother's remains. He stood there a moment, and then he began the treacherous climb down the mountain, the woman's image imprinted in his mind, his heart heavy with the knowledge that, in some way he did not understand, his life had been forever changed.

Chapter One

Los Angeles, CA
April 1997

Susannah Kingston sat staring at her computer's blank blue screen and wondered if her career as a romance writer was over before it had really begun. She'd had dry spells before, days when she just wasn't in the mood to write, when the words didn't flow easily or wouldn't come at all, but never anything like this.

Every day for the past two weeks, she had planted herself in front of her computer, her mind as blank as the screen. Maybe it had been bound to happen. Maybe after ten contemporary romance novels and a couple of short stories, her creative well had gone dry.

She had tried taking long walks in the park,

hoping a little exercise might stir her creative juices. She had tried watching romantic movies like *Somewhere in Time* and *Legends of the Fall*. She had tried reading some of her favorite romance novels over again, hoping for a little inspiration. She had listened to nothing but soft romantic music, and taken even longer walks. Nothing had helped.

She grimaced as she switched off the computer. There was no maybe about it—she was definitely out of ideas.

Leaning back in her chair, she reached for a bite-size Milky Way. When in doubt, eat chocolate.

Susannah stared out the window that overlooked her tiny backyard. Maybe something would click at the next Romance Writers of America workshop. Her best friend, Vivian Hardiman, had talked her into going to the meeting, suggesting that a change of pace might be what she needed.

Susannah unwrapped another dark chocolate Milky Way and popped it into her mouth. Maybe Vivian was right. Maybe it was time to switch from short contemporaries to longer historicals. With any luck at all, the Wild West reenactors who were putting on the workshop might be able to help. If they could just ignite a spark, plant the germ of an idea . . . but she doubted it would happen. She had never cared much for the Old West. All that dirt and grit. She didn't like horses or guns or wild Indians, didn't swoon at the thought of being rescued by some arrogant male, but what the heck, she had nothing to lose.

And maybe, just maybe, something would click and she would come up with an idea that would send her next book flying to the top of the bestseller lists.

The meeting place was more crowded than usual. Susannah wandered through the hall, nodding to several of the writers as she made her way to a display table laden with antique guns and rifles.

Susannah knew several romance writers who wished they had been born back in the days of the wild and woolly West, but she had never been one of them. Why anyone would want to live in the past, in a time before dishwashers and microwaves, indoor plumbing and computers, was beyond her. Not for her the rough-and-tumble life of the Old West. She was perfectly happy living in her air-conditioned condo, driving a car instead of riding a horse, wearing jeans and a sweatshirt instead of mountains of petticoats and high-button shoes. Vivian insisted there was a mystique to the Old West, a fascination for a time gone by, but Susannah was positive that life in the Old West was nothing like the stuff romance novels were made of.

She spent the next two hours listening to the reenactors talk about life on the plains: about clothing, weapons, childbirth and contraception, food storage and preparation.

By the time the workshop was over, she had an even deeper appreciation for the ease of life in the nineties. No wonder women in days gone by had grown old before their time! She tried to imagine what it would be like if she had to draw water from a well, or, worse, a river, if she had to wash her clothes on a scrub board in a wooden tub, gather wood for a fire, bake bread from scratch. She looked down at her jeans and shirt and tried to imagine what it would be like to wear bloomers, a corset, a million petticoats, a bustle, long cotton stockings, and high-button shoes. The very idea was enough to make her shudder. She didn't even like wearing a bra!

"Wasn't it great!" Sandy Browning exclaimed. "I've got so many ideas, I don't know where to start."

"That's terrific." Susannah pasted a smile on her face and tried to look happy. "Listen, I'm going home."

"Yeah, me, too," Sandy said. "I want to get these ideas on paper before I forget. See you at the next meeting."

"Right."

Susannah was about to leave for home when she saw it—a faded 8 × 10 black-and-white photograph of an Indian warrior standing in front of what looked like a jail of some kind judging from the thick iron bars on the window.

Wondering how she had missed it before, Susannah stopped at the table, mesmerized by the warrior's countenance. His eyes were dark and compelling, set in a face that managed to be beautiful and masculine at the same time. His nose was blade straight, his jaw strong and unyielding, his cheekbones high and well-defined. There was an eagle feather tied in his hair—long black hair that flowed like a dark river over his bare shoulders. He wore only a loincloth and moccasins.

"He's something, isn't he?"

Susannah glanced up to see Vivian standing behind her. Susannah and Vivian had met at an RWA meeting four years before and had become instant friends. Viv was a trifle plump, with curly blond hair and gray eyes. She was also one of the most energetic people Susannah had ever known. Like Susannah, she had published a number of romance novels, although Viv wrote historicals.

"He's something all right," Susannah agreed. "Such a strong, handsome face. And his eyes . . ." She laughed self-consciously. "He seems to be looking at me across the mists of time."

"I wonder who he is?" Vivian mused aloud.

"His name was Black Wind."

Susannah smiled at the reenactor who had answered Vivian's question. The man was tall and blond, with a sweeping cavalry-style moustache. He was dressed like an Army officer from 1875 or so.

"Larry Brightman," he said, extending his hand.

"Vivian Hardiman. And this is my friend, Susannah Kingston."

"Pleased to meet you both," he replied politely.

"Where was this picture taken?" Susannah asked.

"Fort Collier, South Dakota. He was a prisoner there."

"Why was he imprisoned?"

"They caught him butchering a cow stolen

from a white man. The Army arrested him and sentenced him to three years hard labor."

"They sentenced him to three years in jail for stealing a cow!" Susannah exclaimed. "Maybe he was hungry."

"I'm sure he was," Brightman said with a shrug. "Back then, they were all hungry."

"What happened to him?"

Brightman shook his head. "No one knows. It was said he killed a soldier in a fight over a white woman. They were going to hang him, but . . ."

"But?"

"Well, no one really knows what happened to him. He could have been hanged, I guess. Records from that far back are sketchy, at best." He glanced across the hall. "Excuse me, I've got to start packing up my gear."

"Is there any chance I could have this photo?"

"No, I don't think so."

"Please. I'm writing a book and he looks just the way I see my hero. I'll be glad to pay you for it."

"Well . . ." Larry frowned. "Twenty-five dollars and it's yours."

"Done," Susannah agreed, and paid him before he could change his mind.

Picking up the picture, she held it against her breast. *Black Wind*. She said his name in her mind, felt a surge of heat flow through her.

"Do you want to go out for coffee?" Vivian asked. "Stu's mom is watching the kids. She won't mind if I'm gone the rest of the day. Heck, she probably wouldn't mind if I left town and never came back."

Susannah grinned. "Are you having trouble with your mother-in-law again?"

"No more than usual," Viv replied with a melodramatic sigh. "I'm too fat, Stu's too thin, I don't pay enough attention to the girls, my house isn't clean enough, I spend too much time writing." She grabbed Susannah by the arm and dragged her toward the coffee shop. "Come on, Suse. Humor me."

"Why not?" Susannah said. "There's no one waiting for me at home." Any excuse to put off sitting down at the computer, she mused.

In the restaurant, they took a booth in the back and ordered pie and coffee. For a moment, they talked about writing and about Viv's kids. And then came the topic Susannah had been dreading.

"So," Vivian said, leaning back in her seat, "still looking for Mr. Right?"

Susannah shook her head. "There's no such thing."

"Of course there is! Everyone has a perfect match somewhere."

"Yeah, right."

"Listen, Suse, Stu's got a cousin . . ."

Susannah held up her hand. She had just ended a two-year relationship and she wasn't quite ready to start over again. It still hurt to think of her ex, to know that Troy had been unfaithful to her.

"I'm not ready to get on that merry-go-round again, Viv. Not yet." Perhaps never.

Susannah smiled to take the sting out of her words. Vivian meant well. She was happily married, with two darling little girls and a thriving career. And like all happily married women, Vivian wanted the same thing for everyone she knew.

"More coffee?"

Susannah glanced up at the waitress. "No, thank you." She looked down at the photograph on the seat beside her. Silly as it sounded, she wanted to go home and be alone with her Indian.

She tossed a couple of dollars on the table, then stood up and gave Vivian a hug. "I'm out of here, girlfriend. Give my love to Stu and the kids."

Susannah spent the next five days haunting every library and historical museum in town, searching for more information on Black Wind, but to no avail. She learned quite a bit about Crazy Horse, Sitting Bull, and General George Armstrong Custer along the way, as well as a good bit of Lakota history and lore, but nothing about the man called Black Wind.

And then, quite by accident, she saw an ad in the newspaper for a powwow. She quickly jotted down the time and place, thinking that she might go if nothing better turned up.

Chapter Two

The following Saturday morning, bright and early, Susannah drove to Orange County.

The parking lot was already crowded by the time she arrived. Joining the crowd, she crossed the pavement toward the fairgrounds.

She heard the sudden crackle of a PA system announcing that the dancing was about to start. The distant beat of a drum could be heard over the rising din of voices as she made her way to the dance area. She passed numerous booths along the way, pausing to look at brightly colored kachina dolls, at paintings done on canvas and deer hide, on rocks and wood. There were a variety of rattles, gourds, and ceremonial masks. There were buckskin shirts and colorful calico dresses, feathered war bonnets and beaded moccasins, spears, and knives of all sizes, the handles

21

made of wood or bone or metal. Several booths sold audio cassettes of Indian music, as well as flutes and drums in assorted shapes and sizes.

At the dance arena, Susannah sat down on a wooden bench next to a young Indian woman and three small children. The woman wore jeans, a T-shirt, and boots. Her long black braids were tied with red ribbon. The kids wore shorts and tank tops.

The youngest, a girl of about four with enormous black eyes, smiled shyly at Susannah, revealing a pair of dimples. "My daddy is going to dance," she announced proudly.

Susannah smiled back at the little girl, then turned her attention to the dance arena as the emcee asked everyone to please rise and remove their hats. Then a single high falsetto rose on the air, to be followed by several others.

Susannah glanced at the people nearby, wondering if they understood what was being said.

"This is the grand entry song."

"What?" Susannah turned toward the Indian woman.

"You looked confused," the woman said, smiling. "Is this your first powwow?"

"Yes."

"I thought so. After the grand entry song comes the flag song."

Susannah listened to the Lakota words, wishing she knew what the singer was saying.

The Indian woman translated for her. *"Tun'ka-s'ilayapi, tawapaha kin'han'oihan'ke s'ni najin'kte lo. Iyohlateya, oyate kihan'wicicag'in'kte ca, leca-mon'welo.* It means the Grand Father's banner

22

will stand forever. Underneath it, the people will grow, so I do this."

"Do this?"

"It means he will honor the flag."

"Oh, thank you," Susannah said. Following the others, she sat down. "I, that is . . ." Susannah paused, afraid she might be committing some terrible breach of etiquette if she asked the woman what tribe she belonged to.

"My name is Cindy Two Crows," the Indian woman said.

"Susannah Kingston."

"What brings you here today?"

"I'm a writer," Susannah replied.

"Oh?"

"I write romance novels," Susannah explained. "I'm here doing research for my next book."

"It's about Indians?"

"Well, sort of," Susannah said, suddenly embarrassed. "My hero is going to be Sioux."

"Oh, one of those kinds of books," Cindy said, grinning broadly. "I love them."

"Do you read romance novels?"

"Of course. How many books have you written?"

"Ten."

The woman lifted her eyebrows, clearly impressed. "What name do you write under?"

"My own. Susannah Kingston."

"Kingston, sure, I've read some of your books."

"Really?"

Cindy nodded. "I read the last one, *Marriage on Her Mind*. It was really good."

"Thank you."

Cindy nodded toward the dance circle. "This is called the Rabbit Dance. It's sort of like an Indian waltz. The words are usually about unfulfilled love, or a loved one who is far away. There are also honoring songs and giveaway songs."

Susannah nodded, her eyes drawn to the circle where several young women were dancing, their bodies moving in graceful rhythm to the beat of the drum. Bending slightly, they made subtle movements as they slowly turned from side to side. Their costumes were beautiful buckskin dresses with heavily beaded yokes. Each girl carried a shawl over her arm and held a fan and a matching beaded purse.

As the morning wore on, she saw that Indians of all ages danced, from children barely able to walk to elderly men and women. Susannah was mesmerized by the multicolored costumes, the willowy movements of the women in their long fringed shawls, the intricate steps of a handsome young man doing a hoop dance. He twirled and bent and twisted every which way, his body moving fluidly as he passed the hoops over his body— two hoops, four, six, then eight, each movement producing a different effect, each one more complex than the last.

The sun beat down upon her head, the scent of dust and fry bread filled her nostrils. She heard the whir of a snow cone machine.

In need of something cool to drink, she thanked Cindy for explaining the dances to her and made her way to the refreshment stand. She bought a large cup of root beer, heavy on the ice, then went to stroll through the booths, wanting to buy a souvenir of some kind to take home with her.

She bypassed T-shirts and vests and scarfs, dreamcatchers in a variety of sizes and colors, Indian dolls, brightly beaded chokers, baskets, a wide assortment of jewelry crafted in silver and turquoise, fetishes carved in onyx. She saw much that was pretty, but nothing she wanted to take home.

Disappointed, she was about to turn away when she saw a single black-and-white feather attached to a loop of rawhide. Hanging from a post, it fluttered in the breeze, as if beckoning her.

Lifting the feather from a hook, she ran one finger lightly over the spine, surprised by the warmth of it, the way it seemed to conform to her hand, inviting her touch. She knew, in that moment, that she had to have it, knew, somehow, that it was meant to be hers.

"Can I help you, miss?"

Susannah smiled at the man standing behind the counter. Tall and lean, he was dressed in a pair of faded blue jeans, moccasins, a long-sleeved Western shirt, and a buckskin vest that had a moon and stars painted on one side and a slash of lightning painted on the other. He wore his long gray hair in twin braids that reached his waist.

"How much do you want for this?" Susannah asked, holding up the feather.

The man shook his head. "It is not for sale."

"It isn't? Why not?"

"It is a Lakota prayer feather," the man explained, taking it from her wrist. "It is very old, and sacred to my people."

"But I've got to have it."

He looked at her intently, his deep black eyes seeming to look at her and through her, almost as though he could read her mind, her heart. "Give me your hand."

"What?"

"Your hand," he repeated, and extended his own.

Susannah felt a chill of unease skitter down her spine. She was almost tempted to tell him to just forget it. Almost. She stared at his hand. His skin was brown and wrinkled, like sunburned leather. His palm was heavily calloused.

Her heart began to beat faster as she placed her hand in his, felt his fingers, surprisingly strong for such an old man, curl around hers. He closed his eyes, his grasp tightening. Susannah's breath caught in her throat as the image of a man standing atop a high mountain flashed through her mind. For an instant, she thought she heard someone chanting to the sound of a distant drum.

With a nod, the old Indian released her hand and opened his eyes. "You are the one," he murmured, his voice thick with wonder.

"Excuse me?"

"Take the feather. It is yours."

"Oh, thank you," she said, disconcerted by the man's intense gaze. "How much do you want for it?"

The man shook his head. "It is yours."

"That's very nice of you," Susannah said, puzzled by the man's peculiar attitude, "but I couldn't . . ."

The man silenced her with a wave of his hand. "This is no ordinary feather," he said somberly. "It is *wakan*."

"*Wakan?*"

"Holy. You must be careful with it."

"I will. Are you sure I can't pay you for it?"

"Very sure. Things that are sacred must not be sold." His dark-eyed gaze met hers again. "Eagle feathers are sacred to the Lakota people. This is a medicine feather. If you are worthy, it will bring you that which you most desire." Reverently, he placed it in her hand. "Remember," he warned, his voice solemn, "it is a prayer feather."

"Yes, I will," Susannah replied, wondering what, exactly, he was warning her to be careful of. "Thank you so much."

At home, she went immediately to her office and placed the feather beside the photograph of the Indian, which she had framed. They looked well together, she mused as she sat down and switched on her computer.

For a moment, she stared at the blank screen, thinking of Western movies she had seen and historical novels she had read in the past, and then, like a flood that could no longer be restrained, the story unfolded in her mind. She saw it clearly, from beginning to end. Words began to pour out of her, almost faster than she could type them.

Four hours later, feeling pleased and weary, she sat back in her chair. It was going to be the best story she had ever written, the break-out book that would make her name a household word.

Stretching her arms over her head, she glanced at the picture of the Indian and smiled. Tomorrow, she would have to call Vivian and tell her she had been right, after all. Changing from contemporary to historical had been just the boost she needed.

Susannah ran a finger over the Indian's picture. Having a handsome hunk for inspiration hadn't hurt, either.

A breeze wafted through the open window beside her desk, stirring the feather. With a smile, Susannah picked it up and twirled it between her thumb and forefinger. The Indian who had given it to her had told her it was old. How old, she wondered? Or had he just said that? There had been no reason for him to lie; he hadn't been trying to coax her into buying anything. And what was all that nonsense about her being the one? She frowned. What else had he said? Something about the feather being holy and bringing her the desires of her heart.

She ran her finger lightly over the feather, wondering why it felt warm to the touch. Little frissons of heat seemed to travel from her hand all the way up her arm to settle in the region of her heart. Maybe it really was magic . . .

She shook off the notion, certain she was just being fanciful. She was a writer, after all, blessed with an extremely vivid imagination. After backing her work up on a floppy, she switched off the computer.

Susannah fixed a big salad for dinner, rinsed

the dishes and put them in the dishwasher, took a long bubble bath. After drying off, she slipped into a long white cotton nightgown that she had ordered from a catalog. It looked old-fashioned, with its high neck, long sleeves, and ruffled hem.

Feeling suddenly melancholy, Susannah picked up the feather and slipped the rawhide loop over her wrist, then walked out into the small side yard that opened off the kitchen.

It was a beautiful night. A cool spring breeze had blown the smog out of the city. A full moon hung low and yellow in the sky, shining like amber glass in a sea of black velvet.

A beautiful night, she mused, meant to be shared with someone you loved. Someone who loved you . . .

With a sigh, Susannah stretched her arms over her head and gazed up at the night sky. A million stars winked back at her, as if they shared a secret she would never know.

A faint breeze caught the feather dangling from her wrist. She stared up at it, watching it rotate in the gentle wind. The black and white of the feather reminded her of the black-and-white photograph she had bought at the workshop. There had been an eagle feather in the warrior's hair, one that looked just like this, she thought, and then grinned. Surely one eagle feather looked pretty much like another.

Lowering her arms, she ran her finger over the feather again. The warrior in the painting had looked handsome and brave, the kind of man women dreamed of and writers brought to life in the pages of their books.

Where was *her* knight in shining armor? she wondered. Where was the man of *her* dreams?

With a sigh, Susannah sank down on the chaise longue and closed her eyes, the words of an old song playing in the back of her mind.

"Mr. Sandman, send me a dream . . ."

Yes, she thought, drawing the edge of the feather across her lower lip. Send me the man of my dreams.

Chapter Three

With a low moan, Susannah rolled over, trying to find a more comfortable position. When had her bed gotten so hard? She shivered as a cool breeze whispered over her face. She was certain she had left the heater on last night. Why was her room so cold? And what on earth was that racket? It sounded like . . . like a bugle!

Sighing with irritation, she opened her eyes, blinked. And blinked again.

She was dreaming, Susannah thought as she sat up. It had to be a dream. But never, in all her life, had she had a dream quite as vivid as this one.

Men in blue uniforms were emerging from long wooden barracks, forming lines, standing at attention. The bugle blared again. There was the sound of drumming. Someone raised a flag, and she stared at it for several moments, thinking it seemed to have fewer stars than it should have. She had seen a flag just like it not long ago. Of course, she thought, it looked just like the old flag she had seen at the reenactment workshop.

Feeling confused, she brushed a lock of hair from her forehead. It was then that she noticed the feather dangling from her wrist. Frowning, she glanced around. Numerous wood and adobe buildings were grouped around a large stretch of empty ground. Susannah heard a man shouting orders. Dust filled the air as the soldiers broke ranks and headed toward a long low building on the far side of what she decided must be the parade ground.

She heard the whinny of a horse, and then the sound of footsteps coming closer. Alarmed, she scrambled to her feet.

"Excuse me, ma'am, but what are you doing here?"

Susannah whirled around and found herself face-to-face with a man who looked as if he had just stepped out of an old Western movie. He wore a dark blue sack coat, trousers, and black boots, as well as a black slouch hat set at a rakish angle. A wide black belt circled his waist.

Maybe she *was* on a Hollywood back lot, she thought, except Hollywood's forts always had high wooden walls with catwalks and lookout towers. She didn't think she had ever seen a fort without walls before.

"Dorothy, I don't think you're in Kansas anymore," she muttered.

"Ma'am?"

"Nothing." Susannah folded her arms over her breasts, careful not to crush the feather, and wished she was wearing something a little more concealing than a cotton nightgown.

The man's gaze ran over her, curious and slightly suspicious. "I don't recall seeing you here before, ma'am."

"No. Well, I've never been here before," Susannah replied, wondering where, exactly, "here" was.

He nodded, his expression puzzled. "What are you doing out here at this time of the morning, ma'am?"

"I'm not sure." She glanced around again. "I think I . . . that is, I . . ."

"Do you . . . ah, excuse me for asking, but do you walk in your sleep?"

"I never have before," Susannah replied. She glanced at the flag fluttering in the morning breeze. "But if I didn't know better, I'd think I'd walked all the way back to the nineteenth century."

"Ma'am?"

"Nothing. Where am I?"

"Fort Collier, ma'am."

Susannah frowned. Why did that name sound so familiar? "Who are you?"

He snapped to attention. "Lieutenant Elliott Carter, at your service, ma'am."

She smiled uncertainly. Elliott Carter was a handsome young man, probably in his early thirties, with close-cropped blond hair, a thin moustache, and light blue eyes.

Susannah shook her head. Fort Collier. Lieutenant Carter. She closed her eyes, willing herself to wake up. She had to be dreaming! But the ground felt cold and hard and damp beneath her feet, and the sun felt warm upon her face.

"Ma'am?"

She opened her eyes to find him staring at her.

Carter removed his coat and draped it over her shoulders. "I think I'd better take you to Colonel O'Neill."

The colonel was seated behind a large mahogany desk. He was making notes on a sheet of paper and didn't look up when they entered the room.

The lieutenant cleared his throat. "Excuse me, Colonel O'Neill."

"In a minute, Carter."

Feeling like a child about to be reprimanded, Susannah stood in front of the colonel's desk, waiting for him to acknowledge her presence. It reminded her of the time her father had kept her standing at the dinner table for ten minutes while he decided what her punishment should be for spending the day at the mall instead of going to school.

With a sigh, she folded her arms and glanced around the room. It was small and square. A wooden filing cabinet stood in one corner. There was a picture of President Ulysses S. Grant on the wall behind the desk. A small table held several rolled-up papers that looked like maps. Pegs held a bayonet and a hat similar to the one Elliott Carter was wearing.

She turned her attention back to the colonel.

He was a tall, gray-haired man with skin like leather. He chose that moment to look up and she saw that his eyes were gray.

The colonel's expression remained impassive as his gaze skimmed over Susannah from head to foot. He glanced at Carter. "Who's this?" he asked brusquely.

"My name is Susannah Kingston."

The colonel grunted softly. "What are you doing running around my post in your nightclothes?"

"I'm not sure."

One thick gray brow rose in annoyance. "Not sure?" He glanced at Carter again. "Lieutenant, what's going on here?"

"I don't know, sir. I found her near the trading post, sir."

The colonel transferred his gaze back to Susannah. "Do you have family here?"

"No."

O'Neill tapped his fingertips on the top of his desk, and then, between one breath and the next, his eyes turn cold and hard. "What are you doing with that?"

"With what?"

"That feather. Unless I'm badly mistaken, it's a Lakota prayer feather."

Susannah shrugged. "So what?"

"Two possibilities come to mind. You've run away from the Indians, or you're spying for them."

"Spying!" Susannah squeaked. "Me? That's ridiculous. I don't even belong here."

"Yes," the Colonel replied dryly. "I think we've

established that. Well, miss," he asked briskly, "what do you propose I should do with you?"

"Do with me? I don't think you need to do anything with me, thank you very much. I'm quite capable of looking after myself."

"Indeed? This is an army post, miss. I have several hundred soldiers under my command. I can't have a single young woman running around unchaperoned." He cleared his throat. "Especially attired in her nightclothes. Lieutenant Carter, take her to Sud's Row. She can stay in the Pedersons' hut. Oh, and find her something more suitable to wear. Try MacDougal's wife. They, ah . . ." A faint flush tinged the colonel's cheeks. "They seem to be about the same size. Miss Kingston, you are to consider yourself confined to quarters until I decide what to do with you."

"Confined to quarters! You can't do that. I'm not in the Army."

"Everyone on this post is under my command, ma'am, and that includes you. You are not to try and leave this post until the reason for your being here is established to my satisfaction."

"Now wait just a minute . . ."

O'Neill leaned across his desk, his gray eyes as hard as flint. "Is that clear, Miss Kingston?"

"But I . . ." Her voice trailed off as she caught sight of the calendar on the colonel's desk. The month read April, but it was the year that held her gaze and caused her stomach to drop to the floor. 1870.

Carter saluted, then grabbed Susannah by the arm and hauled her out of the colonel's office.

"Let me go!"

"You'd best do as the colonel says, miss."

"Who are the Pedersons? I don't want to stay with someone I don't even know, and I'm sure they don't want me, either."

"The Pedersons were transferred off the post three days ago. Their hut is empty."

That bit of information had her feeling a little better.

Until she noticed the hut. It was a small square building exactly like a half-dozen others, all sitting side by side in a neat row on the north side of the parade ground.

Smoke was rising from all the chimneys but one.

Carter opened the door for her and motioned her inside. Hands fisted on her hips, Susannah glanced around the room. It was virtually empty save for a lumpy sofa and a straight-backed chair. White ruffled curtains hung at the window, looking incongruous against the bare wood walls.

Grimacing, she walked into the kitchen, which was nothing more than a cast iron stove, a sink with a pump, and a few crudely made shelves.

"Lovely," she muttered, thinking of her bright economy kitchen at home. "Just lovely."

The bedroom was devoid of all furniture. Limp yellow curtains hung from the single window.

"You don't really expect me to stay here, do you?"

"Colonel's orders, miss."

"Well, I don't care what he says. I'm not staying here."

Carter cleared his throat. "I'd do as he says, miss."

"Really?"

"Yes, miss. I know this place doesn't look like much, but the guardhouse is a lot worse."

"The guardhouse!"

"Colonel O'Neill doesn't tolerate disobedience, ma'am."

"But . . . the guardhouse. He'd really do that?"

Carter nodded. "Yes, miss. You stay here and make yourself at home," he said with a crooked grin, "and I'll be back as soon as I can with some clothes and some breakfast."

"Thank you, Lieutenant."

"My pleasure, miss."

"Susannah."

"Yes, miss."

With a sigh, Susannah watched him leave, then closed the door after him.

It was April. 1870.

Brow furrowed in thought, she wandered through the three small rooms. Bare wood floors with wide gaps between the boards, bare wood walls, a fireplace made of rough stone. This place was beyond rustic, she thought. It was downright primitive!

So, what was she supposed to do now? If seeing was believing, then she had been transported into the past, with no recollection of how she'd gotten here or any clue as to how to get back where she belonged.

If she wasn't in the past, she was having the mother of all nightmares.

Too nervous to sit still, she paced the floor for

several minutes, then went to look out the small front window, her fingers absently stroking the feather. The wavy glass didn't reveal much of a view—a corner of the parade ground, the barracks, and an open stretch of ground where two soldiers stood with their heads together while a third man chopped wood. Unlike the others, he wasn't wearing Army blue. Indeed, he wasn't wearing much of anything at all, just a breechclout and moccasins. Heavy iron shackles hobbled his feet. Sweat dripped down his back. His long black hair fell halfway to his waist.

A chill slithered down Susannah's spine as the third man turned around. With a gasp, she drew back, one hand clutching her throat. It was him! The Indian in the photograph.

He looked up then, his gaze finding hers, holding hers, for a moment that seemed to stretch into an eternity. His image imprinted itself on her mind: high cheekbones, well-defined; a broad slash of a nose, a stubborn jaw, straight black brows above deep black eyes. Sweat dripped down his chest, glistened on a pair of well-muscled arms.

As she watched, one of the soldiers said something, then jabbed his rifle butt into the Indian's side, apparently ordering him to get back to work.

The Indian continued to stare at her for several moments and then hefted the ax and went back to the task of chopping wood. He grimaced as he lifted the ax, and Susannah wondered how hard the soldier had struck him even as she wondered why such a thing was permitted.

He turned, and she noticed the spiderweb of scars that crisscrossed his broad back and shoulders, overlaid with ugly red welts and half-healed lacerations. A thin trickle of blood oozed down his right side. How cruel, she thought, to make him toil in the hot sun when he was injured!

She stayed by the window, watching the Indian work, admiring the rhythmic play of muscles in his back and shoulders. There was an unconscious grace to his movements, a sense of power tightly leashed. Even covered with dirt and sweat, his feet hobbled, there was something about him, some indefinable air of confidence, that made her think he was a man of some importance among his own people.

Susannah had never been one to swoon over rippling male muscles, preferring a man with brains to one with brawn, but she couldn't seem to draw her gaze away, couldn't help wondering what it would be like to be held in those powerful arms.

She might have stood there all day if Lieutenant Carter hadn't returned carrying a covered tray and a small valise.

He smiled at her when she opened the door. "Breakfast," he said. He dropped the valise on the floor. "Mrs. MacDougal sent you something to wear. I'm afraid you'll have to make do with company chow."

"That's all right," Susannah said. Removing the feather from her wrist, she placed it carefully on the mantle, then sat down on the sofa.

Carter smiled at her as he handed her the tray. Her enthusiasm quickly died away when she lifted the lid and found herself staring at a lump of beef hash, a thick slice of dry brown bread, and a cup of black coffee.

Carter shrugged. "It's been said that Army cooks have killed more soldiers than redskins," he said apologetically. "I'll see if I can't rustle you up something from the officer's mess for dinner."

"Thank you."

"Well, I've got to go. Remember, stay inside."

"Yes," she agreed, remembering his threat of the guardhouse. "I will. Thank you, Lieutenant."

"I'll bring you some wood later."

Susannah frowned. Wood? "Thank you."

He offered her a quick smile, then left the house.

Susannah poked at the hash with her fork. It didn't look the least bit appetizing—or even palatable, for that matter. She'd seen dog food that looked more appealing. Disregarding the urge to hold her nose, she took a bite, swallowed, and put her fork aside. She would make do with bread and coffee and hope for something better for lunch.

When she finished eating, she put the tray aside and picked up the valise. Inside, she found a long-sleeved white cotton blouse, a long calico skirt, a corset, a beribboned corset cover (which she recognized thanks to her recent visit with the reenactors), white cotton drawers, three white ruffled petticoats, a blue dress with a high neck and long sleeves, a pair of black shoes, and two pairs of white cotton stockings. Mrs. MacDougal had thoughtfully included a hairbrush and a bar of lavender-scented soap.

Slipping off her nightgown, Susannah put on the drawers, the corset cover, the blouse, one petticoat, the stockings, and the skirt. She was muttering under her breath by the time she tried on the shoes, which were the right size, but were hard and stiff and uncomfortable.

She ran the brush through her hair, wishing she had a mirror so she could see how she looked.

And then, unable to resist the urge any longer, she went back to the window.

The Indian was out there, currying a horse. It was, Susannah thought, the biggest, blackest, meanest-looking horse she had ever seen. Cross-tied between stout wooden posts, it twitched its tail and wiggled its ears in a most irritable fashion as the Indian brushed its coat.

They looked well together, Susannah thought, the wild-looking horse and the wilder-looking Indian.

Again, as if sensing her presence, the Indian glanced her way, his gaze locking on hers. She felt a swift surge of heat, like an electrical current, flow through her as their gazes met and held.

Susannah had a sudden, unreasoning urge to go to him, to ask his name, to touch him and see if he was truly flesh and blood, for no other man had ever affected her so strongly. Could it be he? she wondered. Could it really be the warrior from the photograph?

And, if so, what, exactly, did it mean?

And how in the world was she ever going to get back home?

Chapter Four

Tate Sapa grunted softly as one of the soldiers set to watch him lifted his rifle and struck him across the back.

"Back to work, chief," the *wasichu* said with a sneer.

Tate Sapa forced his attention from the white woman and went back to brushing the colonel's horse. It was not the stallion's sleek black coat he saw, but the woman he had seen at the window. The woman in his vision. What did it mean?

He spent an hour brushing the stallion. Of all the tasks he was required to do, this was his favorite. The stallion was a beautiful animal, with large intelligent eyes, long legs, and a deep chest. Powerful muscles quivered beneath Tate Sapa's hand as he drew the brush over the animal's neck and shoulder.

He spoke softly to the horse while he worked, and all the while he thought of the white woman and wondered who she was and if he would see her again.

At dusk, they took him back to the iron-barred house and locked him inside. He stood in the middle of the floor, taking slow deep breaths. He hated this small closed place, hated the fetid smell of the prisoners who had been there before him. The floor, the walls, the very air itself reeked of sweat and urine, of fear and desperation. Sometimes, late at night, when sleep would not come and he longed for home, he sensed the restless spirits of those who had died in this wretched place hovering around him.

Fighting back a wave of hopelessness, Tate Sapa went to the small, iron-barred window. Hands fisted around the thick bars, he stared across the compound. He could see the white woman's house from here. Why had he never seen her before?

With a sigh, he rested his forehead against the cold iron bars and closed his eyes. Time passed so slowly in this place. He had been here since *Waniyetu Wi*, the moon of falling leaves, and now it was *Wihakakta Wi*, the moon of tender grass. The Lakota would be repairing their lodges from the ravages of a harsh winter, preparing to move to higher ground. The young men would be speaking out for war, arguing for vengeance as only the very young can, and he would not be there to dissuade them. Of all the voices in the village, his had been the only one that counseled patience, that spoke for peace.

44

Feather in the Wind

"Wakan Tanka Tunkaschila onshimala ye," he murmured. Grandfather Spirit, pity me so that my people may live.

Minutes passed and still he stood there, the same prayer repeating itself in his heart over and over again, until a gentle warmth spread through him, and he knew she was nearby.

Lifting his head, Tate Sapa peered into the darkness. And she was there, a slender figure walking in the pale light of the moon. She clutched a blanket around her shoulders to ward off the chill of the night; a long white gown fluttered around her ankles like morning mist. Moonlight silvered her hair.

Who was she, this white woman? Was she *wiyan wakan*, a holy woman? She had come to him in a vision, and now she was here, walking in the shadows of the night.

As though feeling his gaze, she turned toward him. Transfixed, Tate Sapa stared at her, his heart pounding like a war drum, his palms sweating though the night was cold.

His hands tightened around the bars as she moved toward him, and he fought the urge to turn away, to hide. He was a warrior, a man who had counted coup on the enemy, slain *matohota*, the grizzly bear. He would not cower before one tiny *wasicun winyan*.

Lifting his chin and squaring his shoulders, Tate Sapa stood his ground, and waited.

Susannah couldn't explain the overpowering urge that had her walking toward the guardhouse. Tired of being cooped up in the hut all day, she had decided to go out for a breath of air. And then she had felt it, a sudden warmth that had dispelled the chill of the night. She had turned toward the source and seen his face at the window.

Of their own volition, her legs had carried her across the compound until she stood at the small, iron-barred window.

Up close, she could see that the black-and-white photograph had not done him justice. His hair was as thick and black as midnight. His skin was the color of sun-burnished copper, but it was his eyes that held her spellbound. Black eyes, as restless as the wind, as fathomless as the ocean. The most beautiful, compelling eyes she had ever seen.

Time ceased to have meaning as Susannah stood there. She had an almost overpowering urge to reach out and touch his hand, to see if he was real, or merely a figment of her all too active imagination.

Mr. Sandman, send me a dream . . .

"I'm Susannah," she said, and then wondered if he spoke English.

Clutching the blanket in one hand, she tapped her fingertips to her chest. "Susannah."

"Micaje Tate Sapa."

Susannah frowned. "Do you speak English?"

He stared back at her, his expression blank.

"I guess it was too much to hope for," she muttered ruefully. "In the movies, the Indians always manage to speak English. Oh, well, another Hollywood myth shattered."

She smiled self-consciously, unable to look

away from his enigmatic gaze.

A gust of wind blew over the parade ground. She should have been shivering, she thought, but the fire in his eyes held the cold at bay, held the world at bay. In this place, at this moment in time, there were only the two of them. Like a magician, he held her trapped in the power of his eyes, and she wondered if she would stand there forever, warmed to the innermost core of her being by his presence, helpless to move, to think, to speak.

The sound of heavy footsteps broke the spell between them. Susannah's heart seemed to jump into her throat as she realized someone was coming. Remembering the lieutenant's dire warning against venturing outside, she turned and ran for the hut.

Tate Sapa stared after her until she was out of sight, and then, with a melancholy sigh, he stretched out on the dirty blanket that served as his bed.

"Su-san-nah." He whispered her name into the darkness.

Wrapped in a blanket, Susannah sat on the lumpy sofa and stared into the fire she had built in the hearth, only it wasn't the dancing flames she saw, but a pair of ebony-colored eyes set in a ruggedly masculine, ruggedly beautiful face. If he was indeed the Black Wind in the photo, she thought, he was well named, for he had looked at her and she had felt as though she were caught in the middle of a hurricane.

She snuggled deeper into the blanket. Impossible as it seemed, she had been transported into the past. How or why she didn't know; for how long, she didn't know.

Susannah closed her eyes, and the Indian's image sprang quickly to mind. And suddenly she didn't feel so alone, or quite so far from home.

Susannah smiled at Elliott Carter. He had come calling on her that afternoon, inquiring after her health, asking if she would care to go for a walk. She had accepted eagerly.

They had left the fort to stroll along the narrow stream that meandered through a copse of trees a short distance away.

It was a lovely day. She couldn't remember ever seeing a sky so big, so blue and clear. It seemed to stretch away forever. Wildflowers bloomed in colorful profusion along the banks of the stream, the trees were bright with new spring growth, the grass spread over the prairie like a carpet of plush emerald velvet. She took a deep breath, inhaling the scent of crushed grass and earth and wildflowers.

"Miss Kingston, may I ask you something?"

"Of course, and please, call me Susannah."

"What are you doing here?"

"I don't know."

"What do you mean?"

"Just what I said. I don't know what I'm doing here, or how I got here."

Carter shook his head. "It doesn't make sense, miss."

"Susannah."

"Susannah," he repeated with a smile. "I mean,

48

you had to come from somewhere."

Indeed, Susannah mused. *But you'd never believe me if I told you.*

"Have you been in the Army long?" she asked.

Carter hesitated, as though he wasn't quite ready to change the subject, and then he said, "Almost six years."

"You must like it."

Carter shrugged. "It's a living."

"A hard one, I should think."

"At times. I must admit that life on an Army post is monotonous, even boring at times, but . . ." He shrugged again. "Being an officer has its advantages. The pay isn't all that bad, and I feel like I'm serving my country the best way I know how."

"I don't see how it can be boring," Susannah remarked. "It seems that bugle blows almost constantly, calling the men to do this or that."

Carter chuckled. "Yeah, it's a busy life."

"Well, it seems that way to me. Reveille's at what, six? Breakfast at six-thirty, all those other calls. What are they anyway? Seems like your men spend all day running from one place to the next."

"Well, let's see," Carter said. "There's fatigue call at seven-thirty, sick call at eight, assembly for guard detail at nine. Boots and saddles is called at ten of the hour, and drill is at ten. There's recall at noon, and mess at one. Then there's drill for target practice and stable call, dinner, and then retreat at nine, and lights out at nine-thirty."

"Makes me tired just to think about it," Susannah muttered. "When do the men ever have time for themselves?"

"They're free to do whatever they want when they're not on duty, so long as they stay within bugle call."

Cavalry life had seemed much more interesting and romantic in the movies, Susannah mused as they walked along. Men in neatly pressed dark blue uniforms, crisp red and white guidons snapping in the wind, smiling women in brightly colored calico dresses and wide-brimmed sunbonnets, high-stepping horses. Reality was much more . . . gritty.

"They're aren't many women here," she remarked.

"No," he agreed. "It's a hard life for a woman. Not many take to it."

"I noticed an Indian chopping wood yesterday."

Carter grunted softly. "Tate Sapa."

"Is that his name?"

"Yes."

"What does it mean?"

"Black Wind."

The name hit her with the force of a blow. The man who had sold her the picture had told her the Indian's name was Black Wind. "What did he do?"

"Killed a cow."

"That's all? He's in chains, doing hard labor, for stealing one cow?" And even as she said the words, she remembered saying almost the same thing to the man at the reenactment workshop.

"He's lucky they didn't hang him."

"Is he? Maybe he was hungry."

"I'm sure he was. Most of them are, now that the buffalo herds are dwindling."

"How long has he been locked up?" Susannah asked, remembering that Brightman had told her Black Wind had been sentenced to three years of hard labor.

"I'm not sure. About six months, I think."

"I think it's horrible, treating him like that."

Carter shrugged.

"Why was he whipped?"

"Insubordination."

"I'd like to go back now," Susannah declared, and began walking briskly back the way they had come.

"Miss Kingston! Susannah, wait!"

She stopped abruptly, her arms folded over her chest. "What do you want?"

"I didn't arrest him. I didn't beat him." Carter took a deep breath. "And I don't understand your concern. He's just a damned savage."

"He's a human being!"

"I could argue that with you, but I won't." He smiled at her as he offered his arm. "Don't be angry."

She glared at him a moment, then, with a sigh, she took his arm. She didn't agree with what he'd said but, given the time and the place, she could understand it. "I'm sorry."

"Forget it."

"I want to thank you again for the bed and the other things you brought me."

"My pleasure."

"I appreciate it." Carter had showed up at her

hut that morning, along with four other soldiers. They had set up a bed, carried in a small table and a chair, a couple of lamps, rugs for the floors, a few dishes and utensils.

"The other women were glad to give you what they could."

"It was very nice of them."

"You'll meet them all tonight. The colonel is celebrating his anniversary, and the officers and their wives have been invited. He asked me to invite you, as well."

"Oh."

"With your permission, I shall call for you at seven."

Susannah nodded. "Seven."

He walked her to her door, bowed over her hand. "Until tonight, Miss Susannah."

"Thanks for the walk."

"My pleasure."

She watched him as he walked briskly away, thinking she really didn't want to go to a party at the colonel's. For one thing, she wasn't comfortable meeting strangers; for another, she didn't have anything suitable to wear. But she had the feeling that an invite to the colonel's was like a command from the king.

The O'Neills' hut was as different from Susannah's as sunlight from moonlight. Thick carpets covered the ugly wooden floors, colorful paintings brightened the drab walls. The furniture was comfortable but elegant. Pictures of the O'Neills' children and grandchildren were everywhere.

Mrs. O'Neill reminded Susannah of a bird. She

was small and quick and cheerful, an amazing contrast to her tall, rather staid husband. She welcomed Susannah with a smile and a hug and made her feel as if they had been friends for years.

"My husband tells me you don't remember how you got here," Mrs. O'Neill said. "Well, don't you worry, I'm sure it will come back to you. And in the meantime, it'll be nice having another woman on the post. Come along and meet the others."

The other women present took their cue from the colonel's wife. All four of them came forward and introduced themselves to Susannah, saying she must be sure to let them know if she needed anything, inviting her to join them in their reading circle, which was to be held at the colonel's house the following day.

"We're reading *Les Miserables*," Barbara Nethington told Susannah. "Have you read it?"

"Yes." And seen the Broadway show, Susannah thought, stifling a grin.

"Do join us," Lily Sweeney urged with a smile. "It will be *so* refreshing to have a new face to look at."

"And hear a new opinion," Louise Riva replied with a wry grin.

"I'd like to. Thank you."

As in every gathering Susannah had ever attended, the women eventually ended up in the kitchen, talking about their husbands and babies, while the men sat in the living room. Susannah was surprised by the numerous ways the frontier wives had found to keep themselves entertained.

There was an activity almost every day of the week. They had a reading group, a sewing circle, a day when they met to play cards. They went on picnics and nature walks with their children. Louise Riva was teaching them to speak French. There was a dance once a month.

Dinner was served at eight. Susannah, who had always felt nervous and uneasy with strangers, found herself feeling right at home.

After dinner, the men went outside to smoke while the ladies took sherry in the parlor. Later, they played charades, then everyone toasted the colonel and his wife, congratulating them on forty years of marriage and wishing them forty more. Carrot cake and champagne followed. Mrs. O'Neill insisted everyone take a piece of cake home.

Lieutenant Carter walked Susannah back to her hut.

"Did you have a good time?" he asked.

"Yes, thank you."

"I'm glad. Do you think you could get to like it here?"

"Yes, why?" she asked. But she already knew why. Women were scarce on the frontier. Barbara Nethington had told her that single women didn't last long. Old or young, pretty or plain, they were inevitably quickly married. It was so hard to keep help that, in some instances, people looking for hired help advertised for homely girls in hopes they would stay single longer.

They had reached her house now. Carter took her hand in his. "Miss Susannah, I know this is sudden, but I find you most attractive and I was wondering, that is, if you don't mind, I should like your leave to court you."

With an effort, Susannah stifled the urge to bat her eyelashes. She couldn't help it—she felt like she was caught up in an old B Western.

"I've offended you, haven't I?" Carter said, clearly mistaking her silence for rejection.

"Not at all," Susannah said quickly. "It's just that, I mean, we've only just met."

"Then you wouldn't mind?"

"No, Lieutenant, I'd be honored."

"Thank you, Miss Susannah." He squeezed her hand. "Good night."

"Good night, Lieutenant. Thank you for a lovely evening."

"My pleasure."

Smiling, she watched him walk away.

For a time, Susannah stood in the moonlight, pondering the twist of fate that had brought her here. And then, inevitably, she found herself thinking of the Indian. Black Wind.

Before she quite realized what she was doing, she found herself hurrying toward the guardhouse.

Chapter Five

He came awake suddenly and knew, without knowing how he knew, that she was nearby.

Tate Sapa stood up, grimacing as pain lanced through the half-healed lacerations on his back and shoulders. He chided himself again for his lack of self-control, for continuing to defy the soldiers who guarded him. It was foolish to do so, but he could only endure their ridicule and their insults for so long before his pride rebelled, before the urge to strike out against his enemies overcame his reason and rage smothered logic.

In the past five months, he had been whipped on several occasions, denied food and water on others, but he refused to cower before them, refused to surrender his pride. It was the only thing of value left to him.

The muscles in his back and shoulders ached

from the hours he had spent felling timber late that afternoon.

Feeling old beyond his years, Tate Sapa moved to the window and peered into the darkness.

And she was there, walking toward him in the moonlight. He drank in the sight of her, wondering, as he did so, why her mere presence had the power to soothe the anger and frustration that tormented him.

His hands curled around the cold iron bars as her steps slowed. *Come to me,* he thought. *Let me see your face again, hear your voice again.*

He took a deep breath, his nostrils filling with myriad scents—damp earth, sage, the stink of his own unwashed body, but, overall, the sweet fragrance of the woman.

"Hi," she said. A tentative smile played over her lips as she held out her hand. "I brought you something."

Slowly, he reached for what she offered. Unfolding the cloth, he frowned at the triangular shaped lump in the palm of his hand.

"It's cake," the woman said.

He sniffed it suspiciously, his stomach growling at the thought of food. He was hungry all the time. In the morning, the guard brought him a bowl of mush and a cup of black coffee; at night, he received a hunk of overdone meat, a piece of dry bread, and a glass of water. At noon, if he was lucky, he got meat and cheese and something to drink.

"Taste it," the woman urged, lifting her hand to her mouth. "It's good."

He took a bite, smiled, wolfed down the rest,

and wished for more. *"Pilamaya,"* he said, and returned the cloth to the woman.

"I wish you could speak English," she said. "Not that we have anything to say to each other."

Tate Sapa remained mute. No one knew he spoke English, and he preferred to keep it that way. He had learned much by feigning ignorance of the white man's language. But he was not thinking of that now. He watched the way the moon-dappled shadows played over her face. She frightened him, this woman from his vision, made him feel things he had never felt before.

"Nituwe hwo?" he mused aloud. Who are you?

Her beauty mesmerized him. She was small and delicate, her skin was smooth and clear. He wished he dared touch her skin and discover for himself if it was as soft as it looked. He yearned to touch her hair, feel it curl around his fingers. He had never seen anyone with hair like hers before.

She took a step closer, her gaze seeking his. "I wish I knew who you really were," she whispered. "I know it's silly, but I feel like you're the reason I'm here. I wish . . ."

Her words emboldened him. Knowing it was dangerous, knowing he would be severely punished if she betrayed him, he reached through the bars.

Susannah's mouth went dry as his calloused hand cupped her cheek.

"Cocola," he said, a note of wonder in his voice. Soft, so soft. And warm.

She didn't pull away but stood there, her gaze locked on his, as he drew his knuckles over her cheek, then lifted a lock of her hair. He made a soft sound in his throat as her hair curled around his finger.

Susannah swallowed hard, bewildered by the rapid beating of her heart. Her legs felt suddenly weak; there seemed to be butterflies dancing in her stomach.

He ran his thumb over the curl of hair wrapped around his finger, then, with obvious reluctance, took his hand from her hair.

"Su-san-nah."

The fact that he remembered her name made her feel ridiculously happy.

"Tate Sapa," she replied.

He nodded, a faint smile touching his lips.

Susannah felt her heart turn over. His hair was unkempt, his face streaked with dirt, but none of that mattered. He was the most handsome of men! Just the merest smile, yet it changed his countenance completely, softening the hard lines, erasing the bitterness from the depths of his eyes. No doubt a full-blown smile would render her unconscious, she mused.

She looked at his hands, large capable hands that were wrapped around the bars, and yearned to feel his fingertips against her cheek once again.

Heart pounding, Susannah reached up and took one of his hands in hers. He had big hands, the palms calloused, the fingers long.

Tate Sapa frowned, surprised that she would touch him of her own free will. In the distance, he heard one of the sentinels calling out the post number and the hour, reminding him again that he would be severely punished if anyone knew he had laid his hands on her. It wouldn't matter that she had come to him. He would be the one to suffer for it.

Susannah glanced at their joined hands, at her fingers entwined with his, and gently pulled away. "It's late. I'd better get back."

"Ye sni yo," he murmured softly. Don't go.

She heard the gentle pleading in his voice and wished she knew what he was saying. "Good night."

Tate Sapa watched her walk away, the gentle swaying of her hips making him yearn for things that could never be.

"Su-san-nah." He whispered her name into the darkness, and knew he would find no rest in his bed that night.

They came for him early the next morning, ordering him out of his cramped cell. Thrusting a shovel and a rake into his hands, they marched Tate Sapa to the stables and put him to work mucking the stalls that housed the officers' horses.

The chains that hobbled his feet rattled annoyingly with every move he made. His ankles were raw from their constant chafing.

He worked steadily, removing soiled straw and replacing it with fresh.

The smell of manure, old and fresh, filled the air, mingling with the odor of his own sweat.

Thoughts of home crowded his mind—the sun-swept prairies, the clean scents of earth and sage and sweet grass, the aroma of roasting buffalo hump.

The scent of flowers that clung to the hair of the white woman . . .

Since the moment he had first seen her in a vision, she had never been far from his thoughts. And now she was here. Again, he wondered who she was, and what had brought her to this place. Was it possible she had been sent here to rescue him? If so, she was truly *wakan*. Tate Sapa had tried twice to escape, and failed both times.

He grimaced at the memory of the punishment that had followed: days of being chained to the wall, forced to stand for hours on end with his hands shackled high above his head, denied food and drink.

He put his shovel aside and stroked the neck of the colonel's big black horse. Mounted on such an animal, he could ride like the wind for home. No one would be able to catch him.

He glanced at the shackles that hobbled his feet day and night. Save for the manacles, he would vault onto the animal's back and make a run for it.

And he would take the white woman with him.

The thought made him smile.

"Hey, redskin, get back to work!"

Wiping the smile from his face, Tate Sapa took hold of the stallion's lead rope and led the horse from the stall. Outside, he tethered the black to the hitch rack.

He was about to go back into the barn when he caught a glimpse of Susannah. She was walking around the parade ground with several other

61

white women, but he had eyes only for her. She moved with the grace of a young doe. He saw her smile, and then, like a gift from *Wakan Tanka*, the breeze brought him the soft sound of her laughter.

"What are you doin', starin' at those women, buck?" The harsh voice of the duty sergeant grated on Tate Sapa's ears even as the man's crop fell across his back. "I told you to get to work!"

Hands clenched, Tate Sapa went back into the barn, yearning for his freedom, for the chance to vent his anger on the white men who rode him so mercilessly, treating him as if he were some kind of inhuman creature without heart or mind or feelings.

He stared at the pitchfork propped against one of the stalls. It would make a formidable weapon. But even as he considered it, he knew it would be suicide to strike out against his guards. They would shoot him down without question or qualm.

And yet, maybe that would not be so bad. Surely he could kill or injure several of the *wasichu* before they killed him. He could die fighting, as a warrior should. *Hoka-hey.* Perhaps it was a good day to die.

He shook the thought from his mind. Death would always be there, waiting. For now, he would bide his time. He might yet find a way to escape this place.

At dusk, Susannah stood at the window, listening to the company bugler blow retreat. Impossible as it seemed, she'd been at the fort a week now. She had made friends with the other women and actually enjoyed their company. They were a close-knit group, bound together by circumstances and proximity. It amazed Susannah that they managed to keep busy and seemed quite content to live in this dreary place.

The bugle sounded again, drawing her attention back to the men. Attired in their dress uniforms, the entire garrison, save for those men standing guard, were assembled on the parade ground.

She had learned much of army routine in the last few days. It seemed the bugle was constantly calling men to duty. She had never realized that the soldiers took turns cleaning the stables and working in the kitchen. They spent time on the rifle range, and time drilling on the parade ground. Something called guard mount took place every morning. The men detailed for duty were assembled in front of their company quarters, inspected by the first sergeant, then marched to the parade ground, in front of the guardhouse, where they were inspected by the sergeant major. When he was satisfied with the old and new guard formations, he reported to the officer of the day that the guard was formed. The officer of the day then inspected the guard, ordering them through the manual of arms. Passwords were given, and the new guard replaced the old for the next twenty-four hours.

During this time, the post prisoners were paraded to the left of the old guard.

She was shocked by the various punishments doled out to the men in the guardhouse. Men arrested for drunkenness were made to walk back and forth in front of the guardhouse while carrying heavy logs on their shoulders.

Carter had told her he had once seen a man staked out "spread eagle." It had been a cruel thing. The man had been forced to lie in the hot sun for hours with the flies swarming over him, eating him up.

Other punishments included being trussed up to a caisson wheel, or having a man strung up by his thumbs, wrists, or arms. Sometimes a man was gagged, then tied so he couldn't move. This was called "bucking and gagging."

The most common offenses were drunkenness and desertion. Susannah could understand the motivation for both. The men worked hard under arduous conditions for little pay.

Once, she had overheard several of the soldiers singing as they worked. The words, sung with feeling, had made her smile.

"A dollar a day is damn poor pay, but thirteen a month is less!"

She sighed as the men were dismissed.

What the heck was she doing here, and how was she ever going to get home?

Brow furrowed in thought, Susannah began to pace the floor until her eye was drawn to the feather. Lifting it up, she ran the tip over her chin, marveling at its smooth texture.

Of course, she thought, the feather was the answer. She had been stroking it and wishing for her dream man. And somehow, she had been thrust back in time.

A rush of excitement swept through her as she

sat down on the sofa and slipped the loop over her wrist. Closing her eyes, she ran her fingertips over the edge of the feather.

"Home," she murmured. A quick mental image of Dorothy clicking the heels of the ruby slippers together darted through her mind. "I want to go home . . ."

She woke with a start. Had it worked? A quick glance around told her she was still in the past.

With a sigh of disappointment, she stood up and stretched the kinks from her back. Had she really expected it to work, really expected to be whisked back to her own time? And yet, if it wasn't the magic supposedly contained in the feather that had brought her here, what had?

Hardly aware of what she was doing, Susannah left the hut and made her way toward the guardhouse, thankful that the guard was inside. She could hear him snoring softly.

Black Wind was waiting for her. She felt a peculiar flutter in the pit of her stomach when she saw his face at the window.

She felt herself smile and wondered what there was about this man that made her feel warm inside. *Home*. The word whispered in the back of her mind.

"Hi."

"*Hau.*"

Susannah smiled. That was one word she did understand. She had heard it in practically every cowboy movie ever made.

"I don't know why I keep coming here," she said with a shrug.

He didn't know why she came either, but he

was glad for her company. He loved the slightly husky sound of her voice, the way her dark brown eyes met his, open and honest. The other white women at the fort looked at him as if he were less than human, as if he were some repulsive creature that walked on two legs, yet had no sense, no feeling.

"*Tanyan yahi yelo,*" he murmured softly. I am glad you came.

"I wish I could understand you," she said. "I wish you could speak English."

He let his gaze move over her face, thinking how beautiful she was. Who are you? he wondered. Where have you come from?

"It's a pretty night, isn't it?" Susannah mused. "The sky seems so much bigger here than it did at home."

Home. Sadness dragged at his heart as he wondered if he would ever see his home, his people, again.

She lifted a hand to brush a wisp of hair from her face, and he saw the feather dangling from her wrist.

He reached through the bars and took hold of her hand.

Susannah tried to pull away, but his grip was like iron, holding her fast. "Let me go!"

In a quick move, he slipped the rawhide loop over her wrist, then released her hand.

"Give me that!" she exclaimed. "It's mine."

He shook his head. "*He mitawa.*" It is mine.

Susannah frowned. "Damn, I wish I knew what you were saying."

He smoothed the edges of the feather and she

had a quick mental image of the photograph she had seen of this man, of the eagle feather tied in his hair. Could this feather really be the same one? But surely all eagle feathers looked pretty much alike.

And yet, there had been a look of recognition in his eyes when he saw the feather.

"Is it yours?" she asked. She pointed at the feather, then at him. "Yours?"

He frowned at her a minute, then thumped his chest and smiled. *"Han. Mitawa."* Yes. Mine.

"But I need it." She reached through the bars, silently asking for the feather's return. She had to have it. Somehow, it had brought her here. She was sure of it. She remembered that the old man who had given it to her had said it contained much magic. Had he known what it was capable of? Was that why he had admonished her to remember that it was a prayer feather? But surely, if he had known what power the feather held, he would not have parted with it.

"Please," Susannah said, "please give it back. I need it."

Tate Sapa shook his head. Questions raced through his mind. How had this white woman come into possession of his sacred eagle feather? Why did she say she needed it? How had she found it in the first place? He had left it at his mother's burial site five winters before, the same winter his father's brother had disappeared. Tate Sapa looked at her sharply, wondering if she had desecrated the holy ground of the Lakota.

In the distance, one of the sentry posts called out the hour.

"I guess I'd better go," Susannah said. She glared at him a moment. "Are you sure you won't give me the feather?"

"*Mitawa,*" he said firmly.

"I know, I know," she muttered. "It's yours. But mark my words, Mr. Black Wind, I intend to get it back!"

He waited until she was out of sight, and then he smiled. "You will not, Su-san-nah. But I will enjoy watching you try."

Chapter Six

Susannah let out a heavy sigh and pulled the covers up to her chin. She had been at the fort for two weeks now, and still had no idea of why she was there, exactly how she had gotten there, or how she would ever get home. Elliott Carter continued to call on her each evening, taking her for walks, escorting her to the colonel's house to play cards or charades. Once he arranged for the colonel's striker to serve them a quiet dinner for two. But it was the Indian, Black Wind, who occupied her thoughts and made her heart pound in a most alarming way.

The Army worked him mercilessly. He was hard at work from early morning until dusk, mucking stalls, currying horses, carrying water, cutting wood, digging trenches, scrubbing the barracks floors, raking the parade ground, burning the trash.

He worked steadily, his face an impassive mask. The soldiers taunted him relentlessly. She had heard them call him names, cursing him, ridiculing his people, calling him a dog-eating redskin and a dirty blanket-back Indian and other names that didn't bear thinking about. Susannah was glad he couldn't understand what they were saying, though she was certain the disdain in their voices could be understood in any language.

She spent far too much time sitting at her window, watching him when he was working nearby. Far too much time admiring the rhythmic play of his muscles, noting the width of his shoulders, the length of his legs, the way his breechclout covered just enough for modesty's sake, and little else.

He always seemed to know when she was watching him. Inevitably, he would pause in whatever he was doing and look her way, his midnight-black gaze resting on her, making her feel as if they were somehow connected.

The soldiers set to guard him treated him abominably, hitting him with their rifle butts when he didn't move fast enough to suit them. She had seen them take the food meant for Black Wind and eat it themselves, or feed it to the dogs. On more than one occasion they had refused to give him water.

It seemed childish and cruel to Susannah, and she wondered how he endured it, day after day.

At night, lying in her narrow cot, staring at the

ceiling, she fought the urge to go to him, fought her own longing to be with him. And yet she couldn't shake off the feeling that he was the reason she was here, that their lives were fated to be entwined.

And maybe, she thought, maybe it was just her overactive imagination hard at work.

Turning on her side, Susannah stared out the window. It had been cool and cloudy all day, and a brisk wind was blowing across the parade ground. In the distance, she heard the sound of thunder. No doubt it would be raining soon.

The wind rattled the glass in the window and crept up through the floorboards. Shivering, she crawled out of bed and slipped into the heavy cotton robe one of the women had given her. Going into the parlor, she started a fire in the hearth, wishing, for the thousandth time, that she was back home in her cozy apartment with its plush carpets and forced-air heating.

So much had happened so quickly in the past two weeks. Now, shivering in front of the fire, she wondered what her friends thought of her abrupt disappearance. No doubt her editor had been trying to get in touch with her. Vivian would be wondering what had happened to her. Her landlord would be expecting the rent. She had bills to pay and a deadline to meet, and an appointment with her agent. What would her parents think when they got back from their cruise and discovered their only child was missing?

The wind howled around the hut, its cold breath seeping through every crack. Susannah thought of Black Wind, huddling beneath a single blanket in the guardhouse. She had watched him work that afternoon. The men set to guard him had refused to let him take a break, refused him food and water, insisting it was wasted on a dirty Indian. They ridiculed him because he was filthy, yet refused to let him wash. It had been cold today, but he had no shirt to ward off the chill. His only apparel seemed to be his clout and a pair of well-worn moccasins.

Chiding herself for being a fool, she went into the kitchen and brewed a pot of tea. When it was done, she poured some into a tin cup, wrapped two slices of bread in a napkin, grabbed a quilt off the foot of the bed, and left the hut.

The wind crept under the robe, under her gown, as she made her way to the guardhouse. Thankful for the clouds that hid the moon and stars, she crept through the darkness toward the back of the building.

She should have known he would be there, at the window, staring out, staring toward home.

"I brought you something," she said, and thrust the cup and the napkin through the bars.

Susannah heard his stomach growl loudly as Tate Sapa unwrapped the bread. He turned away, and she knew he didn't want her to see him wolf it down. She saw his head go back as he drained the cup in two long swallows.

And then, slowly, he turned to face her again. *"Pilamaya."*

"If that means thank you, you're welcome. Here." She folded the quilt and shoved it through the bars. "I thought you might be cold."

Tate Sapa took the quilt and wrapped it

around his shoulders. It was far heavier and warmer than the filthy, threadbare blanket the Army had given him.

"What the hell's going on here?"

Susannah whirled around, her heart plummeting to her toes, to find the soldier on guard duty glaring at her.

"I . . . that is . . . I mean . . ." She swallowed, her heart beating frantically as she wondered how she could possibly explain being out here in her nightgown in the middle of the night.

The guard walked up to the window and peered inside, then gasped as Black Wind reached through the bars, his hands closing around the soldier's throat.

"Get . . . help." The words were hardly more than a whisper as the guard dropped his rifle and struggled to free himself.

Astonished by the sudden turn of events, Susannah could only stand there, watching, as the soldier went limp. When Black Wind released him, the guard slid to the ground.

"What have you done?" she exclaimed. "Don't you realize they'll flog you for this, if they don't hang you?"

"Su-san-nah."

"What?"

He gestured at the soldier, then himself, then pointed at the distant hills.

She shook her head. "No, I can't."

"*Iyokipi,* Su-san-nah."

She stared at him, trying to see his face in the darkness. He wanted her to help him escape. She knew it, just as she knew he hated having to ask for her help.

Muttering a very unladylike oath, she knelt beside the soldier. If he was dead, there was no way in hell she was going to help the Indian escape. But he wasn't dead, only out cold.

She searched his pockets, but couldn't find a key. Calling herself a hundred kinds of a fool, she went around to the front of the building and peered inside. There was no one there.

Closing the door behind her, she went through the desk until she found a ring of keys.

Black Wind was waiting for her, his hands fisted around the bars set in the heavy wooden door. She could feel his gaze as she put first one key and then another into the lock until she found the right one.

Instead of unlocking the door, she withdrew the key and took a step backward. "You won't hurt me, will you?"

He stared at her hard for a moment, then shook his head.

"Shoot, you don't even know what I'm saying."

Certain she was making the biggest mistake of her life, Susannah unlocked the cell door, then stepped back as Tate Sapa opened it and stepped into the room, ankle chains rattling.

Taking the keys from her hand, he squatted on the floor and unlocked the shackles from his ankles. They were raw and red from the iron's constant chafing. Rising to his feet, he tossed the manacles aside.

Moving toward the back of the room, he took several boxes of ammunition from a shelf, then went through the drawers of the desk. He grunted softly as he removed a knife in a beaded sheath, then pulled an amulet of some kind out of the drawer. He slipped it over his head, shoved the knife into the waistband of his clout, then left the building.

Susannah followed Black Wind outside, then stood in the shadows, watching, as he bent over the unconscious guard. Removing the man's jacket, he shrugged it on, slipped the ammunition into the pockets of the coat, then picked up the rifle.

Motioning for her to follow him, he headed toward the stables.

As if she had no mind of her own, Susannah trailed after him, her heart pounding wildly. She knew she should cry out, call for help, but she couldn't. No man deserved to be locked up for three years just for butchering a cow.

Tate Sapa dispatched the stable guard with a blow to the back of the head, then dragged the man inside and dumped him into an empty stall.

Moving quickly, he found the black stallion, slid a bridle over its head, and led it outside.

"I hope you make it back home," Susannah said.

He stared at her a moment, his dark gaze moving over her face. She shivered, wondering if it was caused by the cold wind stirring the dust, or by the sudden desire that blazed in the Indian's black eyes.

She swallowed hard, knowing she would never see him again, wondering why the thought filled her with such sadness. She didn't really know him, after all.

"Su-san-nah." He closed the distance between them. Slowly, he lifted his hand and caressed her cheek. She had not realized how tall he was. The top of her head barely reached his shoulder.

Oh, Lord, she thought, he's going to kiss me. She swayed toward him, then gasped as he caught her around the waist and thrust her onto the stallion's back.

Before she could think or cry out, he was up behind her, his heels drumming into the horse's sides. The stallion bolted forward.

There was a shout from one of the sentries, a warning to halt and be recognized, followed by a gunshot, more shouts, more gunfire.

She heard Black Wind grunt softly as they raced by one of the sentries. For a moment, she thought he had been shot, but then he kicked the horse again, demanding more speed, and she decided she had been mistaken.

The sounds of gunfire and shouts were swallowed up in the whoosh of the wind and the pounding of the stallion's hooves.

And then there was only the darkness of the night and the sound of her own heart hammering in her chest, a quick tattoo that seemed to echo the sound of the stallion's hoofbeats.

As fear subsided, Susannah became aware of the cold wind tunneling through her hair, stinging her eyes, of the big horse beneath her. Thunder reverberated through the heavens, unleashing a torrent of rain. But, most of all, she was conscious of the strong arm locked around her waist, the solid wall of flesh at her back.

Tate Sapa urged the stallion on, seemingly unmindful of the wind, the cold, the rain that pelted them with ever-increasing intensity, until she was cold and wet clear through.

"Stop, please," Susannah begged, but he continued onward until, too cold and tired to care, she rested against him and closed her eyes, not caring if the horse stumbled and broke all their necks.

She came awake with a start, wondering what had awakened her, wondering how on earth she had managed to fall asleep on the back of a moving horse.

She realized it was the cessation of movement that had roused her. At the same time, she realized she was alone on the horse. It had stopped raining, and dawn was just brightening the edge of the horizon.

"Black Wind?"

She glanced behind her, but saw only darkness and a distant flash of lightning.

Hanging onto the horse's mane, she slid to the ground, turned, and stumbled. Over the Indian.

He was lying face down on the ground, not moving.

For a moment, she stared at him. She had read her share of Westerns, seen her share of cowboy movies. Indians were supposed to be one with their horses. They weren't supposed to fall off.

Kneeling beside him, she shook his shoulder. "Black Wind."

No response.

She shook him again, a little harder, and he groaned softly.

"Are you all right?" she asked dubiously. Her hand slid down his right shoulder and encountered something warm. And sticky. "No." She shook her head, refusing to believe what she knew to be true. There was blood on her hands.

She sat there, unmoving, while night turned to day. The rising sun painted the clouds with broad streaks of crimson and ocher. Thunder rumbled overhead, unleashing a soft, gentle rain.

Black Wind stirred. He groaned softly as he opened his eyes.

He muttered something that sounded very much like a curse as he sat up.

"You look awful," Susannah observed. He looked remarkably pale; his eyes were dark with pain.

"I feel awful."

Susannah blinked at him in astonishment. "You . . . you speak English."

He nodded. "I need your help."

"What kind of help?"

He looked at her as if she had just asked the world's stupidest question, which, she supposed, she had.

"I need you to bandage my wounds."

"Wounds?" Plural.

He nodded again, wincing.

"What do you want me to do?"

He removed his coat. Susannah swallowed the bile that rose in her throat when she saw the blood leaking from his right side.

But there had been blood on his back, too.

Clenching her jaw, Susannah edged around behind him. He had been shot twice. The bullet that had caught him in the side had gone through the meaty part of his back and exited in front. Since there was no corresponding bullet hole in the front of his shoulder, she assumed the bullet was still in there somewhere. She knew what that meant. She had seen Shirley MacLaine dig a bullet out of Clint Eastwood's shoulder in *Two Mules for Sister Sarah*.

She also knew she couldn't do it.

Black Wind pulled the knife from its sheath, and before she quite realized what he meant to do, he cut the ruffle off the hem of her nightgown and wrapped the cloth tightly around his middle to stop the bleeding.

Then he offered the knife to her.

Susannah shook her head. "No, I can't. I'm sorry."

"I cannot reach it myself."

"I know, but . . . you see . . ." She shook her head again. "I'm sorry, I just can't."

"Please, Su-san-nah," he said quietly, and placed the knife in her hand.

"But . . ."

"Take it out."

She stared at the knife, unable to believe she was actually sitting in the rain out in the middle of nowhere, soaked to the skin, getting ready to pry a bullet out of a man's shoulder.

She glanced at the prayer feather he wore tied in his hair. *Please,* she thought, *if there's any magic in you at all, please send me back home where I belong.*

She waited, but nothing happened.

"Su-san-nah, are you going to let me bleed to death?"

His words, and the thought that he might die and leave her out there in the middle of nowhere, alone, jolted her out of her stupor.

Sitting behind him, her lower lip clamped between her teeth, she lifted the knife. "If Shirley MacLaine could do it, so can I," she muttered.

The next few minutes were the most tense of her entire life. His skin was slick with rain—rain that ran red with his blood. She thanked God that the bullet wasn't embedded too deeply, that after three nerve-wracking tries, she managed to dislodge it.

She tore a strip of cloth from her nightgown and made a square that she pressed over the wound. Sixty-five-dollar bandages, she thought as she ripped another strip of cloth to hold the first one in place.

Good thing I'm wearing a long gown, Susannah mused ruefully. *I can spare a few feet for bandages and still maintain my modesty, if not my dignity.*

"Here," she said, holding the jacket for him. "You'd better put this on."

She helped him slide the coat over his wounded shoulder, wondering if he would die of pneumonia or infection or both.

She began to shiver as the cold and the realization of what she had just done set in.

Tate Sapa took the knife from her hand and replaced it in its sheath; then, sucking in a deep breath, he stood up. He swayed unsteadily for a moment, then reached for her hand and helped her to her feet.

"What now?" Susannah asked, noting the ashen hue to his skin, the thin lines of pain that bracketed his mouth.

"We need to find shelter." Taking hold of the horse's mane, he swung onto the animal's bare back.

Pain flickered in his eyes. He sat there a moment, breathing heavily, then reached for her hand.

She wished suddenly that she could get on the horse without his help, but the animal looked as tall as a mountain.

"I'm sorry," she muttered, and placed her hand in his.

A low groan rumbled in his throat as he lifted her up in front of him.

And then they were riding across the vast empty prairie.

Chapter Seven

They rode for what seemed like days, pausing only briefly to rest the horse. Susannah was acutely conscious of Black Wind's hard-muscled arm around her waist. She couldn't remember ever being so cold, or so afraid, in her whole life.

As the hours passed, his skin grew increasingly warm to the touch. Heat radiated from his body, warming her back. It occurred to her that he probably had a fever, but there was nothing she could do about it now. At least he didn't have to worry about being cold.

At long last, he drew rein under a rocky ledge that was just big enough to shelter them from the storm. Glancing around, she saw a house in the distance. Smoke rose from the chimney. Several horses stood head down in a peeled pole corral.

There was a small barn, as well as a couple of other small buildings.

She couldn't help wondering what it was that possessed people to settle in the middle of the wilderness, surrounded by wild animals and wild Indians, and then complain when they were attacked.

"Black Wind, let's go down there," she said, glancing over her shoulder. "You need help."

"They will not help me."

"Of course they will."

He looked at her a long moment, then shook his head. "I am Lakota. They are *wasichu*."

"*Wasichu?*"

"White." There was no mistaking the scorn in his eyes, or the disdain in his voice.

"So?"

"We are enemies, Su-san-nah."

Comprehension dawned slowly, but when it hit, it hit hard.

He nodded when he saw that she understood, and then, very slowly, he slid from the back of the stallion. For a moment, he stood there, his forehead resting on the horse's flank, the rifle cradled in the crook of his arm. He drew several deep breaths, and then offered her his hand.

It was a large calloused hand, cold and wet, yet the touch of his fingers curling around hers sent a bolt of heat racing up her arm.

As soon as her feet hit the ground, he released her and stepped back. His dark eyes narrowed as his gaze swept over her.

And then, as if he was a puppet and someone

had cut the strings, he sank to the ground.

"Black Wind!" Kneeling beside him, she placed her hand on his forehead. The fever was much worse than she'd suspected. He felt like he was burning up. His brow was sheened with sweat; his eyes were glazed when he stared up at her.

She removed her wet robe and covered him with it, wondering, as she did so, what good it would do. She tried to take the rifle from him, but he refused to let it go.

She sat there for what seemed like hours, watching the rain, listening to the thunder, wondering what she would do if he died, wondering how she would ever get home again.

When she was certain he was asleep, she removed the eagle feather from his hair and slipped the loop over her wrist. Then, stroking it lightly, she closed her eyes and thought of home—hot running water and forced-air heating, cold milk and a warm bed, jeans and T-shirts and comfortable shoes . . .

Please, please, just let me go home. Even as the words crossed her mind, she wondered if she really wanted to go back to her own time now. How would she live with herself if she suddenly found herself back in her own cozy blue and white bedroom, knowing she had left Black Wind alone and unconscious.

When she opened her eyes, the rain had stopped. The sun was going down. Susannah looked at the house in the distance. A faint yellow light glowed like a welcoming beacon in one of the windows.

A loud rumbling in her stomach reminded her

that she hadn't eaten since the night before. There would be food in the house. Dry clothes and blankets. Some sort of medicine . . .

Black Wind stirred restlessly as the fever burned through him. He needed help, and soon. Susannah stuck the feather into the pocket of his coat for safekeeping and put on her robe. With great trepidation, she approached the stallion. The horse was so tall, she couldn't see over its back when she stood next to it.

For a brief moment, she considered trying to climb into the saddle and riding toward the house, but she quickly changed her mind when the horse snorted and shook its head at her. Better a long walk than to risk being thrown, or having the animal run away with her.

Muttering under her breath about being burdened with wounded Indians and bad-tempered horses, Susannah squared her shoulders and started walking.

Dogs began barking as soon as she neared the house. She came to an abrupt halt, intimidated by a big black shepherd that sniffed at her heels, its teeth bared, while the other, smaller dogs continued yapping wildly.

A moment later, Susannah saw a movement at the window, then the front door eased open a little, revealing a tall, lanky man.

"Blue, Patch," he hollered, "shut up!"

Immediately, the dogs stopped barking.

"Who are you?" the man demanded brusquely. "What are you doing out here?"

"My name's Susannah Kingston. I'm lost and I need help."

"Who is it, Abe?" a female voice called.

"Some woman. Says she's lost."

"Well, don't just stand there. Bring her on in. It's cold outside."

Abe shook his head. "I don't know, Hester. She's in her nightclothes."

Susannah heard the sound of footsteps, and then a woman appeared in the doorway, standing a little behind her husband.

"Come on in, deary," the woman said. She opened the door wider. "You're gonna catch your death standing out there in the cold."

"I need help," Susannah said. "The man with me is badly hurt."

"Go get him, Abe," Hester said. She gave him a little shove. "Hurry along now."

"Damn it, woman . . ."

"Abe Micklin, you do what I say, and you do it now!"

"I'll go with you," Susannah said.

"Damn right," Abe muttered. "Can he ride, or do I need to hitch up the wagon?"

"A wagon would be a big help."

Grumbling loudly, Abe lumbered off to hitch up the team.

"Come inside, deary," Hester said. "Let me get you something dry to wear."

"Thank you."

"Come along."

Susannah stood inside the bedroom doorway while Hester rummaged in a trunk at the foot of the bed.

Hester looked to be in her early forties, Susannah thought. She had black hair just turning gray, sharp brown eyes, and the wrinkled skin common to women who spent a lifetime on the plains.

Susannah glanced around. The house was small but clean, sparsely furnished with a few pieces of rough-hewn furniture. Rag rugs covered the floor, cheerful gingham curtains fluttered at the window. A bouquet of wildflowers arranged in a rusty tin can made a bright spot of color on the kitchen table.

"Here we go," Hester said. Rising clumsily to her feet, she handed Susannah a warm wool dress and a pair of boots.

"I reckon that dress'll be a mite big on you, deary, but at least it's dry."

"Thank you so much."

Susannah had changed and was ready to go by the time Abe returned with the wagon.

He was a crusty old coot, Susannah mused. Tall and fence-post thin, he sat hunched over on the wagon seat, his battered hat pulled low on his forehead. He had skin like leather and pale green eyes that didn't miss a trick. She thought he looked like an old Ichabod Crane.

They reached Black Wind a short time later. Susannah jumped from the wagon seat and rushed to his side, praying that he was still alive.

"A redskin!" Abe exclaimed, coming up beside her. "You brought me out here for a dirty redskin!"

"He's hurt. He needs help."

"I ain't helpin' no Injun. And I sure as hell ain't havin' one in my house."

"Please, mister, he'll die."

"Good riddance, I say."

"You've got to help him," Susannah said. "He's . . . he's my husband."

"Husband!" He stared at her in disbelief.

"Yes, he's a scout for the Army at Fort Collier," Susannah said, making the story up as she went along. "We were on our way back to the fort when we were attacked by Indians. My husband was shot."

"Scout, huh? Long way from the fort, ain't ya?"

"I got lost trying to find my way back."

Abe studied her for several moments, his eyes narrowed, his expression dubious.

"Su-san-nah?"

She glanced at Black Wind. He was looking up at her, his eyes dark mirrors of pain. And then, slowly, his eyelids closed again. Fearing he had died, she knelt beside Black Wind and felt for his pulse. Thank God, he was still alive.

"Please, Mr. Micklin. We need help."

"All right, all right," Abe said. "Long as he's an Army scout . . ." He thrust the rifle into Susannah's hands, muttering under his breath as he did so.

He lifted Black Wind with remarkable ease for such a skinny man, displaying a wiry strength that took Susannah by surprise. Black Wind appeared to be unconscious, which was probably a blessing, Susannah mused as Abe plopped him over one shoulder and carried him to the wagon. She hurried forward and lowered the tailgate, stood there chewing on her lower lip as Abe placed Black Wind, none too gently, into the bed of the wagon.

"I think I'll ride back here, with him," she said.

"Suit yourself," Abe muttered. Taking up the stallion's reins, he tied the horse to the rear of the wagon, leaving Susannah to climb into the bed of the wagon as best she could.

She put the rifle beside Black Wind, then climbed aboard, scraping her knee on the rough wood as she did so. Pushing the rifle out of the way, she sat down beside Black Wind and cradled his head in her lap, her hand idly stroking his brow.

He groaned softly as the wagon hit a bump.

"It'll be all right," Susannah said, wondering if he could hear her. "You'll be dry and warm soon."

Abe drove the wagon to the barn, then vaulted to the ground.

"You can bed down in the barn," he said sourly. "I ain't havin' no redskin under my roof, Army scout or no."

Susannah didn't argue. She was too thrilled at the prospect of having a roof over her head again.

Abe carried Black Wind inside and settled him on a bed of sweet-smelling straw in an empty stall. Susannah followed on his heels, lugging the heavy rifle.

"I reckon Hester'll be out directly," he said curtly. "I'll put your horse in the corral."

"Thank you."

Muttering something unintelligible, Abe left the barn.

Susannah propped the rifle in a corner, glad to be rid of it. She had never liked guns; this one was almost as long as she was tall.

A short time later, Hester Micklin limped into the barn carrying several blankets, an oil lamp, and a large basket.

"There's some hot water in there, and some salve you can use to treat his wounds," she said, setting the basket on an upturned milk pail, "and cloth for bandages."

"Thank you, Mrs. Micklin."

"Hester, dearie, just call me Hester."

"Thank you, Hester."

"Ain't nothing. Just bein' neighborly. When you get done tendin' your man, you come on up to the house. I've got some soup warmin'."

Susannah nodded, touched by the woman's generosity.

"Don't mind my Abe too much," Hester said. She spared a fond glance for her husband as he led the horses into their stalls and forked them each some hay. "Injuns killed his brother last year."

"I'm so sorry."

Hester nodded. "Pawnee found Sam out huntin' and kilt him. My Abe ain't been the same since. He hates 'em all now. I tried to tell him you can't blame every Injun alive for what happened, but he says he can. You come get me if you need help with yer man."

"I will."

She watched as Abe took Hester's arm and walked her toward the house. For all his gruffness, she noticed he treated his wife gently enough.

Setting her mind to the task at hand, Susannah eased Black Wind out of his jacket.

90

"My man, indeed," she muttered as she stripped off his wet moccasins. She bit down on her lower lip as she contemplated removing his breechclout. "No way," she decided. It was only a little damp, after all.

There was a covered bowl of hot water and a chunk of yellow soap in the basket. Susannah washed Black Wind's face, chest, arms, and legs, then carefully dried him with a length of toweling. She tried to remove the bandages from his back and shoulder, but the cotton was stuck fast to the dried blood. Her stomach knotted as she soaked the cloth, then peeled the cotton away.

She washed the dried blood from the wounds, then studied the ugly holes carefully. She didn't see any of the red streaks that were supposed to indicate infection. Breathing a silent prayer, she spread a thick layer of smelly yellow salve over the wounds, bandaged them with strips of clean cloth, then sat back on her heels.

"Well, I've done all I know how to do," she muttered. "I guess the rest is up to you."

Rising wearily to her feet, she spread his jacket over the stall door to dry, then walked up to the house and knocked on the front door.

"Come in, come in," Hester said. She ushered Susannah into a tiny kitchen. "Sit down before you fall down, dearie."

"Can I help you with that?" Susannah asked.

"No, you just rest. You look all done in."

In no time at all, Hester served up a bowl of soup, a thick slice of fresh baked bread, and a cup of hot tea.

"I'll fix a bowl of broth for yer man," Hester

said, bustling around the kitchen. "I've got some willow bark tea, here, too. You make him drink all he can hold."

The soup was hot and delicious, the bread sweeter than manna from heaven. Susannah ate ravenously, nodded when Hester asked if she wanted seconds.

With a sigh, Susannah sat back in her chair, feeling as content as a kitten after lapping up a bowl of cream. "Thank you, Hester. That was wonderful."

The other woman waved off her thanks. "Bah, it was just a bowl of soup."

"Well, it was the best I've ever tasted. The bread, too."

Hester's plump cheeks flushed with pleasure, and Susannah had the feeling Abe probably didn't hand out too many compliments in the course of a day—or a year.

"Here," Hester said, placing a tray on the table. "There's a bowl of soup and a pot of tea. You make sure he eats. Fever's bound to set in if it hasn't already."

"He's burning up," Susannah said.

Hester nodded. "Well, then, you need to make sure he drinks plenty of that willow bark tea. It's good for fever."

"Thank you," Susannah said. Rising, she took up the tray and left the house.

This was a fine turn of events, she thought crossly. The Indian had stolen a horse and kidnapped her, and now she was playing nursemaid when what she ought to do was to have Abe throw Black Wind's butt into the wagon and haul him back to the fort.

Stepping into the stall, she placed the tray on the overturned milk pail, wondering how she was supposed to get him to eat or drink anything when he seemed to be unconscious.

Kneeling beside him, she placed her hand on his brow. It was still much too hot. A fine sheen of sweat covered his face and chest.

"Black Wind? Wake up."

He mumbled something incoherent under his breath.

"Black Wind? Tate Sapa, wake up."

His eyelids opened and he stared at her for a long moment before recognition flickered in his eyes. "Su-san-nah?"

She poured a cup of tea, then slid her arm behind his neck and lifted his head. "Here, drink this."

She'd been afraid he would refuse, but he drank greedily.

"*Sanpa.*"

"What?"

"More."

"Oh." She poured another cup and held it for him. "I've got some broth for you."

He shook his head, too weary to eat.

"You've got to eat something," Susannah said. She uncovered the bowl, picked up the spoon, and dipped it into the broth. Sitting beside him, she slid her arm under his head again. "Come on, open your mouth."

He stared up at her, his black eyes dull with pain.

"Just a little," she urged.

"Not . . . hungry."

"I know, but you need to eat to keep your strength up."

Slowly, he opened his mouth and let her feed him. One bite, two, three, and then his eyelids fluttered down and he was asleep. It frightened her, how hot he was. She could feel the heat rising off his body.

She covered him with a blanket, then sat beside him, wishing that she could do more.

His fever worsened during the night. Wracked with pain, he tossed and turned, murmuring words she could not understand. She sponged him with cool water, offered him a drink when he was coherent, held him down when he started to thrash about. Chills followed the fever. She covered him with more blankets, but he continued to shiver uncontrollably.

She thought of all the movies she had seen where the hero and heroine huddled together, sharing their body warmth.

Muttering "What the heck," she slid under the covers and pressed herself against him. After a moment, he turned toward her, his arms wrapping around her, drawing her close, until she could hardly breathe. Gradually, the shivers that wracked his body quieted and his breathing grew less labored.

With each minute that passed, Susannah became more aware of the body pressed so intimately against her own. His skin was warm and smooth. She could feel his hard-muscled thighs entwined with hers. His hair was thick and soft.

She put her hands on his arms, intending to push him away. Instead, she let her fingertips slide over his biceps. She knew men who worked out every day who would kill to have arms like these, she mused, to have a hard flat stomach ridged with muscle.

She closed her eyes, her nostrils filling with the scent of sweat and man, hay and straw, the pungent scent of horses and cows and manure.

She was aware of his every movement, the feather-light touch of his breath on her cheek, his long bare leg that had somehow found its way beneath her skirts to nestle against her own. She noticed that her heart seemed to be beating in time with his, that his chest was solid and unyielding against her breasts.

Swallowing hard, she opened her eyes. Light from the lamp bathed his face in a warm golden glow, and she thought again how handsome he was. He moaned softly, his face contorting with pain. His arms tightened around her as a tremor shook him from head to foot.

The fever returned with a vengeance. He pushed her away, threw the blankets aside.

"Stop it," she said. "Black Wind, stop thrashing about like that."

He stilled at the sound of her voice, and then he was staring at her from fever-bright eyes. *"Mni."*

"What?"

"Woyatke."

"I don't understand. Speak English."

He frowned, as though trying to recall the word in her language. *"Woyatke."*

"You want a drink?" she guessed.

He nodded weakly.

Scrambling out from under the blankets, she poured him a cup of tea, held his head up while he gulped it down.

"*Sanpa.*"

"More?"

He nodded, and she refilled the cup. He drank more slowly this time, then, with a sigh, he closed his eyes, apparently falling asleep between one breath and the next.

Gently, she lowered his head, drew the covers up to his chin. And then, because she was too tired to make up another bed, she crawled under the covers, but sleep eluded her. Thoughts buzzed around her mind like bees around a honeycomb. How was she going to get back home? Was it the magic in the eagle feather that had brought her here? What if she could never go back to her own time? Her friends would be worried by now, her parents in a panic. What if the Army was following them?

Black Wind tossed restlessly beside her, scattering her thoughts.

"This is all your fault," she muttered irritably. "I don't know how or why, but it is. I just know it."

It would be so much easier to hate him if he was old and ugly, she mused, or if he was mean-spirited and obnoxious. Instead, he was just the kind of man she liked to write about—tall, dark, and handsome, strong, yet tender. The kind of man she had always hoped to marry.

Feather in the Wind

With a sigh, Susannah closed her eyes. Maybe tomorrow she would wake up in her own bed and find out she had dreamed the whole thing. She wouldn't miss this place one bit, she thought, but if she could remember it when she woke up, it would make a hell of a story!

Chapter Eight

Tate Sapa woke abruptly, plagued by a terrible thirst. His body felt as though it were on fire, his mouth was dry, it was hard to breathe, to think. He brushed a hand across his face, his fingers tangling in long silken strands.

Frowning, he opened his eyes to find Susannah cuddled up against him, her head resting on his uninjured shoulder, her arm lying across his chest. He wrapped a lock of her hair around his finger, marveling at how soft it was. His own hair was thick and coarse; hers was like dandelion down.

She stirred in her sleep. Though she slept fully clothed, he could feel the warmth, the softness, of her feminine curves brush against his bare skin. The pain in his back and shoulder receded as a new ache made itself known. He did not want to admit that he cared for her, did not want to acknowledge that her nearness had the power to affect him in such a way. He was a Lakota warrior. She was his enemy.

His enemy. . . . If that were true, why had she appeared to him in his vision? What did it mean?

He groaned deep in his throat as her hand slid down his chest and over his belly, coming to rest just above the waistband of his clout.

Tate Sapa took a deep, steadying breath, and his nostrils filled with the warm, sleepy scent of her. He resisted the urge to caress her cheek, to trail his finger over the fullness of her lower lip.

With an effort, he dragged his thoughts from her lush flesh and tried to concentrate on going home. His people would be leaving their winter camp, bound for higher ground. The women would be repairing tepees ravaged by a harsh winter, the men would be readying their weapons for the hunt.

And he was lying here, helpless as a newborn foal, his body hard and aching for the woman sleeping at his side.

Wakan Tanka, unshimalam ye oyate. Great Spirit, have mercy on me.

Susannah stirred at his side again, and he found himself gazing into her eyes, warm brown eyes hazy with sleep. A wave of color washed into her cheeks when she realized how intimately she was pressed against him.

Overcome with embarrassment, Susannah scrambled out from under the covers. Murmuring something about getting breakfast, she hurried out of the barn. Outside, she took several deep breaths while the crisp morning air cooled her flushed cheeks.

She had been having one of the most erotic dreams of her life moments before she woke to find herself pressed up against the very man she had been dreaming about.

She took another deep breath, willing her heart to stop racing, but she couldn't shake off the memory of that dream. She had been alone in a hide lodge with Black Wind, lying with him on a pile of soft furs while they took turns exploring each other from head to heel. Susannah's palms tingled with the memory of touching his bare flesh, of running her hands over his well-muscled arms, over his chest and belly. How much had been a dream, she wondered, and how much had been reality? And how would she ever face him again?

With a shake of her head, she walked swiftly up the path to the house. Hoping she looked calmer than she felt, she knocked on the door.

Hester opened the door, a smile of welcome spreading over her ruddy face.

"No need to knock," Hester said, "just come on in whenever you've a mind to." She stepped back so Susannah could enter, then headed toward the kitchen. "Breakfast is almost ready," she called over her shoulder.

Susannah followed Hester into the kitchen, wondering if the woman was always so cheerful. Clad in a yellow gingham dress and a huge white apron, with her hair piled on top of her head, Hester Micklin reminded Susannah of a daisy.

"Sit down, dearie," Hester invited, waving a

hand in the direction of the table. "Here you go." She pushed a steaming cup of coffee in front of Susannah. "This will take the chill out of your bones right quick."

"Thank you. I'm sorry to be so much trouble."

"Landsakes, child, you're no trouble at all. It's nice having another woman on the place for a change. How's that man of yours doing this morning?"

"He's better," Susannah murmured, and felt her cheeks flush at the memory of waking up practically lying on top of him.

Hester nodded. "I'll have to find you another dress. That one's powerful wrinkled. Must have been uncomfortable, sleeping in your clothes. I'll see if I can't find you a nightgown, too."

Susannah sighed with regret as she thought of her beautiful nightgown. It wasn't good for anything but rags now.

She sipped the hot bitter brew that passed for coffee on the frontier. She had always heard Western coffee was strong enough to float a horseshoe; now, she believed it. Only a generous helping of sugar and cream made the stuff palatable.

She had passed Abe on her way to the house. He had scowled at Susannah as she walked by, then went back to forking hay into a corral. She wondered if the man ever smiled, and why Hester, who seemed always cheerful, had married such a grouch.

"Here you go," Hester said.

Susannah stared at the plate that Hester set in front of her. It was piled with scrambled eggs, several thick slices of ham, a mountain of fried potatoes, biscuits and gravy. It was more food than she usually ate in a day.

"Go on, dig in. I heated some beef broth for your man, although if he's anything like my Abe, he won't put up with broth and weak tea for long."

Susannah had barely made a dent in her breakfast when Abe stomped into the kitchen.

"Sit down, love," Hester said, smiling at him. "Breakfast is ready."

With a grunt, Abe dropped into the chair across from Susannah. A few minutes later, Hester handed him a plate, then joined them at the table.

Abe ate in silence, all his energy apparently focused on his breakfast, which disappeared at an alarming rate.

Hester filled up the silence, talking about her garden, the possibility of planting fruit trees, their nearest neighbor who lived over the rise.

"Well," Hester said, sitting back and regarding Susannah with a smile, "you look like you could use a bath, a clean dress, and a hairbrush. Abe, bring the tub in for me before you go back outside, will you? Oh, and a bucket of water, too. That's a dear."

With a scowl, Abe pushed away from the table. "You don't see me taking no bath in the middle of the week," he muttered as he stomped out the door.

"Hester, I don't want to be a bother."

"Landsakes, child, it's no bother."

"But . . ."

"Oh, don't you pay Abe no mind. He just likes to complain." Hester stood up and began clearing the table.

"Here," Susannah said, rising to her feet, "let me do that."

"Why, thank you, dearie."

"It's the least I can do."

"It's mighty nice, having another woman in the house," Hester said.

The back door slammed open as Abe came in carrying a bucket of water.

"Thanks, love," Hester said. "Don't forget the tub."

With a grunt, Abe left the room.

Hester fetched a large pan out of a cupboard and filled it with water, then put it on the stove to heat.

"Uh, Hester?"

"Something wrong?"

"I . . . that is . . ." Susannah fidgeted. "I need . . ."

"Landsakes, the necessary's out behind the house. I plum forgot to tell you that last night, didn't I?"

Susannah nodded, then hurried outside. As she made her way to the outhouse, she quietly cursed the fates that had sent her to this place, this time. Last night, she had squatted behind a bush, thinking she would write her next book for free in exchange for a roll of toilet paper.

When she returned to the kitchen, Hester was washing the dishes. Another pan of water was heating on the stove. A large round wooden tub sat in one corner of the room.

Susannah picked up a cotton dishcloth and began drying the dishes.

"I'll take care of the dishes," Hester said. "Why don't you go give your man some breakfast? By the time he's taken care of, your bath should be ready."

With a nod, Susannah dropped the towel over the back of a chair.

"Oh, I found an old chamber pot, too. It's there, by the back door."

"A chamber pot?"

"For your man, so's he don't have to go outside."

"Oh." Susannah stared at the chamber pot. It was round, with a handle on one side. A sudden rush of color heated her cheeks as she imagined offering Black Wind the pot.

Holding the pot gingerly by the handle, she picked up the bowl of soup and the spoon and left the house, thinking that Hester Micklin was one of the nicest women she had ever met.

He heard her footsteps long before she entered the stall. The scent of cooked beef filled the air, but he had no appetite for food, only an agonizing thirst. He watched her place a bowl on the overturned bucket. Her dress was badly wrinkled, her hair mussed, and there was a flush on her cheeks.

Susannah took a deep breath. "Do you have to . . ." Her gaze slid away from his as she plopped the chamber pot down beside him. "That's in case you have to . . . you know."

He looked at her quizzically for a moment,

then stifled a grin as recognition dawned. He did, indeed, have to.

Muttering under her breath, she left the barn.

Tate Sapa could hear her pacing just outside the door while he relieved himself.

Her cheeks were redder than the wildflowers that grew in the valley of the Little Big Horn when she returned to take the pot away.

She wouldn't meet his gaze when she returned to the barn. "How are you feeling this morning?"

He shrugged, then winced as the movement sent a sharp pain through his injured shoulder.

The hand she placed on his brow felt cool.

"You've still got a fever," Susannah remarked. She picked up the bowl of soup and removed the cloth that covered it. "Do you want me to feed you?"

"No."

She handed him the bowl, but he shook his head. "I do not want it."

"You've got to eat."

"No."

With a sigh of exasperation, she covered the bowl and set it down on the bucket. "Fine. Starve. See if I care." She glared at him a moment. "I guess I'd better check your wounds."

When he didn't protest, she removed the bandage from his shoulder. To her untrained eyes, it appeared to be healing. In the movies, people always looked for red streaks, but she didn't see anything that looked ominous. She applied a fresh dressing and rewrapped his shoulder, then drew back the blanket to check the wound in his side. There were fresh blood stains on the cloth swathed around his middle.

Swallowing the bile that rose in her throat, she removed the bandages. Blood seeped from the ragged hole.

"I think it needs stitching," she remarked.

"Do it then."

"I can't. I'll get Hester."

"Su-san-nah . . ."

But she was already out of the barn and running for the house.

Hester listened intently to what she had to say, gathered up her medical supplies and a fresh pot of tea, and followed Susannah to the barn.

"This is Hester," Susannah said. "She's going to help you."

Hester smiled at Black Wind reassuringly as she examined the wound, front and back.

"Don't worry," she said. "Shouldn't take more than a half-dozen stitches to put you to rights. The entry wound's closed up nice."

Quickly and efficiently, she wiped away the blood and washed the wound, disinfected his side with carbolic, threaded a slender silver needle.

Nausea churned in Susannah's stomach. She was thinking maybe she had better wait outside when Black Wind reached for her hand.

"Su-san-nah, do not go."

She stared into his eyes, deep black eyes filled with pain, eyes that begged her to stay. With a sigh of resignation, she settled herself beside him, her back turned toward Hester, Black Wind's hand cradled in her lap.

"This will likely hurt a bit," Hester told Black

Wind. "Try not to move."

Tate Sapa nodded, his gaze fixed on Susannah's face.

Susannah squeezed his hand, felt his fingers tighten around hers as Hester began to stitch the ragged edges of the wound together. Sweat dotted his brow; his jaw was rigid, but he didn't move.

Susannah swallowed hard, certain she was going to vomit up the big breakfast she had consumed earlier. She could hear the soft whisper of the thread being drawn through Black Wind's mutilated flesh. His fingers were crushing her hand. His face was scored by deep lines of pain. His gaze never left her face.

She tried to smile reassuringly though she felt like crying. She'd had stitches once, a long time ago, but they had given her a shot to numb the pain so that she hadn't felt anything at all. And then the nurse had given her a big red lollipop to make her smile. Knowing it was silly, Susannah wished she had a red lollipop to give to Black Wind.

"There," Hester said. "All done." She dabbed at the wound, mopping up the blood, then bandaged his side once again. "It don't seem to be infected," she said cheerfully. She glanced at the untouched bowl of broth, then looked at Susannah. "You make sure he drinks all that broth and the tea, and you make him drink as much water as he can hold."

"I will. Thank you, Hester."

"*Le mita pila,*" Tate Sapa said. "My thanks also."

"Glad to help out. You mind what I said, young man. You eat, then get some rest," Hester said, and gathering up her things, she left the barn.

"*Pilamaya*, Su-san-nah."

She looked down at their linked hands, his so big and brown, hers so much smaller. "I didn't do anything."

"You could have left me to die."

"No, I couldn't." She drew her hand away from his and reached for the bowl. "I want you to drink this, then get some sleep."

He nodded, and she uncovered the bowl and began to feed him. When he had eaten all he could, she held the cup for him. He started to refuse but, seeing the look of determination in her eyes, he drank it down, deciding it would be quicker to do it than to argue.

When he was settled back on the blanket, Tate Sapa reached for her hand again. Susannah could feel the tension thrumming through him as he closed his eyes, felt a wave of tenderness surge through her as he drifted off to sleep, her hand still tightly held in his.

With a sigh, she eased her hand from his and went up to the house, drawn by the promise of a hot bath and a change of clothes.

He began to heal quickly after that, as he slept most of the time. Susannah spent much of her time simply sitting beside him, watching him sleep, surprised that she felt the need to do so.

Some afternoons she spent up at the house with Hester. She learned to make a cake from scratch, learned now to make candles, and how to bake bread.

Now, it was morning and she was standing at the stove, stirring a pot of oatmeal that she had prepared entirely on her own. She ladled some into a bowl, sprinkled it with brown sugar, then covered it with a cloth and set it on a tray next to a thick slice of bread and a cup of tea.

Humming softly, Susannah walked down to the barn.

Black Wind was sitting up, scowling.

"Are you hungry?" she asked.

Black Wind stared up at her, thinking how pretty she looked as she sat down and spread her skirts around her. He had never known anyone who moved with such unconscious grace.

"I thought maybe you were tired of broth, so I made you some oatmeal." She uncovered the bowl, then dipped the spoon into the bowl, frowning when he refused to open his mouth. "What's wrong?"

"I am not a child. I do not need you to feed me." He regretted the words as soon as they were spoken, but he could not call them back. It angered him that he was weak; he resented the fact that he was dependent upon her. He was a man, a warrior—not an infant. He did not want her mothering him or feeling sorry for him.

"Oh, well, fine. Here, feed yourself then." Susannah dropped the spoon into the bowl, then thrust the bowl into his hands. Then, her lips drawn in an angry line, she scrambled to her feet and flounced out of the barn.

Tate Sapa swore as she slammed the heavy

door behind her, cursed the Blue Coats who had shot him, cursed his own helplessness.

He ate all the oatmeal, intrigued by its sweetness, ate the bread, drank the tea, made use of the chamber pot, then settled back on the blanket and closed his eyes.

Scattered images flickered through his mind: the majestic peaks of the *Paha Sapa*, the vast rolling prairie awash with sunlight, quiet nights along the Tongue River, when the air was still and the earth was at peace.

He thought of his father, crippled in the last battle against the Army, and wondered how his father had survived the winter without him.

He thought of Wakinyela, and wondered if she was still waiting for him, or if, in his absence, she had turned to another.

Belatedly, he wondered if the Army would come looking for him.

But mostly he thought of Susannah, his body hardening at the memory of the morning he had awakened to find her lying beside him. Susannah, with her pale golden skin and curly brown hair; Susannah, with her expressive brown eyes and husky voice. She had plagued his thoughts since the day he saw her in vision. And now she was here. What did it mean?

Hearing the sound of her footsteps, he struggled to sit up. Without knowing why, he dragged the soldier's coat toward him and searched the pockets for the feather. When he found it, he slipped it under the straw behind his head.

Susannah regarded him for a minute, then, with a grimace, she picked up the chamber pot, took it outside, and emptied it in the outhouse. *Disgusting,* she mused as she rinsed it out under the pump, then made her way back to the barn.

"I'm sorry I got angry," she said. She placed the pot in a corner of the stall.

She waited a moment, hoping he would apologize, too, and then shrugged when no apology was forthcoming. "How are you feeling?"

"I have been better."

A faint smile tugged at the corners of her lips. "Can I get you anything else?"

"I want to go outside."

"I don't think you should get up yet."

"I do not care what you think, woman. I am going outside."

"Suit yourself."

She stood back, her arms crossed over her breasts, while he struggled to his feet.

Tate Sapa was breathing heavily by the time he managed to stand up. Feeling light-headed, he stood with his back against the side of the stall. Sweat dripped from his brow; his stomach felt queasy.

Susannah looked up at him. He towered over her, tall and broad-shouldered. Still, for all his bulk, she thought she could probably knock him over with no more than a harsh look.

"Still want to go outside?" she asked.

Gritting his teeth, he nodded.

"Men," she muttered, and stepping forward, she slipped her arm around his waist. "Lean on me, then."

It was not a totally unwelcome idea. Stooping a little, he draped his arm around her shoulders.

Side by side, they walked slowly out into the sunlight.

Tate Sapa tilted his head back and took a deep breath, basking in the warmth of the sun on his face, the fresh clean smell of earth and wind.

Abe was chopping wood down by the stream. Susannah saw Hester hanging clothes on the line that stretched between the back of the house and a solitary tree.

Susannah glanced at Black Wind. "Do you want to sit down?"

"No. I must walk."

"Walk? If I let go of you, you'd probably fall flat on your face."

He looked at her for what seemed like an eternity, his dark gaze holding her own, until she felt as if her insides were melting like chocolate left too long in the sun.

"Then," he said, very softly, "do not let me go."

Do not let me go. Black Wind's words, innocent as they were, sent shivers down her spine. His skin was warm beneath her hand. She could feel his hip pressed intimately against her own, feel the weight of his arm resting on her shoulders.

Susannah took a step forward, and his thigh brushed against hers. Taking slow steps, they made their way toward the narrow stream that cut behind the house.

Susannah slid a furtive glance in Black Wind's direction. There were fine lines of pain around his eyes, a determined set to his mouth. Men, she thought disgustedly. Always needing to prove how macho they were. She knew every step had to be causing him pain, yet he walked doggedly onward.

He was breathing heavily by the time they reached the stream. A fine sheen of perspiration coated his brow.

Susannah jerked her chin toward a deadfall near the water's edge. "You'd better sit down before you fall down," she muttered.

This time he didn't argue. She wanted to help him, but she had a feeling he wouldn't have appreciated the gesture just now.

With a shake of her head, Susannah viewed the countryside. It was peaceful, here by the river. Lacy cottonwoods grew near the stream, their leaves fluttering in the breeze. Long-stemmed plants and tiny flowers in rainbow colors grew along the banks. Early-morning sunlight danced over the water, sparkling like diamonds tossed by a careless hand. A chorus of birds chirped in the treetops.

"It's pretty here," Susannah remarked. Sitting down, she removed her shoes and stockings and tested the water with her toes. With a yelp, she jerked her foot from the river. "Geez, it's freezing cold!"

"It is always cold," Tate Sapa remarked with a grin. "The water comes from high in the mountains."

"Well, you could have warned me," Susannah muttered. "It feels like it came from an iceberg." Drying her feet, she pulled her heavy cotton stockings back on. "Where did you learn to speak English so well?"

"From a white boy that we took prisoner. I

taught him to speak Lakota, and he taught me to speak his language. My friends ridiculed me for learning the *wasichu* tongue, but it came easy to me. My uncle encouraged me. He said it would be a good thing, for one of our people to speak the white man's language."

"I would think more of your people would have wanted to learn."

"Why?"

Susannah shrugged. "I don't know. I guess I'm guilty of feeling that everyone should speak English. It's quite a sore spot where I come from. What happened to the boy?"

"He was killed by the Crow when they raided our village two summers ago."

"Oh." She plucked a blade of grass and twirled it between her thumb and forefinger. "How long were you in jail?"

"Since last winter."

Susannah pictured the grimy little cell. The idea of being locked up in such a place made her shudder. "That's a long time."

Tate Sapa nodded. He had endured the lack of food, the hard work, the derision of the soldiers, the cruel beatings, without complaint.

He was a warrior, accustomed to hardships. But he had never been forced to endure anything as loathsome, as humiliating, as being shackled and confined in the white man's iron-barred house. Being imprisoned had stripped him of his dignity. He was Lakota, accustomed to the freedom of the plains. It had cut deep into his pride to be locked up, to have his steps curbed by a length of thick chain.

He was a warrior, unaccustomed to taking orders, to being forcibly compelled to obey or be whipped like a dog. Among the Lakota, a man was free to travel whatever road he chose, to fight or make peace, to be a warrior or to sit with the women. The idea of one Lakota giving orders to another was unheard of.

Head back, he drew in a deep breath. He was free now. Soon, he would return to his people. . . .

A movement caught his eye. Turning his head, he saw Susannah walking downstream, pausing now and then to pick the flowers that grew in scattered clumps along the shore.

Her hips swayed provocatively as she walked. Her movements were graceful as she bent to pluck a bright pink bloom. Heat spiraled through him, pooling in his groin.

Tate Sapa's mouth went dry as she turned and started walked toward him. The sun streaked her hair with gold. There was a smile on her lips as she bent her head to smell the colorful bouquet in her hands.

As she approached, he rose slowly to his feet, his heart pounding like a Lakota war drum.

"Su-san-nah."

"Are you ready to go back?" she asked. "I think . . ." Her words trailed off as she saw the heat smoldering in his eyes.

And then he was reaching for her, his movements slow and deliberate so as not to surprise or frighten her, giving her plenty of time to back away.

"Oh," she murmured, and knew she had been

waiting, hoping, for just this moment since the first day she had seen him in the guardhouse.

He placed his hands on her shoulders and drew her toward him, until all she could see were his eyes—deep, dark pools of liquid ebony. Susannah swayed toward him, the flowers tumbling from her hands as she wrapped her arms around his waist, tilted her head back, and closed her eyes.

After a moment, she opened her eyes to find him staring down at her. "Kiss me," she whispered.

She saw the confusion in his eyes. Did Indians kiss? If not, it was time he learned. And before she could change her mind, she drew his head toward hers and pressed her lips to his.

His lips were warm and firm and hesitant. For a man who probably had never kissed a woman before, he learned quickly. Between one breath and the next, he was pressing his lips to hers. Mindful of his injured side, she tried not to hurt him as she pressed against him, wanting to be closer. His skin was hot beneath her fingertips as she stroked his back and shoulders. Some small part of her brain that was still functioning told her it was madness to kiss him like this, but her body had no interest in what her mind had to say.

Rising on tiptoe, she deepened the kiss, her tongue sliding over his lower lip. He drew back in surprise, then slanted his mouth over hers and explored her lips with his tongue.

Tate Sapa gasped when her tongue met his, and then, with a low groan, his mouth devoured hers, making her heart soar and her insides turn to jelly.

His hands moved restlessly up and down her back, then cupped her buttocks and held her tightly against him, letting her feel the hard evidence of his desire.

Susannah moaned softly. She had been kissed many times, but none had ever affected her like this. She felt as though she were spinning out of control, as if she had no mind or will of her own, no thought save to yield her heart and soul to the man whose kiss turned her thoughts to mush and had every nerve in her body humming with pleasure. She ran her hands over his arms, arms that were rock-hard and quivering with tension.

"Su-san-nah?" He drew back, his dark eyes smoldering with passion.

She stared up at him, her thoughts in turmoil as her conscience struggled to make itself known. She wanted him, she thought, wanted him desperately. But there could be no future for the two of them. The question of morality aside, she would only be asking for heartbreak if she gave herself to this man, because there was no way they could ever have a life together.

Susannah took a deep breath and then, slowly, shook her head. "No, I can't."

He went very still, his gaze fixed on hers. "Because I am Lakota?"

"No."

"Do not lie to me, Su-san-nah." His voice was harsh, edged with anger.

"I'm not lying! I . . . I just can't."

He looked at her for a long moment, then he

turned his back on her and began walking toward the barn.

"Black Wind, wait." She grabbed her shoes and stockings and hurried after him. "Let me help you."

"I do not need your help, white woman."

Feeling as though he had slapped her, she came to an abrupt halt. She hadn't meant to hurt him. Why couldn't he understand? Surely he must know they could have no future together. And then she frowned. He might be an Indian, but he was a man, too, and like every other man, he wasn't interested in the future, only in what he wanted now.

She waited until he had a good lead on her, and then she followed him. He walked slowly, one hand pressed to his wounded side. It annoyed her no end to realize she wanted to run after him, to slip her arm around his waist and have him lean on her again.

When they reached the Micklins' place, Susannah veered off toward the house, suddenly feeling the need to be with Hester.

"Oh, there you are," Hester remarked as Susannah stepped into the kitchen. "I sent Abe down to the barn to fetch you for dinner, but he couldn't find you."

"We went for a walk."

"Oh," Hester said, beaming. "Your man—what's his name, anyway?"

"Black Wind."

Hester nodded. "He must be feelin' better."

"Much better," Susannah muttered dryly.

"Well, now, that's good. I kept a plate warm for

the two of you." She reached into the oven and removed a covered platter. "This should tide you over until supper time."

"Thank you, Hester." Susannah took the plate and silverware the other woman offered her. "I don't know how I'll ever be able to repay you for your kindness."

Hester dismissed her thanks with a wave of her hand. "No need to thank me. I'm glad to be able to do it."

"Well, I just want you to know how much I appreciate it."

"Hush, now, I ain't done anything more than anybody else would have done."

"Well, where I come from, people aren't quite so neighborly," Susannah said, thinking of home, where people hid behind locked doors and carried automatic weapons.

"I found another dress you might be able to wear," Hester said. "Of course, we'll have to take it in, and it's a little out of style, but I think the color will suit you. You can try it on later."

"Thank you," Susannah said, thinking she had never known anyone as generous as Hester Micklin.

"You'd best get that down to your man while it's still hot," Hester said, smiling.

With a nod, Susannah left the house.

Thoughts of Hester fled her mind as she neared the barn. She found Black Wind inside. He was standing by the stallion's stall, lightly stroking the horse's neck.

She shivered, felt her cheeks flame as she re-membered Black Wind's hands moving over her back and shoulders, cupping her buttocks, drawing her up against him.

Long and lean, with copper-colored skin and long black hair, he was by far the most handsome man she had ever seen. She watched the play of muscles in his back and shoulders as he scratched the stallion behind the ears, felt her heartbeat speed up at the sound of his voice speaking words she did not understand.

She might have stood there forever, admiring the way he moved, the long clean lines of his back, if he hadn't turned to face her.

Their gazes met and held, and it was as if sparks flew between them. She saw the yearning in Black Wind's eyes and feared he would read the same wanting in her own.

"I brought you something to eat," Susannah said, thrusting the platter toward him.

He took the plate from her hands, his gaze never leaving her face.

She looked into his eyes, eyes as deep and black as a midnight sea, and felt herself drowning in their depths.

"Eat it while it's hot," she said, and practically ran out of the barn to keep from throwing herself into his arms.

Chapter Nine

She hid out up at the house the rest of the day.
Hester went through an old trunk, pulling out a
couple of dresses she had long ago outgrown,
and the two of them spent the afternoon altering
them to fit Susannah. Sewing had never been
high on her list of favorite things to do, but Hester made it fun.

"How long have you lived out here?" Susannah
asked. She was standing on a stool while Hester
pinned the hem of a blue muslin dress.

"Nigh onto four years," Hester replied. "We
come out after the war. We lost our place in Virginia. Yankees took it all."

"Don't you get lonesome out here all alone?"

"Oh, we're not as alone as it looks. There's
other spreads here 'bouts. The Cramers live a
couple miles to the east, then there's the Babbitts

and the Hallidays to the south, and the Mortons over to the north. We all get together now and then."

"Don't the Indians bother you?"

"Naw. Oh, they steal some stock now and then, but mostly they leave us alone."

Susannah thought about Black Wind, who had been sentenced to three years at hard labor for stealing one cow. "But you said Indians killed your brother-in-law last year."

"Pawnee," Hester said. "Monroe was huntin' on their land. Course, they could have just run him off. They didn't have to kill him."

A trickle of fear skittered down Susannah's spine. "Are there Pawnee near here?"

"Mostly Sioux and Cheyenne. They ain't never give us no serious trouble. Turn a mite to your left," Hester said. "I'm just about through."

"Black Wind is Lakota," Susannah said.

"Sioux. Lakota. Same thing."

"Oh, I didn't know that." Knowing he belonged to an apparently peaceful tribe made Susannah feel better somehow. There was a lot she didn't know, she thought ruefully, like why she was here.

She stared out the window and looked at the barn in the distance. What was he doing?

"There. All done." Hester stood up. "You look pretty as a picture in that old dress of mine."

Susannah smiled her thanks. It was a pretty dress. The neck was square and edged with lace, the sleeves were short and puffy, the skirt full and ruffled.

Stepping down from the stool, Susannah

Feather in the Wind

twirled around, liking the way the skirt belled out around her. Wearing yards of muslin and lace had its compensations—it made her feel pretty and feminine.

Hester shook her head. "Hard to believe I was ever skinny enough to wear that dress. Well, I'd best be seeing to supper. And you'd best go down and see how your man's doin'."

Susannah felt oddly shy and excited as she walked down to the barn. She waved at Abe, who was sitting on a stump fussing with a piece of harness, grinned when he just looked at her and shook his head. How on earth did Hester put up with such a bad-tempered husband?

She paused outside the barn and ran a hand over her hair, smoothing it back from her forehead, wishing she had a tube of lipstick and some eye shadow. She frowned when she realized what she was doing. Giving herself a swift mental shake, she stepped into the barn. She looked fine the way she was, and if *he* didn't think so, well, that was just too bad.

She found Black Wind walking up and down the long aisle that ran between the stalls, one hand pressed against his side.

"What are you doing?" Susannah exclaimed. "You were shot, twice, remember? You're supposed to be resting."

"I do not need any more rest. Too much rest makes a man weak."

Hands fisted on her hips, Susannah glared at him. Stubborn man!

He nodded toward the door. "Will you walk outside with me?"

123

"Don't you think you've done enough walking for one day?"

"No. Will you walk with me, Su-san-nah?"

"Yes." Why did her name on his lips make her go all soft and squishy inside?

She heard the sound of pounding hooves as they reached the doorway. She felt Black Wind stiffen beside her and then she peered out the doorway and saw the reason why. Soldiers!

"You've got to hide." Slowly, she pulled the heavy barn door shut. "Up there," she said, pointing to the loft. "Hurry. You can hide under the hay."

With a nod, Black Wind grabbed the rifle, then climbed up the ladder and pulled it up after him.

"Black Wind, here."

Picking up the Army coat that had been draped over the stall, she wadded it into a ball and tossed it up to him.

She hid the dishes under a clump of hay in one of the stalls, folded the blankets Black Wind had been using for a bed and laid them over one of the saddles, took a last look around, and left the barn.

Hester and Abe were standing on the porch when she reached the house.

"What's going on?" Susannah asked.

"An Injun escaped from the fort," Hester said. "They're lookin' fer him."

"Oh?" Susannah glanced at Abe. He had made no secret of his feelings for Indians, or his irritation at having one on his property. She held her breath, waiting for him to tell the Army that the Indian they were looking for was in the barn.

"Miss Susannah, is that you?"

She felt a moment of panic when she saw Lieutenant Carter. With an effort, she fought for a calm she was far from feeling and summoned a smile. "Hello, Elliott."

"What are you doing here?" he asked, swinging out of the saddle. "Where's the redskin?"

She forced herself to meet his gaze. "I don't know where he is."

"We know you rode off with him."

"Yes, that's true. He kidnapped me, and then he . . . he left me here in the middle of the night and took off."

"That's right," Hester said quickly. "Ain't that right, Abe?"

"If she says that's what happened, I reckon it's so," Abe replied gruffly. "I got work to do." He jabbed a finger in Carter's direction. "You keep them horses out of my crops, hear?"

"Yes, sir. Do you mind if we have a look around?"

"Look all you want. Just don't be disturbin' nothing. And keep them animals out of my wife's garden."

"We'll be careful, sir. Thank you, sir." Carter watched Abe walk off toward the corrals located alongside the house, then turned his attention back to the ladies on the porch. "This is our last stop, Miss Susannah. You can ride back to the fort with us."

"She ain't goin' back to the fort," Hester declared. "She's stayin' here." She placed her arm around Susannah's shoulder, as if daring the lieutenant to try and take her away.

125

"Miss Susannah?"

"Thank you, Elliott, but Mrs. Micklin has offered me the hospitality of her home, and I've decided to stay."

"Are you sure?" Carter glanced around, his expression dubious as he took in the rough-hewn house, the crude corrals and barn, the empty plains beyond.

"Yes. It was nice to see you again, Elliott."

"Would you mind if I called on you when I get the chance?"

"Of course not," Susannah replied. She smiled as if she had nothing in the world to hide. "I'll look forward to it."

"It might not be for some time," Carter said. "We'll be out patrolling for several weeks."

"I'll be here."

Carter smiled at her, then tipped his hat in Hester's direction. "Good day to you, Mrs. Micklin."

"Good day, young man."

"Are we gonna have a look around, Lieutenant?"

"No need, Sergeant. Let's ride." Carter nodded at Susannah, then reined his horse around and rode out of the yard, followed by his men.

"Well, that was a close one," Hester remarked when the dust settled.

Susannah nodded. "Bless you, Hester, for not saying anything."

"Soldiers! They're almost as much trouble as the Injuns. Landsakes! I got bread in the oven!" Catching up her skirts, Hester ran into the house.

Blowing out a sigh of relief, Susannah hurried

to the barn. "Black Wind? You can come down now."

He poked his head over the edge of the loft. "They are gone?"

Susannah nodded.

He looked at her a moment more, then lowered the ladder and climbed down. "You did not tell them I was here. Why?"

"Why should I?"

"I took you from the fort."

She nodded again, unable to speak when he was so near, unable to draw her gaze from the intensity of his eyes.

"Su-san-nah . . ." He whispered her name as he took a step toward her, closing the distance between them until they were almost touching. "Why, Su-san-nah?"

"I couldn't let them take you. I was afraid. Afraid they would beat you again."

Slowly, his mouth descended on hers. Her eyelids fluttered down as his lips claimed hers. She swayed against him, her hands clutching at his shoulders. His arms went around her waist, drawing her up against him, holding her tight, tighter, until she could scarcely breathe. She felt the sweep of his tongue against her lower lip, found herself thinking that no one had ever kissed her quite like this before, or made her feel as though hundreds of butterflies were dancing in her stomach.

She pressed against him, wanting to be closer, closer, reveling in the strength of his arms. She was swimming in dangerous waters, about to sink into their swirling depths, when she heard

127

a loud "humph" behind her.

Black Wind muttered something that sounded very much like a curse as he released her and took a step backward.

"I got work to do in here," Abe said curtly.

Heat washed up Susannah's neck and flooded her cheeks. Without a word, she turned on her heel and ran out of the barn, and then she stopped. She couldn't go up to the house, not now. She needed some time alone.

Lifting her skirts, she ran toward the stream, thinking a good cold soak was just what she needed.

"Women," Abe muttered as he began shoveling soiled straw into a wheelbarrow. "Contrary creatures at best."

Tate Sapa nodded, thinking that perhaps Susannah was, indeed, a holy woman. She had certainly worked her magic on him. He thought of her constantly, missed her when they were apart, dreamed of her at night.

"You'd best go after her 'fore she gets lost," Abe remarked as he tossed another forkful of straw into the wheelbarrow. "She looks like a city gal to me, and they ain't got the sense God gave a goose."

Tate Sapa was out of the barn before the old man finished speaking.

He found her at the stream, sitting on the bank with her feet dangling in the water. There was a peculiar catch in his heart as he saw her sitting there, looking small and lost and alone.

"Su-san-nah?"

Slowly, she turned to face him, and he saw that

there were tears in her eyes.

"Do you wish to be alone?"

She shook her head. "Not really."

He sat down beside her, close enough that he could feel the heat of her beside him. "Why are you crying?"

"I guess I'm homesick."

"Where is your home?"

"A long way from here."

"I would take you home if I could."

"You can't. No one can."

"I do not understand."

"I don't know how to get back there."

He frowned, confused by her words. "You do not know the way?"

She shook her head, took a deep breath, and dissolved into tears.

"Su-san-nah." Gently, he gathered her into his arms and held her close while she wept. *"Ceye sni yo,"* he murmured. Don't cry.

He stroked her hair, thinking how soft it was, how small she was, how easily she fit into his arms, how right it felt to hold her and comfort her. He should not be holding her at all. For the first time in days, Tate Sapa thought of Wakinyela. He had asked for her hand shortly before he had been captured by the Blue Coats. It had been his father's wish that he marry Wakinyela. Everyone in the village knew that she would one day be his wife. He tried to summon her image to his mind, but all he could see was the woman in his arms, her sun-kissed cheeks damp with tears.

Gradually, Susannah's sobs quieted. And still

129

she sat there. And still he held her, the need to protect and comfort her strong within him. And he knew, in his heart, that he would never willingly let her go.

Susannah let out a long, shuddering sigh. "I'm sorry."

"It is all right." He brushed away the last of her tears with his fingertips. Her eyes were luminous beneath long dark lashes. "Do you feel better now?"

Susannah nodded. "Yes, thank you."

"I am leaving here tonight."

"Leaving! Why?"

"I have been away from my people for too long. I must go home."

"I'll miss you."

"Come with me, Su-san-nah."

His words took her by surprise. Go with him? For a moment, she let herself think what it would be like to stay with Black Wind, to love him . . . And then she shook her head. "No, I can't."

"I will care for you."

"I know, but I don't belong with your people. I have to find my way home."

"You have someone waiting for you there?" Jealousy burned within him at the thought that she might belong to another. "A husband?"

"No. But my parents will be worried. And my friends. I have a house, and a career."

"What is career?"

"I work. You know, a job."

He frowned at her. "Why do you not have a man to take care of you?"

"I don't need a man to take care of me," she

retorted, but she couldn't help thinking how nice it was to be held in Black Wind's arms, how right it felt for him to soothe her tears.

"The ways of the white man are foolish. He builds big fires that he cannot sit close to. He lives in a square house when all the earth is round. He digs in the dirt for yellow iron and kills the buffalo for its tongue and its hide while my people starve for lack of meat. He lays miles of track across the prairie. The smoke from his iron horse turns the air black. The noise frightens the animals."

Tate Sapa shook his head. "They do not look after their women. Truly, the *wasichu* are a strange breed. I will never understand them."

Susannah sighed heavily. Everything he said was true, and only served to emphasize how different they were. "I'd better go help Hester with dinner."

Reluctantly, he let her go. Rising, he helped her to her feet. "I hope you find your way home, Su-san-nah."

"Me, too." She forced a smile, wondering if she would ever see her home again, wondering if she would be happy there without him.

He watched her walk back to the house and then, his mind made up, he returned to the barn. There were things to do before nightfall.

Chapter Ten

The moon was low in a cloudless sky when Tate Sapa led the black stallion out of the barn. He had donned the soldier's coat against the chill of the night. The pockets sagged with the weight of the ammunition he had stolen from the fort. He had tied the eagle feather in his hair, praying its magic would see him safely home.

He did not like stealing from those who had helped him, but necessity had driven him to it. He had taken an old canteen he found in the barn, two of the white man's blankets, as well as an old saddle and saddlebags that looked as though they hadn't been used in a long time.

Outside, he slid the rifle into the boot, draped the blankets over the stallion's withers, hooked the canteen over the horn.

Standing in the shadows beside the corral, he

stared up at the house. Susannah was there. She had not returned to the barn after the evening meal. All night, he had waited for her, wanting to see her one last time.

No lights shone from the windows; no smoke rose from the chimney.

And still Tate Sapa stood there, staring at the house, knowing he should go, yet needing to see her again, hold her again, tell her good-bye.

Susannah. He knew, in that moment when he contemplated a life without her, that he could not tell her good-bye.

Not now.

Not ever.

With a sigh, Susannah flounced over on her stomach and closed her eyes. He was leaving, she was staying, and that was that. But she would miss him.

Abruptly, she sat up, fully awake. The feather! He had the feather. Even though it hadn't transported her home the last time she had tried, she knew, *knew*, that she would never get back to her own time without it.

Swinging her legs over the side of the bed, she stood up. She was about to leave the room when she heard a scraping noise near the window. Susannah's heart jumped into her throat as she whirled around.

"Oh, it's you. You scared the crap out of me. What are you doing sneaking in my window in the middle of the night?"

"Come with me, Su-san-nah."

The soft plea in his voice moved over her as

softly and gently as a caress. "I wish I could, Black Wind, truly. But I just can't."

She was glad for the darkness that hid his face from her. She didn't think she could look into his eyes and refuse him again.

"You are sure?"

"Yes. I'm sorry."

He moved toward her, to kiss her good-bye, she thought. Instead, he took hold of her hands and before she quite knew what he was doing, he had tied her hands together with a piece of rawhide.

"What are you doing?" Susannah exclaimed.

"I am kidnapping you again," Black Wind replied, the trace of a smile in his voice.

Before she could argue or scream, he stuffed a wad of cloth into her mouth, draped her over his shoulder as though she were a sack of meal, and carried her across the floor and out the ground-floor window.

Susannah struggled in vain. She kicked and scratched with all the force at her command, but she might as well have been trying to tear down a granite wall with her bare hands for all the good it did her.

She heard him groan once as her fist struck his injured side, and she hit him again, and then again, hoping the pain would make him let her go, but he held on tight. And then he was thrusting her onto the back of the stallion, swinging up behind her.

Susannah raised her hands to rip away the gag, but by then it was too late to scream, too late to do anything. The horse bolted forward and they were galloping through the night, the hem of her nightgown flapping like a sheet drying in the wind.

She had a strange sense of déjà vu as they raced through the darkness. *I've done this before*, she thought, and wondered how many times she was going to be abducted in the middle of the night and carted off wearing nothing but a nightgown.

It was frightening, riding hell-bent through the night, unable to see where she was going. Sort of like being on Space Mountain at Disneyland, she mused wryly. Hurtling through the dark at breakneck speed with no control over how fast or how far you went, trusting that you would arrive at your destination safely.

It was near dawn when Black Wind reined the big stallion to a halt.

Susannah looked around, but there was nothing to see for miles in any direction except tall grass. Far in the distance, she could see mountains.

Tate Sapa dismounted, then reached up to help her from the horse.

Disdaining his help, she slid from the saddle and held out her bound hands. "Untie me."

"No."

"No? No! Why not?"

He didn't answer; instead, he spread the blankets on a stretch of flat ground.

"Lie down, Su-san-nah."

"No."

"Lie down, Su-san-nah."

He spoke quietly, but she heard the steel will

underlying his soft tone. Deciding it would be wise not to argue, Susannah did as she'd been told.

Lying there, she watched Black Wind unsaddle the horse, saw him wince as he lifted the heavy rig from the horse's back. He tied a long strip of rawhide to the horse's reins, then tied the loose end of the rawhide to his wrist.

He let out a sigh as, very carefully, he stretched out beside her. She saw the dried blood then, a dark red stain against his sun-bronzed skin.

"You've been bleeding!" she exclaimed, and then felt a wave of guilt sweep over her as she remembered purposely hitting him there again and again.

"It is all right," he said wearily. "Go to sleep, Su-san-nah."

"But . . ."

He fixed his dark gaze on her and she fell silent, afraid of him for the first time. A breath of wind stirred the eagle feather tied into his long black hair, silently mocking her with the promise of home.

Turning her back on him, she stared out at the sea of grass and wondered if she would ever see her home again. With a sigh, she realized she'd been a fool to fight with Black Wind. As long as he had the feather, she had to go where he went.

Susannah woke stiff and sore and angry. Her wrists ached from being bound, her back was sore from lying on the hard ground, and she was mad clear through. She had saved Black Wind's life. How could he do this to her? He would probably be dead if she hadn't helped him. And what thanks did she get? He had kidnapped her again and tied her up as if she was his prisoner. Or his slave . . .

She groaned softly. How many movies had she seen where the handsome Indian warrior kidnapped the beautiful white woman and carried her away to his lodge? A dozen? A hundred? The movie, *Winterhawk* immediately came to mind, only she didn't have an uncle and a bunch of mountain men to come to her rescue. She didn't have anybody.

Gradually, she became aware of Black Wind's back pressing against hers, of the heat radiating from his body.

Not wanting to care, she rolled over and sat up. "Black Wind?"

He jerked awake, took a deep breath, and sat up, one hand pressed hard against his side.

"Are you all right?"

He nodded.

"Sure you are," she muttered sarcastically, feeling his forehead. "You've got a fever."

Tate Sapa shrugged. "Get up."

Susannah held out her hands. "Untie me." When he made no move to do so, she lifted her gaze to his. "Have you forgotten so quickly what it's like to be a prisoner?"

A muscle twitched in his cheek; then, muttering under his breath, he untied the thong that bound her wrists.

She bit back the urge to thank Black Wind as she rubbed the circulation back into her wrists.

Head cocked to one side, she watched him

stand up. He was hurting. She knew it from the way he moved, from the grim set of his mouth.

Wordlessly, he handed her the canteen, then began to saddle the horse.

The water was tepid but welcome. Susannah capped the canteen, then stood up and folded the blankets. Black Wind took the bedding from her and draped it over the stallion's withers, then offered her his hand.

A jolt of awareness arced between them as she placed her hand in his. His palm was large and calloused, his fingers long as they curled around hers. Their eyes met and held, and Susannah had a sudden inexplicable urge to take him in her arms and comfort him.

Reminding herself that she was mad at him, she put her foot in the stirrup and he helped her into the saddle, then, moving stiffly, he mounted behind her.

She stared straight ahead, conscious of his arm around her waist, of the hard-muscled chest at her back, of his breath fanning her cheek when she chanced to turn her head. She could feel the heat of his body; his thighs cradled her buttocks.

She felt flushed and nervous and vulnerable as never before. She was accustomed to looking out for herself, had always considered herself to be self-sufficient, but now, for the first time in her life, she was completely at the mercy of another human being. It was a frightening feeling, more frightening than it had been to wake up and find herself in another time.

Anything could happen out here in this land of snakes, wild animals, and wilder Indians. She could get sick, snakebit, shot, and no one would ever know what had happened to her. Black Wind could use her or abuse her and there would be no one to defend her. Her parents would never know what had happened to her . . .

Tears of self-pity welled in her eyes, and she blinked them back. She wouldn't cry. She wouldn't give him the satisfaction of knowing how frightened she was.

"I will not hurt you, Su-san-nah."

His words, softly spoken, toppled her defenses and unleashed a flood of tears.

Tate Sapa brought the horse to a halt, dropped the reins, and drew Susannah into his arms.

"I will not hurt you," he said again, and she felt his lips move against her hair. "Do not be afraid of me."

He lifted Susannah's left leg over the horse's withers so she was sitting sideways in the saddle. Gently, he drew her head to his shoulder and stroked her hair.

"Please take me back to Hester's."

"I cannot."

"Why?"

"Five years ago, I went up into the *Paha Sapa* in search of a vision. I stayed there for three days and three nights, praying to *Wakan Tanka* for help."

She wiped away her tears, interested in what he was saying in spite of herself. She had never known anyone who spent three whole days praying. She thought three minutes was a long time.

"I asked for help," he said again, "for guidance, and *Wakan Tanka* sent me a vision." He took her chin in his hands and lifted her face toward his. "I saw you in my vision, Su-san-nah."

"Me?" Her voice emerged in a barely audible squeak.

Tate Sapa nodded. "You were dressed in a white shirt and blue pants." She heard the wonder in his voice, a wonder that matched her own disbelief. "You were holding a piece of paper in your hands."

In spite of the heat of the day, a sudden shiver snaked down Susannah's spine as she recalled the day at the reenactment workshop. She had been wearing a white blouse and blue jeans.

"And on that paper was the image of a man." Tate Sapa paused, his gaze searching hers. "I was the man."

She shook her head. "That's not possible."

"I saw you, Su-san-nah, as clearly as I see you now. I do not know what it means, but I will not, cannot, let you go until I find out."

Susannah was tired and hungry by the time they stopped for the night. "What's that?" she asked, pointing at the faint glow of light in the distance.

"There is a town ahead."

A town, she thought. Food and shelter and a bed . . . only they didn't have any money to pay for those things.

Tate Sapa dismounted and lifted her from the saddle. Heat flowed through her at the touch of his hands at her waist. Her body slid down over his as he lowered her to the ground. Murmuring her name, he drew her into his arms, his chin resting lightly on the top of her head.

She told herself to push him away. He had kidnapped her and tied her up, but her body craved his touch, and she melted against him, a wave of contentment sweeping over her as she rested her head against his chest and closed her eyes.

She didn't know how long they stood there. A minute, an hour—time had lost all meaning. Maybe it had ceased to exist. At that moment, she didn't care, so long as she could stay there, in his arms.

Susannah heard him sigh, and then Black Wind released her and pulled a length of rope from one of the saddlebags.

Her whole body went on instant alert. "What's that for?"

"I must go down there," he said, nodding toward the town.

"So?"

"You will stay here."

Susannah stared at the rope in his hand, her heart pounding with trepidation. "You haven't answered my question."

"I do not want you to follow me."

"I won't."

"Can I trust you to stay here until I return?"

She nodded, her gaze darting from his face to the rope in his hands.

"I would like to believe you."

Some of the tension drained out of her. Perhaps he was going to be reasonable after all.

"But I cannot."

She'd had no idea he could move so fast. In spite of her struggles and her promises not to try to run away, he quickly lashed her hands behind her back, then tied her to the tree.

"I hate you for this," she cried. "I'll never forgive you. Never."

"Never is a long time." Black Wind slid his knuckles over her cheek, then removed his coat and draped it around her shoulders. He regarded her for a long moment and then turned away, and she had the feeling he had put her out of his mind.

Gathering the reins, he swung into the saddle and rode away, leaving Susannah there with nothing but the wind and her own dark thoughts for company.

Thoughts of home flooded Susannah's mind as she sat there. How long had she been gone? Was the passage of time in the past the same as it was in the present? If she found her way back home, would she find that she had been gone for months or for only a few days? If she found her way back home, how would she explain where she had been, and who would believe her? She had always thought time travel to be right up there with alien abductions and stories of Bigfoot.

With a sigh, she sank down to the ground, rested the back of her head against the tree trunk, and closed her eyes.

She didn't want to go to Black Wind's village and live with his people. She wanted to go home. She missed sleeping in her own bed. She missed going to the movies and listening to the radio. She missed her parents and Vivian. She missed writing every day. She had missed a Michael Bolton concert and the meeting with her agent.

Yet if she found herself miraculously at home again, she would miss Black Wind.

Damn the man! Opening her eyes, Susannah took a deep breath and stared toward the town. Where was he?

She didn't know how long she'd been asleep when she heard the sound of hoofbeats. Straightening, she peered into the darkness, and he was there, riding out of the shadows of the night like some phantom warrior.

Black Wind rode into a patch of silver moonlight, and she felt her breath catch in her throat. How magnificent he looked. Regal was the word that came to mind. Like a knight of old, he sat the stallion with easy grace. For a moment, their eyes met, and then he swung out of the saddle. Only then did she notice he was leading a second horse.

He bent over her and cut the rope that bound her to the tree, then untied her hands.

She stood up, rubbing her wrists, wondering where he had gotten the horse.

He withdrew something from his saddlebags and thrust it into her hands.

"What's this?" she asked.

"Clothes. Get dressed."

She unrolled the bundle and found a pair of men's corduroy pants, a dark green wool shirt, and a pair of boots. "That's all?"

He frowned at her. "What more do you need?"

"Something to wear underneath."

His frown deepened.

"Don't Indian women wear . . . Never mind."

He turned away while she dressed. The pants were too snug and the shirt too big, but they were warmer than her nightgown and far more suitable to riding. She pulled on the boots, wishing for a pair of socks. They were a little too big, but not much. She rolled her nightgown into a ball and tucked it under her arm.

"Here." He thrust what looked like a hunk of beef jerky into her hand. "Let's go."

"Where did you get all this stuff? The horse?"

"I stole it."

"You didn't!"

He shrugged. "Among my people, it is considered a coup to steal from the enemy."

"Not where I come from."

"You are here now," he reminded her with a wry grin. "Hurry. We must go before someone misses the horse."

Susannah stuck the jerky in her mouth, stuffed her nightgown into one of the saddlebags tied behind her saddle, then stared at the horse. It was brown, with a black mane and tail and black on its legs. Grabbing hold of the pommel with both hands, she shoved her foot into the stirrup and pulled herself onto the horse's back. Black Wind adjusted the stirrups for her, handed her the reins, then mounted his own horse.

"Su-san-nah?"

"What?"

"Do not try to run away. There is no place for you to go."

She nodded curtly to show she understood.

He studied her face for a moment and then, apparently satisfied, he reined his horse east. For

144

a moment, she gazed longingly at the town. It wasn't much, just a tiny island of civilization in a vast sea of grass, but at least it was civilization of a sort.

She glanced at Black Wind. He was riding away, seemingly unaware that she wasn't following. Yet she knew, *knew*, that he would be after her quicker than a hungry cat chasing a mouse if she didn't follow.

Heaving a sigh, she gave her horse a nudge in the side with her heel and the animal lurched forward, then broke into a bone-jarring trot as it hurried to catch up with the stallion.

"He might have at least asked if I knew how to ride a horse," she muttered.

Certain she was going to be bounced out of the saddle with every step, she clung to the reins with one hand and the horse's mane with the other.

She didn't know where they were going, but she hoped it wouldn't take long to get there.

Chapter Eleven

They rode until late afternoon, stopping every hour or so to rest and water the horses. Susannah marveled at the vastness of the plains, the endless blue vault of the sky. The rolling grassland seemed to stretch away into forever. Here and there, stands of timber rose up from the midst of the prairie. Sometimes they passed depressions in the earth that Black Wind told her were buffalo wallows. Once, they crossed a narrow stream.

Black Wind handed her a hunk of dried beef at their second stop.

"Jerky and water," Susannah muttered under her breath. As lunches went, it wasn't much, but at least it took the edge off her hunger.

She was bone-tired, stiff and sore in muscles she'd never known she possessed by the time they made camp. Feeling as if she was a hundred years old, Susannah climbed out of the saddle. Her legs felt like rubber, and she would likely have fallen flat on her face if Black Wind hadn't been there to catch her.

"What is wrong?" he asked, his brow furrowed. "Are you sick?"

"No, I am not sick." She tried to push him away. It was like trying to move a mountain.

"Tell me what is wrong."

"Wrong! Wrong! You want to know what's wrong?" She pounded her fists against his chest. It was like *hitting* a mountain, too. "I'm tired. I'm hungry. You've dragged me over a million miles of grass. I'd never been on a horse in my whole life until I met you. My legs hurt. My back hurts. My neck hurts. My shoulders hurt. My . . . my backside . . ."

She broke off, glaring up at him as a slow smile curved his lips. "What?" she shouted. "Why are you looking at me like that, you big jerk?"

He lifted one black brow. "Jerk? I do not know this word."

"It means stupid male chauvinist idiot." She tried again to escape his grasp, but he held her against him, exerting just enough power to hold her in place without hurting her.

Black Wind frowned down at her. "You are angry with me."

Well, she thought, that was the understatement of the year. "Angry doesn't begin to describe it."

"Su-san-nah . . ."

"Don't call me that." No one else had ever said

147

her name the way he did, slowly, almost reverently.

"It is your name."

"I know," she said, feeling miserable. "Please, just let me go. I have to find my way home."

"I cannot let you go." He lifted one hand, let his fingertips slide through the silkiness of her hair. He was captivated by the fire in her eyes, the angry flush in her cheeks.

Susannah felt her anger fade at his touch. How could she stay mad at a man who touched her so gently, who looked at her with such obvious concern? "Did you really see me in a vision?"

Black Wind nodded.

The eagle feather fluttered at the movement, drawing Susannah's gaze. "And you don't know what it means?"

"No."

"What will your people say when they see me?"

"The women will be jealous because you are so beautiful," he replied, grinning, "and the young men will look at me with envy."

"Ohhh . . ."

She tried to summon her anger, to remind herself that he had kidnapped her, that she wanted to go home, but as Black Wind lowered his head and claimed her lips with his, none of that seemed to matter.

She slid her arms around his neck, holding on for dear life as he deepened the kiss. She felt the length of his body against her own and pressed closer, closer, and thought how well they fit together, how smooth his skin was beneath her hands, how beautiful his eyes were. Her fingers delved into his hair, long black hair that felt like coarse silk.

His tongue dueled with hers in sweet intimacy, making her forget everything, making her think of sparkling champagne and satin sheets and moonlight dancing on the ocean.

She heard a low moan and wondered if it had come from his throat or hers.

"Su-san-nah?" His lips slid down her throat, lingering at the pulse beating there.

It would be so easy to give in, to surrender to the touch of his hands and lips, to let him ease the fierce desire burning through her. No other man had ever made her feel the way he made her feel, but if she let him hold her and kiss her, she feared she would never be able to leave him. And she didn't want to stay here, in this time. She didn't belong here. She never would.

"Let me go."

Black Wind went suddenly still and then, slowly, he released her and took a step backward, his hands clenched at his sides. He was breathing heavily, but no more heavily than was she.

"We need wood for a fire," he said gruffly.

Susannah looked at him blankly for a moment, then nodded and walked away, wishing, per-versely, that he had refused to let her go. *Coward*, she thought, hating herself for it. But it would be so much easier if he would just force himself on her. She wouldn't have to make the decision then.

She walked along, picking up kindling as she went. She knew she would never find her way home, never be able to leave him, if she let him make love to her.

When she returned to camp, he had the horses unsaddled and hobbled and was sitting cross-legged on the ground, skinning a small animal that looked suspiciously like a bunny. She dumped the wood on the ground and turned away, unable to watch him gut the furry little thing.

It was full dark by the time he finished.

"Build a fire," he said.

"I don't know how." She pointed at the skinned carcass. "And before you ask, I don't know how to cook whatever that is over a fire, either."

He looked at her skeptically for a moment, then cleared a patch of ground, laid a fire, and had the meat on a spit and cooking in practically no time at all.

Susannah sat down, warming her hands, while he disposed of the entrails. The aroma of roasting meat made her stomach growl. She tried not to think that the rabbit had been alive, whiskers twitching, only a few minutes ago.

He didn't look at her, didn't acknowledge her presence in any way, yet the tension between them was palpable. She was aware of every breath he took, every move he made. She watched him take the rabbit from the spit and split the carcass down the middle. He placed one half on a tin plate, uncapped a canteen and filled a tin cup with water, then handed both to her.

"Black Wind . . ."

"Eat."

Susannah hated the silence between them; it

wore on her nerves. But if he could stand it, so could she. Determined to ignore him, as he was ignoring her, she tore a piece of meat from the chunk on her plate and popped it into her mouth. It burned her tongue and brought tears to her eyes. Refusing to let him know, she gulped it down, then took a long drink of water.

Muttering under her breath, she pulled the meat apart so it would cool faster. She couldn't believe she was here, sitting on the ground, eating one of Thumper's relatives. She couldn't believe Black Wind had seen her in a vision, and yet it had to be true. He had described her, had described his photograph, perfectly. He couldn't have made it up.

So, he had seen her in a vision. What did it mean? Why was she really here? How would she ever get home?

She slid a furtive glance in his direction. The feather. It was the key. Somehow, she had to get it back. And then what? It hadn't zapped her back to her own time the last time she had tried. Maybe the feather had nothing to do with her being here at all.

Overcome with a wave of homesickness, Susannah set her plate aside and stared into the fire. Never, in all her life, had she felt so lost, so alone.

She wouldn't cry. She wouldn't! What was the use?

She stiffened as she felt Black Wind's arm slide around her waist. She wanted to resist, to tell him to go away and leave her alone. Instead, she slid onto his lap and laid her head against his shoulder. And suddenly all the pain and loneliness melted away.

He didn't say anything, just held her close, his strong arms gentle around her, his breath caressing her cheek. She wished it didn't feel so good to be cradled in his arms, that it didn't feel so right. Because they could have no future together. He belonged in the past and she didn't, wouldn't, couldn't . . .

Thinking about it made her head ache.

He was still holding her close when she fell asleep.

Chapter Twelve

They reached the Indian village two days later. Looking at the hide lodges spread along the banks of a slow-moving river, Susannah was reminded of a scene from *Dances with Wolves*.

"Do not be afraid, Su-san-nah," Tate Sapa said. "My people will not hurt you."

She tried to look unconcerned, but she grew increasingly more nervous as they neared the village.

Dogs of all sizes ran forward, barking furiously as Black Wind reached the first hide lodge. Men, women, and children stopped whatever they were doing and turned in his direction. Susannah felt their stares as she passed by.

By the time they reached the center of the village, a large group of men had gathered around them.

Tate Sapa reined the stallion to a halt in front of a large tepee, then slid from the back of his horse. Susannah watched the crowd part for an elderly man who limped toward Tate Sapa and embraced him.

They spoke softly for a few minutes. Susannah listened to the harsh guttural sounds, wishing she knew what they were saying.

After a time, Tate Sapa lifted Susannah from the saddle. He had told his father only that she had saved his life, nothing more.

"Su-san-nah," he said, "this is my father, He Wonjetah."

"Pleased to meet you," Susannah said.

"He does not speak English, but he bids me welcome you to our lodge."

"Tell him thank you."

"You tell him. The Lakota word for thank you is *pilamaya*."

"Pilamaya," Susannah repeated.

He Wonjetah nodded at her. He was a tall man, with an austere countenance and long black braids tinged with gray. He wore a rawhide shirt, leggings, and moccasins, and leaned heavily on a walking stick. He looked familiar somehow, though she knew that was impossible.

"This is my lodge," Black Wind said. "Go inside and wait for me."

Susannah didn't argue. She was only too glad to get away from the curious stares of the Lakota.

The inside of the lodge was dim. Furs covered the floor. There were two backrests made of woven wood, several large packs that she assumed held clothing or supplies of some kind, a few pots and bowls. Near the back of the lodge was a small earthen mound that looked like an altar. The lining of the lodge was decorated with drawings of horses and men. Susannah studied them for a minute, trying to decipher their meaning, then turned away.

She whirled around, her heart pounding, as the door flap lifted.

"Oh," she said, relieved to see Black Wind, "it's you."

He looked at her, one black brow arched in amusement. "Were you expecting someone else?"

"Kevin Costner?"

Tate Sapa frowned. "What?"

"Never mind. So, what am I supposed to do now?"

"You will do as I say."

"Will I?"

Tate Sapa nodded slowly, emphatically. "I have told my people that you are my captive."

Susannah shrugged. "Big deal. That's what I am."

"They will expect me to punish you if you do not obey me."

"No doubt you'd enjoy it," she replied waspishly.

"Su-san-nah . . ."

"I'm sorry. I didn't mean it."

Crossing the floor, Tate Sapa gathered her into his arms, thinking again how small she was, how fragile. "I will not hurt you."

"I know."

He tilted her chin up, forcing her to meet his gaze. "Tell me you do not feel what I feel when I hold you close, and I will leave you alone."

"Will you let me go?"

"I cannot. Not until I know why you were sent to me."

"What if you never find out?"

He shook his head. "I do not know. We will speak of that later. I want to know what you feel when I hold you, Su-san-nah."

Her gaze slid away from his. "I don't know what I feel."

"*I* know. Your heart pounds when I am near. Your body warms and longs for my touch. You think of me when we are apart. You dream of me at night."

His voice spun a silken web around her heart. His eyes were dark, burning with a fierce inner fire that threatened to burn away her resistance.

She shook her head. "No."

"You are lying, Su-san-nah. You can lie to yourself, but you cannot lie to me. I see the truth in your eyes." His hands slid down her arms, making her shiver. "I know what you want. It is what I want."

She looked up at him, helpless to resist as he lowered his head and kissed her. Fire. Rivers of fire racing through every vein. Oceans of fire engulfing her, consuming her, until she couldn't think of anything but his kisses. The touch of his hands on her skin inflamed her, making her yearn for more.

"Black Wind . . ." She drew back and gazed up at him, gasping for breath, and then, standing on her tiptoes, she pressed her lips to his. They stood close, close enough that she could feel every inch of his body against her own. Caught up in a maelstrom of desire, she forgot where she was, forgot everything but the need this man aroused in her.

She thought the kiss might have lasted forever if someone hadn't chosen that moment to rap on the lodge flap.

Tate Sapa drew his mouth from hers, his breathing ragged. *"Tima hiyuwo,"* he called hoarsely. Come in.

Susannah had eyes only for Black Wind until she heard a startled gasp that was decidedly feminine.

Guilt flickered in Black Wind's eyes as he stepped away from her.

Glancing around, Susannah saw a slender girl with long black hair standing near the door. The girl was young and beautiful, with large dark eyes and dusky skin. She wore an ankle-length dress Susannah guessed was made of doeskin. Long fringes dangled from the sleeves. A colorful design fashioned of beads was worked into the yoke.

"Wakinyela," Tate Sapa murmured. He released Susannah and took a step toward the other woman.

The woman's eyes narrowed, sparking with jealousy as she looked Susannah up and down. "Who is this?" she asked.

"Wakinyela, this is Su-san-nah. She saved my life."

"Why is she here?"

Tate Sapa squared his shoulders. "Because I want her here."

"I do not."

"We are not yet married," Tate Sapa said, his voice cool. "This is still my lodge."

"She is staying here?"

"She is mine."

Wakinyela made a sound of disgust in her throat. "We are betrothed, Tate Sapa. I will not share you with a *wasicun winyan,* or let you shame me in front of our people."

"If there is any shame here, it is yours," Tate Sapa replied curtly. "Su-san-nah saved my life. She is my captive, but also a guest in my lodge. You will treat her with the respect she deserves."

"I will treat her as the enemy!" Wakinyela exclaimed, her voice rising. "Have you forgotten that the *wasichu* killed my father and your mother and sister? I will not make her welcome."

Wakinyela reached behind her and withdrew the knife sheathed behind her back. "She should die, as my father died. As my brother died!"

Susannah listened curiously to the heated exchange, wishing she could understand what they were saying. Now, she took a hasty step backward. The hatred blazing in the woman's eyes transcended language.

"Wakinyela!" Eyes flashing fire, Tate Sapa plucked the knife from the woman's grasp. "Does my life mean so little to you that you would kill the woman who saved it?"

"Does my pride mean so little to you that you would bring a *wasicun winyan* into your lodge to mock my grief? I have sworn on the graves of my loved ones to kill any *wasichu* I meet."

Tate Sapa took hold of her shoulders. *"Wachin-ksapa ya!* You will not avenge yourself on Su-san-nah."

Wakinyela glared up at him, her black eyes like cold fire, her lips compressed in a thin angry line.

"I will have your word that you will not try to harm her."

"I will not give it!" With slow deliberation, she put her hands on his and removed them from her shoulders. "You are no longer my betrothed. *Hecheto aloe.*" It is finished.

"Nunwe," Tate Sapa replied quietly. So be it.

Wakinyela sent a last, fulminating glance at Susannah, then, her head high and proud, she stalked out of the lodge.

"What was that all about?" Susannah asked.

"She is angry because you are here. We were to marry, but she has thrown me away."

"I'm sorry," Susannah said, knowing, even as she spoke the words, that they were a lie.

Tate Sapa shook his head. "It is not your fault."

"I didn't know you were engaged."

He shrugged. "It was my father's wish that I marry Wakinyela."

"Are you . . . Do you love her?"

"No, Su-san-nah, I do not love Wakinyela. I never did."

For some reason, that knowledge pleased her a great deal.

Tate Sapa let out a deep breath as he drew Susannah into his arms again. "Do not be afraid, Su-san-nah. I will not let anyone harm you."

Susannah nodded, but she couldn't forget the

hatred in Wakinyela's eyes, or the fervor in the woman's voice.

Her gaze darted toward the door as she heard someone enter the lodge. At first, she feared Wakinyela had returned, but it was He Wonjetah, Tate Sapa's father. She was struck again by the feeling that she had seen him somewhere before.

The old man stared at Susannah for a long moment before turning his attention to his son. "What is this you have done?"

Susannah felt Black Wind's arms tighten around her. She couldn't understand what the old man was saying, but she was certain it concerned her presence in his lodge.

"What do you mean?" Tate Sapa asked.

"Wakinyela tells me she no longer wishes to marry you. She says you have shamed her by bringing this *wasicun winyan* into your lodge."

"I have shamed no one," Tate Sapa replied.

"What does this *wasicun winyan* mean to you?"

"She saved my life, *Ate*."

"That is all you feel for this white woman? Gratitude?"

He Wonjetah's keen black eyes held his son's gaze, as if daring him to lie.

Tate Sapa shook his head. "I am not certain what I feel. Do you remember the vision I had five winters ago?"

He Wonjetah nodded. "*Han*, I remember."

"Su-san-nah is the woman I saw."

Susannah looked up at Black Wind as she recognized her name. He smiled down at her, his gaze tender and reassuring.

"You are certain of this?" He Wonjetah asked.

Tate Sapa nodded. "She came to me at the fort where I was imprisoned." Lifting his hand, he removed the eagle feather from his hair. "She had this with her."

He Wonjetah took the feather from his son's hand. "How did she come to have *Wanbli*'s sacred feather?"

"I do not know."

"Ask her."

"Su-nan-nah?"

She looked up at him, her expression apprehensive. She didn't have to understand Lakota to know that Black Wind's father was less than thrilled with her presence.

Black Wind smiled at her reassuringly. "Where did you get the prayer feather?"

"An Indian gave it to me."

"What Indian? What was his name?"

"I don't know." Susannah licked her lips, wondering if he would believe what she was about to say. "There's something I have to tell you."

"Tell me, then."

"I'm afraid."

"Do not be. I will let no one harm you."

"My home is far from here," she said. "Far in the future."

"I do not understand."

"The future. Do you know what year it is?"

He frowned at her, then shook his head.

"The white men number the passage of time in days, weeks, months, and years. This is the year 1870. I come from the year 1997. That's over a hundred years from now." She frowned a moment. "A hundred summers from now," she explained, recalling that the Indians counted their time in moons and summers instead of months and years.

Tate Sapa shook his head. "That is not possible."

"I know. I don't believe it, either, but here I am. I don't know how I got here, and I don't know how to get back where I belong."

Tate Sapa stared down at her. He understood her words, but was such a thing possible?

"You said you saw me in a vision."

"Yes."

"Did you see anything else?"

Brow furrowed, he recalled the vision. At the time, he had not considered the other things he had seen; he had had eyes only for the woman who had captured his likeness on a piece of paper. Now, other things came to mind.

"There were many women milling about, strangely dressed."

"They were romance authors. Women who write books. That's what I do. What else?"

"Long glass tubes hung from the ceiling. Light came from them."

"Those are fluorescent lights," Susannah said. "People in my time don't use candles or oil lamps anymore. We have something called electricity."

"How can this be?"

Susannah sighed. "I don't know."

"The feather—where did you get the feather?"

"I went to a powwow to look around and I saw it hanging from a pole. It really is yours, isn't it?"

Tate Sapa nodded. "When my mother was

killed, I left it at her burial place."

Susannah looked at He Wonjetah. She knew suddenly why he looked familiar. "The Indian who gave it to me looks very much like your father. Maybe he's one of your descendants."

"Perhaps. Prayer feathers are *lila wakan*. Very holy."

"That's what the Indian who gave it to me said. He told me to be careful how I used it."

Tate Sapa nodded. "*Wanbli*'s feathers carry strong magic."

Strong magic, indeed, Susannah thought, if it could carry her back through time.

Black Wind glanced at his father, who was waiting patiently for an explanation. He could not tell his father what Susannah had told him, could not expect his father to believe such a story. He could hardly believe it himself.

"So," He Wonjetah said. "What did the white woman say? How does she come to have the feather that was left at your mother's burial place?"

"She says an Indian gave it to her, but she does not know his name, or from where he obtained it."

She listened as Black Wind translated her words for his father.

The old man studied Susannah, his expression thoughtful. After a time, he shook his head. "I fear our young men will no longer follow your council if you keep this woman in your lodge. She may be *winyan wakan*, but I fear their hatred for the *wasichu* may prove stronger than their respect for you, my son. Think carefully on what you do, for, once done, some things cannot be undone."

"I hear you, *Ate*."

"Does she cook?"

Tate Sapa grinned wryly. "No, but she will learn."

Chapter Thirteen

Susannah had never liked being the center of attention, and she liked it even less now. Every time she went outside, people stared at her, pointing at her skin, which was pale next to theirs, gawking at her curly hair, her curious clothing. She was pretty certain the Indians had never seen a woman wearing men's pants before. At first, she stuck her nose in the air and tried to ignore the looks and whispers. She knew they didn't mean to be cruel, knew she was an oddity in their midst, but the curious looks, the gestures, the laughter all took their toll.

She had been in the village almost a week when she stopped going outside except early in the morning and late at night to answer nature's call. Squatting in the dirt behind a bush made her long for home as nothing else had.

Black Wind treated her kindly enough. She knew the warriors taunted him and made crude jokes when they caught him gathering firewood or drawing water from the river, tasks that were clearly women's work. His father accepted her in his lodge with stoic resignation.

She had often heard the term "a fish out of water." Now she knew what it meant. She didn't belong here, in this place, with these people; she would never belong here.

If Black Wind knew how unhappy she was, he didn't remark on it. He hunted their meat and prepared their meals, asking only that Susannah wash their dishes and tidy the lodge.

They were not tasks that required a great deal of time or effort, which left Susannah with many hours to fill and nothing to fill them with.

Sometimes she stood in the doorway of the lodge and watched the people of the village. For all that was strange to her, she could see that daily life in an Indian village was much like life anywhere, even though the means to the end were vastly different. The men didn't go to the office and bring home a paycheck so their wives could go to the store; instead, they brought the meat home whole and the women skinned it and butchered it and cooked it.

The women didn't take the MasterCard and shop for a new dress—they tanned the hide and cut the skins and sewed the pieces together. The men hunted and protected their families; the women cooked and cleaned and sewed. Children were loved and cherished. Grandfathers taught their grandsons how to make bows; grandmothers taught their granddaughters to make moccasins. Aunts and uncles and cousins were all involved in the rearing of a child. Often, a grandparent lived with one of his grandchildren.

A lodge was like a big one-room house with no walls, which made Susannah wonder how Indian couples ever managed to be alone. The movie *Dances with Wolves* came to mind again, and she recalled how the couple in that movie had made love while surrounded by two other adults and their own sleeping children. No wonder Lakota families were small, she thought with a wry grin. There was no way she could ever make love with someone else lying three feet away!

The Indian people worked hard during the day and then, often, played at night. There were dances and games, feasts to celebrate the birth of a child.

And always, she was on the outside looking in.

Now, it was late at night, and Susannah was sitting on a rock overlooking the river. She had visited her favorite bush and then, seeing how beautiful the night was, with the moon shining like a lighthouse beacon on the water, she had decided to stay out a little longer.

The river looked like a sheet of black glass, reflecting the full moon and the stars, the silver-barked trees that grew along the banks. It was quiet, she thought, so quiet. And so peaceful.

Thoughts of home flitted through her mind. Home. She would probably never see her family or her friends again. Turning slightly, she gazed at the lodges behind her. The village made a pretty scene in the moonlight, reminding her of a Leanin' Tree birthday card she had once seen. Firelight cast dancing shadows on the lodge skins. Horses stood silhouetted against the night. She heard a baby's soft cry. The sound of laughter drifted on the breeze.

With a sigh, she turned her gaze toward the river again. She couldn't stay here. If she had to remain in the past, then she wanted to do it in a big eastern city where they had at least a modicum of civilization. In the East, there would be shops and libraries and museums, places that were familiar, a lifestyle more like the one she had left behind. They might not have movies, but there would be operas and plays and music. She could get a job somewhere, maybe writing for a newspaper, or teaching school. She would be able to speak the language, dine in a restaurant, bathe in a tub with hot water and soap . . .

There was nothing for her here—except Black Wind. With a sigh, she rested her head on her bent knees and closed her eyes.

Black Wind. His father had been right. The warriors would not listen to him now. They scorned him for taking a white woman into his lodge. If she went away, he could lead his people again. He could marry Wakinyela, although why any man would want to marry that sharp-tongued shrew was beyond her.

The thought of Black Wind holding another woman, any woman, sent a sharp stab of pain through her heart. Just thinking of him filled her with happiness. He looked at her, and she found herself wondering if staying here would be so bad.

"Su-san-nah."

As if she had conjured him from her thoughts, he was there beside her. Clad in only a breechclout, he looked dark and dangerous and wild. Her insides seemed to melt like butter left too long in the sun as his gaze met hers. He held out his arms in silent invitation, waiting.

Why fight it? she thought, and slid off the edge of the rock into his waiting arms.

Contentment washed over her, soothing, peaceful, as he drew her close. His skin was smooth and warm beneath her cheek. A long shuddering sigh escaped her as she wrapped her arms around his waist and lifted her face for his kiss.

Fire and honey flowed through Susannah's veins as Black Wind's mouth claimed hers in a kiss that scorched her lips like a brand and sent fingers of flame shooting along every nerve. And she knew in that moment that, no matter what the future held, she was his, always and forever his.

She lost track of time as his hands and his lips drifted over her until she was floating on a sea of sensation, every nerve ending quivering and alive, aching to be touched. His hands slid down her bare arms, making her shiver with delight. She moaned softly as his tongue caressed her neck, the sensitive place behind her ear. He dropped feather-light kisses on her eyelids before returning to savor her mouth in another long, lingering kiss that made her heart race and her toes curl with pleasure.

Somehow, they were lying on the grass, arms and legs entangled. Her hands explored his back and chest. The taut muscles in his arms quivered beneath her questing fingertips. She heard the sharp intake of his breath as she slid her hand over his flat belly. Like satin over steel. She had read that phrase in a book once. Now she knew what it meant.

"You are truly *winyan wapiya,*" Black Wind murmured, his breath warm against her ear. "Only a woman who possesses great magic could have bewitched me so completely."

Susannah smiled at him. "Are you bewitched, Black Wind?"

He nodded. "What kind of *wihmunge* do you wield that binds me to you?"

"Wihmunge?" she repeated. "What's that?"

"Witch medicine."

"Are you calling me a witch?"

"You are offended?"

"Well, where I come from, it's not usually a compliment."

"I only mean that I am under your spell, Su-san-nah," he amended. Being called a witch was a serious thing. Witches were feared, and were killed when discovered.

She ran her hands over his chest. "Are you complaining?"

"Have you truly come from the future?"

"I'm afraid so. Does it matter?"

Slowly, he shook his head. "Tell me you will not leave me."

170

"I will not leave you," she replied quietly.

His gaze never left hers as he slowly shook his head. And then he kissed her again, a kiss of such gentle passion that it brought tears to her eyes.

"Oh, Tate," she murmured, "I think you have some very strong *wihmunge* of your own."

He kissed her again, lightly this time. "Come," he said, taking her hand and helping her to her feet. "We should go back."

"Back?" She blinked up at him, her senses still reeling from his kisses.

"I am a warrior. I would not defile you, Su-sannah, nor take advantage of you when you have no male relations to protect your virtue."

He slid one finger down her cheek. "When I plant my seed within you, you will be my woman, my wife."

"Wife?"

Tate Sapa nodded. "You will marry me, Su-san-nah."

She was a woman of the nineties, and as such, she was tempted to say, Oh, I will, will I? Instead, she nodded her acceptance. Who was she to argue with fate?

Wakinyela smiled to herself as she slipped away from her hiding place. She knew how to get rid of the white woman now. Tate Sapa himself had given her the idea.

Susannah woke feeling wonderfully refreshed the following morning. She smiled at He Won-jetah, and even offered to try and prepare the morning meal. Black Wind had performed some magic of his own, she mused as she stirred the ashes from last night's fire, for she no longer felt like an outsider. He loved her, and it made all the difference in the world. If she put her mind to it, she could learn his language, his ways. Pioneer women had followed their men into the wilderness and managed to survive and be happy, and so could she.

She glanced down at the corduroy pants and wool shirt Black Wind had stolen for her. Today, she would ask him to bring her a piece of doeskin so she could make herself a tunic like the Indian women wore. Granted, she had never been much of a seamstress—had hated sewing in high school—but if she was going to stay and make the best of things, it might be easier if she dressed like the other women.

She sang as she prepared breakfast, thinking how outrageous it was to be singing "Heartbreak Hotel" while she knelt beside a firepit in a Lakota lodge in the heart of the Black Hills.

She felt her heart leap with joy as Black Wind entered the lodge, felt the touch of his gaze clear to her toes.

"*Hihani washtay,* Su-san-nah."

She looked at him askance.

"It means good morning."

"*Hihani washtay* to you, too."

He smiled, pleased at her use of his language.

He Wonjetah grunted softly as he sat cross-legged on his blankets. He wrinkled his nose as he took the bowl Susannah handed him. For a moment, he regarded the contents as if he feared it might contain some kind of poison instead of broth and vegetables, then, with a heavy sigh of resignation, he tasted a spoonful.

Susannah waited, hardly daring to breathe.

He took another spoonful, swallowed slowly, then nodded. *"Washtay,"* he decided.

"It means good," Tate Sapa told her.

Susannah let out the breath she had been holding, thinking that, at that moment, He Wonjetah's praise meant more than the top spot on *The New York Times* bestseller list.

"Thank you," she said.

"The word is *pilamaya*, Su-san-nah."

"Pilamaya," she repeated.

He Wonjetah nodded, then quickly finished his soup. He left the lodge a few minutes later, leaving Tate Sapa and Susannah alone.

As soon as the door flap closed behind the old man, she was in Black Wind's arms.

"Su-san-nah," he groaned, "what have you done to me? I can think of nothing but you."

"What have *you* done to *me*?" She slid her hands over his back and down his arms, unable to keep from touching him. "I've never felt this way before."

His lips caressed her cheek. "You were in my mind when I woke this morning."

"I dreamed of you last night," she confessed. A little moan of pleasure escaped her lips as his tongue stroked her neck.

"What did you dream?"

"That we made love by the river last night."

A slow smile spread across Black Wind's face. "My dream was the same."

Susannah rested her head against his chest,

the sure, steady beat of his heart the sweetest music she had ever heard.

For a timeless moment, there was no one else in all the world, only the two of them, cocooned in the warmth of the love growing between them.

"What will you do today?" he asked.

"I don't know." She looked down at her clothing. She'd worn this shirt and pants for days now. Both were wrinkled and dirty. "Try my hand at sewing, I guess. What will you do?"

"My father wishes to go hunting. He has asked that I go with him."

"Oh." She couldn't keep the disappointment from her voice as she thought of spending the day alone.

"Will you miss me?"

"You know I will."

He smiled a decidedly pleased masculine smile, then bent his head and kissed her. "I will not be gone long."

A sudden commotion from outside drew them apart.

"Wait here," Tate Sapa said. He kissed her once more, then moved toward the door. Before he reached the entrance, the flap was thrown back and several warriors burst into the lodge.

Tate Sapa glared at Mato Mani, the medicine man. "What is going on here?"

The tribal shaman pointed an accusing finger in Susannah's direction. *"Wakanka!"* he exclaimed.

"What's he saying?" Susannah asked, alarmed by the tone of the man's voice.

"He claims you are a witch."

A witch! Susannah took a step backward, inwardly flinching from the accusation in the medicine man's eyes.

Tate Sapa put himself between Susannah and the warriors crowding into his lodge. "Where did you hear such a thing?"

"Wakinyela overheard you talking to the *wakanka winyan* by the river last night. She said the *wakanka* has put you under her spell."

"And you believe her?"

"I saw the white woman in vision last night," the medicine man said. "I saw her standing in two worlds. She held a drawing in her hands, Tate Sapa, a drawing with your likeness upon it. I fear she has captured your soul."

"Black Wind, what is he saying?"

Susannah felt her insides grow cold with fear as Black Wind translated the medicine man's words. How could the medicine man have known about that picture?

"Wakinyela said you admitted the white woman has bewitched you," Mato Mani declared.

"Wakinyela is behaving like a jealous child," Tate Sapa retorted. "She is angry with me and seeks to destroy the white woman."

"We will discuss it in council," the medicine man decided. "Until we reach a decision, you will have nothing to do with the white woman."

"She is here as my guest."

Mato Mani jerked his head in Susannah's direction. "Take her."

"No!" Tate Sapa struggled against the three warriors who restrained him while Susannah was taken from the lodge. "Let me go!"

"Black Wind!" Susannah cried his name as she was hustled out of the lodge. She had no idea what was going on or where they were taking her.

"Su-san-nah! *Hey-ay-hee-ee!*"

"Bind him," the medicine man said.

"Let me go!" Tate Sapa fought against the men holding him, but it was no use. In minutes, he was alone in the lodge, bound hand and foot. Desperate with concern for Susannah, he cursed under his breath, the swear words he had learned while at the Army fort coming readily to mind. What would they do with her?

Minutes passed like hours. He worked his hands back and forth, trying to loosen his bonds, but succeeded only in abrading the skin on his wrists.

Where was she? What were they doing to her? Where was his father?

Frustration rose up within him. How long since they had taken her away? An hour? Two?

Susannah . . .

She was more frightened than she had ever been in her life. One of the Indians had bound her hands behind her, and now she stood in the center of a large tepee, surrounded by a dozen grim-faced men and one smug-looking female. She would have given anything to know what Wakinyela was saying, what accusations she was making.

The warriors nodded, their expressions grave, when the Indian woman finished speaking.

There was a moment of taut silence, then two of the warriors grabbed Susannah by the arms and hauled her out of the lodge.

"Tate Sapa, let me see Tate Sapa," Susannah begged as they dragged her across the village toward a lone cottonwood tree.

Careful not to meet her gaze, the two men quickly secured her to the tree, then hurried away, as though they were afraid of her.

Of course they are afraid, Susannah mused bleakly. They think I'm a witch.

What did the Lakota do to witches? It was said that witches had been burned during the Salem witch trials, although Susannah wasn't sure if that was fact or fiction.

She had never been so afraid. Time passed with exquisite slowness. Her arms grew numb, her throat was dry, her legs ached. No one ventured near her or so much as looked in her direction. It was almost as if she had ceased to exist.

She closed her eyes and tried to pray, but fear seemed to have choked off all thought so that she could only murmur, "Help me, Lord, please help me," over and over again.

Where was Black Wind? Why didn't he come to her?

Hours passed. She was hungry and thirsty and sick-to-her-stomach afraid. The shadows lengthened. Smoke rose from numerous cooking fires as the women prepared the evening meal. She heard the familiar sounds of the village as it settled down for the night, mothers calling their children to come home, a baby crying, dogs fighting over scraps of meat.

And still he didn't come.

Darkness descended on the village, taking her last shred of hope with it.

Chapter Fourteen

He Wonjetah stood outside his lodge, his gaze fixed on the distant horizon. The council had decided to destroy the white woman witch. As a people, the Lakota were strong believers in otherworldly powers. *Ptesan-Wi,* the White Buffalo Woman; *Iktomi,* the trickster; *Wakinyan,* the Thunderbird; *Unktehi,* the water monster, all possessed power. There were men and women among the people themselves who were believed to possess magic, but it had been the belief of the council that magic in the hands of a white woman could only bring trouble to the lodges of the Lakota.

He Wonjetah feared that the white woman had indeed cast a spell on his son to make him turn away from his people, from Wakinyela. Tate Sapa was a respected leader, wise beyond his years. Even before he had reached manhood, others had looked to him for guidance. All who knew him believed he had been blessed by *Wakan Tanka*. By the time Tate Sapa had become a warrior, the young men would listen to no other, would follow no other.

He Wonjetah took a deep breath, then stepped into the lodge, feeling far older than his years as he prepared to give his son the council's decision.

"*Ate*, what have they done to Su-san-nah?"

"She is well. For now."

The cold hand of fear curled around Tate Sapa's insides. "What did the council decide?"

"They have declared her to be a witch."

Tate Sapa swallowed the bile that rose in his throat. "No."

He Wonjetah nodded. "She will be destroyed tomorrow morning."

"Destroyed?" Tate Sapa choked on the word. "How?"

"It will be done quickly and mercifully," He Wonjetah said reassuringly.

"How?"

"Mato Mani will slit her throat."

"No." Tate Sapa shook his head, sickened by the images his father's words evoked.

"It is for the best, *cinks*."

"No!" Tate Sapa shook his head again. "You cannot let them kill her. She saved my life."

He Wonjetah hunkered down on his heels beside his son. "What are you not telling me?"

Tate Sapa shook his head. "It is as I told you. I saw Su-san-nah in vision before I was captured by the Blue Coats. She held a paper bearing my image, just as Mato Mani said."

"*Ee-hee!* She is truly a witch."

"No! She is my destiny."

"*Heyah!*" He Wonjetah exclaimed. "No, that is not possible."

"It is true, *Ate*."

He Wonjetah shook his head. "Our people will never accept her now. Even if you could persuade Mato Mani to release her, she would never be trusted."

"You must release me."

"*Heyah*, I cannot. There is nothing you can do. There is nothing I can do." He Wonjetah stood up. "I am sorry, Tate Sapa."

"*Ate* . . ."

"Sleep, *cinks*. When you wake, it will be over."

Tate Sapa stared after his father, his mind in turmoil, his stomach churning as he imagined Mato Mani putting a knife to Susannah's throat. He closed his eyes, and the images grew brighter, more vivid, terrifyingly real. He could see the terror in her eyes as the blade touched her skin, hear the fierce pounding of her heart, her last anguished cry as she called to him for help. And then the vision dissolved in a sea of crimson.

"No!" He opened his eyes, his heart hammering in his ears. Had he slept through the night? He glanced up at the smoke hole, relieved to see that the sky was still dark.

Heedless of the pain, he struggled against the rope that bound his wrists. He felt the skin give way, felt the warmth of his blood drip down his hands, and still he fought to free himself. Time and again, he gazed up at the sky, judging the time, feeling it slipping away from him.

The rope was wet with his blood by the time Tate Sapa managed to free his hands. He cursed softly as he fumbled with the rope that bound his feet. He filled a parfleche with as much pemmican and dried venison as it would hold, shoved in a buckskin shirt and leggings, a pistol taken from the body of a white man. He took a couple of trade blankets and a buffalo robe, grabbed his knife and the rifle and ammunition he had stolen from the fort, then crawled under the back wall of the lodge. He stood in the shadows a moment, listening, then merged into the darkness.

On silent feet, he made his way toward the far end of the village. In the light cast by the moon, he could see Susannah. She was tied to a tree, her head bowed. Tate Sapa searched the surrounding shadows before creeping slowly toward her.

A dog growled as he passed by, then, apparently recognizing Tate Sapa's scent as a familiar one, lowered his head and went back to sleep.

Dropping the rifle and other supplies on the ground, he cat-footed up behind her, one hand covering her mouth before she could cry out.

"Su-san-nah, it is me," he whispered. Drawing his knife, he cut her hands free. "Let us go."

Weak with relief and gratitude, she followed him into the trees beyond the village, her heart pounding like thunder in her ears.

"Wait here," Black Wind said, and disappeared into the darkness.

She stared after him, every nerve on edge, all

her senses alert. Where had he gone?

Five minutes passed. Ten. Susannah rubbed her aching wrists, stretched her back and shoulders. Where was he? Had someone seen him release her? Was he being restrained even now while they looked for her? She peered into the darkness. All seemed quiet. Where was he?

Fifteen minutes later, Black Wind returned, leading their horses. Wordlessly, he lifted her onto the back of the bay. He secured the parfleche behind the bay's saddle, draped the buffalo robe over the horse's withers, slipped a waterskin over the horn. If anything happened to him, if they were separated, she would have food and water, a gun with which to protect herself.

"We are going to ride north," he whispered. "Whatever happens, do not stop. If we get separated, keep riding north. I will find you."

"Black Wind . . ."

"There is no time to argue, Su-san-nah, no time to explain. Just do as I say."

She nodded, the urgency in his voice communicating itself to her.

She watched him swing onto the back of the stallion with effortless grace. "Stay close."

She had expected him to ride out as fast as he could, but he held the black to a slow walk, keeping to the trees. Once they reached the river, he turned north. Only when they were well away from the village did he urge the black into a gallop.

The bay needed no urging to follow the stallion. Susannah clung to the saddle horn for dear life as her horse lined out in a dead run. At any moment, she expected to hear war cries rise up behind her, hear the thunder of hooves as the Lakota gave chase. But all she heard was the wind rushing by and the thudding of her own heart.

As the miles went by, new fears crept into her mind. What if the horse ran into a tree? What if it stepped into a prairie dog hole? What if the bay made a quick turn and she tumbled out of the saddle? What if her horse lagged behind his and she got lost?

What if, what if . . . You could drive yourself crazy wondering what if.

She kept her gaze on Black Wind's back, confident that he would take care of her.

The prairie stretched ahead of them, flat, endless, looking gray in the moonlight.

She saw a dark shape silhouetted on a rise. Thoughts of wolves sent a quick chill down her spine.

Just when she thought they were going to ride through the night forever, Black Wind reined his stallion to a halt. The bay came to an abrupt stop, and Susannah grabbed onto the horn to keep from being pitched over the horse's neck.

Stillness settled around them, broken only by the sound of the horses blowing through their nostrils. Susannah patted the bay's neck. It was hot and sweaty and covered with lather.

Tate Sapa lifted his leg over the stallion's neck and slid to the ground, then helped Susannah from her horse.

She collapsed against him, her legs and back

aching from the hard ride. "Do you think they'll follow us?"

"I do not know."

His hands slid down her neck, then gently massaged her shoulders. Susannah sighed as his strong fingers kneaded the soreness from her muscles.

His lips brushed her hair. "Do you need to rest?"

The thought of sleeping, even on the hard ground, sounded like heaven. "I can go on if you think we should."

"There is a small canyon not far from here. We would be safer there than out here in the open."

Climbing back into the saddle was the last thing she wanted to do, but she didn't want to slow him down, didn't want him to think she was weak. "Let's go, then."

He placed his finger beneath her chin and tilted her face up. Murmuring "My brave one," he lowered his head and kissed her.

Heat flared through her and at that moment, Susannah thought she would gladly ride a thousand miles if Black Wind would kiss her like that when they were through.

She moaned softly when he drew away. "It is not far," he promised as he lifted her into the saddle.

One step was too far, she thought wearily, but she forced a smile as she picked up the reins. If her poor tired horse could make it, so could she.

They rode into the canyon just as the sun climbed over the horizon. Susannah stared in awe as the rising sun streaked the sky with bold slashes of crimson and lavender and bright pink. Sunlight spilled into the canyon, reflecting off the sides, transforming the smooth stone walls into a fairy tale fortress reminiscent of a scene from *Beauty and the Beast*. A narrow stream cut through the canyon, fed by a waterfall that tumbled down one side of the cliffs. A small pool was located near the base of the falls.

"Oh, it's beautiful."

Tate Sapa nodded, pleased that she found it so. Dismounting, he lifted her from the back of the bay.

It was then that Susannah saw his wrists, the skin rubbed raw and crusted with dried blood. "Black Wind, what happened?"

"It is nothing."

"Nothing! Nothing! Oh, Black Wind."

He was surprised by her tears. "Su-san-nah . . ."

"Don't 'Susannah' me, you silly man." Jerking the waterskin from the saddle horn, Susannah splashed water over his wrists, rinsing away the blood. Muttering under her breath, she went searching through his saddlebags, an exclamation of surprise rising to her lips when she found her nightgown stuffed inside. She had forgotten all about it. Ripping a strip of material from the hem, she tore it in half and bandaged the wounds in his wrists. Sniffing back her tears, she tied off the second bandage, then stared up at him, confused by the emotions churning within her.

Tate Sapa brushed his knuckles over her cheek. "*Pilamaya*, Su-san-nah," he murmured, and lifting the buffalo robe from the bay's back, he spread it beneath a tree. "Sleep now."

She looked up at him, trying to read his thoughts. "You need to get some rest, too."

"I must look after the horses first. Sleep now, Su-san-nah."

Sleep. Suddenly, it sounded like the sweetest word she had ever heard. With a sigh, she sank down on the robe, asleep almost before she closed her eyes.

Tate Sapa sat on his heels, motionless, as he watched her sleep. She claimed to have come to him from the future. Was it possible? He touched the feather tied in his hair. Eagle feathers were believed to hold powerful medicine. Had his prayer feather been strong enough to bring her back through time? He had told his father that Susannah was his destiny. He had not realized how deeply he believed that until now.

Lifting his head, he gazed at the canyon walls. They had left a trail that would be easy to follow. Would his people come after them, or would the Lakota consider themselves well rid of them both?

He lowered his gaze to the woman sleeping so peacefully on the buffalo robe. They could stay here indefinitely. There was water, grass for the horses, game was plentiful. He could build a rough shelter to protect them from the elements.

Unable to keep from touching her any longer, he brushed a lock of hair from her brow. Her hair was silky, her skin warm and smooth. He had never known a woman with such soft skin, or one who had curly hair. He touched one springy curl, smiled as it coiled around his finger.

"Su-san-nah." Tate Sapa whispered her name, silently thanking *Wakan Tanka* for bringing her into his life, wondering if she considered being in his time a curse or a blessing, wondering what he would do if she should be taken from him. He had known her such a short time, yet she was already a part of him, woven into the very fabric of his life, so that he could not imagine what it would be like should she suddenly disappear.

Needing to hold her, he stretched out on the robe and put his arms around her. She snuggled trustingly against him, sighing as he drew her close.

The sun climbed higher in the sky, bathing the canyon with its warmth, its golden haze settling over them like a benediction.

Susannah sighed as she shifted on the bed, and then realized she wasn't in a bed, she wasn't at home, and she wasn't alone. She opened her eyes and found herself almost nose to nose with Black Wind. He was asleep, his arms locked around her waist.

Drawing back a little, she studied his face. His lashes were short and thick, his mouth sensual even in sleep. There was a faint scar near his hairline that she hadn't noticed before. He was, quite simply, the most beautiful man she had ever seen.

One of the horses whinnied. Before the sound had completely died away, Tate Sapa had rolled to his feet, rifle in hand.

Susannah sat up, amazed that anyone could

wake and move so quickly.

Tate Sapa breathed a sigh of relief when he realized they were still alone in the valley. He stretched the kinks out of his back and shoulders, then turned to face Susannah.

"Well, I'm impressed," she said, grinning.

"Impressed?"

"I've never seen anyone move so fast in my whole life."

Tate Sapa shrugged. "I thought . . ."

"I know." She yawned, then stood up. "How long have we been asleep?"

He glanced up at the sun. "About five hours."

She remembered the security of lying in his arms.

He remembered wondering how he would live without her.

She looked up, felt her gaze caught in his. His eyes were black, a warm beautiful black, like liquid velvet. She had the strangest feeling that she could dive into those eyes and lose herself forever.

Mr. Sandman, send me a dream . . .

Standing there, basking in the heat of his eyes, she knew that Black Wind was the embodiment of every dream she had ever had, every hope, every wish.

She knew then that she had been in love with this man since that day she first saw his photograph. She had never believed in fate or kismet, but now she was thoroughly convinced that some mystic power had sent her to the powwow, had guided her feet toward the booth where she had found the eagle feather that Black Wind wore in his hair.

"Su-san-nah?"

"Do you believe in karma?"

"Kar-ma?"

"You know—destiny, fate, kismet?"

"I believe you were meant to be mine."

Susannah nodded. "Me, too. I believe we were fated to be together." She smiled faintly. "I guess I must have been born in the wrong century, since I came here, to you."

"Will you stay, Su-san-nah?"

"I want to." The lack of modern conveniences didn't seem as horrible as it once had. Her ancestors had managed to survive without microwaves and washing machines and had been perfectly happy. If they could do it, so could she. Looking at Black Wind, feeling the love radiating from his eyes, she decided she wouldn't trade what she had now for a mansion in Beverly Hills. She only hoped she would be able to stay, refused to consider that she could be whisked back to the twentieth century.

She took one of his hands in hers and ran her fingertips over the bandage on his wrist. "What happened?"

"They tied me up to keep me away from you."

"Oh, Black Wind, what have I done? I've alienated you from your father, from your people. Will they take you back?"

"It does not matter."

"Of course it does!"

"Su-san-nah . . ." He put his arm around her waist and drew her up against him. "It does not matter," he repeated firmly. "You are all I need. Will you be my woman, Su-san-nah? My wife?"

"Yes."

The word slid easily past her lips. No doubts. No hesitation.

Tate Sapa captured her hands in his, then took a step backward so he could see her face. "I will love you and protect you so long as I live."

Susannah gazed into his eyes, warmed by the love she saw there, by the sincerity in his voice. Birds chirped in the treetops. Sunlight bathed the canyon in a golden glow, and she knew she would remember this moment for as long as she lived.

"And I will love you, Black Wind, and honor and cherish you so long as I live."

"Ohinniyan, wastelakapi."

"What does that mean?"

"Forever beloved."

With a sigh, she melted against him. *"Ohinniyan, wastelakapi."*

"Su-san-nah . . ."

"Yes," she murmured, "Oh, yes."

His kiss was as soft as dandelion down, warmer than a thousand suns. Without taking his lips from hers, he lifted her into his arms and carried her toward the waterfall.

She wrapped her arms around his neck, welcoming the sweet invasion of his tongue.

He carried her effortlessly, and she gloried in his strength, in the fall of his hair over her hands, in the touch and the taste and the smell of him.

She was breathless when he set her on her feet. Only then did she notice her surroundings. It was

191

a fairy place. New grass made a soft green carpet beneath her feet. Wildflowers bloomed in bright profusion near the water's edge. Slender cotton-woods and willows provided a leafy canopy. Shimmering rays of sunlight danced through the leaves, warming the grass, making the water sparkle.

"Oh, Black Wind, it's so beautiful."

"You are beautiful, Su-san-nah, the most beautiful woman I have ever known."

"Kiss me." She moaned. "Kiss me, kiss me, kiss me!"

"*Wiwasteka,*" he murmured, and taking her in his arms, Tate Sapa drew her down to the ground, his body molding itself to hers, heat to heat and heart to heart.

Time lost all meaning as he slowly undressed her. "*Wiwasteka.*"

"You said that before. What does it mean?"

"Beautiful woman."

"Am I? Black Wind, there's something I have to tell you."

He looked at her expectantly, and her gaze slid away from his. "I . . ." She bit down on her lower lip. "You see . . . I'm not . . . that is, you're not the first. . . ." There was no easy way to say it, yet she felt he had a right to know, and so she said it all in a rush, hoping it wouldn't sound so bad. "I'm not a virgin."

A muscle twitched in his jaw, and then he let out a long sigh. "It does not matter."

"I wish I were. I wish I'd never known anyone else."

"It does not matter, Su-san-nah. Nothing that

happened before we met matters now."

Tears stung her eyes as he cupped her cheek in his palm. "You are my woman now, as you were meant to be."

She nodded, unable to speak, as he kissed her. And then he began to undress her, his hands gentle, almost reverent, as he caressed her out of her clothing. She was smooth and soft from head to foot, delicate, beautiful. Growing up, Tate Sapa had caught glimpses of young girls bathing in the river, but he had never seen a grown woman completely nude. Lakota mothers were zealous in guarding the chastity of their daughters.

Tate Sapa had never been in love, had never made love to a woman. Now, as he gazed at Susannah, he knew he had never seen anything as lovely, that never before had he been given a gift as precious as the one before him.

Susannah trembled with delight as his hands stroked her flesh. His hands were big, calloused from years of hard work, yet his touch was tender. He rained kisses on her face, her neck, lower, lower, until his mouth brushed her breast. He paused, looking up at her, and she dragged his head down, wanting him to touch her and taste her.

She ran her hands over him, exploring every wonderful inch. His skin was the color of dark bronze, sun-warmed and smooth. His muscles rippled beneath her fingertips as she ran her hands over his arms and back.

She seemed to be drowning in sensation, every nerve and fiber vibrantly alive, every sense attuned to the world around her—the grass beneath her, the feel of Black Wind's body lying over hers, the heat of the sun on her face, the cool whisper of a soft summer breeze. His hair teased her breasts, his lips tantalized her, and his hands—oh, those wondrous hands—like a master musician, he knew which chords to pluck to make her hum with desire.

"Now," she whispered when the torment became more than she could bear. "Now, Black Wind."

"Su-san-nah . . ." Her name was a low groan on his lips as his body merged with hers.

She arched up to meet him, her arms wrapping around his waist to hold him close, and in that moment, when they became one flesh, she knew a soul-deep regret that she had given her innocence to a man who hadn't deserved it.

But that was in the past, and there was no point in dwelling on it. She closed her eyes as Black Wind kissed her and kissed her until her head was spinning and she clung to him as the only solid thing in the world, the only thing that mattered.

And Susannah knew, knew, that heaven was smiling down on them. No matter how it had been accomplished, no matter by what means she had found her way to this place, she knew without a doubt that she had been born for this man and no other.

Chapter Fifteen

"I did not hurt you?" Tate Sapa regarded her anxiously, his dark eyes tender with concern.

"Hurt me? Oh, no, you didn't hurt me."

"It was over too quickly."

She couldn't help grinning. True, it had been quick, but it had been incredible.

"Su-san-nah . . ."

She ran her hand through his hair. "What?"

Propped on one elbow, Tate Sapa gazed down at her. How beautiful she was, with her skin flushed from his lovemaking and her soft brown eyes smiling up at him. "I have no words, no way to tell you . . ."

Heart swelling with tenderness, Susannah brushed a lock of hair from his brow. "I know." A soft sigh escaped her lips. "It was wonderful, wasn't it?"

"Wonderful," he agreed, smiling. His hand cupped her cheek, then drifted down her neck to cup her breast. "Wonderful."

"I like you, too." With a seductive smile, she dragged her fingernails over his chest, down his flat belly.

He sucked in a breath, desire kindling in his eyes. "Is it too soon to do it again?"

Susannah slid a glance at his manhood. "Doesn't look like it," she remarked dryly. Laughter bubbled in her throat as a dark flush rose in Black Wind's cheeks. "You're blushing!"

He grinned as he tucked her firmly beneath him. "You dare to laugh at me, woman?"

"I'm not laughing at you," she said, though she was nearly choking. "Honest."

Straddling her hips, he began to caress her. His gaze never left her face as his hands moved over her body, boldly stroking the secret places that made her come alive, until she was writhing beneath him, moaning with need.

"You are not laughing now," he murmured.

She raked her nails over his inner thighs, caressed his chest, then cupped her hand around his neck and drew him down toward her.

"Tell me," he demanded softly.

"I love you."

"Again."

"I love you."

With a groan, he covered her body with his, his face buried in the hollow of her shoulder, as her warmth enveloped him.

* * *

Later, they bathed in the pool, taking turns washing one another. She was surprised when he wanted her again and took her, there, in the pool. It was wonderfully primal, sensual. She clung to him, her whole body quivering with desire, aware of the sunlight on her face, of his strong arms supporting her, of the water swirling around her legs as his life poured into her, filling her with liquid heat.

For a time, they stood pressed together, the heat of their bodies warming the water.

"I'm turning into a prune," Susannah murmured, and when Black Wind looked perplexed, she held up her hand and wiggled her fingers. "See? All wrinkled, like a prune."

"I do not know of prunes," he replied with mock gravity, "but I do not want a wrinkled woman." And so saying, he swung her into his arms and carried her out of the pool.

Sometime later, Susannah washed her clothes, wishing, as she did so, that she had something else to wear. She was heartily sick of wearing a baggy shirt and men's pants. She supposed, if worse came to worst, she could wear Hester's nightgown. Instead, she donned Black Wind's extra shirt, which fell past her knees, and they went for a walk in the woods. It was cool under the trees. The air was fragrant with the scent of earth and foliage. Birds darted among the branches, singing and scolding as they passed below. She saw a bushy-tailed gray squirrel and a chipmunk, several lizards. Tate Sapa pointed at a tree and she saw a fat raccoon peering at her through the leaves.

Tate Sapa found some berry bushes, and they picked handfuls of plump berries, feeding them to each other until their mouths were stained purple and juice dripped from their chins. They picked wild onions and turnips for dinner. Tate Sapa set a snare for a rabbit, then fashioned a spear from a tree branch.

Susannah sat in the shade while he stood on the edge of the stream, the spear poised. He stood there, unmoving, looking like a statue cast in bronze. Sunlight cast blue highlights in his hair. A spiderweb of fine white scars marred the symmetry of his broad back and shoulders. Her stomach clenched as she thought of the beating he must have endured, the pain, the humiliation.

There was a sudden blur of movement as Black Wind threw the spear. She clapped her hands as he lifted a fat trout from the water. My husband, the fisherman, she mused, and felt joy rise up from the very depths of her heart, bright and bubbly, like fine champagne on New Year's Eve.

This must have been how Adam and Eve felt in the Garden, she mused. Just the two of them, alone in paradise. She wondered what Eve had thought when she first saw Adam. Had she found him irresistible and exciting? Had his smile warmed the very deepest part of her being? Had his kisses made her pulse race and her heart beat like thunder? Had the prospect of being in his arms turned her insides to mush?

Tate Sapa caught another fish, gutted the pair, strung them on a strip of rawhide, and left them soaking in the water.

Susannah's heartbeat increased as he walked

toward her, his long legs quickly covering the short distance between them.

Susannah stood up and stepped into his embrace, her arms wrapping around his waist. They had made love only a short time ago, but she wanted him again.

He smiled when she told him so. "Can you not tell that I want you, too?" he asked.

She nodded, acutely aware of his growing desire. They had few clothes to dispose of. His clout. The shirt she was wearing.

Murmuring her name, he swung her into his arms and carried her to their blankets. They made love slowly this time, arousing each other, backing off, tasting and tempting, until Susannah thought she would burst with need. For a man who had never made love to a woman before, Black Wind had quickly discovered how to please her, how to take her to the very edge of bliss, until the pleasure became the most exquisite pain. And then he entered her, filling her with ecstacy. Light and heat exploded within her, making her feel as though she had somehow captured the sun.

Susannah lifted her hips, drawing him deeper, watching his face as his own release came. The sound of her name on his lips, his long shuddering sigh of satisfaction, pleased her beyond words. He collapsed on top of her, his heated breath fanning her neck.

"Am I heavy?" he asked after a while.

"Yes." She wrapped her arms around him when he started to move. "But I like it." Indeed, it was a wondrous weight. She could feel the beat of his heart, his every breath.

Sated and happy, heart swelling with love and tenderness, she stroked his back and thought she would ask nothing more of life than to stay here, in this place, with this man, for as long as she lived.

Days passed, and Susannah's love for Black Wind grew deeper, stronger, as did her respect and admiration for his ability to provide for them. They had fresh meat each night. He built a snug shelter and thatched the roof with tree branches. He taught her how to skin game and cook over an open fire, how to find the fruits and vegetables that grew wild in the canyon.

He insisted she learn how to load and fire the rifle and the pistol, praising her lavishly whenever she managed to hit the target. She had never liked guns, didn't relish the thought of taking a life, animal or human, but she could see the wisdom in knowing how to use a gun. They were alone in the wilderness, after all, and the time might come when she would need to defend herself. She tried not to think of the wild animals that inhabited the canyon, the enemy tribes that could wander into their sanctuary, or the Army, which might still be looking for them.

After a great deal of trial and error, she fashioned an ankle-length tunic of buckskin. She made herself a pair of moccasins by using Black Wind's for a pattern.

Daily, they swam in the pool; in the evening, they took long walks, or sat side by side, enjoying the peace and beauty of the night.

They made love often. Inside the shelter, beside the stream, in the cool depths of the placid pool, on top of a sun-warmed rock, under a canopy of twinkling stars. Always, Black Wind treated her with a tenderness that bordered on awe. It pleased Susannah to know that she was the first woman he had ever loved, and she wished again that she had listened to her mother, that she had saved herself for the man she would spend her life with. . . .

Susannah frowned as she stirred the coals, then added wood to the fire. She had not thought about home in days. Her parents must be frantic with worry, her friends, too. Her rent was overdue. It occurred to her that she could find herself back in her own time with no place to live.

There was no point in dwelling on what could not be changed. For all she knew, she was here to stay.

"Su-san-nah."

She looked up, smiling when she saw Black Wind walking toward her.

"Riders are coming," he said. He thrust the rifle into her hands. "Go into the woods. Stay there."

"Riders?" Susannah glanced toward the entrance to the canyon. "Who are they?"

"They are too far away to tell. Do as I say."

"What are you going to do?"

"They will have seen the smoke from the fire. They know someone is here."

"So you're just going to wait around until they get here?"

"There is no other way out of the canyon. If we

both hide, they will search until they have found us both."

"Black Wind . . ."

"They will be here soon. Find a place to hide." He gazed deep into her eyes. "Do not come out until I tell you it is safe."

"No, I want to stay with you."

"Do not argue with me, woman!"

She bristled at his tone, but she couldn't be angry, not when his eyes were filled with concern for her well-being.

"Please, Su-san-nah," he begged softly.

"Oh, all right. Promise me you'll be careful. You won't do anything stupid."

He arched one brow, as if the thought of his doing anything stupid was ludicrous. "I promise." He kissed her quickly, then gave her a little nudge. "Go. Hurry."

Tate Sapa watched her run toward the trees, watched her until she was out of sight, then he turned back to their camp, checking to make sure there was nothing in evidence that indicated a woman had been there.

He made sure the pistol was loaded, then placed it within easy reach.

He saw the plume of rising dust before he saw the riders. Six of them, and his father riding at the head.

Did his people want to destroy Susannah so badly they had sent warriors to find them?

He Wonjetah reined his horse to a halt a few feet from where Tate Sapa stood. *"Hau, cinks."*

Tate Sapa nodded. *"Hau, Ate."* He glanced at

the warriors spread out behind his father. "Why have you come here?"

"To ask you to return to our people."

"No."

"Our people have need of you. The Blue Coats have sent messengers to discuss a treaty. The young men have taken them prisoner. They are arguing for war. Mato Mani has spoken for peace, but they will not listen to him."

"Why do you think they will listen to me?"

"You have always been their leader."

"I have taken a white woman to my lodge. Did you not tell me they would no longer respect me?"

"Where is the white woman?"

"There is no need for you to know."

"Come back with us, *cinks.* I fear the young men will kill the Blue Coats and bring the soldiers down on us." He Wonjetah dismounted and placed one hand on his son's shoulder. "Our tribe is small. We cannot stand against the Blue Coats. Would you see your people destroyed at the cost of your pride?"

"What of the white woman?"

"I have spoken to Mato Mani. He has convinced the council that Wakinyela was mistaken. I give you my word, as your father and a warrior, that the white woman will not be harmed."

"I must think on it." Tate Sapa glanced at the other warriors. "Sit. Rest. There is food inside the shelter."

"Where are you going?" He Wonjetah asked.

"I must discuss this with Su-san-nah. This decision involves her also. I cannot make it on my own."

Susannah watched Black Wind walk toward her. Her nerves were stretched like fine wire by the time he reached her hiding place. She had recognized his father. Had the Lakota come to finish what they had started? Was she to die here, in this place?

She searched Black Wind's face, but could determine nothing from his expression.

"Su-san-nah?"

She had an almost overpowering urge to run away from him, to find a hole and crawl into it, to bury her head in her hands and hide in the darkness.

"Su-san-nah, it is all right."

She stepped into view, the rifle heavy in her hands, afraid that nothing would ever be all right again. "What do they want?"

He took the rifle from her and cradled it in one arm. "They want me to return to the village and speak to the young men."

"Are you going?"

He blew out a sigh that seemed to come from the soles of his feet. "I think I must."

She looked up at him, waiting for him to go on, afraid to ask what would happen to her if they went back. She had seen her share of cowboy movies. She knew what happened to unwanted white captives.

He must have seen the trepidation in her eyes. Slowly, he lifted his hand and caressed her cheek. "You are in no danger, Su-san-nah. I would not go back with them if I thought they meant to harm you."

"They were going to kill me a few days ago."

"But now they need me alive more than they want you dead," he replied matter-of-factly. "My people need me, Su-san-nah. I cannot refuse."

"Would you refuse if I asked you to?"

He put his free arm around her waist and drew her up against him. "Yes, Su-san-nah. If you ask me to refuse, I will." He gazed deep into her eyes. "The decision is yours. What shall I tell my father?"

"Tell him you'll go, of course." She slid her hand down his chest, deeply moved that he would choose her over his own people. "You've got to help, if you can."

"I knew I had chosen wisely when I took you for my wife," Tate Sapa said. "Truly, the gods were kind to send you to me."

"I don't know who sent me," Susannah murmured, "but I'm glad they did."

"As I am," Tate Sapa replied fervently. "As I am." He brushed his lips against her cheek. "Come, let us go tell my father our decision."

They rode out of the valley late that afternoon. Susannah couldn't help feeling uneasy as they rode toward the Lakota village. Only a few days ago, the Lakota had been insisting she was a witch and screaming for her death.

Black Wind's father rode on her left, Black Wind rode on her right. The other warriors were spread out behind him. She glanced at them over her shoulder. These were men who knew how to fight, and they had the scars to prove it. They were not rash young men, nor aged veterans, but seasoned warriors in their prime.

Clad in buckskin leggings and moccasins, their faces as unyielding as granite, their long black hair blowing slightly in the wind, they were an awesome sight. Susannah was glad she was on their side.

At dusk, they stopped at a waterhole to water the horses and fill their waterskins, then they went on for another hour before making camp near a copse of trees.

The warriors set about making camp with a minimum of fuss or effort. One of the men started a fire, another produced jerky and some little flat cakes that were soaked in water and produced something Black Wind called *wojapi*, which was similar to a cherry pudding. Blankets were spread around the fire, the horses were hobbled nearby. One warrior took sentry duty, and the others wrapped up in their robes and turned in for the night.

Susannah lay beside Black Wind, too keyed up to sleep. All around her came the soft sounds of sleeping men. How had they managed to find sleep so quickly?

She shifted on the hard ground, wishing for her bed at home, for the familiar sounds of the city to lull her to sleep. It was so quiet here. No car horns blaring. No sirens. No dogs barking. No television to fill the emptiness, no radio turned low to fill up the sound of silence. Just the soft snuffling of the horses grazing nearby and the on-again, off-again song of a cricket.

Feather in the Wind

"Sleep, Su-san-nah," Tate Sapa urged. "We will be leaving before dawn."

"I'm not tired."

He held out his arm, inviting her to join him in his blankets. She didn't wait to be asked twice. Scooting across the short distance between them, she snuggled against him, her head resting comfortably on his shoulder.

"It will be all right," he said reassuringly.

"No," she said sadly. "It won't."

"What do you mean?"

Susannah bit down on her lip, wishing she hadn't said anything. But maybe he needed to know. "Be careful of any treaty the Army offers you," she said quietly. "Whatever promises they make, they won't keep them. They never kept any of them."

"What are you saying?"

She shrugged. "Just that you can't trust the Army, or anyone else. They'll make you promises they won't keep. All you can do is try to stay out of their way."

Tate Sapa rolled onto his side, his gaze searching hers in the semi-darkness. "Go on."

"I don't remember names and dates," Susannah said apologetically. "I never paid much attention to history when I was in school. But when I was trying to find out who you were . . ."

"What do you mean?"

"When I saw your picture, I went to the library to try and find out who you were."

"What is library?"

"White people keep their history in books, sort of like the Lakota winter count."

Black Wind nodded. "Go on."

"Well, I did quite a bit of reading, and I seem to remember that the government promised to give the Sioux the Black Hills and then, when gold was . . . is discovered, the politicians will change their minds. There's going to be a big fight. It will be a tremendous victory for the Sioux and the Cheyenne, but it won't matter. In the end, your people will be defeated and sent to live on reservations."

"When does this happen?"

Susannah shook her head. "I'm not sure. I didn't pay much attention to dates." She frowned. "In the mid-1870s, I think, somewhere around there."

"What does that mean? 1870s?"

"Well, according to the white man's reckoning, it's 1870 now."

Tate Sapa frowned. "How much time is there until the mid-1870s?"

"About five years."

It was a long time, he thought bleakly, and yet not long enough. "What can I do to help my people?"

"I don't know. Urge them not to fight, I guess. You can't win."

He knew she spoke the truth, knew his people could never win against the *wasichu*. It was why he spoke for peace, why he urged the young men to avoid the war trail. Perversely, he did not like hearing the same words from Susannah.

"I'm sorry, Black Wind," she murmured.

"It is not your fault."

"I know, but . . ." She let the words trail off. It

wasn't her fault. The fate of the Indians had been determined long before she had been born.

"Go to sleep, Su-san-nah," Tate Sapa whispered. "The fate of our people rests, as always, with *Wakan Tanka*."

With a sigh, she closed her eyes, wondering if what she had told Black Wind would somehow change the future.

Chapter Sixteen

Susannah's nerves grew increasingly taut as they rode into the village. People stopped what they were doing to stare at her as she passed.

The first time she had ridden into the village, the Lakota had viewed her with blatant interest and curiosity. But that was gone now, replaced by suspicion and animosity that was so strong, it was like a living, breathing thing, threatening to overwhelm her if she let it.

She lifted her chin and squared her shoulders, refusing to let them know how frightened she really was. Black Wind had promised to protect her, but he was only one man, after all. He might not be able to stop them should they decide to do away with her after all.

As soon as they reached his lodge, she slid off her horse's back and ducked inside. The interior was cool and dim. She took a long drink from a waterskin hanging from one of the lodge poles, then sank down on Black Wind's buffalo robes and closed her eyes. When she was alone with him, she knew she was where she was meant to be, but now, in the heart of Indian territory, in the midst of dozens of Lakota lodges, doubts assailed her. His people didn't want her here—they had accused her of being a witch.

She looked up as someone stepped into the lodge. "Oh, Black Wind . . ."

Crossing the floor, he took her hands and drew her to her feet and into his arms.

"Do not be afraid, Su-san-nah. Mato Mani has given me his word that you will not be harmed."

Susannah nodded. She didn't know if Mato Mani's word could be trusted, but it made her feel a little better just the same.

"I must go talk to the soldiers," Black Wind said. His gaze caressed her. "Will you come with me?"

"You want me to be there?"

"Yes."

"All right."

The soldiers who had come to parley with the Lakota were being held in a large tepee on the outskirts of the village. Two warriors stood guard outside. Tate Sapa spoke to them briefly, and Susannah wondered if he were explaining her presence.

She followed Black Wind into the lodge, then stood near the doorway while her eyes adjusted to the dim interior. There were three soldiers, all bound hand and foot. Two of them seemed to be in their early thirties; the youngest, who was surely no more than eighteen or nineteen, had been wounded. Dried blood made a dark stain on his left shirt sleeve just above his elbow. His face was sheened with sweat, his eyes were dull with pain.

The two older men stared up at Susannah. Recognition flickered in their eyes. Recognition and curiosity. They were wondering what she was doing there, she thought, wondering if she was there of her own free will.

Tate Sapa studied each man. The youngest of the three stared blankly at the ground. The other two met his gaze defiantly.

"Why have you come here?" Tate Sapa asked brusquely.

"Colonel O'Neill sent us to make peace."

The reply came from a ruddy-faced man wearing captain's bars.

"My people *are* at peace," Tate Sapa replied.

The captain nodded. "Colonel O'Neill wants you and your chiefs to come to the fort and sign a treaty."

"Why?"

"He wants you to guarantee safe passage for any settlers that cross Sioux land."

"Do you think that I am a fool, that I would return to the fort so that you can lock me up again?"

"Colonel O'Neill has promised all charges against you will be dropped if you will cooperate."

"I cannot speak for the Yankton, or the Brule, or the Oglala, or the Teton," Tate Sapa replied.

"I speak only for my own people, and only as long as they wish to listen."

The captain nodded. "I understand that, but we've got to start somewhere. If your people will agree to sign the treaty, Crazy Horse and the others might follow."

"I will speak to my people. That is all I can do."

"And if your people say no?"

"If they say no, you and your men will be the first to know it."

The captain lifted his chin and squared his shoulders. "You mean we'll be dead."

Tate Sapa nodded.

"I've got a man here who's hurtin'," the captain remarked, cool as you please. "Do you think you could help him?"

"I will send the medicine man to look after him."

"Obliged to you."

With a nod, Tate Sapa left the lodge.

"Ma'am?"

Susannah had turned to follow Black Wind outside. Now, she glanced over her shoulder. "Yes, Captain?"

"Colonel O'Neill was right about you, wasn't he? You are a spy."

"No, Captain . . . What's your name?"

"McCarin."

"I'm not a spy, Captain McCarin."

"Then what are you doing here, with him?"

"I'm not really sure."

"If they let us go, you're welcome to go back to the fort with us."

"Thank you, Captain, but my place is here, with him."

"I'd think it over, if I was you."

"Believe me when I tell you I've thought of nothing else, Captain," Susannah replied, and ducked out of the lodge.

Tate Sapa was waiting for her.

"What are you going to do?" she asked.

"I will speak to the young men." He took her hand and they walked toward the river.

"What about the other men?"

"Most of our people want peace. It is only the young men eager to count coup who speak for war."

"The captain said they wanted your chiefs to go to the fort. You won't go, will you?"

"If I must."

"You can't! How can you even think of it?"

"I am the only one here who speaks and understands the white man's tongue."

"I don't care! I wouldn't trust that colonel any farther than I can throw him."

A faint smile moved over Tate Sapa's face. "I do not trust him, either, Su-san-nah, but I cannot turn my back on my people. I must try and insure a lasting peace before it is too late."

Susannah blew out a soft sigh as she slipped her arm around his waist. She'd known she wouldn't be able to talk him out of it, had known that his love for his people, his honor, would compel him to do what he felt was right.

They had reached the river now. It was cool and quiet near the water. A gentle breeze stirred the leaves of the cottonwoods. Tate Sapa listened for a moment, wishing the sacred talking trees would tell him what to do, which way to go.

He gazed into the distance, his thoughts troubled. How could he convince the young men that peace was the answer?

Was it the answer? As far as he could tell, the whites did not want peace. A peaceful band of Cheyenne had been massacred at Cedar Canyon only a few years earlier. Another band of Cheyenne had been massacred at Sand Creek that same year.

Only the year before, Custer's cavalry had attacked a camp composed of Cheyenne, Kiowa, Arapaho, and a wandering band of Apache who had chosen to make their winter headquarters in a small valley near the banks of the Washita River. The Army had attacked at dawn, killing over a hundred people, including women and children. Chief Black Kettle, who had long been known as a man of peace, had been slain trying to defend his people.

Susannah laid her hand on Black Wind's arm. "Black Wind?"

With a sigh, he turned toward her. "What is the answer, Su-san-nah?"

"I don't know. All I know is that, in the end, your people will be defeated and forced to live on reservations."

"I would rather be dead," Tate Sapa said vehemently. "I will not live on the reservation."

"Are you going to vote for war, then?"

"I do not know." He blew out a long sigh. "Is it better for us to die now, in battle, or to have the Army hunt us down and kill us a few at a time?

What of our children, Su-san-nah? Our old ones? Will I condemn them to death if I say fight? Will they not die on the reservation if we surrender? How can I speak for them?"

"I don't know." She drew him into her arms and held him tight. She didn't know what kind of life the Indians had led after their defeat. She only knew that, in her time, they lived on reservations where unemployment, alcoholism, and suicide were at an all-time high.

Tate Sapa rested his chin on the top of Susannah's head. Her arms were warm and comforting, and for a moment he took solace in her touch. And then, resolutely, he took her hand.

"Come," he said, "I will walk you back to our lodge. It is time for the council to meet."

Susannah jumped to her feet when Black Wind entered the lodge three hours later. "What did they decide?"

"I have told the soldiers I will not go to the fort. They have agreed to meet with me two moons from now at Rock Tree Creek. If we can agree on a treaty, I will bring it back to the village to be signed."

"What about the soldiers who were captured?"

"The injured man's wound has been taken care of. We have given them food and water. Two of our warriors will ride with them until they reach the safety of the fort."

"Do you think your chiefs will sign the treaty?"

Tate Sapa nodded. "We will try for peace one last time."

"I'm afraid. What if . . ." She swallowed past

the fear rising in her throat. "Tate . . ."

"We will not speak of it now."

"But—"

"Not now, Su-san-nah."

He reached for her, wrapping his arms around her waist and holding her close. His lips brushed the top of her head, sending little shivers down her spine.

Even though he didn't want to talk about it, Susannah couldn't help wondering what would happen if the Indians decided not to sign the treaty. What if the solders tried to arrest Black Wind? So many things could go wrong.

"Su-san-nah?"

She heard the wanting in his voice, the unspoken question, the longing. The yearning in his eyes consumed every other thought, the heat of his desire burned away every doubt and fear.

Standing on tiptoe, she answered his question with a kiss.

His arms tightened around her. She felt his body tense, felt his rising desire as he kissed her back. His tongue was a warm, welcome invasion.

With a low groan, he carried her down to the buffalo robes, his mouth never leaving hers.

Desire flowed over her and through her, heating her blood, her flesh. She stirred restlessly beneath him, her hands moving over his broad back, down his chest, over the muscles that rippled beneath her fingertips. He was so beautiful, a study in male perfection, and he was hers. The knowledge made her heart sing with happiness.

A low moan of pleasure rose in her throat as his hands caressed her, fanning the embers of desire. She pressed against him, wanting to be closer, closer.

"*Skuyela*," he murmured.

"What?" She breathed the word into his mouth as he kissed her again.

"Sweet," Tate Sapa replied, his tongue gliding over her lower lip. "So sweet." He began to undress her, his mouth never leaving hers.

"Not fair," Susannah said. She slid her hand between them and unfastened the ties of his clout. It fell away and there was nothing between them but desire.

Murmuring her name, Tate Sapa eased himself on top of her, his dark eyes scorching her as he slid between her thighs.

"Su-san-nah."

"Yes," she murmured, "oh, yes."

She ran her fingertips over his chest, then drew his head down toward her and kissed him, their mouths fusing as their bodies joined.

There was no way to describe it, no words to convey the joy that spiraled through her, the wondrous pleasure, the soul-deep sense of belonging that engulfed her. She was his, had been born to be his. In this time and place, or any other, she would be his. Always and forever his . . .

With a sigh, Tate Sapa rolled onto his side, carrying Susannah with him, their bodies still joined together.

"I did not hurt you?" he asked.

Susannah smiled. It was so sweet of him to worry about her. "No."

"I am so much bigger than you."

Feather in the Wind

Laughter bubbled up inside her. "Yes," she said, "and I love it."

He frowned at her. "What if there is a child?"

Susannah blinked at him. A child! She had never even thought of getting pregnant. "What do you mean?"

"You are so tiny."

Comprehension came swiftly. He was afraid she might have trouble giving birth. It was a possibility that had given her cause for concern in the past. When she had been engaged to Troy, they had gone to see a doctor, who had told her not to worry. If she got pregnant and the baby was too big to deliver normally, they would simply do a C-section. His words had not given her the comfort they should have. Childbirth had always scared her a little. The thought of being cut open terrified her.

"Su-san-nah?" Tate Sapa frowned down at her. "What?"

"I did not mean to frighten you."

"You didn't." She forced a smile. "I'm fine. It's just that we never discussed children . . ."

He didn't move, but she felt suddenly alone, as if a vast gulf had opened between them. "You do not want my child?"

Susannah felt a sudden lurch in her stomach, as if the floor had just fallen out from under her.

"Tate . . . I . . . Wait a minute. Don't go putting words in my mouth."

He drew away from her, his dark eyes empty of expression. "Tell me your words, Su-san-nah."

She realized then that he hadn't been asking if she wanted his child. He was asking if she

219

wanted to bear an Indian's child.

"If you do not want to bear my child, you have only to tell me and I will not touch you again."

"No, it's not that. Please don't think that. I've always been afraid of having a baby. Any baby. My doctor told me I would probably have a difficult time, but not to worry because they would take the baby if they had to."

"Take the baby?"

"It's called a caesarian." She drew a line across her stomach. "They would cut me open and take the baby out when it was time for it to be born."

Tate Sapa stared at her stomach, his frown deepening. He had heard of such a thing being done once. It had saved Otter's child, but his woman had died.

"I'd love to have your child, Tate," Susannah said.

He shook his head. "Perhaps it is not a good idea."

"What are you saying?"

"I'm not sure." He did not want to cause her pain or put her life at risk, but he knew of no sure way to keep her from getting pregnant other than abstinence. Could he live with her and not touch her?

"We could try the method the Catholics use," Susannah suggested, "although you probably won't like it."

"What is it, this Catholic method?"

As best she could, she explained it to him. She had expected him to object flat out, but, after a moment's consideration, he nodded his agreement.

"We will try it," Tate Sapa said. It would not be as pleasurable as finding his release within the warmth of her body. But being able to make love to her only at certain times during the month was better than not being able to make love to her at all.

"Maybe we should try it now?" Susannah asked.

A smile curved the corners of his mouth and chased the darkness from his eyes. "I think that would be a good idea," he mused as he drew her into his arms. "A very good idea."

Chapter Seventeen

Because the Blue Coats now knew where the Lakota were camped, Mato Mani decided it would be prudent to move the village.

Susannah had watched in wonder as the women packed up their household belongings, then dismantled the lodges. The horse herd was rounded up, and within a matter of hours, the Indians were on the move.

Tate Sapa had dismantled their lodge and done most of the work in getting ready to go. Susannah had helped as much as she could, but, at best, she had done very little.

Now, riding alone near the rear of the vast column, she felt a sudden wave of homesickness. The other women rode in groups of two and three, talking and laughing as they went along. Young mothers nursed their infants. Older children raced their ponies along the edge of the caravan. The warriors rode at the front, scouting the way. Teenage boys rode drag behind the herd to make sure none of the horses strayed away.

Susannah looked for Black Wind. He was riding up ahead with his father and a couple of other men. She spent a few minutes admiring Black Wind—the way he sat his horse, looselimbed yet regal somehow. He wore a wolf skin clout, a buckskin vest, and moccasins. Of all the men in the village, she thought him far and away the most handsome.

As though feeling her gaze, he turned around, a smile touching his lips when his gaze met hers. For a moment, time ceased to exist. She felt his love reaching out to her, felt her heart skip a beat as the warmth in his eyes washed over her, and she knew she could endure anything—the suspicion of his people, Wakinyela's hatred, the hardships of living with the Indians—if she could see that look in his eyes every day.

His smile grew wider, as though he were reading her mind. He waved, then turned his attention once more to what his father was saying.

They rode for hours, never faster than a walk. Just when Susannah began to wonder if they were ever going to stop, the column came to a halt.

Tate Sapa rode back to Susannah. Helping her from the saddle, he took her by the hand and led her away from the others.

"Let us sit here," he said.

Susannah sat down beside him. For as far as

she could see, there was nothing but endless prairie.

"Here," Tate Sapa said, handing her something that looked a little like a long egg roll.

"What is it?"

"Wasna."

"And what is that?"

"Pemmican. It is made of jerky, chokecherries, and suet." He grinned at her dubious expression. "Try it, Su-san-nah."

She took a small bite. It was rich and sweet. "It's good," she said, the surprise evident in her voice.

Tate Sapa nodded.

"How do you make it?"

"Meat is roasted until it is very brown, then it is pounded very fine, as are dried berries. They are mixed together, then melted suet is mixed in. The Blue Coats are very fond of it."

"You're kidding?"

"Kidding?"

"You're not serious."

"Ah. Yes, very serious. My people have been known to trade pemmican to the soldiers in exchange for blankets and even ammunition."

Later, after everyone had eaten and rested and taken care of their personal needs, and the people were ready to go on, Tate Sapa helped Susannah mount her horse.

"Are you all right, Su-san-nah?"

"Yes, why?"

"I know it is hard for you to be here."

She shrugged. What could she say? It was hard.

"We will camp at dusk."

Susannah nodded, felt her heart swell with emotion as he reached up to caress her cheek.

She sighed as she watched him walk away.

"Where are we going?" Susannah asked.

The Indians had ridden until late afternoon, then stopped by a narrow stream to make camp for the night.

Because the weather was warm, the people had not taken time to set up their lodges; they would sleep outside, under the stars.

So many stars, Susannah mused, glancing up at the sky. The moon hung low in the sky, as yellow as a pat of butter.

Numerous cooking fires made little beacons of light across the plains. Susannah had gone on an overnight camp out once when she had been in the Girl Scouts. She remembered hearing one of the leaders say "White man build big fire, sit far away. Indian build little fire, sit close."

Now, sitting beside Black Wind, she saw that it was true.

"We are going deep into the *Paha Sapa*," Tate Sapa replied. "The Black Hills."

Susannah frowned. The name sounded familiar. Unless she was mistaken, she seemed to recall reading somewhere that Colonel George Custer had found gold there during some fact-finding tour. She couldn't remember the year, or what had happened after that. She wasn't sure of the exact year, sometime in the early 1870s, she thought. She had seen pictures of the Black Hills. It had looked like a beautiful place, the hills covered with pines, the sky a bright clear blue. Her father had gone fishing there once and sent her a postcard. Even in Susannah's time, over a hundred years later, the Black Hills were often in the news as the Indians continued the neverending battle to reclaim their ancient hunting grounds. The only difference was that, in the future, they did their fighting in court.

Susannah wrapped her arms around her knees, her gaze fixed on the fire. "How long will it take to get there?"

"A few days."

"And then what?"

"We will stay there until it is time for me to leave to meet with the soldiers."

"Please let someone else go in your place," Susannah said earnestly.

"I cannot. You know that no one else speaks the white man's tongue as well as I do."

Susannah sighed as Black Wind took her by the hand and drew her to her feet. "Let us not look for trouble, Su-san-nah," he said, draping a blanket over his shoulder. "It will find us soon enough."

Hand in hand, they walked away from the camp into the darkness. Her heart was pounding with anticipation when Black Wind stopped. He spread the blanket on a flat stretch of ground, then drew her into his arms and kissed her. On a scale of one to ten, his kisses definitely rated an eleven.

His hands slid up and down her arms, sending little shivers of pleasure running through her. His lips were warm, possessive, drawing her into a place where nothing mattered but the two of them. Reality fell away, leaving them alone in a world of wonder.

Susannah felt the slight tremor in his hands as Black Wind undressed her, moaned with soft delight as his hands brushed her bare skin, making her tingle with pleasure.

She removed his vest and moccasins, untied the string that held his clout, then pressed against him, marveling anew at how perfectly her body fit to his.

He drew her down on the blanket, his hands caressing the contours of her breast, the curve of her hip. Kisses trailed in the wake of his hands. He whispered to her, tender words of love spoken in English and Lakota. She strained toward him, wanting him to possess her, but he refused, his hands and lips continuing their sweet torture, until she was wild with need.

He rose above her, his long dark hair brushing against her breasts.

"Su-san-nah . . . *wastelakapi* . . ."

"Yes," she sighed. "Yes, now. . . ."

The wonder of it, the sheer ecstacy, flowed through her like warm sweet honey. Eyes closed, her arms and legs twined around him, she gave herself over to the intense waves of pleasure that washed over her, like breakers crashing against the shore, higher, higher, until, gradually, ecstacy receded like the outgoing tide, leaving breathless fulfillment in its wake.

With a sigh, Tate Sapa rolled onto his side, carrying Susannah with him. Never had he imagined that loving a woman could be so exhilarating, or so humbling. He had known, from early childhood, what mating was all about. One did not grow up in a Lakota village surrounded by dogs and horses without learning how puppies and foals were created. There was little privacy in a Lakota lodge. He had, on more than one occasion, seen his parents in an intimate embrace. But he had never realized the soul-deep satisfaction that resulted from the union of flesh to flesh, had never considered that the act of love was more than merely a joining of bodies. He knew now that it was a melding of minds and hearts as well. A perfect blending of two spirits.

He felt her heart beat in time with his, heard the little contented sounds she made as she snuggled closer. Again, he stood in awe of the magic that had carried her across time to this place, to his arms.

Knowing their being together was nothing less than a miracle, he closed his eyes and offered a silent prayer of thanks to *Wakan Tanka*.

Susannah felt her breath catch in her throat when she caught her first glimpse of the Lakota's sacred Black Hills, an island in a neverending sea of grass. The hills were truly an imposing sight, granite peaks that rose hundreds of feet above the surrounding plains. Black Wind had called the hills the "heart of everything that is." It was here that he had seen her in a vision, here that his people had come to pray for hundreds of years.

They had ridden through lush meadows, through a forest of pine cut with rushing streams filled with fish she thought were trout. There were rolling hills and ridges covered with ponderosa pine, silver-barked birch, quaking aspens, cottonwoods, and ironwood. She had caught glimpses of deer and beaver, a fat porcupine.

"It's beautiful," she murmured. "No wonder your people fought so hard to keep this place."

Tate Sapa frowned. Fought? They were still fighting. And then he remembered that Susannah had told him that, at some future time, the hills would be lost to his people. He could not imagine such a thing, could not imagine how his people could survive if their very heart was taken from them.

They made camp in a meadow near a slow-moving stream. Susannah watched in amazement as the women raised their lodges. In no time at all, the village looked as though it had been there for days instead of hours.

Children ran through the meadow, exuberant in their youth. Dogs were everywhere, barking, fighting, chasing after the children.

The horse herd grazed in the distance, covering the ground like a huge, multicolored blanket.

Soon, cooking fires were lit, and the scent of roasting meat permeated the air.

Susannah helped Black Wind erect their tepee, her awe for the Indian women increasing. How did they manage on their own? The poles—she learned there were twenty of them, eighteen for the frame and two for the smoke flaps—were heavy. The lodge cover was large and awkward to handle. She knew she could never have raised the tepee on her own, yet none of the other women needed men to help them.

Several of the warriors came by to watch Black Wind. She couldn't understand what they said, but she knew by the looks on their faces and their gestures that they were teasing him for doing "women's work." She overheard the words *win-yan wasichu*, and guessed they were saying derogatory things about her because she needed a man's help.

The lodge went up much faster than she would have imagined. When it was up and the smoke flaps set, Black Wind left her to set up house-keeping.

She was glad to be able to go inside, away from curious stares. She carried their belongings into the lodge, then stood there a moment, trying to remember where everything went. The tepee was quite roomy, probably about twenty feet in diameter.

She spread the sleeping robes along the back wall, dug a small fire pit in the center, arranged the cooking utensils on one side of the lodge. There were two willow-bark backrests with furry covers. She would have to ask Black Wind to make one for her, too, she thought. A tripod held Black Wind's shield and lance. Large parfleches held their extra clothing; smaller ones held Black Wind's war paint, extra bridles, strips of rawhide. She piled He Wonjetah's belongings on his bedroll, certain he would not want her going through his things.

When she was finished, she gathered her courage and went outside. They would need wood for the fire, and she was determined to get it. Black

Wind had suffered enough ridicule on her account. Finding wood was something she could do on her own.

Susannah was conscious of being watched as she made her way toward the forest that grew on the edge of the meadow. She tried to tell herself she didn't care that the Indians didn't like her, didn't trust her, but she knew it was a lie. She'd never had trouble making friends, never been on the outside looking in, until now.

Back straight, shoulders square, she kept walking, not relaxing until the trees hid her from view. With a sigh, she began to gather the small branches and twigs that littered the ground. Birds twittered in the treetops; a squirrel watched her pass by. The hum of insects blended with the sighing of the wind.

When she'd gathered an armful of wood, Susannah turned around and headed back the way she'd come, only then realizing that she wasn't sure which direction to go. She hadn't walked in a straight line and now, deep in the heart of the forest, she had no idea which way to go. She fought back a rush of panic.

"Think, Susannah," she muttered, cheered a little by the sound of her own voice. "You can't be very far from camp."

She glanced around one more time, then started walking, hoping to see a familiar landmark. But the trees all looked the same.

When she'd been walking for about fifteen minutes, she realized she had to be going the wrong way. Veering to the left, she took off in that direction.

Twenty minutes later she admitted she was hopelessly lost. Her Girl Scout leader had once told them that if they got lost, they should sit down and wait for someone to find them. Thinking that sounded like good advice, Susannah found a fallen log and sat down, then dumped her load of firewood on the ground.

She wouldn't panic. Black Wind would find her.

For a time, she studied her surroundings. The forest reminded her of the story of Hansel and Gretel. She grinned as she cast Wakinyela in the part of the Wicked Witch.

She listened to the breeze whisper to the trees, and wondered what was happening back home. Susannah hated to think of the worry her disappearance must be causing her parents, her friends, her editor. Had she been declared missing? Dead? Abducted by aliens?...

She blew out a sigh, knowing it was useless to worry and wonder. There was nothing she could do about it now.

Unable to sit still any longer, she picked up her load of wood and started walking again. Even if she was going in the wrong direction, at least she was doing *something*.

The forest seemed to get thicker as she went along, and the panic she had being trying so hard to ignore hit her full force. Well and truly frightened now, she began to walk faster. That was when she heard it, a rustling in the brush to her left. Some deep-seated instinct halted her in midflight and she froze, her gaze darting toward the noise.

Her mouth went dry and her heart plummeted to the ground as a brown bear rose up behind a clump of bushes. Berry juice, as red as blood, dripped from its mouth and stained its enormous paws. Nostrils flaring, it stared at her through black beady eyes.

Time stretched into infinity as she stood there, waiting, afraid to move, afraid to breathe. She recalled a TV show she'd seen where a bear had suddenly turned on a woman and started mauling her. But that bear had been muzzled and on a leash. This one looked quite capable of tearing her to shreds. Did bears eat meat? Did it matter?

She thought she heard footsteps behind her, but she was too terrified to risk a glance over her shoulder. And then she heard Black Wind's voice, soft and soothing.

"Do not move, Su-san-nah."

She tried to speak but she couldn't form the words, couldn't push them past the lump of terror lodged in her throat.

The bear stood there, unmoving, for minutes without end. She noticed how long its claws were, that it was missing a piece of its left ear, that there were gray hairs mixed in with brown.

It seemed as though years passed and then, abruptly, the bear dropped to all fours and ambled away.

"Su-san-nah?"

She watched death walk away from her, and then, feeling suddenly dizzy, she went limp. The firewood she had gathered tumbled from her arms.

"Su-san-nah!" Tate Sapa dropped his rifle and

caught her before she fell. "Su-san-nah, it is all right."

She looked at him blankly for a moment, then, with a strangled sob, she buried her face in his shoulder as tears welled in her eyes and violent tremors shook her body.

"It is all right, *wastelakapi*," he murmured. "It is all right. *Mato* has gone."

"I was so afraid." Her teeth were chattering now. "So afraid."

"I know." Effortlessly, he swung her into his arms and held her close, rocking her as if she were a child.

"What if . . . if it comes back?"

"He will not. He is an old warrior, long past fighting."

"He . . . he didn't look so old to me."

"He has wandered these woods for many years, Su-san-nah. He has never harmed anyone." He smiled at her. "I hunted him when I was very young. My arrow did not fly straight. Instead of his heart, I hit his ear. Old *Mato* and I have crossed paths many times since then."

His voice, low and soothing, calmed her. She tried to imagine what Black Wind had been like as a child, a teenager, a young man.

He carried her back to where he had left his horse and lifted her onto its bare back; then, leading the horse by the reins, he walked back and picked up his rifle and the wood Susannah had gathered. He placed the wood in her lap, then vaulted up behind her, his arm wrapping around her waist and holding her close.

Feather in the Wind

"How did you know where I was?" Susannah asked.

"My father saw you leave the village. He said you had been gone a long time."

"I got lost."

"It is easy to do."

Susannah looked doubtful. Somehow, she couldn't imagine Black Wind getting lost.

They reached the village a short time later. Black Wind slid off the back of the horse and took the wood from Susannah's hands. He carried it inside the lodge, then came back to lift her from the horse.

She buried her face against his shoulder so she wouldn't have to see the faces of the people who were staring at her.

"I'm never going to fit in here," she murmured as he lowered her feet to the ground. "Never!"

"In time . . ."

Susannah shook her head, her gaze fixed on the feather tied in his hair. "I want to go home."

His dark eyes reflected the hurt her words caused him. His hands fell away from her waist, and he took a step backward. "I will not keep you here against your will."

"Oh, Tate," she sighed, "it isn't you I want to leave. But you have to admit I don't fit in here. And you know your people will never trust me. They think I'm a witch! The only reason I'm even allowed to be here is because they need you."

He wanted to argue with her, to tell her it wasn't true, that, in time, his people would learn to love her, but he didn't believe it himself. "What do you want me to do, Su-san-nah?"

"I don't know. I wish I did."

Susannah was still pondering Black Wind's question the following afternoon as she walked down to the river for water. What did she want him to do? She had told him she wanted to go home, but she knew he couldn't do anything about that. And, deep down, she wasn't sure she wanted to go back, not unless Black Wind could go with her.

There were several women and children gathered near the river. Susannah wished she could join them, sit down and spend a few minutes chatting with them. But even if she could speak Lakota, she knew she wouldn't be welcome in their midst. The women glanced her way, then ignored her.

Susannah knelt beside the water and filled her container, pretending to ignore them, too. She smiled as she watched a couple of toddlers splashing in the water. On shore, two little boys were wrestling. A little girl sat on a blanket, chewing on a piece of jerky while she watched the boys.

With a sigh, Susannah stood up. She was about to head back to the village when the little girl started to choke. The women quickly gathered around her, thumping her on the back, but to no avail.

Seconds ticked by. Unable to stand there and do nothing, Susannah ran forward, grabbed the girl, praying that she remembered how to do the Heimlich maneuver.

The women stood there, astonished, as a piece of jerky flew out of the little girl's mouth.

"I think she'll be all right," Susannah said. She glanced at the women, who were staring at her in awe. When she heard the word *wakanka*, she decided it was time to go.

When Susannah returned to the lodge, Black Wind was sitting outside, honing the blade of his hunting knife. He smiled at her as she dropped the waterskin and sat down beside him.

"What has happened?" he asked. "You look worried."

"Oh, Tate." She sighed, and quickly told him about the incident at the river.

"You did the right thing, Su-san-nah. You could not let the child die."

"I know, but I heard that witch word again. It scares me. Black Wind, look."

Tate Sapa glanced up to see several men and women walking toward them. He stood up, then offered Susannah his hand and drew her up beside him. "Do not be afraid."

Easier said than done, Susannah mused as the Indians came to a halt in front of the lodge.

A man leading a horse stepped forward. He began to speak. Susannah watched Black Wind's face, hoping to find a clue to what the man was saying in Black Wind's expression. Everyone looked so solemn, she was sure it wasn't good news.

When the man finished speaking, he handed Susannah the horse's reins, then stepped back. Two women came forward. One handed Susannah a dress made of doe hide and a pair of soft moccasins, the second offered her a buffalo robe.

"Are these for me?" She looked at him blankly. "Why?"

"They are gifts from the girl's father and mother and grandmother for saving her life."

"They don't have to give me anything for that."

"It is our way, Su-san-nah." He took the buffalo robe, which was quite heavy, and draped it over the horse's back, then took hold of the horse's reins. "It would be an insult for you to refuse."

"Oh, well, tell them thank you for me."

"You tell them."

Susannah nodded, one hand stroking the dress, which was as soft as velvet. What was that word? Oh, yes. *"Pilamaya."*

The man and the two women nodded at Susannah, then turned away. The others followed.

"Does this mean they don't think I'm a witch anymore?"

"No," Tate Sapa said, smiling, "but they have decided that you are a good witch."

"Like Glinda," Susannah murmured.

"What is Glin-da?"

"The good witch of the North," Susannah said, then laughed. "Never mind." She lifted the reins. "What am I supposed to do with a horse?"

Tate Sapa lifted the robe from the horse's back and tossed it inside the lodge, then tethered the horse to a stake driven into the ground near the lodge.

"It is a fine animal," he remarked, running his hands over the horse's neck and over its back.

"Is it a boy or a girl?"

"It is a mare."

"Oh." It was a pretty horse, sort of a cinnamon color with a dark mane and tail and one white stocking. "I think I'll call her Broomhilda."

Tate Sapa frowned. "What does Broom-hil-da mean?"

"It's the name of a witch," Susannah said, grinning. "Fitting, don't you think?"

Chapter Eighteen

Over the next few days, Susannah found herself being more readily accepted by the Lakota. True, no one was beating down her door in an effort to be her best friend, but at least the people no longer looked at her with dark suspicious eyes. Mothers didn't hold their children close when she passed by. She had saved the life of a Lakota child, and there was nothing of greater worth to the Indians than their children.

She remembered seeing a bumper sticker once that said something about it taking a whole tribe to raise a child; here, in the land of the Lakota, she saw that saying in action. Mothers, fathers, brothers, sisters, grandparents, aunts, uncles, cousins—all played a role in the raising of a child. Babies weren't left with strangers; there was always a member of the family ready and willing to look after an infant. Children didn't have to look far for someone to play with. If Father was away hunting, Grandfather was there to teach a young boy how to use a bow and arrow. If Mother was nursing the baby, Grandma or an aunt was there to make a new dress for a little girl's doll.

Now that she was no longer on the outside looking in, Susannah's entire view of the village changed. She saw the love and concern the people felt for one another, she heard their laughter, saw their sorrow when an aged parent passed away. The Lakota weren't savages—they weren't cold and cruel and heartless—they were just people trying to survive and make a home in the most primitive of circumstances.

She looked at Black Wind with new eyes, too, and felt a warm affection for the people who had raised him, who had made him the wonderful man he was. She wished suddenly that she could have met his mother.

These were busy days for the people. Acquiring food seemed a neverending task, yet, in the evening, there was always time to play. Some nights there were dances, some nights were filled with storytelling.

One evening there was an ear-piercing ceremony. Black Wind told her this was a big event in a young girl's life that took place sometime between the ages of four and ten. It was a way for the parents to show how much they loved their daughter. A man who was well respected in the tribe was asked to pierce the girl's ears. The grandmother put on a big feast.

Black Wind explained that there were spirits who watched over food; if a person was selfish, the spirits would go away, but if a person was generous with what he had, then the spirits would remain.

Later, the girl sat on a blanket surrounded by all the gifts her parents would give away in her honor. The man who pierced the girl's ears was given the most valuable gift. Susannah thought it a charming tradition.

The days passed quickly now. Black Wind was teaching her to speak Lakota. It was not an easy language to learn, but she was determined to master it. Few people in the village spoke any English; until she could communicate with them, she would always be an outsider. She quickly learned a few basic words—*cinks*, pronounced chinks, meant my son; *ciye*, pronounced chee-YAH, meant a man's brother; *skuyela* was pronounced skoo-YAH-lah and meant sweet; *heyah*, which was pronounced hee-YAH, meant no.

The best times, her favorite times, were when Black Wind took her riding. The country was so beautiful, she never tired of looking at it. They rode through lush meadows, up mountains thick with trees, along slow-moving streams.

They made love on a bed of soft green grass in a lush meadow, or beneath the sheltering boughs of a windswept pine high on a mountainside, or under a blanket of stars beside a slow-moving stream.

Susannah could not get enough of Black Wind. She reveled in his kisses, in the touch of his hand, in the husky tremor in his voice when he whispered that he loved her.

Sometimes, as now, it amazed her that she could be so happy in this place; she, who had never liked camping or roughing it outdoors, who had loved long hot baths and dining in expensive restaurants. Such a short time ago, she had wanted only to go back home; now she wished only to stay here, in this time, in this place, with this man.

"What are you thinking, Su-san-nah?" Black Wind rose up on one elbow so he could see her face. Gently, he dragged a finger over the tip of her nose, along the curve of her cheek.

"How happy I am," she replied.

"Are you, truly?"

She nodded, loving the way he looked at her, the way his gaze caressed her. "I never want to leave this place."

"Or me?"

"Or you." She smiled up at him, thinking how handsome he was, how sexy he looked wearing only shadows and a smile. "Do you think your father will ever like me?"

Tate Sapa blew out a breath, then shrugged. "Perhaps, in time. He has not yet forgiven me for refusing to take Wakinyela as my wife."

"It's more than that. It's because I'm white, isn't it?"

Tate Sapa nodded. "He has a strong hatred for the *wasichu*."

"Well, I guess I can't blame him for that." White men had killed his wife and daughter together with many of his friends. "It bothers me,

243

though, knowing he wishes I wasn't here."

"Let us not think of that now," Tate Sapa said. He brushed kisses over her face and neck and breasts. "Let us think only of each other."

Susannah sighed, only too willing to do as he asked. She felt like a pagan, making love to Black Wind in the deep shadows of a wooded glen beneath a bright blue sky. She could hear birds singing, the wind whispering soft secrets to the trees, the humming of insects, the beating of her own heart as Black Wind's kisses became more intense. She was like clay in his hands, her body molding itself to his, soft and pliable, willing to be shaped to his needs and desires.

She rose up to meet him, welcoming the sweet invasion of his flesh, drawing him deep inside her, her eyelids fluttering down as fulfillment washed over her and through her, and she knew, in that moment, in the deepest part of her being, that they had created a new life between them. . . .

The next day, a group of hunters returned to the village. There was a feast that night. Everyone dressed in his finest, then met near the center of the village. Women had been cooking all day—ribs and hump meat and tongue. There were wild onions and potatoes and turnips, berries and nuts and *wojapi*, the cherry pudding.

After the feast, there was dancing. Susannah watched in fascination as the Indians danced. Sometimes just the women, sometimes just the men, sometimes the children joined them. Some of the steps were so intricate, she wondered how anyone mastered them; some were slow and simple.

The men were dancing now. Susannah watched Black Wind, mesmerized by the way the firelight played over his tall, bronze body. He wore a clout, moccasins beaded in red and black, and a fringed vest. His hair flowed down his back like a river of black silk, save for one braid that fell over his left shoulder. The eagle feather was tied to the end of the braid. He moved with infinite grace, his whole body dipping and swaying to the beat of the drum. He was beautiful, so beautiful, and when his gaze met hers, she felt the touch of it clear down to her soul. Those eyes, dark liquid black eyes that held secrets only she would ever know, promises that only the two of them could keep.

He was dancing for her, only her. It was the sexiest, most romantic thing any man had ever done. Desire flared to life in the deepest part of her as she watched him. The firelight played over Tate Sapa's copper-hued skin, loving him, caressing him, reminding Susannah of a Greek statue come to life.

When the dance was over, she was waiting for him, ready for him.

Taking her by the hand, he led her away from the dance circle. She stopped him once, needing to feel his arms around her, his lips on hers. He hugged her close, his lips fusing to hers, kissing her as if he would never stop.

Gasping her name, he swung her into his arms and carried her deeper into the shadows of the night until they came to a secluded glen near the river.

He was a warrior that night, a man who knew what he wanted and would not be denied. But she had no thought to deny him. She gave him her heart and soul that night, the promise of forever . . .

It seemed unfair that, just as she was beginning to feel as though she had found her place in the village, it was time to leave.

"How long will it take us to reach Rock Tree Creek?" Susannah asked.

"Seven days, maybe eight."

She glanced over her shoulder. Three warriors rode behind them. She wasn't sure how she felt about spending a week out on the plains with four men. Black Wind had decided not to bother with a lodge, so they would be sleeping outside. Privacy would be minimal.

What can't be changed must be endured. She couldn't remember where she'd heard that, but it seemed fitting. She grinned as she recalled a line of dialogue from *Steel Magnolias*, something about that which doesn't kill us can only make us stronger.

Attitude, Susannah mused. It was all attitude. If she looked on this trip as a trial, then it would be. On the other hand, if she decided it was going to fun—well, then, it would just be an adventure.

They rode at a leisurely pace. Susannah was struck anew by the beauty of the countryside. It was lush and green, the sky a sharp clear blue. Miles of rolling grassland stretched ahead of them, tall enough to brush the bellies of the horses. It was sad to think that, in only a few years, everything would be changed. The Indians would be rounded up and confined on reservations, their way of life forever gone. They would be forbidden to live as they had always lived. Their religion would be outlawed, their children sent away to boarding schools, forbidden to speak their native language.

Such inhumanity was beyond her comprehension. Surely it could have been handled differently, she thought. Had it really been necessary to take children away from their parents, to forbid them to speak the only language they knew? Why did her people think their way was the only way?

She shook off her morbid thoughts. She was only one person; there was nothing she could do to change things. This piece of history had already been written long before she was born. And yet she was here, in the middle of Indian country . . . It was mind-boggling.

They rode for several hours, then paused to eat and rest the horses.

Susannah watched Black Wind. He moved with an air of confidence that she had never noticed in the men of her acquaintance. He belonged here, in this place. He knew who he was, what he was, where he fit in the scheme of things. She had learned that the Lakota believed that everything was alive. Rocks, trees, each blade of grass, the mountains themselves, all were alive. When an Indian killed an animal, he thanked the animal for giving up its life so that the hunter might live, and then he left a part of the meat behind to appease the *wanagi*, the spirits.

She watched Black Wind lead their horses to a small stream to drink. She never tired of watching him. He moved with such assurance, such innate grace. She knew he was aware of everything around him—the horses, the direction of the wind, the small animals that scurried through the grass.

Chewing on a hunk of jerky, Susannah studied the other warriors. Two of them were squatting on their heels, sharing a waterskin; the third was standing a little apart, obviously keeping watch.

Susannah looked out over the grassland, thinking it would be virtually impossible for anyone to sneak up on them. There were no rocks or trees to shield an enemy, yet one man stood guard.

A short time later, they were riding again. Leaning forward, Susannah patted Broomhilda's neck. In retrospect, she had decided it was a silly name for a horse, so she had taken to calling the mare Hildy, which probably wasn't much better. Hildy had a nice, rocking-chair walk, a rather bumpy trot, and a smooth, easy lope.

There was something remarkably pleasant about riding across the plains. She had heard some of her girlfriends talking about how wonderful horseback riding was. Until now, she had never understood their enthusiasm, but she had to admit there was something relaxing about it. Maybe it was the sense of being in control of such a large animal, although she wasn't sure she really *was* in control. Maybe it was the sense of well-being that came from exercising out in the open. Whatever it was, she was beginning to feel a sort of bond with Hildy.

She slid a glance at Black Wind. Susannah felt a bond of another kind with him, a deep, everlasting bond, as if they had been promised to each other before time began, mated before the foundation of the world.

"Are you all right?" Tate Sapa asked. "Do you need to stop?"

"No, I'm fine." She smiled as happiness bubbled up inside her. "I'm wonderful!"

Tate Sapa grinned, baffled by her sudden exuberance.

"It's so beautiful here," Susannah exclaimed. "And I'm so happy."

"You do not wish to go back to your own time, then?"

"No. I want to stay here with you, forever and ever." Needing to touch him, she reined her horse closer to his and placed her hand on his thigh. "I'm pregnant, Tate, I just know it."

He stared at her, speechless. Pregnant!

"You are sure?"

Susannah nodded. It had been seven weeks since the night they had made love in the glen. She had known that night that their union would produce a child, and now she was certain.

She withdrew her hand from his thigh, stung by his silence, by his apparent disapproval. "Don't you want a baby?"

"Of course, but . . ." He shook his head. A child. It was too soon, and his life was too unsettled. If an agreement could not be reached with the

Army, the Lakota would soon be at war.

He felt Susannah watching him, waiting for him to say something. He glanced over his shoulder, then met her eyes. "We will talk of it later, when we are alone."

"Fine." Blinking back her tears, Susannah urged Hildy into a lope. She was glad when Black Wind let her go. She needed to be alone.

He didn't want the baby. She let her tears fall, felt them dry on her face as the warm wind brushed her cheeks. She drew Hildy to a walk. Maybe she shouldn't have told him so soon. Maybe she should have waited until they were alone. It wouldn't have changed anything, she told herself angrily. If he didn't want it, then he didn't want it, and there was nothing she could do about it. She was pregnant and that was that. . . .

Oh, Lord, pregnant! The Indian women didn't have doctors and hospitals. They had midwives and tepees. And she'd always been such a coward, determined to be out cold if she ever had a baby. Natural childbirth in a hospital was one thing she had never wanted to experience; natural childbirth in an Indian village was unthinkable, frightening beyond words. What if there was a problem? So many things could go wrong during childbirth—the baby could come early, the baby could die, *she* could die . . .

"Su-san-nah."

She turned toward the sound of his voice. She'd been so lost in a nightmare of her own making, she hadn't even been aware of Black Wind beside her.

"What is wrong?"

"I'm afraid! I don't want to have a baby, not out here."

One look at Susannah's face, and Tate Sapa decided they would camp where they were for the night. There were a few trees for shelter, and a small stream would provide water. He sent the other men off to see if they could find fresh meat, then lifted Susannah from the back of her horse and sheltered her in his arms.

"What is it, *wastelakapi*?" he asked quietly.

"I'm not ready to be a mother!" She clutched at his shirt, her fingers curling around the material. "I don't know anything about babies. You don't want it, and I don't want to have it out here, in the wilderness."

"Su-san-nah . . ."

"No, no, I'm afraid. I've always been afraid."

"Su-san-nah, it will be all right. Our women have strong, healthy babies. They will help you when the time comes."

"You don't want it. I thought you'd be glad."

"I am glad." Lightly, he stroked her hair. "I hope to give you many children. Many sons."

She looked up at him, her gaze searching his. He meant it. She could see it in his eyes, hear it in his voice. "Sons?" she repeated with a teasing smile.

"Sons."

Susannah folded her arms over her stomach in an age-old protective gesture. "It could be a girl."

"She will be welcome."

"You're not mad then?"

"No, Su-san-nah, how could I be angry?" His

eyes smiled at her. "You did not make this child by yourself." He dragged the tip of his finger down her cheek. "It is not the child that concerns me."

"It's the timing, isn't it? You'd rather it hadn't happened now."

Tate Sapa nodded. "I would have hoped our child would be born in a time of peace." A deep sigh escaped his lips. "But I fear those times are gone from us."

Susannah rested her head on his chest and closed her eyes. She didn't know a great deal about history, but she was afraid Black Wind was right. He held her close, as if he could shield her and their child from the trouble that was sure to come.

That first day set the pattern for the rest. They rose early, rode until noon, stopped to eat and rest the horses, rode another few hours, stopped to rest the horses, then rode until dusk. They always found a campsite located near a waterhole or a stream but never camped too close to the water.

"We do not want to scare away the animals that come to drink," Tate Sapa explained when Susannah asked why they didn't camp closer to the river. "Our enemies, too, may stop here for water. It is safer not to be too close."

"Enemies?"

"The Crow."

Susannah glanced around, as if expecting to see a hundred warriors descending on them. "Here?"

"They often sneak onto our land to steal our horses."

At her stricken look, Tate Sapa grinned. "They are our ancient enemies, Su-san-nah. They steal from us, and we steal from them. It is considered a great coup, to steal an enemy's warhorse."

"Really?" she asked weakly. She thought of the horse Tate Sapa kept tethered near their lodge. "Sounds dangerous."

"It can be."

"Have you ever stolen from the Crow?"

Tate Sapa nodded. "When I was a young warrior, my friend and I went into the land of the Crow. We captured two war ponies, then drove off the Crow horse herd. The Old Ones made a song for us, and our parents held a giveaway to honor our bravery."

"You don't do things like that anymore, do you?"

"Not too often."

In the evenings, the men told stories, which Black Wind explained to her. Sometimes they spoke of battles, sometimes they told funny stories, and sometimes they told what Susannah thought of as Lakota Bible stories. One of her favorites was the Lakota version of the creation. Genesis began "In the beginning . . ." and so did Black Wind's story.

"In the beginning," he said, "there was *Inyan*, who dwelt with *Hanhepi*, the Darkness. *Inyan* was soft but without form, but he was all powerful and he was everywhere. His powers were in his blood, and his blood was blue. His spirit was *Wakan Tanka*.

"*Inyan* wanted to use his powers to rule others, but there were no others, and so he took a part of himself and created *Maka*, the Earth. But he used so much of himself that his veins opened and his blood flowed, and his blood became the waters of the earth. The powers could not live in the water, so they became the great blue dome of the sky and became *Skan*.

"After a time, *Maka* grew angry because she was not a separate being, but a part of *Inyan*. She said she could not control the waters, and she could not see herself because it was always dark. She demanded that *Inyan* banish *Hanhepi*, but *Inyan* replied that he had used all his blood in creating her and now he was powerless.

"*Maka* took her complaint to *Skan*, who divided *Hanhepi* in two—one half remained in darkness and was banished to the regions under the earth. The other half became *Anpetu*, the Light, and *Maka* commanded that she make all things visible. And now there was light everywhere, but no shadow and no heat.

"*Maka* saw herself and cried that she was cold and ugly. Then she saw the blue waters and divided them into lakes and seas and rivers and used them to adorn herself.

"But she was still unhappy, and she complained to *Skan* that she was tired of the brightness, and she was cold. So *Skan* created *Wi*, the Sun, and he placed *Wi* above the blue dome and commanded him to shine and give heat.

"But there was still unrest. *Maka* complained that the world was too hot, and asked *Skan* to bring *Hanhepi* back to the world to give relief from the sun. And *Wi* complained that he had no rest. So *Skan* decreed that there should be nighttime and daytime, and *Wi* should rule over the day, and *Hanwi*, the Moon, would rule over the night.

"And so there were four Sacred Beings—*Skan*, *Inyan*, *Maka*, and *Wi*, and these four became *Wakan Tanka*, which no one can understand. *Skan* became the source of all power, and his domain was everywhere; *Wi* became the chief of the Sacred Beings; from *Maka* would come all creatures of the world; *Inyan* ruled over the rocks and mountains. Colors were assigned to each of the powers: *Inyan*'s color was yellow, *Maka*'s was green, *Wi*'s was red, and *Skan*'s was the blue of the sky."

Feeling as content as a child after a bedtime story, Susannah curled up in Tate Sapa's arms and went to sleep.

Chapter Nineteen

Seven days later, they reached the appointed place. Tate Sapa and his men had dressed with care for the occasion, donning their best clouts, moccasins, leggings, and shirts.

Susannah wore an ankle-length doeskin dress that was as soft as velvet. There was a bright red sash at her waist.

Her gaze moved lovingly over Black Wind. He looked every inch the proud warrior in fringed leggings, a wolf-skin clout, and a shirt that had been bleached white. Long fringe dangled from the sleeves; the yoke had been beaded in yellow and black.

Her gaze lingered on the black-and-white eagle feather tied in his hair. It reminded her of the photograph she had bought at the powwow, which reminded her of home. She wished she had some way of contacting her parents and letting them know she was all right.

If time passed in the future at the same rate it did in the past, then she was in deep trouble with her editor. Her landlord had most likely boxed up her clothing, put her furniture in storage (or sold it!), and rented her apartment to someone else, and everyone she knew must think she had met with foul play or dropped off the end of the earth. . . .

All Susannah's worries about home fled her mind, replaced by a sense of foreboding, when she saw the two large tents set up in the grassy hollow between two gently sloping hills. Flags fluttered in the breeze that blew over the prairie. Horses were tethered to ropes strung between trees; numerous blue-clad men could be seen engaged in various activities.

She heard Black Wind mutter something under his breath. Following his gaze, she saw several Indians dressed in the garb of Indian police.

"I don't think we should go down there," Susannah said. She placed her hand on Black Wind's arm. "Let's go back."

Tate Sapa shook his head. "I must try for peace one last time, Su-san-nah."

"How far is the fort from here?"

"Not far." He pointed eastward. "No more than a hard day's ride."

"Then the Micklins are close by?"

"That way," Tate Sapa said, pointing over his shoulder.

Somehow, knowing that Hester and Abe were nearby made Susannah feel better.

"Ready?" Black Wind asked.

She wasn't, but there was nothing to be gained in delaying any longer.

Tate Sapa gave her a smile of encouragement, then led the way down the hill.

"Riders comin'!"

The shout went up from one of the troopers as they approached the encampment. There was the sound of a bugle. Soldiers grabbed their weapons and formed a line, standing at attention.

Susannah stared at the tall, gray-haired man who emerged from the larger of the two tents. It was none other than Colonel William Henry O'Neill, who had once accused her of being a spy.

"Just like old home week," Susannah muttered as she reined her horse to a halt. Silently, she prayed that the colonel would not recognize her since she was dressed like a Lakota woman. Her hair had grown a little longer in the last few months, and the sun had turned her skin a dark golden brown.

Colonel O'Neill stepped forward, followed by his interpreter.

"Tell them I bid my Sioux brothers welcome," O'Neill said, his voice stiff and formal.

Tate Sapa nodded curtly. "I understand your language."

"Oh, well, that's good," the colonel replied. He dismissed the interpreter with a wave of his hand.

Dismounting, Tate Sapa lifted Susannah from the back of her horse.

"Where are your chiefs?" O'Neill asked. "Why

didn't they come with you?"

"They sent me in their place. I will carry your words back to them."

"I see."

It was obvious to Susannah that O'Neill was upset by the news, but he covered it well. "You're just in time for dinner," he said. "Maxwell, Wilkinson, see to their horses." Two troopers stepped forward and led the horses away.

Susannah kept her head down as she followed Black Wind into a large tent. The other warriors followed. Three soldiers brought up the rear.

A table large enough to seat six people occupied the center of the tent. "Please, sit down." The colonel gestured to one of the chairs.

Tate Sapa glanced around the tent, then sat down in the chair that faced the entrance. He placed his rifle on the ground, within easy reach. Susannah stood to his left, the warriors to his right.

O'Neill looked at Susannah. "Please, have a seat."

She did so reluctantly, afraid to refuse for fear of drawing undue attention to herself. Thus far, she didn't think the colonel had really paid her any mind.

"Do your braves also speak English?" O'Neill asked.

"No."

"Tell them to join us."

"They prefer to stand."

O'Neill looked momentarily taken aback, then he shrugged and took a seat across from Tate Sapa. Minutes later, the colonel's striker entered the tent bearing a large tray. The scent of venison filled the air when the striker removed the tray's cover, revealing a half-dozen thick steaks and all the trimmings.

Susannah couldn't help being impressed with how well the colonel ate, even out in the middle of nowhere.

The colonel's striker served the food, then left the tent. It was a silent meal. Susannah could feel the tension coming from Black Wind and the warriors in waves.

The warriors ate standing up. Ignoring the silverware, they ate with their knives. They glanced repeatedly at the tent flap, making her wonder if they expected to be attacked. And then she remembered that such things had happened frequently in the past. Indians had often been invited to meet with the Army. Some had been poisoned. Some had been shot. Perhaps they were right to be cautious.

Susannah slid a glance at Black Wind, wondering if he had ever eaten a meal at a table before. And then she realized that he was watching her from the corner of his eye, observing how she used her knife and fork.

Colonel O'Neill did not offer his men anything to eat. They stood at attention to one side of the tent door, their gazes fixed on the tent wall.

When the meal was over and the dishes cleared away, O'Neill filled a pipe and offered it to Tate Sapa, who took a puff and passed it to one of his men. When all the men had smoked, the colonel put the pipe away.

"Now, then," he said brusquely, "let's get down

to business. You understand, business?"

"I understand," Tate Sapa replied, his voice equally curt.

"Good. I came here today to establish peace with your people."

"The Lakota are at peace," Tate Sapa replied evenly.

O'Neill nodded. "Yes, of course, but we want your assurances that our people will not be attacked for crossing your land. More and more settlers are arriving every day. Your people must stop attacking the wagon trains. The settlers must be allowed safe passage to the West."

"My people have attacked no settlers."

O'Neill looked skeptical. "Two wagon trains were attacked in the last month. The people were massacred, their stock stolen, the wagons burned."

"I cannot speak for the other tribes. Nor can I blame them for defending their hunting grounds."

A dark red flush stained the colonel's cheeks. "Be that as it may, I want your word that your people will not attack the settlers."

"And do I have your word in return that they will not hunt in our territory, or attack our village?"

"Well, you can't expect them not to hunt," O'Neill replied. "They've got to eat."

"The buffalo herds are growing smaller. The *wasichu* kill more than they need, and leave what they do not want to rot in the sun. They cross the plains with their noisy wagons and chase away the game. They muddy the water and dig in the earth for yellow iron. These things must stop."

"See here, you can't lay claim to the plains in their entirety."

"This is our land. We will allow you to cross it if you do not take from it what is not yours."

Anger flickered in the colonel's gray eyes. He stared hard at Tate Sapa. "I thought you came here to speak for peace."

Tate Sapa nodded. "It is my wish that my people be allowed to live as they have always lived. We want nothing you have. All we ask is that you do not take what is ours."

O'Neill blew out a deep breath, then stood up. "I think we should discuss this again tomorrow, after we've all had a good night's sleep."

Tate Sapa stood up. "There is nothing more to discuss."

"I think there is, when heads are cooler." O'Neill smiled, but Susannah thought it looked rather forced. "Please, stay here and rest. Is there anything you need?"

Tate Sapa shook his head.

"Very well." With a curt nod, O'Neill stalked out of the tent, followed by his men.

"You were right, Su-san-nah," Tate Sapa said. "We should not have come here."

"What are you going to do now?"

"We are leaving this place. I will tell our chiefs to be prepared to fight. It is what the *wasichu* want. They do not want peace. They want our land, and they will not rest until they have it."

"There must be another way," Susannah said, but she knew what he said was true. The government and the settlers would drive the Indians from their lands, then pen them in on reservations. Crooked Indian agents would steal their food allotments and swindle them out of reservation land, as well. She wished she knew how to change history, wished there was something she could do to make the future better for the Lakota.

She listened while Black Wind spoke to his warriors. They nodded, their faces dark with anger, as he told them what the colonel had said.

"Come," Black Wind said, taking up his rifle. "We go."

Darkness had fallen. Small campfires glowed like fireflies. Susannah stayed close to Black Wind as they started toward the horses, which had been tethered near the Army mounts.

"Hey, there, where do you think you're going?"

Tate Sapa turned around. "We are leaving."

"I don't think so," the soldier said, lifting his rifle. "Colonel wants to talk some more."

"We are through talking."

"Drop your weapons. Hackett, go get the colonel."

Susannah was standing close to Black Wind. She could feel the tension radiating from him as he glanced around the camp. Several soldiers had risen to their feet. All were armed, their expressions hostile. She had the feeling they were just itching for a reason to shoot.

A moment later, Colonel O'Neill was striding toward them. "One of my men tells me you want to leave. Is this true?"

Tate Sapa nodded. "There is nothing more to discuss."

"I'm afraid I must insist you stay."

"And if I refuse?"

The colonel smiled. It was a cold smile, one that did not reach his eyes. "I don't think you want to do that, now do you?"

Tate Sapa's hands tightened on his rifle as a dozen soldiers gathered around them, circling like wolves around a kill.

"Why don't we all go back into the tent and see if we can't reach an understanding."

"You have made your feelings quite clear," Tate Sapa replied. "As always, the white man wants everything his way, and will do whatever is necessary to obtain it."

"Now, now, we're willing to give your people food and blankets in return for their guarantee not to harass the settlers."

"I know of other tribes who have made treaties with the whites. Their people went cold, their young ones starved to death, while waiting for blankets and food that never came."

O'Neill stiffened. "Occasionally that happens."

"Occasionally? Every tribe that deals with the white man loses his freedom and ends up on the reservation. I will not let that happen to my people."

"Have I said anything about the reservation?"

"Not yet."

Susannah kept her head lowered, watching the confrontation from the corner of her eye. She felt a wave of apprehension as O'Neill stared at her. Recognition came slowly. "Ah, Miss Kingston, I believe."

With a sigh of resignation, Susannah looked up.

"I thought it was you." O'Neill remarked, looking pleased. "I knew you were a traitor. Take her to my tent."

"No. She is my woman and under my protection."

"She is a traitor, and will be dealt with as such."

Susannah cried out as one of the soldiers reached for her.

Tate Sapa reacted instinctively. Lifting his rifle, he sighted down the barrel and fired at the man who was trying to drag Susannah away.

With a cry, the man dropped Susannah's arm and crumpled to the ground, his hands clutching his shoulder. Immediately, every soldier in the vicinity was in the fray. Two men grabbed Susannah and hauled her toward the colonel's tent. Shoving her inside, they warned her to stay put, then shut the door flap.

The sound of gunshots made Susannah cringe with fear. She heard shouting, the high-pitched yelp of a man in pain, hoofbeats, and then everything grew still.

She was pacing the tent, her concern for Black Wind's safety growing by the second, when O'Neill entered the tent.

"Where is he?" she asked. "Where's Black Wind?"

"He escaped."

"And the others?"

"Two are dead. We have one in custody. The one you call Black Wind got away, but we'll get him."

Susannah closed her eyes as relief washed over

her. Thank God, Black Wind was safe. "What happens now?"

"We'll be leaving for the fort in the morning." O'Neill stared at her, his eyes filled with disdain. "You may consider yourself under arrest for treason."

"Treason!"

"Consorting with the enemy. Spying." O'Neill nodded, his expression smug. "We are at war, Miss Kingston. I shouldn't like to be in your shoes."

"I'm not a spy!"

"I think you are. Captain McCarin told me you stayed with the Indians when you had a chance to return to your own people. I warn you, don't try to escape. Spies are shot."

Shot! Susannah blinked at him, her arms folding protectively over her abdomen. Shot . . . Before she could collect her thoughts enough to speak, the colonel was gone.

She sat down in one of the chairs, afraid her legs would no longer support her. They thought she was a spy. It was incredible, would have been laughable, if she weren't so frightened, not only for herself, but for the future of her unborn child.

Surely Black Wind wouldn't let them take her back to the fort and yet, what could he do? He was outnumbered fifty to one.

Thoroughly discouraged, she folded her arms on the table, put her head down, and cried.

The Army broke camp first thing the following morning. There was no doubt in Susannah's mind that she was a prisoner, as much as the wounded warrior who rode beside her, even though her hands weren't tied behind her back, as his were. Tonkalla had been shot in the shoulder. A bloody bandage was wrapped over the wound. A soldier led his mount.

The men who had gone after Black Wind the day before had returned empty-handed. Black Wind, at least, had gotten away unscathed.

Susannah slid a glance at the soldiers riding beside her. They were looking straight ahead, but she was aware of their scorn, their derision. They thought she was an Indian lover, a spy. She had no doubt that they would shoot her down without a qualm if she tried to escape.

As the day wore on, she found herself searching the countryside, looking for Black Wind. She couldn't believe that he would go off and leave her, yet there was no place for him to hide, no way he could follow her without being seen.

As the miles went by, she became more and more convinced that he had gone back to the village.

It was near dusk when the Army made camp for the night. They would reach the fort tomorrow. And then what? Susannah wondered, as she watched the men set up the colonel's tent. Would she get a trial, or would they just lock her up in the guardhouse and throw away the key?

She thought of the small iron-barred cell where Black Wind had been held prisoner and tried to imagine herself living there for the rest of her life.

It was full dark by the time the soldiers had set up camp. One of the men handed her a tin plate of bacon and beans and a cup of coffee.

Susannah stared at the greasy mess and thought she might throw up. The coffee was hot and black and bitter.

She put the plate and the cup aside and wished, futilely and fleetingly, for a cup of hot chocolate topped off with whipped cream.

One of the soldiers, an older man with a slight paunch and graying hair, escorted her into the shadows so she could relieve herself. Susannah thought she would die of embarrassment as she squatted in the bushes, knowing an armed man stood only a few feet away.

When they returned to the campfire, she wrapped herself in the blanket that had been given to her, lay down, and closed her eyes.

She didn't think she'd be able to sleep. She could hear the men talking softly, the crackle of the flames, snores coming from those who had turned in for the night, horses stamping their feet, the howl of a coyote. Whoever had written praises to the quiet of the prairie night had obviously never slept under the stars with fifty snoring men, fifty restless horses, and a lonely coyote!

She was drifting in that netherworld between wakefulness and sleep when a hand dropped over her mouth. She came awake instantly, her heart in her throat.

"Su-san-nah, it's me."

She turned her head and saw Black Wind lying belly down on the ground beside her. His face and chest were smeared with dirt so that he seemed to be a part of the earth itself.

"Follow me," he said.

Susannah glanced over her shoulder. All the men were sleeping. The two men standing guard were visible at the far end of the camp, sharing a cigarette. She could see the tip glow as one of the men inhaled.

Moving as silently as she could, she crawled after Black Wind, certain that, at any moment, one of the sentries would shout for her to stop.

She followed Black Wind for what seemed like miles, scraping her elbows and knees on the ground, certain every living creature within a hundred miles could hear her moving through the thick yellow grass, could hear the beat of her heart, echoing like thunder in her ears.

Just when she thought they were going to crawl through the night forever, Black Wind slipped over the edge of a depression in the ground. When he reached the bottom, he stood up. Turning, he helped Susannah to her feet, then lifted her onto the back of his horse, which was tethered to a clump of sagebrush.

Untying the reins, he handed them to Susannah, then vaulted up behind her.

"Are you all right?" he asked.

"Yes, fine. Hurry, let's get out of here."

"I do not like to leave Tonkalla behind," Tate Sapa said quietly.

"Maybe you should go back and get him."

Slowly, Tate Sapa shook his head. The soldiers had let Susannah bed down apart from the others so she could have a little privacy, but they had shackled Tonkalla to the supply wagon. There was no way to get to his old friend without being seen, no way to remove the iron cuffs.

And then there was no time for thought.

Susannah glanced over her shoulder as the sound of hoofbeats filled the silence of the night.

She heard Black Wind mutter something in Lakota, and then they were riding through the darkness.

Susannah couldn't help thinking that, if he'd been alone, Black Wind would have been able to outrun his pursuers easily. As it was, with his horse carrying double, she knew it was only a matter of time before the soldiers overtook them.

Black Wind urged his horse faster, increasing their lead. When they reached a rocky outcropping surrounded by a tangled mass of brush, he reined the horse to a halt. Dismounting, he pulled Susannah from the back of the horse. Lifting his gun, he smacked the horse across the rump with the rifle butt; then, grabbing Susannah by the hand, he headed for the cover of the rocks.

She was breathless by the time they took shelter behind a large boulder. Frightened, hardly able to draw breath, Susannah crouched beside Black Wind, waiting to hear the shout that would mean their hiding place had been discovered.

She could feel the tension radiating from Black Wind as he peered over the top of the boulder, and then, miraculously, she felt him relax. Moments later, he sat down beside her, the rifle within easy reach.

"Are they gone?" she asked anxiously.

"For now. Are you all right?"

"I'm fine. What are we going to do?"

"I am going to take you to the Micklins."

Susannah knew a moment of relief at the thought of seeing Hester and Abe again. And then she frowned. "Where are you going?"

"I must go back and warn my people."

"I'm going with you."

"No, Su-san-nah."

"Why not?" She turned to face him, but, in the darkness, all she could see was his profile, sharp and clean.

"This is what the young men have been waiting for. They have been eager for war. Nothing will stop them now. I want you to stay with Hester, where you and our child will be safe."

"I'm not leaving you."

"Do not argue with me, Su-san-nah. You do not know what it will be like when the fighting starts. Our people cannot hope to win. The *was-ichu* have more warriors than the Lakota, more weapons, more of everything. I have seen war before, Su-san-nah. I will not put you at risk."

"No, Black Wind. Either we both go back to the village, or we both go to the Micklins. I won't let you send me away. We have to stay together."

He lifted a hand to the eagle feather in his hair, felt a faint warmth on his fingertips as he untied the thong that held it in place. "Take this, Su-san-nah. Perhaps it will see you safely home."

She shook her head, refusing to take the feather. "No. My place is here, with you."

His gaze rested on her face, and then he nodded. "Perhaps you are right."

"I know I am."

Tate Sapa tied the feather into his hair again, then stood up, peering into the darkness, his head cocked to one side as he listened to the sounds of the night. All was quiet.

"Come," he said, taking Susannah by the hand and lifting her to her feet.

They walked all that night and then, just as dawn was brightening the horizon, they took refuge in a small thicket not far from a shallow stream.

"How much farther is it to the Micklins'?" Susannah asked.

"Many hours. We will rest here today, and continue our journey tonight, when it is cool and there is less chance of discovery."

He ran his hand over the ground, brushing away bits of leaves and debris. Sitting down, he drew Susannah into his lap and kissed her cheek. "Are you well, *wastelakapi*?"

Susannah nodded. "Just tired."

"Sleep, Su-san-nah."

"What about you?"

"I will keep watch."

"You need to rest."

"I will." He drew her head down to his shoulder, then began to massage her back. "Sleep, Su-san-nah."

Cradled in his arms, she closed her eyes, the gentle touch of his hands stroking her back lulling her to sleep.

It was dark when Susannah woke. She felt a rush of panic when she realized she was alone in the thicket. Scrambling to her feet, she looked around.

"Black Wind? Black Wind, where are you?"

"Here, Su-san-nah."

She whirled around to see him enter the thicket, his rifle in one hand, his shirt in the other. He propped his rifle against a tree, then sat down and spread his shirt, revealing a half dozen prairie turnips, wild onions, and something that looked like lettuce.

"Looks healthy," Susannah remarked as she sat down across from Black Wind.

He shrugged. "I would prefer meat, but I dare not use the rifle." Drawing his knife, he quickly peeled a turnip and handed it to Susannah.

She had never been overly fond of raw vegetables, but she was too hungry to be picky. After they'd eaten, they walked to the stream. Susannah drank her fill, then sluiced water over her face and arms, glad that it was summer and not winter.

"Ready?" Black Wind asked as stood up.

"Yes." She smiled at him as he reached for her hand.

Tate Sapa returned her smile, proud of her courage, of the fact that she never complained, humbled by her trust in him, in his ability to protect her, to get them to safety.

"Nice night for a walk," Susannah remarked as they set out across the plains. "Reminds me of *An American Werewolf in London*.

"What is Lon-don?"

"It's a big city."

"They have wolves there?"

"Not really. *An American Werewolf in London* is the name of a movie." Susannah frowned, wondering how to explain moving pictures.

273

"Movies are pictures that . . ." She shrugged. "That move."

"Pictures that move? How is this possible?"

"Well, I'm afraid I don't know exactly how they work, but I bet you'd love them. I do. Back home, I used to go to a show at least once a week. More, if I could."

He frowned, confused by her words. "What do these pictures that move show?"

"Different things. Some movies are comedies, stories that make you laugh."

"Like *Iktomi*?"

"Well, sort of. Other movies are mysteries— you know, someone commits a crime and you try to figure out who did it. And then there's science fiction, stories about things that haven't happened yet, like *Star Wars*."

"Star wars?" Tate Sapa glanced up. "The white man has wars, even up there?"

"Well, in science fiction they do. There are lots of movies about what life on other planets might be like."

Tate Sapa frowned. "You believe there is life on the stars?"

"I don't know, but some people do. There are Western movies, too, with cowboys and Indians."

Tate Sapa grunted softly, frowning as he tried to imagine pictures that moved and told a story at the same time. "I think I should like to see these pictures that move."

"I wish you could."

"Tell me of your time, Su-san-nah."

"Geez, I don't know where to start. Hardly anything in my time is the way it is here. We don't ride horses anymore. There are hardly any empty spaces left. Everyone is always in a hurry. We have machines that do practically everything . . . I don't know how to explain what a machine is, except to say they do most of the work nowadays. Women don't have to wash their clothes in the river, or cook over an open fire, the way the Indian women do. You just put your clothes in the machine, add some soap, and the machine washes your clothes for you. Same with cooking. You put the ingredients in a dish, put the dish in the microwave . . ."

"If people do not ride horses, how do they get from one place to another?"

"More machines. Some are called cars. And we have trains. . . . Have you seen a train?"

Black Wind nodded.

"Well, trains in my time are a lot faster than the ones you've seen. And we have airplanes." Susannah pointed upward. "Airplanes travel across the sky, and can take you hundreds of miles in a short time."

"Machines that travel through the air?" Tate Sapa shook his head. "That is not possible."

"But it is. Let's see, what else is different? Oh, we have telephones that let you speak to someone clear across the country, and computers . . ." Her voice trailed off. There was no way to explain computers. "In my time, women work."

"Our women work," Tate Sapa remarked.

"I don't mean that kind of work. In my time, women don't just stay home and look after their children. They hold down jobs. In my time, women are doctors and lawyers and police officers."

"Who cares for their children?"

"We have places called day care centers that look after their kids."

"I do not understand. Why do your women have children if they do not want to care for them?"

"Well . . ." Susannah began, and then stopped. It was a question she had often asked herself. Of course, there were women who worked because they had no other choice, but she knew a lot of women who didn't have to work to put food on the table or clothes on their backs. They worked because they felt they were missing something by staying at home, as if being a "housewife" was something to be ashamed of. Personally, Susannah couldn't think of anything she'd rather do. What could be more rewarding that staying home and watching your children grow up? How awful, if some baby-sitter saw her child take its first step, some stranger heard her child's first word. Of course, she realized that, these days, when everyone was urging women to go out and "find themselves," her views were definitely out of date. She had always been grateful that her mother didn't work outside the home, that her mother was there, waiting, when she got home from school.

"It isn't that they don't want children," Susannah said at length. "It's just that some women like working outside the home. It doesn't mean they don't love their children."

"It seems a strange kind of love to me," Tate Sapa mused.

Feather in the Wind

For a time, they walked in silence. It was eerie, to be walking across the plains in the dead of night while the earth was asleep. Fluffy white clouds drifted across the sky, playing hide and seek with the moon and the stars. Moonlight silvered the grass.

"Do you need to rest?" Tate Sapa asked after a while.

"I think so."

"We will be there in a few hours," Tate Sapa remarked. He found a smooth place and indicated Susannah should sit down, then he sat down beside her. Laying his rifle aside, he drew her into his arms. "Rest, Su-san-nah."

She closed her eyes, grateful for the strong arms around her. Even out here, in the middle of nowhere, he made her feel safe. His love cocooned her, shutting out the rest of the world. Susannah placed one hand over her belly, smiling as she imagined her child growing there. Would it be a boy, she wondered dreamily, or a girl? She thought of the pictures she had once seen that depicted a fetus in the womb, sucking its thumb, and she was overcome with a sudden surge of love, a need to protect the tiny life growing beneath her heart.

Tate Sapa held her close, his hand lightly massaging her back as he thought of all the strange things she had told him about. Pictures that moved. Machines that flew through the air, cooked food, washed clothes and dishes. It was beyond his comprehension that such things could exist. Yet he had no doubt she was telling him the truth, that she had come to him from the future. How long would she be here, with him, and what would he do if she should go out of his life, if she should return to her own time?

"Su-san-nah?"

She blinked up at him. "Is it time to go?"

"I am afraid so."

She nodded, then yawned, wishing she could sleep just a little longer.

Tate Sapa helped her to her feet, then took up his rifle. "Ready?"

Susannah forced a smile, determined not to complain.

It was, she decided, the longest walk she had ever made in her life. But, finally, the Micklin place came into view, the house looking like a huge beast crouched in the darkness.

A half-dozen dogs started barking the minute they approached the house. A short time later, a light appeared, then Susannah saw Abe peering out the window.

"It's me, Mr. Micklin," Susannah called, shouting to be heard above the incessant barking of the dogs. "Susannah Kingston."

A short time later, the door swung open and Abe stepped out on the porch, holding a rifle in one hand and a lantern in the other.

"What the hell are you doing prowling around my place in the middle of the night?" he said, his voice as much a growl as that of his hounds.

Susannah spread her hands in a gesture of appeal. "We need a place to spend the night."

"Agin?" Abe squinted into the darkness. "That Injun with you?"

"Yes."

"Landsakes, Abe, it's Susannah." Hester bustled out onto the porch, pulling a robe on over a voluminous white nightgown. "Come on in, you two."

Five minutes later, they were all seated at the kitchen table while Hester warmed a pot of coffee.

"So, tell me, what brings you back this way?" Hester asked. She took Susannah's hand in hers and patted it. "I've missed you, child."

"I missed you, too," Susannah said, and related, as briefly as possible, all that had happened since they had been gone.

Hester shook her head. "Well, I don't know what to say. A traitor, indeed! I never heard of anything so foolish."

"I didn't see no horses out there," Abe remarked. "How'd you all get here?"

"We walked," Susannah said. She glanced at Black Wind and smiled. He hadn't said anything since they entered the house.

"Walked! Landsakes, child, you must be exhausted."

"I *am* a little tired," Susannah admitted, although a little tired didn't begin to describe how she felt.

"Well, I should think so. Finish your coffee while I get some bedding."

Abe stared out the window. "Gonna be daylight soon," he said sourly. "Long as I'm up, I might as well go tend the stock. I'll leave the lantern in the barn for ya."

"Thank you, Mr. Micklin."

"Might as well call me Abe," he said gruffly.

Rising from the table, he clapped his hat on his head and left the house.

Susannah regarded Black Wind over the rim of her cup. "Are you all right?"

Tate Sapa nodded. "Why do you ask?"

"Well, you haven't said a word. And you seem sort of . . . distant."

"I have much on my mind, *wastelakapi*."

"I know." She leaned across the table and took his hand in hers. "Promise me that you won't leave me."

"Su-san-nah . . ."

"Promise me, Tate. If you leave me here, I'll just follow you."

"Su-san-nah!"

"Well, I will. You just think about that before you go sneaking off in the middle of the night."

"I will remember."

"Say it."

He grinned at her. "I promise not to leave you."

"I have your word, as a warrior?"

"Yes, *wastelakapi*, you have my word, as a warrior and as your husband. I will not leave you."

"Here you go," Hester said. "Sheets and blankets. I'm sorry, I don't have an extra pillow. There's a nightgown there, too. You all get some rest now."

"Thank you, Hester."

"Yes, thank you," Tate Sapa added. "I am sorry I stole from you before."

"Pshaw, don't worry about it," Hester said. "Abe never used that old saddle, and we got lots of blankets. We're just glad to have you both back safe and sound. Go on, now, get some sleep.

280

Come on up to the house when you wake up, and I'll have some vittles waitin'. And hot water for a bath," she muttered, thinking out loud. She glanced at Susannah's stained tunic and shook her head. "I put those dresses you left behind back in the trunk. I'll go dig them out later."

Impulsively, Susannah kissed Hester on the cheek. "Hester, I don't know what I'd do without you."

"Landsakes, child, I got a whole passel of clothes I can't wear no more. You're welcome to all of them. And hot water don't cost nothing."

"Thank you, Hester. You're the best friend I've ever had."

"You're welcome, honey. Now, you go on and get some sleep, the both of you."

Abe had left the lantern in the barn, just as he'd said he would. Susannah quickly made a bed in one of the stalls, wondering, as she did so, if she would ever sleep on a real bed between clean percale sheets again.

She pulled the voluminous nightgown over her head, then crawled beneath the covers of the makeshift bed. She was asleep the minute she closed her eyes.

Tate Sapa stood there a moment, watching her, thinking how lovely she was, how much he loved her and the child she carried.

With a sigh, he stripped off his clothing, stretched out beside Susannah, and drew her into his arms. Later, he would decide what to do about returning to his people. For now, he needed rest, needed to have his woman close beside him.

Chapter Twenty

It was as if they had never been gone, Susannah mused that evening. Once again, she was attired in one of Hester Micklin's calico dresses. The full skirt swished when she moved. It was a pretty dress, a dark green print with a white lace collar yellowed with age. She had kept her moccasins, finding them more comfortable than the foot-wear of the day.

Black Wind had spent the day helping Abe clear some ground behind the house. Abe had been reluctant to accept help, but Black Wind had insisted, saying he wanted to do something in return for Abe's letting them stay. In the end, Abe had given in. Susannah had gone to the window several times during the day, needing to assure herself that Black Wind was still there.

She had spent most of the afternoon helping

Feather in the Wind

Hester put up the last of the summer vegetables. It was a long, hot process, yet it had been fun, too. Hester had a wry sense of humor and a hundred stories to tell. The men had come in at midday, hot and sweaty. Side by side, they had washed up at the sink, then sat down at the table. They made quite a pair, Susannah reflected, the old farmer and the young warrior. Under ordinary circumstances, the two of them would never have met.

She hummed softly as she set the table for dinner. She knew that, sooner or later, they would have to decide about returning to the village, but for tonight, she wanted to pretend everything was all right.

At dusk, the men came in and washed up at the sink, then sat down at the table.

Hester had covered the raw plank table with a bright blue cloth. A glass vase held a bunch of bright yellow daisies.

Hester and Susannah dished up the meal, then took their places. Abe glowered at Black Wind, muttered something about heathens at the dinner table, then bowed his head and said grace.

Black Wind watched as Susannah and Hester bowed their heads and, after a moment's hesitation, did the same.

Abe, as usual, said little during the meal, all his attention apparently focused on eating. Black Wind didn't have much to say either, leaving Hester and Susannah to fill the void.

Hester talked about the letter she had received from her sister back East, about adding a room to the house next year, about the latest book she had received by mail order.

"Well, enough about me. How are you, Susannah? You look a might peaked."

"I'm fine. I'm pregnant." She hadn't meant to say anything, but the words fairly flew out of her mouth as she realized how anxious she was to discuss it with another woman.

"Pregnant! Why, that's wonderful. When's the baby due?"

"I'm not sure."

Hester ran an appraising eye over Susannah. "Well, you don't look to be too far along," she said, then grinned. "Another few months, and you'll fill out that old dress of mine. How are you feeling?"

"Fine. A little nauseous in the mornings sometimes."

"Well, that's normal enough. A baby! Abe, ain't that somethin'?"

"Yeah, somethin'. What's for dessert?"

"Apple pie, love. No, you just sit," Hester insisted when Susannah started to get up to help. "You need to get plenty of rest."

"I feel fine, really."

"I know you do. And I aim to see you stay that way while you're here." Hester smiled at Black Wind. "Congratulations, young man. You take good care of this little gal, hear?"

Tate Sapa nodded, pleased and amused by the older woman's concern for Susannah. He thought it was too bad that all whites weren't like Hester Micklin and her husband. Hester was kind and generous, and, for all his complaining, Abe was a good man, one Tate Sapa felt he could trust.

Feather in the Wind

Hester quickly cut four slices of pie, poured four cups of coffee, then sat down at the table again. "Maybe the two of you should sleep here in the house. Might be more comfortable than the barn."

"We will stay in the barn," Tate Sapa said.

Hester frowned at him, then smiled. "Like your privacy, do you? Well, can't say as I blame you."

Susannah felt her cheeks grow warm at the implication of Hester's words, but she was glad Black Wind wanted to stay in the barn. And for just the reason Hester thought.

Later, after the dishes were done, Black Wind and Susannah took a walk down by the river.

"Susannah, I must go back to my people."

"All right."

"Will you not stay here?"

"Not a chance."

He drew her into his arms and held her close. "Will our child be as stubborn as its mother, do you think?"

"I don't mean to be stubborn, Tate, I'm just so afraid that, if we're separated, we may never find each other again."

Tate Sapa rested his forehead against hers. It was a thought that had given him some concern, too. She had come to him in such a miraculous way, the thought was always there, in the back of his mind, that she might be taken from him, spirited back to her own time, where he would never see her again. He lifted a hand to the eagle feather in his hair and wondered what would have happened if she had taken it when he offered. Had it truly been the means of bringing her to him, or was she a gift from *Wakan Tanka*, sent to fulfil his vision and ease his loneliness?

"When do you want to leave?" Susannah asked.

"Soon."

"How will we get there?"

Tate Sapa blew out a deep breath. He had stolen a saddle and blankets from the Micklins in the past, though it had grieved him to do so, but he could not bring himself to steal their horses. The Micklins had been kind to them; he could not steal from them again, could not take something as valuable as their horses.

"I will ask Micklin if he will let us borrow two of his horses. If not . . ." He shrugged. There were other settlers not far from here.

"If not, what?"

"Perhaps he will let me do some work to pay for the horses."

"What if he won't? Do you intend to walk all the way to the village?"

"No."

Susannah drew back so she could see his face. "What do you intend to do?"

"If necessary, I will steal the horses we need."

"From Abe and Hester? You wouldn't!"

"No," he replied soberly, "but there are other settlers nearby."

"You'd steal their horses?"

"I told you before, it is considered a coup to steal from the enemy."

"But those settlers have done nothing to you."

"They are still the enemy, Su-san-nah," he replied quietly.

Susannah nodded. From Black Wind's point of

view, it wasn't stealing: It was war. Still, she was relieved to know he wouldn't steal from the Micklins.

Hand in hand, they walked back to the barn. It was warm inside, fragrant with the scent of hay and clean straw and sweet feed.

Susannah watched Black Wind strike a match and light the lantern. He placed it on the floor near the stall where their bedding was, then crossed the barn and closed the big double doors, shutting out the night, shutting out the rest of the world.

She watched him turn and walk toward her, his movements innately graceful, sensual. She felt excitement flutter in her stomach as he approached her, felt her heartbeat quicken in anticipation. They stood facing each other a moment and then, wordlessly, she began to undress him.

She loved the feel of his skin beneath her hands, loved to run her fingers over his broad shoulders, over his biceps. She removed his clout, her hands sliding down his thighs and over his calves. He had nice legs for a man, long and straight and well-muscled.

Straightening, she smiled up at him, shivering with delight as he unfastened her dress and slid it off her shoulders. She loved the touch of his hands. His fingers were long and strong, his palm callused, yet ever gentle against her skin.

Tate Sapa cupped Susannah's breasts, imagining them swollen with milk, picturing his child suckling there. Stooping, he ran his tongue over her breast. Sweet, he mused, so sweet. His hands slid down her stomach to rest on her belly. Soon, it would swell with his child. And then he felt Susannah's hands moving over his back, her fingers trailing fire, and he forgot everything but the woman in his arms and the love he felt for her.

Removing the last of her undergarments, he drew her down on the blankets and kissed her hungrily, her smooth brow, the tip of her nose, her cheeks, her lips. His tongue met hers and heat flooded through him. She tasted sweeter than wild honey, more intoxicating than the white man's firewater.

His restless hands caressed her, loving the touch of her skin beneath his hands, the soft, urgent moans that rose in her throat as her body responded to his caresses. He kissed her neck, the pulse throbbing in her throat, the sensitive skin behind her ear, her shoulders. His tongue laved her breasts as he rose above her.

"Su-san-nah, *wastelakapi* . . ."

"Yes, oh yes!" She arched beneath him, welcoming the sweet invasion of his body, her arms folding around him to hold him close, closer, her hips lifting to draw him deeper, deeper, until they were as close as two people could be, bound together body and soul by the love they shared, by the desire that flamed between them, a pure golden fire that warmed them all night long.

Abe Micklin shook his head. "Can't let ya have none of my stock," he said, sounding genuinely sorry. "Only got the three horses, one fer ridin' and the two workhorses. Even if I could spare 'em, one of the workhorses is lame, and ain't neither one broke to ride."

Tate Sapa nodded. "I understand."

"I might be able to buy a couple from Kendall or McCracken," Abe mused, referring to his two nearest neighbors.

"Are you sure you have to leave?" Hester asked as she refilled Abe's coffee cup. "You know you're more than welcome to stay here."

"That's kind of you, Hester," Susannah said. "but we've got to go back and warn the village."

"I hate to see you go. More coffee?"

"Yes, please. And I hate to leave."

Hester filled Susannah's cup, then turned to Tate Sapa. "How about you, young man? More coffee?"

Tate Sapa nodded. "Yes, thank you."

Hester smiled. "You sure have nice manners for a . . . that is, I mean . . ."

"For an Indian?" Tate Sapa suggested mildly. He smiled at her. "My people also say please and thank you."

"Well, of course they do! I didn't mean . . ." A crimson flush stole into Hester Micklin's cheeks. "Please don't take no offense."

"You have not offended me," Tate Sapa assured her, his smile widening. "My people think the *wasichu* are barbarians."

Hester looked offended for a moment, and then she grinned back at him. "Is that right?"

Tate Sapa nodded. "They think the whites are a peculiar people, to live in one place the whole year long. They also think it strange that you build square houses when all of nature is round."

Hester put the coffeepot on the stove, then sat down beside Abe, her arms folded on the table. "Nature is round? Reckon you could explain that to me?"

"The moon is round. The sun is round. The sky is round. The stems of plants and the bodies of animals are round. The four winds circle the earth. Life itself is a circle. We are born, we live, we die, and return to the earth."

"Well, now, ain't that interestin', Abe? Go on," Hester urged, genuinely interested, "tell me more about what the Indians believe."

"What do you wish to know?"

"Do your people believe in God?"

"Yes. We call Him *Wakan Tanka.*"

"That's kind of pretty. Ain't it, Abe?"

"I reckon." Abe stood up and grabbed his hat. "I can't sit here jawin' all afternoon. I still got a day's work to do."

"I will help you," Tate Sapa said. He stood up and offered Hester a smile. "Thank you for the meal."

"You're welcome." Hester beamed at Susannah after the two men left the house. "I like your young man. I really do."

Susannah sighed. "Me, too," she murmured. "Me, too."

Sitting back in her chair, Hester ran a hand through her hair, then smoothed her apron. "A baby," she mused aloud. "It's been years since I held a baby in my arms."

"Do you have any children?" Susannah asked.

Hester nodded, a faraway look in her eyes. "Two boys," she replied, her voice softer than Susannah had ever heard it. "They're buried yonder, up on the rise behind the house."

"Hester, I'm so sorry."

"They died young, my babies. Abraham was only six months old when the Lord took him home. My Joshua only lived a week."

Susannah placed her hand over her stomach, as if she could somehow protect her unborn child. "What happened?"

"Little Abe caught the pneumonia. Joshua was just born sickly. He was such a tiny little thing, hardly bigger than a minute." Hester shook her head. "I tried to have another. My arms felt so empty. But the good Lord didn't see fit to send me another." She stared past Susannah, toward her sons' burial place. "Sometimes I go up and talk to them. It comforts me somehow."

Susannah nodded. She wished she could think of some words of comfort, some bit of universal wisdom that would ease the other woman's heartache. She was a writer, words were her business, but she didn't think there were enough words in all the world to ease the pain in Hester Micklin's placid brown eyes.

Chapter Twenty-one

Susannah sat in the shade of the porch, watching Black Wind split kindling: The heat of the afternoon wrapped around her, making her drowsy; the sound of the axe was oddly soothing; the sight of her husband's long lean body was a feast for the eyes. She admired the smooth play of well-defined muscle beneath copper-hued skin as he swung the ax with steady precision, thinking she would be content to sit there all day, just watching him. A fine sheen of perspiration glistened on his skin, and the sun cast blue-black highlights in his hair.

She marveled at his stamina. He had been chopping wood for the better part of an hour. Earlier, she had gone inside to see if she could help Hester with the chores, but Hester had put a book in Susannah's hands and shooed her outside, telling her to rest. The book was in her lap, unopened. Watching Black Wind make little pieces of wood out of big ones was ever so much more fascinating than reading about Oliver Twist.

She glanced over her shoulder as she heard the door open.

"Thought you might be thirsty," Hester said, handing Susannah a glass of cold buttermilk. "I brought some fer him, too. . . ." Hester's voice trailed off as she stared, open-mouthed, at Black Wind, her awed expression almost comical. "My, my," she murmured. "If he ain't a sight to set a woman's heart a flutterin'."

"Yes, indeed," Susannah agreed.

"Lordy," Hester said, fanning herself with the hem of her apron, "he makes me wish I was twenty years younger." Then, seeing the grin on Susannah's face, she shoved the second glass of buttermilk into her hand. "I may be old, child, but I ain't dead nor blind. Go on now. He could probably use something cold to drink. I know I could."

Filled with a sense of well-being, Susannah went down to join her husband.

Black Wind put the ax aside as she approached and handed him a glass. "What is this?" he asked.

"Buttermilk."

Black Wind frowned as he sniffed it, then took a drink.

"Is it good?" Susannah asked. "I've never tasted it."

He shrugged, then drained the glass in two

long swallows. "When one is thirsty, even muddy water is good."

"I guess." She took a sip, then another. Wrinkling her nose with distaste, she handed him her glass. "Here, you can have mine, too."

She watched him drink it down, thinking how pleasant it was to live with the Micklins. She pictured herself and Black Wind building a little place of their own not far from here, settling down, raising a family. It would be nice to have the Micklins for neighbors, to have Hester nearby when the baby was born.

Later that night, lying in Black Wind's arms, Susannah was still daydreaming. They would have a little cabin at first, just a couple of rooms. She would learn how to sew so she could make curtains for the windows; white ones for the parlor, yellow ones for the kitchen, blue ones for the nursery. In time, she would make friends with the other women, and someday the houses scattered across the prairie would become a town, and then a city. They'd build a church and a school . . .

And then, with just a few words, Black Wind shattered her fantasy.

"Where are you going?" Susannah asked as he slid out from under the covers and stood up.

"We must leave tonight."

"What?" She sat up, watching him pull on his clout and moccasins.

"It is time for us to return to my people. I cannot wait any longer."

"But . . ."

"I will not be gone long."

"Gone?" She looked up at him and knew, in that moment, that he was going out to steal the horses they needed. "Are you sure you have to do this?"

"It is the only way, Su-san-nah."

She bit back the urge to argue with him, realizing that horse stealing was something they would never see eye to eye on. Only the day before, Abe had informed Black Wind that his neighbors didn't have any horses they were willing to sell.

"Injuns been raiding to the south," Abe had said with a wry grin. "Run off with most of their extra stock."

Susannah had wondered then if Abe knew that Black Wind intended to run off with a couple more.

"Be ready when I return," Tate Sapa said. Bending, he brushed a kiss across the top of her head. "I will be back soon."

She wanted to argue; instead, she nodded. "All right."

She kissed him good-bye, then began to dress, her hands smoothing the soft doeskin over her hips. Black Wind had said they would leave as soon as he returned. There would be no good-byes, as Black Wind wasn't sure what Abe would do if he learned about the stolen horses.

With that in mind, she pulled on her moccasins and left the barn. Knowing how the whites felt about horse stealing, Black Wind had warned her not to say anything to the Micklins, but Susannah wanted to see Hester one last time before they left.

She hoped Hester and Abe were awake, as it

was still relatively early. Susannah smiled inwardly. She and Black Wind had retired early that night—though they hadn't gone to sleep.

As she neared the house, she heard voices. Abe's voice, loud and belligerent, demanding that someone "get the hell off my property."

Peering into the darkness, Susannah saw several mounted riders gathered in front of the house. Soldiers!

She was about to turn back toward the barn when one of the men shouted, "Look! There's the woman!"

Susannah froze as all attention was suddenly focused on her.

In moments, she was surrounded by soldiers, all brandishing weapons. Low murmurs reached her ears, accusations that she was a traitor, an Injun lover, and worse.

"Where's the Indian?"

"He's not here."

"Riggs, McCarthy, search the barn. Hamilton, secure her hands."

"See here," Hester called as one of the troopers dismounted and yanked Susannah's hands behind her back. "There's no call to be so rough."

"With all due respect, ma'am, I think you should mind your own business."

"Susannah is a decent, God-fearing woman, and one of the best friends I've ever had," Hester replied sharply. "That makes it my business."

"Is that right? Did she tell you she's a spy?"

"A spy!" Hester exclaimed. "Poppycock! Abe, do something."

"No," Susannah said, afraid her friends might

be hurt. "Please, I'll be fine."

The soldiers who had been sent to check the barn returned. "He's not in there."

"You're sure? He has to be here somewhere."

"He left," Susannah said.

"We found some blankets in one of stalls," the taller of the two soldiers remarked. "Looks like somebody's been sleeping in there."

The sergeant nodded. "Search the house."

Hester planted her hands on her ample hips and glared at the sergeant. "You'll do no such a thing," she declared. "Abe!"

"Best let them do what they want," Abe warned. He took hold of Hester's arm, his gaze focused on the rifle trained in their direction. "Damned redskin," he muttered under his breath. "I knew he was gonna cause us trouble sooner or later."

The sergeant stroked his jaw. "That Injun went through a lot of trouble to come back for the woman the last time," he mused, thinking out loud. "I don't think he'll leave her behind now." He grunted softly, his mind made up. "McCarthy, you take Hamilton, Fint, and Haggerty and hide in the barn. Take the woman with you. McKenna, you take these two into the house and keep 'em quiet. Hambly, get the horses out of sight. The rest of you men take cover."

"No!" Susannah began to struggle as one of the men took hold of her arm and forced her into the barn. "Let me go!"

The sergeant, who had followed them into the barn, pushed Susannah into the stall where the bedding was. "Lie down and keep your mouth shut. One word out of you, and he's dead. You understand me?"

Susannah nodded. There wasn't a doubt in her mind that the sergeant meant every word, or that he was capable of shooting Black Wind in cold blood.

"Good." He squatted on his heels in a corner of the stall, his pistol in his hand. "You men, take cover. Fint, turn out that lamp."

Tate Sapa ran effortlessly through the night, reveling in the cool wind against his face, the feel of the earth beneath his feet. He drew in a deep breath, inhaling the scent of sage and grass, the pungent odor of a skunk.

It was exhilarating, to be running wild and free through the night, bringing to mind the first time he had gone on a horse-stealing expedition. He had been a young warrior then, eager to count his first coup, to steal horses from the Crow, to raid the villages of the Pawnee.

He had soon learned that war had a price, and that it was most often paid by the elderly and the very young. When a warrior was killed, his family sometimes went hungry. When enemy tribes attacked their village, the old and infirm were often struck down. Unable to flee, too old to fight, they sometimes sacrificed their lives to save those who were younger. He had seen men and women too old to fight hurl themselves in front of the soldiers' horses in an effort to slow them down so that children and grandchildren might have time to run to safety. His comrades sometimes thought him a coward because he spoke for peace instead of war. But his bravery in battle, the number of coup he had counted, the horses he had stolen, soon silenced their accusations. Of all the young men in his tribe, none had garnered more honors in battle than he had.

Tate Sapa came to a halt atop a small rise, his gaze running over the buildings situated below. No lights shone in the house.

He stood there until his breathing returned to normal, studying the layout of the house and corrals, silently thanking *Wakan Tanka* that the moon and stars were hidden behind a bank of clouds.

Running lightly, he ran down the slope, slowing to a walk as he moved downwind toward the nearest corral. There were three horses inside. He studied them quickly, picking a dun-colored gelding and a dark gray mare.

Pulling a bridle from the waistband of his clout, he slipped between the bars.

The horses eyed him warily as he moved toward them.

"Easy, *tasunke*," he murmured. "Easy now."

Moving slowly, he approached the gray. She whinnied softly, her nostrils flaring as she breathed in his scent.

"Easy, *tasunke*." He slipped the bridle over her head and fastened it in place, then removed the rope wrapped around his waist, fashioned a loop, and dropped it over the dun's neck.

Leading both horses, he opened the corral gate, then vaulted onto the back of the gray. Drumming his heels into the mare's sides, he rode out of the corral.

* * *

Heart pounding, Susannah lay in the darkness, ears straining for some sound of Black Wind's return. She had to warn him away, but how? Beside her, she heard the sergeant shifting in the straw. She could smell the perspiration clinging to his clothes. She couldn't let these men take Black Wind back to the fort, she thought frantically; she couldn't bear the thought of him being imprisoned again, or, worse, being hanged.

She drew in a sharp breath as she heard the sound of hoofbeats approaching the barn, then the soft tread of moccasins as Black Wind stepped into the barn. He hesitated inside the doorway, and she wondered if he sensed something was wrong. She could feel a sheen of nervous perspiration on her brow, the rapid beating of her heart. The other soldiers were in the loft. If she warned Black Wind now, he had a good chance of getting away before they shot him.

"Run!" She scrambled to her feet as she shouted the warning, screamed with pain as liquid fire seared through her right arm and side.

She reeled forward, striking her head on the edge of the stall, and then blackness engulfed her.

"Susannah? Susannah? Landsakes, child, can you hear me?"

Hester's voice penetrated layers of darkness, calling her from the comfort of oblivion to the awareness of pain. With a groan, she opened her eyes to find Hester hovering over her, a worried expression on her face.

"Thank the Lord," Hester murmured. "You gave me quite a fright."

"Black Wind?" Susannah tried to sit up, then fell back against the pillows as pain slashed through her right arm and side. "Where is he? Is he all right?"

"He's fine." Hester placed her hand on Susannah's brow.

"You've got a touch of fever. Here, drink this." She held a cup to Susannah's lips.

Susannah took several swallows. "What happened?"

"That fool sergeant shot you. He was aiming for Black Wind when you stood up." Hester sniffed loudly. "Landsakes, child, you might have been killed."

It was a sobering thought. If she died here, no one back home would ever know what had happened to her. Of course, unless she found her way back home, they'd never know anyway.

"Seems like you're always doctoring one of us," Susannah said wearily. "I'll bet you're sorry we ever came here."

"Nonsense! I'm glad to do it. Well, not glad to do it," Hester said, grinning, "but glad to be able to help. You get some rest now."

"I want to see Black Wind."

"I'll ask the sergeant."

"They didn't hurt him, did they? He's all right?"

Hester's gaze slid away from Susannah's.

"Hester?"

"Well, I'm afraid he went kind of wild when he saw you go down. Took five of them soldiers to subdue him. I'm afraid he took a bit of a beating

301

'fore they got him quieted down."

"But he's all right?" Susannah asked anxiously.

Hester nodded. "He'll be fine." She started to leave the room, then hesitated. "Why, Susannah? Why did he steal those horses?"

"I don't know how to explain it," she replied, "except to say the Indians don't think of it as stealing when you're stealing from the enemy."

"He could have stolen our horses any time he wanted."

"We wouldn't steal from you," Susannah said. "You've been so good to us."

Hester nodded. "I think I understand. You get some rest. There's nothing either one of us can do for Black Wind right now."

Susannah wanted to argue, to get up and see for herself that Black Wind wasn't badly hurt, but trying to sit up made her feel dizzy and nauseous.

That slight exertion drained what little strength she had. Moments later, she was asleep.

Susannah woke to the sound of someone calling her name. Opening her eyes, she saw Hester standing beside the bed, looking down at her. For a moment, she stared at Hester, wondering why the other woman looked so worried, and then it all came back in a rush. She started to sit up, and felt a sharp stab of pain sizzle through her right arm and side.

"Just take it easy, honey. Everything's gonna be fine."

"Black Wind. Where's Black Wind?"

"He's in the barn."

"I want to see him." She struggled to sit up,

ignoring the wave of dizziness that swept over her. "I've got to see him."

With a harumph of disapproval, Hester helped Susannah to her feet. She muttered under her breath as she helped her get dressed, shaking her head over the stubbornness of some women. In spite of the pain of her wounds and the seriousness of their situation, Susannah had to smile.

When she was dressed, she gave Hester a quick, one-armed hug. "You're the best, you know that?"

"Go on with you, now," Hester said. "If you're determined to do this, let's get on with it."

"You don't have to go with me."

"I ain't lettin' you go traipsin' down there among all them soldiers by yourself, not for a minute."

Abe was sitting on a stump in the front yard, glaring at the soldiers who were grouped together near the barn.

Susannah lifted her chin defiantly as she walked by the men, aware of their smirks and loudly whispered slurs.

"Don't let it bother you none," Hester said.

"I won't," Susannah replied. But being called a squaw and an Injun lover and a traitor hurt just the same.

The sergeant was standing near the barn door, smoking a cigar. "Where do you think you're going?" he asked.

"I want to see my husband."

"Husband, is it?"

Susannah lifted her chin and met his gaze. "Yes."

He snorted contemptuously. "Make it short. Now that you're up and around, we'll be leaving in half an hour. Be ready."

With a curt nod, Susannah stepped past him.

Black Wind was being held in the stall they had shared.

She knelt beside him, the pain of her own wounds forgotten as her gaze swept over him. His arms were tightly bound behind his back, there was dried blood on his nose and mouth, and several bruises on his arms and chest. The left side of his face was swollen and discolored.

"Are you all right?" It seemed a silly question, in view of the way he looked, but she had to ask.

Tate Sapa nodded, his dark eyes intense upon her face. "The baby?" he asked softly, aware of the soldiers standing nearby.

"Everything's okay," she assured him.

His gaze moved to the bandage on her arm. "You should not have tried to warn me, Su-san-nah."

"I had to. Don't worry about me. I'm all right. It's just a scratch, really."

"What will they do to you?"

"I don't know." She didn't want to think about that. O'Neill had warned her that traitors were shot, but surely they wouldn't shoot her while she was pregnant! She wanted to curl up in Black Wind's arms, to tell him how scared she was, but she couldn't do that, not now. He had enough to worry about without her acting like a helpless ninny.

Leaning forward, she kissed him gently. "I love you."

"Su-san-nah . . ."

"Time's up. We're moving out."

At the sound of the sergeant's gruff voice, Susannah kissed Black Wind again, then stood up.

"I love you." She mouthed the words as she backed out of the stall, then stood in the aisle, watching as two of the soldiers grabbed Black Wind and hauled him to his feet.

"Just a minute," Hester said. "You're not taking Susannah away from here until I've checked her wounds and she's had a good breakfast."

"See here, ma'am . . ."

"No, Sergeant, you see here. This woman's been hurt, and I ain't sendin' her off with you until she's been taken care of properly."

Hands fisted on her hips, Hester glared at the sergeant.

He surrendered with a wry grin. "Try not to take too long, ma'am. We've got a long ride ahead of us."

Back at the house, Hester checked Susannah's arm and side, declaring that she was "dang lucky" as she applied a fresh coat of salve, then rebandaged the wounds.

When that was done, Hester fried up a mess of eggs, bacon, and potatoes and insisted Susannah eat every bite on her plate. She sent Abe to the barn with a plate for Black Wind, and told him to stay there and make sure he got to eat it.

"I think maybe I'd best go along to the fort and make sure they treat you right," Hester said as she watched Susannah eat. "Yes, I think that's what I'd better do."

"Hester, I can't let you do that."

"Well, child, I don't see how you can stop me."

As it turned out, Abe couldn't stop her, either, and neither could the sergeant. In the end, Abe decided he couldn't let his wife go by herself, so he hitched the team to a wagon and tied his riding horse to the tailgate. While Hester packed a bag, he filled a couple of canteens and tossed them in the back of the wagon, along with some blankets and a pillow. After closing the barn door, he stood with his back against the wagon box, his arms folded over his chest, while he waited for Hester.

She came out a few minutes later carrying a flowered carpetbag.

"I think Susannah should ride in the wagon," Hester decided. She put on a big yellow sunbonnet, then handed one to Susannah.

The sergeant took one look at Hester's set expression and decided not to argue. Muttering under his breath, he lifted Susannah into the bed of the wagon, then mounted his horse and rode out.

Susannah tied the sunbonnet in place, grateful for the older woman's thoughtfulness. "But Hester, what about your place?"

"It'll be fine," Hester replied, tucking a pillow behind Susannah's back. "The cattle can look out for themselves for a few days. I left a note on the door for anyone who happens to stop by, telling them where we are. Lucy Halliday was supposed to come by tomorrow to help me with some canning. Lucy and her husband will look after things till we get back."

With a sigh, Susannah sat back against the side

of the wagon so she could see Black Wind. Hands secured behind his back, he was riding between two of the soldiers, his face impassive. He was bloody and bound, but not beaten, she thought with a sense of pride. Defiance blazed in his eyes, in the set of his shoulders.

It was a long, hard ride. The bouncing of the wagon jarred Susannah's arm and side, increasing the ache. She wondered if Black Wind was sorry they had met. It seemed to her she had caused him nothing but trouble. The Lakota had rejected him because of her, and now he was on his way back to jail when he should be warning his people to pack up and move the village.

Susannah stared into the distance. The sight of so much empty space still amazed her. Born and reared in the city, she found the vast rolling plains both awe inspiring and frightening. Until she came here, she had never been any place that didn't have a convenience store, a gas station, or a mall within a few blocks. Out here, one could go hundreds of miles before reaching civilization.

Time and again on the long ride, Black Wind's gaze met hers. There was no anger in his eyes when he looked at her, no censure, only love and reassurance.

They'd been traveling for hours when the sergeant finally called a halt near a shallow stream. "Thirty minutes," he said.

The men dismounted and watered their horses, then wandered away to see to their own needs. Two of the soldiers escorted Black Wind.

Abe helped Susannah out of the back of the

wagon. Two troopers were there, waiting for her. They reminded her of Laurel and Hardy, one tall and thin, the other rather stout with a moustache.

"Come on," Hester said, taking Susannah's arm. "I need to find a bush."

Susannah nodded.

Hester scowled at the two men who followed them. "There ain't no place for us to run off to, so you just keep back aways, hear? I don't intend to lift my skirts with you two lookin' on."

The younger of the two men, the one who looked like Stan Laurel, blushed furiously, stammered, "Yes, ma'am," and turned his back, ignoring the laughter of his comrade.

"Humph. Fine thing, when a lady can't be left alone to answer nature's call," Hester complained as she dragged Susannah behind a clump of bushes. "How you feelin', honey?"

"I'm all right." Susannah blinked back the tears that stung her eyes. Lately, it seemed as though she was constantly on the verge of tears. She'd never been such a cry baby in her whole life, and she didn't know whether it was caused by circumstances, the fact that she was hurting and tired, or her pregnancy. With a sigh, she decided it was probably all of the above. "I'm worried about Black Wind, Hester."

"I know, child, I know, but you've got to have faith that everything will turn out for the best."

"I don't see how it can."

"That's why you need faith, child. You've got to cast your burdens on the Lord, and trust that He'll see you through."

"I'll try."

"Well, that's all He asks of us, dearie, that we try."

Susannah pressed her hand over her stomach. "You don't think all that bouncing around will hurt the baby, do you?"

"Landsakes, no. That baby will be fine."

Susannah threw her arms around the other woman and gave her a fierce hug. "Hester, I don't know what I'd do without you."

"You're a strong woman, Susannah. You'd get by." Hester returned Susannah's hug. "Okay now, you put a smile on your face. We don't want to give that man of yours anything more to worry about."

With a nod, Susannah wiped her eyes, then ran a hand through her hair. Hester was right. She had to believe everything would work out for the best.

Returning to the rest site, she accepted a canteen of water from one of the men, then went to stand beside Black Wind. She uncapped the canteen and offered him a drink. When he had quenched his thirst, she took a long drink, then soaked a corner of her skirt with water and washed the blood from his face.

He winced as she ran the cloth over his left cheek.

"Are you all right?" Susannah asked.

He nodded.

"Are you sure?" She ran her fingertips over the left side of his face, down his arm, over his chest. His eye was swollen, the bruises on his arms and chest were a remarkable shade of greenish-purple. "You look terrible."

"I am fine, Su-san-nah." His gaze slid over her from head to foot. "Are you well?"

She forced a smile. "We're both fine. Don't worry."

"How can you tell me not to worry?" he asked bitterly. "I will soon be back in prison. The Army thinks you are a traitor. Should they decide to imprison you, or worse, I will not be able to protect you."

"I'm not afraid." It was a bald-faced lie. She was terrified of what waited for them at the fort, of being separated from Black Wind, of facing a future in this time and place without him beside her. She wished he could hold her, desperately needed to feel the strength of his arms around her, but with his hands lashed behind his back, that was impossible.

He didn't say anything, but his wry smile, the sad expression in his eyes, told her he knew her words for the lie they were. "Truly, Su-san-nah, you have the heart of a Lakota warrior."

Because she had to touch him, she placed her hand on his shoulder. She could feel the tension vibrating through him, the coiled power waiting for the moment to strike out. Her heart swelled with emotion, love and tenderness mushrooming side by side until she ached with it.

"Mount up!"

"Try not to worry," Susannah said. She gave him a quick hug. "You've got to have faith."

She repeated those words to herself as one of the soldiers helped her into the back of the wagon, repeated them over and over again as twilight fell over the plains. One by one, the stars came alive, winking softly against the dark blue sky.

It was near midnight when they reached the fort. Black Wind was hauled off the back of his horse. He tried to turn and face her. She heard one of the soldiers curse as he cuffed Black Wind across the face, then pushed him roughly forward.

Susannah stared after Black Wind, wishing she could go to him, comfort him, but the sergeant took her by the arm and hustled her into the colonel's office, where she was kept waiting for a good half hour.

She paced the floor outside his office, her thoughts turning to Black Wind. Would they beat him before they locked him up? She had to find a way to free him. She couldn't bear to think of him locked up again.

At last, O'Neill opened the door and beckoned her inside. He didn't invite her to sit down.

"So, miss," he said curtly, "what have you got to say for yourself?" Rounding his desk, he sat down, his elbows on the desktop, hands clasped, fingers laced together.

"You're making a mistake," Susannah said. "I'm not a spy."

"Can you prove that?"

"Can you prove I am?"

"We found you sneaking around the fort," O'Neill retorted. "No one knows who you are or where you came from. You helped the Indian escape. You were found in a Lakota village." He shrugged. "That's proof enough for me."

"What are you going to do with me?"

"Nothing, until I hear from Washington. You'll probably stand trial there."

"What's going to happen to Black Wind?"

"He'll finish out his sentence plus another year or two, then be sent to the reservation where he can't cause any more trouble."

"That's not fair!"

O'Neill stood up, his hands flat on the desk, his expression ominous. "Don't be impertinent, miss! Hackett, take her to the guardhouse."

Before she could argue, Susannah was being dragged out of the colonel's office and across the compound. Minutes later, she was locked in the cell adjoining Black Wind's. She spared hardly a glance at her surroundings, noting that, except for a narrow cot and a covered slop jar, the cell was virtually empty.

"Su-san-nah!"

Black Wind moved toward her, and she noticed that his right leg was shackled to a thick iron ring bolted to the wall. She knew how humiliating it must be for him, to be chained up like some sort of wild animal, and wondered if that was the reason for the chain. Not as a precaution against his escape, but simply to humiliate him, to remind him that, for him, freedom no longer existed, nor would it ever again.

The heavy iron chain rattled as he crossed the floor. And then he was reaching for her through the bars.

She went to him gratefully, needing his touch, the sound of his voice.

He held her as close as he could, one hand running up and down her back as he murmured her name over and over again.

"Oh, Black Wind, what are we going to do?"

"I do not know, *wastelakapi*. Do not worry about it now. You need to rest. You must think only of the child now."

The baby. She had almost forgotten about it.

Black Wind dragged his blanket to the bars that separated them. Susannah did the same, though she was loathe to touch the threadbare blanket folded across the foot of the cot, and they lay down facing each other, holding hands through the bars.

Tears burned Susannah's eyes. If they sent her to Washington, she would never see Black Wind again. That thought hurt worse than anything else.

Chapter Twenty-two

Colonel William Henry O'Neill sat back in his chair and tried to keep the mounting irritation from showing on his face as he listened to Hester Micklin rant and rave. The woman had been a constant thorn in his side ever since her arrival at the fort. She had been hanging around his office day and night for the past week, trying to get in to see him. Finally, in hopes that she would say her piece and be on her way, he had agreed to meet with her. It had definitely been a mistake. The woman had been giving him the rough side of her tongue for the better part of half an hour, and he'd had just about all he could take.

He slid a glance at the woman's husband, who stood near the door, his arms crossed over his chest, his weathered face inscrutable.

What a pair, O'Neill thought sourly. The man

was as silent as the grave; the woman chattered like a magpie.

Hester drew herself up to her full height, hands fisted on her ample hips. "I said it before, and I'll say it agin; Susannah ain't no more a spy than I am."

"Yes, well, someone else will make that decision." O'Neill thumbed through the papers on his desk, hoping she'd realize he had other duties to attend to. "Good day to you, Mrs. Micklin."

"I ain't leavin' until you turn Susannah loose," Hester said vehemently. "You can't keep her locked up in that dreadful place."

"I'm afraid I can."

"It ain't right. Not in her condition."

"Condition?" O'Neill looked up, his eyes narrowed. "Is she ill?"

"She's in the family way."

The colonel swore under his breath. That did, indeed, complicate matters. He could just imagine what the Eastern papers would say if they learned he was keeping a pregnant woman in the guardhouse. Every liberal bleeding heart west of the Mississippi would be after his hide.

"You can be sure I'll bear that in mind." O'Neill stood up. "Now, if you'll excuse me, I have business to attend to."

"I said I ain't leavin'."

"Mrs. Micklin, I should hate to have to detain you, as well."

Abe pushed himself away from the wall. "Let's go, Hester. This blue belly don't give a damn about right and wrong."

"I'll thank you to keep a civil tongue in your

head, Mr. Micklin, and remind you that while you're on my post, you'll show a little more respect for me, and for this uniform."

"I got no respect fer you, or fer thet there uniform," Abe retorted. "Let's go, Hester," he repeated, and grabbing her by the arm, he pulled her out of the colonel's office.

"Abe! Let me go!"

"Yer wastin' yer time, Hester. He ain't gonna listen, and he ain't gonna turn Susannah loose, neither."

"Well, we've got to do something! You heard what he said. He thinks Susannah is a spy."

"Hell, woman, maybe she is. We don't know nothing about her, or that redskin."

"Abe Micklin, you shut your mouth this minute! How can you even think such a thing?"

"Shit, I don't know what to think anymore. All I know is, we've been gone from our place too long as it is. I say we hitch up the team and go home."

"I'm not leaving this place as long as Susannah is locked up in that awful jail. I think we should try to see her again. Maybe this time they'll let us in."

"Woman, they ain't gonna let you see her. Ain't you got that through yer head yet? That blue belly colonel gave orders that she weren't to have no visitors. He ain't gonna change his mind, and there ain't nothin' you kin do about it."

Hester scowled at him, the light of battle rekindling in her eyes. "Is that so? Well, we'll just see about that."

And so saying, Hester turned on her heel and

marched back into the colonel's office.

"Women," Abe muttered. "Sometimes I think I'd have been better off if I'd a stayed single."

An hour later, Hester was hugging Susannah through the bars. "Are you all right, child?" she asked. She drew back and looked Susannah over from head to foot.

"I'm fine, Hester. I'm still a little sore, but the Army doctor looked me over and said my wounds are healing, thanks to you."

"Humph! As if anybody could be fine in a place like this."

Susannah smiled. "I'm so glad to see you."

Hester reached into the basket on her arm. "Here, I brought you a few things."

She handed Susannah a bar of yellow soap, a bag of gumdrops, a hairbrush and comb, a packet of hairpins, a small bag of inexpensive cologne.

"Hester, you shouldn't have."

Hester shook her head as she glanced around the crude cellblock, her nose wrinkling with disgust.

"Horrible place," she muttered. "I wouldn't let my dogs stay in here. Next time I come, I'll bring you some decent bedding. Why, that blanket ain't fit fer nothing but rags."

Hester glanced over at Black Wind, who had remained silent after greeting her and Abe with a subdued hello. Her gaze ran over him, noting that he seemed thinner than when she'd seen him last. She could still see the bruises on his face and arms, souvenirs of the beating the soldiers had given him.

"We'll get some better blankets for you, too, young man," she said. "Is there anything else you need?"

Black Wind shook his head. The only thing he needed was his freedom, and that was one thing Hester Micklin could not pull out of her basket.

"Here," Hester said, delving into her basket once more, "I thought the two of you might like something to eat. You're both skinny as church mice. Ain't much now, just some bread and meat and cheese."

"Hester, how can we ever thank you?"

Hester waved her hand in a gesture of dismissal. "Landsakes, child, what are friends for? We'll be back tomorrow. Try not to worry now. I just know everything will be all right."

Susannah nodded. "Thank you, Hester. You, too, Abe."

Abe grunted softly, then sidled closer to Black Wind's cell. "Anything I kin get fer you?" he asked gruffly.

"A rifle would be a big help," Black Wind replied dryly.

A rare grin creased Abe's face. "Yeah," he drawled, "I reckon so. Anything else you need?"

"No, but I thank you for what you have done."

"Yeah, well . . ." Abe glanced at Hester. "Reckon we'll be by tomorrow."

"Count on it," Hester said. "Come along, Abe, the colonel said we could only stay a few minutes. Don't want to make that old grouch angry, lessen he won't let us come back again."

She hugged Susannah through the bars. "Don't get discouraged now, hear? Everything's gonna be just fine."

Her arms filled with Hester's bounty, Susannah smiled through her tears. Never, in all her life, had she had a friend as loyal as Hester Micklin.

It was late afternoon the following day when a trio of soldiers came into the guardhouse. They handcuffed Black Wind's hands behind his back, then opened both cell doors.

It was a routine Susannah had grown used to in the last week. Once each afternoon, they were allowed to spend fifteen minutes outside.

During this time, no one was allowed to get near them, or to speak to them. Occasionally, she had seen Hester and Abe in the distance. Hester had tried to speak to Susannah the first time she saw her outside, but the colonel had heard about it and threatened to have her forcibly removed from the post. Still, it always boosted Susannah's spirits to know Hester and Abe were nearby.

She was looking for some sign of her friends when she saw a soldier escorting a couple of men in their direction. The civilians, who were both dressed in Eastern city-style suits and black bowler hats, were carrying a camera and tripod and other paraphernalia.

One of the men guarding Susannah stepped forward. "What's going on?"

"I'm Wilson B. Royale, and this is my assistant, Louis Hackworth. Colonel O'Neill said I might take a picture of the Indian for my newspaper, *The Dakota Chronicle*.

Black Wind shook his head. "No."

"You'll do as you're told, buck," the soldier said.

"Thank you, Corporal. Would you make him stand over there? Yes, with the jailhouse behind him. Yes, that's perfect. Gritty." He studied his subject while his assistant set up the camera. "Do you think you could remove his handcuffs for a moment? Thank you. We don't want to upset the sensibilities of our lady readers."

Sullen-faced, Black Wind stood where he was told while the photographer set up his equipment. He rubbed his wrists as, furtively, he glanced around, weighing his chances of escape. They were not good, he mused. A number of soldiers who were not otherwise occupied had gathered around to watch the picture taking. The two soldiers in charge of watching him stood nearby, rifles at the ready. He could see Abe and Hester standing near their wagon a short distance away.

"Okay," the photographer said. "This is it."

Susannah stood beside the camera, startled by the realization that the picture being taken was the very one that she had bought at the reenactment workshop. For a moment, it seemed as if she was seeing the photograph of Black Wind for the first time. She remembered talking to the man at the reenactment workshop. She had asked how Black Wind died, and he had said he didn't know, there was no record of his death.

"Susannah? Susannah, is that you?"

Elliott Carter's voice penetrated her reverie.

Glancing over her shoulder, she saw him break away from a column of soldiers returning to the fort and ride toward her.

He swung out of the saddle, the smile on his face fading into a frown when he saw that she was under guard. "What's going on here?"

"I'm under arrest for being a spy."

Carter swore under his breath. "I thought that was all settled." He glanced at Black Wind. "So, they caught him."

"They caught *us*," Susannah said. "Elliott, is there anything you can do?"

"I don't know. I'll have to talk to Colonel O'Neill. How long have you been here?"

"A week."

Carter swore under his breath. "I've been out on patrol. I'm sorry I wasn't here for you." His gaze ran over her. She looked a trifle pale; there were dark smudges under her eyes. "Are they treating you all right? You look a little thin."

"I'm fine." She placed one hand over her stomach. "I'm pregnant."

He didn't try to hide his astonishment. "You're . . . you're sure?"

"Yes."

She waited for his expression to change, waited for his concern to turn to derision. She felt like crying when his eyes continued to reflect only concern for her welfare.

"Did he . . . He didn't . . ." He cleared his throat. "Are you happy about . . . about the baby?"

"Yes, very."

"I'll speak to the colonel, see if he won't consider letting you stay in one of the huts, considering you're in the family way."

Almost, she was tempted to accept. The crude hut she had stayed in before seemed like a palace when compared to her jail cell, but she couldn't go, couldn't leave Black Wind. "Thank you, Elliott, but I'd rather stay in the jail."

"You're sure?"

"Yes."

Carter nodded, knowing she wanted to stay with the Indian. He blew out a long sigh. "I'll see what I can do about making you more comfortable." He glanced at Black Wind, who was standing as stiff as a cigar store Indian, staring into the distance, while the photographer took another picture. "Both of you."

"Thank you, Elliott."

"We're done here," Royale said. "Get our gear, Louis. I want to get these developed as soon as I can."

In a matter of minutes, Black Wind's hands were cuffed again and he was being led back to the guardhouse.

"Excuse me, Lieutenant, but she's got to go back, too."

"In a minute, Corporal."

The corporal cleared his throat. "I don't mean to be impertinent, sir, but I'm obeying the colonel's orders."

"Very well, Corporal." Carter took Susannah's hands in his. "I'm sorry about this, Susannah. Try not to worry."

She nodded, unable to speak past the lump in her throat.

A short time later, she was back in her cell. She flinched as the door was shut behind her, the key turned in the lock. She had never realized how much she abhorred small confined spaces until now. How much worse must it be for Black Wind, who had been born and raised in the vastness of the plains, who had known only freedom his whole life.

"What did the white man say to you?" Black Wind asked. His voice was even, yet she heard the fine edge of anger beneath his quiet words.

"He said he'd try to help us."

"Us, Su-san-nah? Or you?"

"Both of us, Black Wind. Don't be angry. We could use a friend right now."

"I do not need a *wasichu* for a friend."

"Is that right? Well, it seems to me you already have some white people for friends. What about Hester? And Abe? Don't they count as friends? And what about me?"

"What about you?" Black Wind asked softly. He watched her through fathomless ebony eyes, his body motionless, his hands clenched at his sides.

She felt suddenly cold all over. "What do you mean?"

"I saw the way the white man looked at you. He cares for you. You would be better off with him, than here with me."

Susannah crossed the floor, her hands curling around the bars that separated them. "Black Wind, shut up. Do you hear me? Just shut up. I won't listen to that kind of talk. Not now. Not after all we've been through. We're in this together whether you like it or not."

With a sigh, he went to her. Reaching through the bars, he wrapped his arms around her waist and held her close. "Forgive me, Su-san-nah."

"There's nothing to forgive."

"Su-san-nah, I think you should ask the lieutenant if he can get you out of here."

She didn't tell him that Carter had offered her that very thing.

"You need to take care of yourself," Black Wind went on. "You need to think of the child. You should not be here, in this place." He looked over her shoulder, anger churning within him as he took in the narrow cot with its threadbare blankets and uncovered pillow. The stench of human waste filled his nostrils. "You should not be here," he said again. "It cannot be good for you, or the child."

"I'm all right," Susannah said. As all right as she could be living in a small square cell that held nothing but a pot to pee in and a lumpy mattress to sleep on. "Just tired."

Black Wind put her away from him. "Go, rest."

She didn't want to leave the shelter of his arms, but she was tired, so tired. Was it part of being pregnant, she wondered, or a by-product of the hopelessness she couldn't shake off? She wished she had listened more attentively when Vivian was expecting and anxious to discuss all the little aches and pains and discomfort that went hand in hand with being pregnant.

"I'll try to sleep if you promise to get some rest, too," Susannah said, kissing him on the cheek. "You look tired."

Feather in the Wind

She was awakened later that night by the rattle of the key being turned in the lock. Sitting up, she wiped the sleep from her eyes, blinked against the lantern's bright yellow light.

"Dinner time." The guard, whose name was Denkner, set the tray on the foot of the bed. He was a short, stocky man, with a neck like a tree trunk and dark, narrow-set eyes.

"Thank you," Susannah said. She stared at the corporal towering over her. Usually, he brought in her dinner and left. She felt suddenly uneasy as his gaze moved over her, lingering on her breasts.

She reached for the tray, but he caught her by the hand, jerked her to her feet, and hauled her up against him.

"Let me go!"

"Su-san-nah!" She heard Black Wind cry her name.

"Come on, honey, just one kiss."

"Let me go!" She struggled against him but he held her tight, her arms trapped between their bodies as he kissed her. It was a wet, disgusting kiss. Nausea roiled in her stomach as his tongue plunged into her mouth. Panic sizzled through her as she realized she was at his mercy. There was no one but Black Wind to hear her cries for help, and there was nothing he could do.

With a sob, she turned her head to the side and brought her knee up, hard. Denkner was ready for her, though, and her knee only grazed his thigh.

She began to struggle more violently, her nails raking his cheek.

"No!" She screamed the word again and again as she tried to escape his grasp.

Denkner stumbled backward against the bars, dragging her body full length against his. "All I wanted was one kiss," he growled, "but now I'll have it all."

"Let me go!"

"Not yet, missy."

He was leaning forward, his gaze intent on her face. His breath reeked of tobacco. She could feel his arousal pressing against her.

This can't be happening! The words screamed in her mind. Susannah shook her head in denial, praying that this was all a bad dream, that she'd wake up and he'd be gone. And then, suddenly, she was free of him.

Denkner's arms were flailing wildly. His eyes widened, his body convulsing as his hands clawed at his throat.

Susannah reeled backward, gasping for breath, as a horrible choking sound issued from Denkner's lips, lips that were slowly turning blue.

It took her a moment to realize what was happening, and then she stared in horror as she watched Black Wind's hands tighten around the corporal's throat, slowly choking the life out of him.

After what seemed like an eternity, Black Wind released his hold on the soldier and Denkner slid to the floor, limp as a rag doll.

Black Wind spared the dead man hardly a

glance. "Su-san-nah, are you all right? Did he hurt you?"

She shook her head, panic rising up within her as she glanced from Black Wind to the soldier. He was dead, she thought, there was no doubt of that.

There was no hope for them now, she thought dully. Black Wind had killed one of O'Neill's men. They would hang him now.

"Su-nan-nah?"

"I'm fine." She glanced at the cell door. It was standing open, beckoning her.

Crossing the floor, she knelt beside the soldier, going through his pockets until she found his keys.

Hurrying to the other cell, she slid the key in the lock, gave it a quick twist, and opened the door.

She gave Black Wind a quick hug, then knelt down, trying first one key and then another on the shackles that bound his right ankle.

She swore softly when none of the keys fit. "The key must be in the office. I'll be right back."

She started to leave when she heard voices in the hallway. She'd never be able to get the key now.

She watched Black Wind kneel down and reach through the bars, his hand reaching for the corporal's sidearm.

"No," she whispered. "Black Wind, don't."

"I will not let them hang me." With a small cry of triumph, he unholstered the corporal's pistol.

"Put that gun down, redskin! Now, damn it!"

Two soldiers stood in the doorway, guns drawn.

"Put it down," the soldier said again. "Do it now, or I'll shoot the woman."

Black Wind's finger slid around the trigger, caressing it. He looked at the soldiers, felt the hot, angry blood stir within him. He recognized these two. In days past, they had taunted and tormented him along with the others. It would be so easy to kill them. *Hoka-hey! It is a good day today!*

He didn't believe the *wasichu* would kill Susannah, but it was a risk he was unwilling to take. With a sigh of resignation, he placed the pistol on the floor, then stood up slowly, his hands raised to show they were empty.

"Come out of there, miss."

Susannah glanced at Black Wind, at the two soldiers, at the gun on the floor.

"No, Su-san-nah," Black Wind said softly. "Do as they say."

For a moment, she considered trying to get the gun, but she knew she couldn't kill two men, couldn't put the life of her unborn child in danger.

Overcome by a sense of helplessness, she walked back to her own cell and sank down on the cot. Moments later, the dead soldier had been dragged away and she was locked behind bars again.

The two soldiers approached Black Wind's cell.

The taller of the two men waved his gun in Black Wind's direction. "Back away," he ordered brusquely. "Reddick, cover me."

Picking up the gun, the soldier backed out of the cell and locked the door.

"I'll go tell the colonel what happened," Reddick said. "You stay here and keep an eye on these two."

Susannah was hardly aware of the other two men. She had eyes only for Black Wind. He stood with his back to the wall, tension radiating from every muscle. They would hang him now. She knew it, and so did he.

Tears stung her eyes. There was no hope left, she thought dismally, no hope at all.

Carter confirmed her worst fears the next morning. The colonel had declared that Black Wind would be hanged the following morning. There was no hope of reprieve.

"I'm sorry," Carter said. "Is there anything I can do?"

Susannah shook her head. There was nothing anyone could do now.

Carter glanced over at Black Wind, who was standing near the bars that divided the two cells. "Is there anything I can do for you? Anyone I can notify?"

Tate Sapa glared at the white man and then, forcing his anger and pride aside, he nodded. "My father is He Wonjetah. Can you let him know what has happened?"

"I'm not sure. I might be able to get word to him somehow, but I can't promise you anything."

"I understand. Will you look after Su-san-nah for me?"

"Of course."

"She is not a spy, or a traitor."

"I know. I'll think of some way to get her out of this mess. Don't worry."

Tate Sapa nodded, then walked to the far side of his cell and turned his back on them.

"Elliott, I have a favor to ask."

"What is it, Susannah?"

She wanted to beg him to let Black Wind go, wanted to promise him anything he asked if only he would let Black Wind go, but she knew he would never agree. He was an honorable man. Duty to his country would never permit him to turn his back on his honor and turn a condemned man loose. "I want to spend the night with Black Wind."

Carter shook his head. "I don't think I can manage that."

"Please, Elliott." Tears filled her eyes and trickled down her cheeks. "Please. I love him."

Carter swore under his breath. "I'll see what I can do."

"Thank you."

That day was the longest, and the shortest, Susannah had ever known. They had shortened the chain that bound Black Wind to the wall so that he could only take a few steps in any direction. Now, when she yearned to be in his arms, to hold him close, it was no longer possible.

She sat on the floor by the bars that separated them, hardly taking her eyes from his face, memorizing every detail, every line—the thick fall of his hair, the width of his shoulders, the length of his thigh, the rich copper color of his skin, the shape of his eyes, his mouth, his nose. Every minute that passed was like a thorn in her heart. She had heard of people who died of a broken heart and had wondered if it was possible. She knew now that it was.

They had said everything there was to say, much of it spoken in the silent communication of soul to soul. She ached in the very deepest part of her being, ached to hold him, to touch him, to cradle him in her arms, to promise him that everything would be all right.

The setting sun reminded her of how very few hours they had left. Someone brought their dinner trays, but neither of them had any appetite for food and, for once, Black Wind did not remind her that she needed to keep her strength up for the sake of the child.

The child . . . Tate Sapa sat with his back against the wall, his gaze on Susannah's face. She had fallen asleep, and he thought how beautiful she was, how much he loved her, how very much he would miss her and the child he would never see.

He thought briefly of his father, of his people, praying that they would be well, that they would somehow avoid being sent to the reservation.

But mostly he thought of Susannah, of that day, high on a mountaintop, when he had seen her in vision, of the nights he had held her in his arms. He did not regret loving her, only that they would not have more time together, that he would not be there to see his child take his first breath, his first step, that he would not be there to hear him speak his first word.

"*Hee-ay-hee-ee!*," he cried softly. "*Wakan Tanka*, bless my woman and my unborn child. Give me the courage of my brother, the mountain lion, that I may die with honor and not bring shame to my father, or my people." He lifted a hand to the eagle feather tied in his hair. "Please, *Tunkaschila*, help my woman to find her way back to her home. . . ."

He fell silent at the sound of footsteps in the hallway, and then Elliott Carter entered the room and unlocked the door to Susannah's cell.

She came awake instantly, her alarm turning to relief when she saw who it was.

"The colonel wouldn't let you stay the night with him," Carter said. "But he agreed to give you an hour together."

Susannah nodded. It wasn't what she had hoped for, but it was better than nothing. And she would be near him the rest of the night, able to see him, to hear his voice. There was so much to say, things she needed to know, things she wanted to tell him before it was too late.

Rising to her feet, she crossed the floor. "Thank you, Elliott. You've been so kind to me. I'll never forget this."

Carter cleared his throat, his gaze skittering away from hers. "The colonel's moving you out of here later tonight."

"Moving me?" She stared up at him, her eyes twin pools of disbelief and confusion. "Why?"

"He didn't say."

"But I want to stay here!" Even if she couldn't

spend the night in Black Wind's cell, she wanted to be near him as long as she could. She wanted to share this last night, these last hours with Black Wind. She wanted to be there for him in the morning, to share what few moments they might have before . . . She shook away the awful image of Black Wind mounted on a horse, his hands bound behind his back, a noose around his neck. She would not, could not, think of that now.

"I'm sorry, Susannah." Carter opened the door to Susannah's cell. "I don't need to warn you not to try anything foolish, do I?"

"No," she replied dully, "you don't have to warn me."

"Good. There are two men standing guard in the office." He smiled at her, his eyes filled with sympathy. "Just thought you ought to know, in case you change your mind."

"Thank you, Elliott."

He unlocked the door to Black Wind's cell, took a step back so she could enter, then closed and locked the door behind her.

"One hour," he reminded them. "I'll make certain no one bothers you."

But Susannah wasn't listening. She was crossing the floor, throwing herself into Black Wind's arms, lifting her face for his kiss.

Tate Sapa's arms closed around her. It seemed like years since he had held her, touched her. He whispered her name over and over again as his hands reacquainted themselves with her softness. His hands skimmed over her breasts. They felt fuller, heavier. He kissed her, tasting her sweetness as if for the first time instead of the last. He drew in a deep breath, capturing her scent, letting it fill his mind and his heart, wanting to brand the memory of this moment on his soul.

Still locked together, they slid down on his blankets. In haste, they shed their clothes, wanting nothing between them. When he hesitated, she took him in her hand and guided him home, sighing with pleasure as his flesh joined with hers, feeling her heart break as his tears joined with hers.

"I love you," he whispered, his voice hoarse.

"And I love you." She clung to him, holding him tight, until, for a few brief moments, she forgot everything but the ecstacy of his touch. She held him tighter, tighter, sobbing with pleasure as his life spilled into her, moaning softly with the realization that this would be the last time he made love to her.

She had hoped to spend years with this man, to grow old at his side, and now only minutes remained.

He held her close for a long while. She listened to the sound of his breathing return to normal, heard him whisper again that he loved her.

They dressed quickly, aware that their time together was almost up, then Black Wind gathered her into his arms and held her close, his hands resting lightly on the slight swell of her belly. He imagined his child sleeping there, safe and secure.

"My mother's name was Tashina Luta," he

said. "Tell my son who his grandparents were. Tell him I loved him."

"I will."

"Teach him about his people. Help him to be proud to be Lakota."

"I will, you know I will. If I can, I'll take him to see your father. I won't let him forget you, I promise."

"Tell him how much I loved his mother."

She nodded, unable to speak past the burning lump in her throat.

"Su-san-nah . . . so many things I want to tell you."

"I know." She buried her face in his shoulder, not wanting him to see her tears. There would be plenty of time to cry later, but she couldn't stop the flood of tears, couldn't stop her heart from breaking.

And then she heard Elliott Carter's voice in the hallway and she knew her time with Black Wind was almost over.

With a sob, she clung to Black Wind, hugging him to her. How could she live without him? She had heard of countries where women threw themselves on the funeral pyres of their husbands. She had thought it a barbaric custom, had shuddered with revulsion at the mere idea, unable to understand why a woman would want to end her life in such a horrible way, but she knew now. She didn't want to go on living without Tate Sapa. It was unfair that the sun would rise when he wasn't there to see it, that people would go on as before, laughing, living, when he was dead.

As if reading her thoughts, he cupped her face

in his hands, his thumbs wiping her tears. "Remember your promise, Su-san-nah. You must be strong now."

She sniffed back her tears as she gazed into his eyes. His love for her shone in the depths of his gaze, burning strong and bright.

"Death will not part us," she said fervently. "As long as I live, as long as our child lives, you'll live, too, in our hearts and our thoughts."

Black Wind nodded. *"Ohinniyan, wastelakapi."*

"Ohinniyan," she repeated. "Forever."

She ran her hand through his hair, her fingertips brushing against the eagle feather. *Home*, she thought, *if only she could take Tate Sapa and go home . . .*

"Su-san-nah?"

"Black Wind! Black Wind! What's happening . . ."

It was like being caught in the eye of a hurricane. Wind and darkness swirled around her, yet inside there was a great calm, and then it seemed as if the earth fell out from under her, swallowing her in a great black wave.

Chapter Twenty-three

The blare of a distant siren and the high-pitched howling of the Parkers' golden retriever roused Susannah from a deep sleep. She jerked to a sitting position, her eyes widening in shock and disbelief as she took in her surroundings. She was sitting on the chaise lounge in the side yard off the kitchen, and it was early afternoon.

She shook her head. Either she was hallucinating, or she was home again.

She glanced around, her gaze darting from the high brick wall that surrounded the yard, to the trees and flowers she had painstakingly planted shortly after she first moved in. She heard the sound of a door slamming, the roar of a jet passing overhead.

Had it all been a dream then?

The thought flitted through her mind, making

her almost physically ill. But no, it had been real, as real as the old-fashioned calico dress and dusty moccasins she wore.

"Black Wind." She whispered his name as a sadness too deep for tears engulfed her. She was home, she thought bleakly, only it didn't seem like home anymore. Not when he wasn't there to share it with her.

She glanced at her wrist, hoping to find the prayer feather magically returned to her, but it was gone, and with it her only chance of going back in time, back to the man who had claimed her heart and soul.

With a sob, she sank back on the chaise longue and buried her face in her hands while the tears flowed down her cheeks, unchecked.

Black Wind was gone from her, and she would never see him again, never again feel the gentle touch of his hand, never hear his voice speak her name. It was a pain beyond bearing, made worse by the knowledge that he was dead, that he had been dead for almost a century before she had even been born.

Susannah wrapped her arms around her waist, thinking of her unborn baby, lamenting the fact that her child would never know its father. She wept anew as she realized all that Black Wind would miss, all that they would never share: birthday parties and Christmas, the excitement of watching their child take its first step, the joy of hearing its first word, trips to Disneyland and the zoo, sending their son or daughter off to school.

"Black Wind . . ." she murmured brokenly. "Oh, Black Wind!"

"Su-san-nah. What is wrong?"

His voice. Was she only imagining it?

Not daring to believe, hardly daring to breathe, she looked up and saw him striding toward her, tall and lean and handsome.

Joy flooded her heart and soul as Susannah jumped to her feet and flew into his arms.

"You're here!" She ran her hands over his shoulders, slid her fingertips along his cheeks. "You're here, really here. I don't believe it!"

"Here," Tate Sapa repeated, glancing around. He had awakened beside Susannah. Confused and disoriented, he had left her side to explore his surroundings, confused by the strange-looking house, by the high walls that surrounded him. "Where is here?"

Susannah smiled up at him, thinking how incongruous a Lakota warrior looked standing in the small, neatly landscaped side yard of her condo.

"Welcome to the twentieth century," she said and then, unable to help it, she began to laugh, tears of happiness and relief streaming down her cheeks.

"Su-san-nah?"

At the tone of his voice, the laughter stilled in her throat. "This is where I live," she said. She gestured at the house. "This is my lodge."

Tate Sapa shook his head. "It is not possible. I cannot be here." He looked at the small grassy area enclosed by a high white wall, at the three small trees bearing some sort of yellow fruit that grew in one corner, at the unfamiliar flowers that grew in red clay pots. "I do not belong here."

"I know." She lifted one shoulder and let it fall. "I didn't belong in your time, either. But you'll get used to it."

She glanced around the yard, at the shrubs that hadn't been watered since she left, at the purple pansies and bright yellow tulips wilting in their pots. She was home, really and truly home.

"Come on," she said, taking Black Wind by the hand, "let me show you around."

It was almost more than he could comprehend. He listened to Susannah as she took him on a tour of her dwelling, which was larger than many Lakota lodges combined. Following her from section to section, he wondered if he was in the *Paha Sapa*, lost in some sort of bizarre vision. He saw things that left him feeling dazed—a large square brown box that produced pictures and sound, a tall white box that held food in many odd shapes and sizes and spit out frozen water, another smaller white box she claimed cooked food, another that washed her dishes, others that she said washed and dried her clothes.

He tried to remember the names of these objects, but they eluded his tongue. Strange names for miraculous things beyond his comprehension. No wonder his people had been unable to defeat the *wasichu*, when they were capable of creating such magic. Never in his life had Black Wind imagined such wondrous things existed.

Her bed was large and soft and had a room of

its own. When he stepped inside, he was startled to see his image reflected back at him.

"It's a mirror," Susannah explained.

Black Wind nodded. He had seen his reflection in water, had seen his face in a small round mirror a Lakota woman had taken in trade for a beaver pelt, but he had never seen so much of himself so clearly.

She showed him another room—her office, she called it. He stared at the black-and-white picture on her desk, recognizing his own likeness as the image he had seen in his vision. Looking at it sent a shiver down his spine. He remembered the day he had been forced to stand in front of the guardhouse while two *wasichu* took his photograph. Some of his people believed the white man's black box could capture a piece of their spirit. He had scoffed at such a thing. Now, staring at his image, he wondered if it might be true.

He followed Susannah into the section of her house she called the living room.

"This is a sofa," she said. "Sit down. I'll be right back."

Black Wind sat down, running his hands over the backrest. It was soft and comfortable, covered with cloth unlike anything he had ever seen. The floor beneath his feet was covered with strange material that muffled his footsteps.

Susannah returned a few minutes later. He stared at the container she offered him. A glass of orange juice, she called it. Hesitantly, he took a drink, startled by the tangy sweetness.

"Black Wind?"

He looked at Susannah, then glanced around the room again. There were paintings on the walls, colored images of Susannah standing with a tall, dark-haired man and a woman with hair the same color as Susannah's; another of Susannah grinning up at a tall boy with dark brown hair and blue eyes.

"Those are my parents, Steve and Nancy," Susannah said, "and that's my brother, Rob."

Slowly, he shook his head. "I cannot believe I am here."

"I know." She couldn't believe it, either, couldn't believe she was actually home again, that Black Wind was there, in her house.

She took a deep breath. There were so many things she needed to do, calls to make, mail to answer, bills to pay. Where to start? It was the sound of her stomach growling that made the decision.

"Are you hungry? We could order pizza or something."

"Piz-za?"

"Trust me, you'll love it."

Tate Sapa watched her cross the room and pick up a strange-looking object. He frowned when she poked at it a few times, then began to talk into one end. Moments later, she put it down and returned to the sofa.

"I ordered pepperoni with everything," she said, smiling.

He nodded uncertainly.

Susannah grimaced as she glanced down at her wrinkled dress. The days she had spent in the guardhouse had left her feeling unclean in a way that had nothing to do with dirt.

"Would you like to take a bath?" she asked. "I know I could use one. The pizza won't be here for thirty or forty minutes."

Tate Sapa nodded. A bath he could understand. It had been many days since he had bathed, and he was eager to wash away the stink of the white man's iron house. Placing the empty glass on the table, he followed Susannah down a narrow corridor.

Five minutes later, standing at the edge of what Susannah called a bathtub, watching it fill with steamy water, he wasn't so sure.

"You might as well have some bubbles, too," Susannah remarked. She poured some strawberry-scented bubble bath into the tub, then put the bottle back on the shelf.

Tate Sapa watched, fascinated, as a froth of foam spread over the top of the water.

"We'll have to find you something to wear," Susannah mused, thinking aloud. "You can't run around L.A. dressed in nothing but a breechclout."

Tate Sapa glanced down. His moccasins were dirty and well-worn, his clout stained from his time in the white man's prison. "I have nothing else."

"Well, don't worry about it. I'll go to the mall later and get you something."

"The mall?"

Susannah nodded. "It's like . . . hmm, like a big trading post. You can buy almost anything you need there." She studied him carefully, then stood beside him, mentally measuring his size against her own. "Go ahead and take your bath," she said as she turned off the faucet. "I need to go check my messages."

She reached into a cupboard and pulled out a fluffy green towel. "You dry off with this," she said, dropping the towel on top of the sink. "And wash with this." She handed him a bar of Camay. "It's soap," she explained as she turned off the tap.

Tate Sapa nodded, fascinated by the object that brought hot water into Susannah's lodge any time she wished it.

Left alone, he stared at the foamy water, sniffed the soap. His people had bathed in the river, scrubbing themselves clean with sand.

With a sigh, he took the eagle feather from his hair and placed it on a shelf.

Removing his clout and moccasins, he stepped into the water. In all his life, he had never bathed in anything but a cold river. He smiled with pleasure as the hot water closed over him.

In her office, Susannah switched on her computer, checking the date and time. It was three o'clock, May third. Amazing, she thought. She had spent several months in the past, yet she had been gone from the twentieth century for less than three weeks!

Going outside, she collected her mail, then sat down at her desk and listened to the messages on her answering machine. Six from her agent, three from her editor, about a dozen from Viv, one from her mother, two from her brother, and one from her dentist reminding her it was time for her six-month checkup.

Her mail contained the usual—about a ton of ads and mail-order catalogs, a half-dozen bills, a reminder that her rent was overdue, a letter from her cousin in Stockton, an invitation to a baby shower for a friend at church.

Susannah smiled as she pressed her hand to her stomach. She would have to start planning for the baby soon. She'd need a crib and sheets and blankets and diapers . . . Lordy, she had never changed a diaper in her life. Thank goodness Viv lived nearby.

The sound of the doorbell scattered her thoughts. Tossing the mail onto her desk, she left her office, glancing at the bathroom as she passed by. He'd been in there a long time, she mused. Grabbing her wallet, she went to pay for the pizza.

Placing the box and the sodas on the table, she went into the bathroom to tell Black Wind dinner, such as it was, was ready.

She stopped inside the door. Black Wind was lying back in the bath, his eyes closed, his arms resting on the sides of the tub. Her gaze ran over him, admiring the width of his shoulders, the ropy muscles in his arms. She glanced at the soap. It was still dry.

Kneeling beside the tub, she dipped the soap in the water, then rubbed it over his chest.

With a start, Black Wind opened his eyes. He relaxed visibly when he saw who it was.

Susannah smiled at him as she washed his chest. "Feel good?"

He nodded, a soft sound of pleasure rising in

his throat as her hand moved lower, across his belly, and lower still. "Su-san-nah . . ."

"Want me to stop?" she asked innocently.

"No," he said, his voice husky, "never."

She laughed softly. Tossing the soap into the soap dish, she stood up, stripped off her clothes, then slid into the tub, her legs straddling his.

"Is this one of the white man's customs?" Black Wind asked, drawing her down on top of him.

"Uh-huh. Like it?"

"Very much." One hand slid up her back, while the other covered her breast. Her skin was soft, slick with soapy water. His body hardened as desire spiraled through him.

"Bet I know what you're thinking," Susannah drawled.

"Do you?"

She ran her hands over his shoulders and along his chest, down his arms, reveling in the muscles that quivered at her touch. She could feel his arousal against her belly. "Tate . . ."

He caressed the soft curve of her breast, loving the feel of her warm soapy skin against his palm. "Tell me what you want."

Susannah laughed softly. "Don't you know?"

He grinned at her. "I think I can guess."

"Yes," Susannah replied dryly, "I'll just bet you can. Well, never mind." Bracing her hands on his shoulders, she started to get out of the tub. "I think I've changed my mind."

In the blink of an eye, he had positioned her beneath him so that he straddled her thighs.

"Oh, no, *wastelakapi*," he said, his voice husky

with desire. "You have started this, and now you must finish."

Happiness and laughter welled up within Susannah as she gazed into his eyes, deep dark eyes smoldering with need and desire. Never, in her wildest dreams, had she imagined making love to anyone in a bathtub, much less a Lakota warrior fresh from the nineteenth century.

"Persuade me," she whispered.

"Shall I do this?" One hand caressed her breast. "Or this?" Lowering his head, he ran his tongue over her lower lip, then kissed her.

"Yes," Susannah murmured, "oh, yes."

Heedless of the water that sloshed over the sides of the tub and soaked the floor and the bath mat, or of the pizza getting cold and the sodas getting warm, she took him in her hand and guided him home.

Much later, they sat in the living room eating reheated pepperoni pizza.

Susannah tried not to stare at Black Wind. She wished she could crawl into his mind and see what he was thinking. He had been extraordinarily quiet since they'd made love.

She had slipped into a pair of faded Levi's and a white sweater. Black Wind was wearing only his clout, since he had nothing else.

Earlier, she had taken him on a tour of her apartment, showing him the refrigerator, how to turn the water on and off, how the stove worked (though she doubted he'd be doing much cooking). She had demonstrated how the stereo worked, the TV, the lights. She had warmed the pizza in the microwave, had almost laughed out loud at the look on his face when she showed him how it went in cold and came out warm.

Black Wind had said little, obviously stunned by the wonders of the twentieth century. He had marveled at the idea of having running water, seemed somewhat taken aback by the television. Susannah had tried to imagine what it would be like to see moving pictures for the first time.

He had grunted softly at his first taste of pizza, looked somewhat astonished when he took a drink of 7-Up, which he had apparently mistaken for water.

Now, he sat beside her, his gaze wandering around the room. She wandered what he thought of it. The carpet was French blue, her sofa a blue-and-mauve print. There was a small fireplace, a coffee table covered with magazines she never found time to read, an end table, a lamp, an easy chair in the same print as the sofa. There were pictures of her family on the mantle, a bookcase filled with books, a curio cabinet filled with DeGrazia figurines.

"Black Wind?"

Placing his glass on the coffee table, he turned to face her.

"Are you all right? Can I get you anything?"

Slowly, he shook his head. "I do not belong here, Su-san-nah."

"I know how you feel," Susannah said. "Believe me, I know."

A wry grin flitted across his face. "Yes, I suppose you do. I should have been more understanding."

"You made me feel right at home," she said, snuggling up against him. "I'll try to do the same for you."

"Home." He glanced around the room. Though it was three times the size of his father's lodge, he felt closed in by the walls, alienated by the strangeness of it all.

"I'll go to the mall tomorrow and get you something to wear," she said. "What's your favorite color?"

He shook his head. "I don't know."

"Well, I'll just buy one of each."

"One of each?"

"Shirts."

"Ah."

"And you'll need jeans and underwear and shoes and socks, a toothbrush . . ."

Taté Sapa shook his head as she reeled off the things he would need. "Su-san-nah . . ."

"I'm sorry. I'm just so happy to be home, to have you here. I want to take you out and show you everything."

He forced himself to smile. She had embraced his way of life with courage, accepting his customs and traditions as her own. How could he, a Lakota warrior who had fought the *wasichu*, killed a grizzly, and counted first coup on more than a dozen of his enemies, do less?

Chapter Twenty-four

Susannah couldn't help smiling as she walked into the City Mall. She paused inside the door, embracing the familiar scents and sounds and sights that assailed her senses. Michael Bolton was playing over the speakers. She could smell popcorn and cinnamon rolls. Kids were laughing, a little girl was begging for a cookie, a boy was whining for a Gargoyle. She saw a teenage couple necking on one of the benches.

If there had been one thing she had missed while in the past, it was being able to wander through the mall. She loved to browse the shelves at Waldenbooks and Borders, to spend a few minutes in the Disney Store. She never got out of there without spending a small fortune.

Walking briskly, she made her way to a popular men's shop. In the past, she had occasionally shopped for Troy, but never with the enthusiasm she felt now, shopping for Black Wind. Humming under her breath, she picked out two pairs of blue jeans, a couple of pairs of walking shorts, a variety of colored T-shirts, a green plaid shirt, a dark blue cable-knit sweater, a gray sweatshirt and pants, underwear and socks.

At the shoe store, she picked up a pair of tennis shoes.

Going into the drugstore, she went to the men's department and bought a hairbrush, a comb, a bottle of cologne, and a toothbrush for Black Wind, then stopped by the paperback rack and picked up the latest romance by her favorite author.

Susannah was leaving the mall, laden with several shopping bags, when she passed a maternity shop. She paused a moment, then retraced her steps and entered the store, thinking she would have to call Vivian when she got home and tell her the news. Viv would be thrilled, although how she would explain her absence, and Black Wind, was something Susannah hadn't quite figured out. She would have to call her mother, too, she thought glumly.

When she left the shop thirty minutes later, she had a pair of jeans, three pairs of shorts, and four tops that seemed as big as circus tents. She ran her hand over her stomach, which was still almost flat. Hard to believe that she would ever be big enough to fill out the clothes she had just bought.

A baby. It was incredible.

On the drive home, she realized they would

have to find a new name for Black Wind. He would have to learn to drive a car, get a license, find a job . . .

Susannah laughed softly as she imagined Black Wind filling out a job application. Finding employment might be a little difficult. There weren't too many openings for full-fledged Lakota warriors these days. The thought brought her up short. What was she thinking? She couldn't expect Black Wind to adjust to the twentieth century overnight. She would have to take it slow, let him get used to things gradually.

And while she was helping him adjust to life in the nineties, there were other things that had to be done.

She needed to make an appointment with a doctor.

She had to meet her deadline and get the manuscript in the mail.

At home, she parked the car in the garage, wondering what Black Wind had done in her absence. Susannah hoped he would approve of the clothes she had bought for him.

She found him sitting in the living room, flipping through the channels. She couldn't help grinning at the picture he made sitting there: a nineteenth-century warrior clad in clout and moccasins holding a can of 7-Up in one hand and the remote control in the other. What was there about men and their need to hang on to the remote? And did any of them ever watch a program all the way through?

"Hi." She dropped the packages on the floor

beside the sofa, then bent to kiss him. "Did you miss me?"

"Always," he replied. Placing the soda and the remote on the coffee table, he wrapped his arms around her waist and drew her down onto his lap. "The . . ." he searched his memory for the word ". . . phone rang while you were gone."

"Did you answer it?"

He looked at her as if she had suggested he run naked through the streets.

Susannah kissed him on the cheek. "I'd better see who called. It might be important." She gestured at the packages on the floor. "The stuff in the blue bag is for you. Why don't you go into the bedroom and try on your new clothes? I have about a hundred phone calls to make."

Black Wind glanced at the large blue sack dubiously, then nodded.

Rising, Susannah went into her office to check her machine, then sat back in her chair and stared at the phone.

"Welcome back to the twentieth century," she muttered, and picked up the receiver.

Susannah emerged from her office an hour later. She had called her parents, her brother, and her agent, explaining to one and all that she had felt the need to get away for a while and had, on a whim, gone off on a short vacation to South Dakota. She had assured her parents and her brother that she was fine, assured her agent and her editor that she would get to work on the book ASAP and have it in the mail in sixty days.

Viv hadn't been home, so Susannah had left a

message on her machine, and then called her doctor's office and made an appointment for the following day at four.

Relieved that she had managed to touch bases with all the important people in her life, she left the room, curious to hear what Black Wind thought of his new wardrobe.

She found him sprawled face down on her bed, his new clothes scattered over the foot of the bed and on top of the dresser. It was obvious he had tried them all on, and just as obvious he wasn't crazy about them, since he was still wearing nothing but his clout.

For a moment, she stood in the doorway looking down at him, admiring the width of his shoulders, the broad expanse of his back, his long, long legs. She thought of stretching out beside him and kissing him awake, but he looked so peaceful, she decided to let him rest.

Picking up his jeans, she tossed them in the washer to take out the stiffness, then went into her office and switched on her computer. Much as she might wish it, the book wouldn't write itself.

Black Wind woke abruptly. He stared at the pale blue walls around him, momentarily disoriented, and then he remembered where he was.

Getting to his feet, he glanced at the clothes Susannah had brought him. The pants, which had felt stiff and uncomfortable, were missing. He wasn't sure what the white things were. They reminded him of his clout. He had regarded them a moment, then tossed them aside. The shirts were soft, the colors unlike any he had ever seen.

He cocked his head to the side, listening intently. The house was quiet, and he wondered if Susannah had gone out again.

Barefooted, he padded down the hallway to her office and looked inside. She was sitting at her desk. She had showed him her computer, told him it was where she worked. She had even read him a part of the story she was writing. He had been fascinated by her ability to write things down. The Lakota kept an oral record of their stories and lineage, passing them down from generation to generation, but parts were sometimes changed or forgotten.

She was unaware of his presence. Standing in the doorway, he watched her for a long time. Sometimes she spoke out loud; sometimes she sat back in her chair and stared at the computer; once she picked up a book and thumbed through it, muttering something under her breath. She had told him it was a book about the history of the Old West and had promised to read him the parts that referred to his people.

He lost track of time as he stood there, watching her, his mind wandering. It was hard to believe that he was in Susannah's house, that all he knew was gone, swept away by the hand of time, that everyone he had known, everyone he had loved, was long dead. He glanced around her office and saw nothing that was familiar. Only Susannah.

What was he to do here, in this place? He was a warrior, born and bred. Did she expect him to stay here, in her house, day after day, with nothing to do? It was not his way, to be idle. He could not spend his days sitting on her sofa, watching the strange pictures that moved and talked, staring at images he didn't fully understand.

Black Wind thought of his unborn child and wished he knew how to read and write so he could record the stories and legends of his people as he knew them. He would like to preserve his memory of the battles the Lakota had fought and won as well as those that had been fought and lost, to write of the beauty of the *Paha Sapa* while it was fresh in his mind. His child would never know its grandfather, and he wished he had the ability to write about his father's bravery so his child would know what a courageous warrior his grandfather had been. He would like to write of Mato Mani's ability to heal the sick and foretell the future, and of his father's brother, Hehaka Luta, who had gone to seek a vision and never returned. Some said *Wakan Tanka* had spirited Hehaka Luta into another world. Tate Sapa shook his head. Once, he would have said such a thing was impossible, but no more.

There were so many things his son or daughter should know. Songs and stories and legends. He knew Susannah would write them for him if he asked her to, but he felt a sudden inexplicable need to do it himself. Perhaps Susannah would teach him how.

"Black Wind. How long have you been standing there?"

He shrugged. "Not long."

"Well, I need a break." She stood up and

crossed the floor, her arms wrapping around his waist. "How about some lunch?"

He nodded, then followed her into the kitchen. Sitting at the table, he watched her pull things from the refrigerator. She explained what they were as she put them on the counter.

"Mayonnaise, mustard, Swiss cheese, avocado, ham, tomato, onion."

He nodded, repeating each word.

Susannah pulled a loaf of bread from the bread box. "I made an appointment with the doctor," she said as she cut the tomato into thin slices. "Do you want to go with me?"

"Doctor?" He looked at her sharply. "Are you sick?"

"No, but I am pregnant, remember? I need to go in for an examination, and I'd like for you to be there."

Tate Sapa stared at her. Among the Lakota, childbirth was left to the women. Knowing he would only be in the way, a man often went hunting while his woman was in labor. "Is it the white man's way, to take part in such things?"

"Well, not always. You don't have to go with me if you'd rather not. It's just that I'd feel better if you were there."

"I will go."

She smiled at him as she handed him a plate and a glass of iced tea. "It's a sandwich," she said. "Hope you like it."

She sat down at the table across from him, and he watched Susannah pick up the sandwich and take a bite. Following her example, Black Wind did the same, chewing slowly.

Susannah grinned at him. "So, what do you think?"

"It is . . . *waste*," he replied. "Good."

"Wait until you taste my chocolate pie," she said, smiling.

He nodded, but his mind was not on food.

"Su-san-nah, will you take me to see the *Paha Sapa?*"

"Of course."

"Do my people still live there?"

"No, the hills belong to the government now. I have a book about the history of the Black Hills somewhere. Do you want to see it?"

Tate Sapa nodded.

Susannah left the table, returning a few minutes later with a small book. Sitting down, she opened to the first page. "It says here that the Lakota signed a treaty at Fort Laramie in 1868 that set apart a large tract of land known as the Great Sioux Reservation."

Tate Sapa nodded. "I know of this treaty."

"It says that the Sioux were guaranteed 'absolute and undisturbed use and occupation.' Then, in 1874, Custer and a military expedition went into the hills to survey the area and found gold." She skipped down a few sentences. "In 1875, President Grant sent the Allison Commission to negotiate with the Sioux to purchase the Black Hills. They offered the Sioux six million dollars, but the Lakota refused to sell. After that, prospectors started pouring into the hills in search of gold. It says here that in 1876 a handful of Lakota signed an agreement to sell the hills . . ."

"My people sold the *Paha Sapa* to the *wasichu*? I do not believe it."

"Well, the sale wasn't considered valid since most of the adult males refused to sign."

Tate Sapa nodded. He could not imagine his people selling the sacred hills. They were the heart of the People, the spiritual center of the Lakota.

"Anyway," Susannah went on, "in 1877, the United States Congress passed the Black Hills Act, which put ownership of the hills in white hands. From 1920 to the present, the Lakota have been trying to regain ownership of the hills. According to this, the battle is still being fought."

"When can we go?"

"Do you need to go right away? I've got to get this book finished."

"There is no hurry," he replied with a wry grin. "The *Paha Sapa* will wait."

Later that day, after finishing up a chapter on her book, Susannah thought again about finding a Christian name for Black Wind. She didn't want to hurt him, didn't want to offend him in any way. She knew how hard it was going to be for him to adjust to her lifestyle, harder for him, perhaps, than it had been for her. She, at least, had had some knowledge of life in the past.

Shutting down her computer, she sought him out. He was looking at the pictures in the book on the Black Hills.

He glanced up as she entered the room. "It is a good thing, to know how to read and write. Will you teach me?"

"Sure. You'll have to be patient with me, though. I've never tried to teach anyone." She smiled, pleased that he wanted to learn, that he seemed to be willing to accept her way of life. Perhaps it wouldn't be as difficult a transition as she feared. A new name would be a good place to start.

"Black Wind, what would you think of taking a Christian name?"

He frowned at her. "What is that?"

"A first name, like my first name is Susannah and my last name is Kingston."

"I have a name."

"I know, but I think most Indians today have a Christian name and an Indian name, like, well, like this." She pointed to a page in the book. "See, this is a quote by an Indian named John Two Bulls."

"You think I should have a Christian name?"

"Well, it might be easier to introduce you to people."

"What name?"

"Gee, I don't know. . . . I've always liked the name Daniel. I was thinking it would be a nice name for the baby, if it's a boy."

"Daniel." He repeated it slowly. It felt strange on his tongue.

"If you don't like Daniel, I have a whole book full of names," Susannah said. "We could look at them later."

"I will be Daniel for you," he said, "if that is what you wish."

Susannah's shoulders slumped. "I'm not trying to change you, or steal your identity, honest. It's just that it's going to be hard enough to explain who you are, and I thought it would be easier if you had a Christian name like everyone else."

"It is all right, Su-san-nah," he said bleakly, and rising to his feet, he left the room.

Susannah stared after him. "Damn, that didn't go well at all," she muttered, and then wondered if maybe her timing had been wrong. After all, he'd barely had a chance to get used to being in a different century, and she was after him to change his name, which was practically the only thing he had left.

With a sigh, she went after him.

He was in the living room, staring out the front window, watching three boys playing catch in the street.

"I'm sorry," Susannah said. She put her arms around him and placed her cheek against his back. "You don't have to take a new name. It was wrong of me to suggest it."

He placed his hands over hers. "It is all right, Su-san-nah. I will have to get used to living here, in your time, as you learned to live in mine."

"Black Wind, please don't be unhappy."

"I am not unhappy." He turned in her arms. "I just feel . . . lost."

"I know, but it'll get easier in time. I promise."

He nodded, but she had the feeling he didn't believe her.

Just then, the phone rang. She felt Black Wind start at the sound, then relax. She gave him a quick kiss on the cheek, then went to answer the phone. It was Vivian.

"Where have you been, girl?" Viv asked. "I've

been calling you for days."

"I went out of town unexpectedly," Susannah replied, grinning.

"Well, you might have called. I imagined all sorts of terrible things."

"No, I'm fine." She looked at Black Wind and smiled. "Better than fine."

"So, where'd you go?"

"I took a trip to South Dakota."

"Really? Whatever for?"

Susannah hesitated a moment, then grinned. "Research."

"What aren't you telling me?"

"I met a man while I was there," Susannah said, glancing over at Black Wind, who was watching her curiously.

"Tell me everything!"

"Well . . ." Susannah drawled, her gaze moving over Black Wind, "he's got long, long legs and the broadest shoulders I've ever seen. His hair is black, and his skin is a dark copper color. He's the most handsome man I've ever seen, and I love him desperately."

"Tall, dark, and handsome," Viv said, and Susannah could hear the smile in her voice. "Are you going to see him again?"

"Well, actually, I brought him home with me."

"Well, that's some souvenir," Vivian remarked dryly. "Sounds serious, girlfriend. Is it?"

"Very."

"When do I get to meet him?"

"Soon, I promise. Listen, I've got to go. I'll call you tomorrow, okay?"

"Okay. You behave yourself now, hear?"

"Right. Bye, Viv."

"Bye."

Susannah hung up the receiver, frowning. She had only been gone for a couple of weeks, yet she was more than a couple of weeks pregnant. How was she going to explain it? She supposed she could always fall back on the old explanation and say the baby was premature. Since she hadn't begun to show much yet, she might get away with it.

She looked up to find Black Wind watching her intently. "That was Vivian. She's my best friend."

Tate Sapa nodded. "Am I?" he mused, "the most handsome man you've ever seen?"

"Definitely." Crossing the room, she slid her arms around his waist. "You've been here for two days. Would you like to go out and take a look around?"

"Yes, I think I would like that."

Pulling back a little, she looked him up and down, then grinned. "Maybe you'd better put some clothes on first."

A short time later, they left the house. Black Wind looked virile and handsome in a pair of jeans and a dark blue T-shirt. He had tried on the tennis shoes, then put on his moccasins.

He stared at her car, obviously reluctant to get inside.

"Unlike that horse you made me ride, my car won't bite you," she said, sliding behind the wheel. "Come on, get in."

Taking a deep breath, Black Wind ducked inside and sat down.

"Shut the door."

She arranged his seat belt, patted his arm reassuringly. "Don't be alarmed by the noise the engine makes, okay? It's a little loud, but harmless."

He flinched as the engine hummed to life, clenched his hands as she backed out of the garage. "Where do you want to go?" she asked.

"Go?"

"The mall? A movie? Or just for a drive?"

Black Wind shook his head. "You choose."

"The mall, I think."

Black Wind nodded. She had mentioned this place several times, had gone there to buy his clothes. He was curious to see what it was, this mall. He stared straight ahead as she pulled out of the driveway onto the street, his hands clutching the edge of the seat. His trepidation turned to amazement and then delight as the car picked up speed. The fleetest pony he had ever owned had not been able to travel at such great speed.

Susannah smiled at the look of enjoyment on Black Wind's face. Bypassing the mall, she decided to take him for a short ride on the freeway, then circle back.

He looked a little alarmed as cars began whizzing by on both sides, but he was soon urging her to go faster. Men and cars, she thought, and knew there was at least one thing about the nineties that he was going to love.

Later, they walked through the mall. Susannah tried to see it through Black Wind's eyes—the bookstores, the dress shops, the Candy Factory, the Disney Store. He stopped at every window, peering inside, asking dozens of questions. She took him into the bookstore and showed him her book on the shelf. From there, they went into the Candy Factory, where she bought several varieties of chocolates so he could try them out. They stopped in one of the men's shops and he walked up and down the aisles, staring at the mannequins, examining the suits and ties, touching everything. She heard him mutter something about the white man wearing too many clothes.

They took the escalator to the second floor. Black Wind was hesitant to step on it at first, and then, when they reached the top, he wanted to go back down. Susannah was happy to oblige, and they rode up and down the escalator three times.

"Remarkable," Tate Sapa remarked.

At the food park, Susannah bought a double scoop of chocolate ice cream for herself, a scoop of chocolate and one of vanilla for Black Wind. He watched her take a lick of hers, then did the same.

"Good?" she asked, and he nodded, too busy eating to reply.

He watched the people coming and going, amazed at their number, stared at a young woman who had purple hair. The man with her had shaved his head except for one long yellow strip in the middle. He saw women wearing hardly anything at all, and others who wore long flowing robes that covered them from their neck to their ankles.

"It is quite amazing, this world of yours," he remarked when they were on the way home. "So many strange things to see. No wonder you were so anxious to come back to your own time."

"Well, I did miss it," Susannah admitted, "but I'd have been happy to stay in the past with you." She bit down on her lower lip. "But you're not going to be happy here, are you?"

"I am happy to be with you."

"That's not what I asked."

"I do not think I will ever belong here."

"Don't say that. You've only been here a couple of days. Give yourself some time to get used to it."

"I have no other choice," he replied, his voice wistful and resigned at the same time.

Susannah nodded, but, deep inside, she wondered if that was true. She thought of the prayer feather hanging on a nail in her bedroom. The feather had carried her to the past, and brought Black Wind to the present. Might it not also take him home again if he wished to go?

Dr. Fries smiled as Susannah entered his office and sat down next to Black Wind.

"Well," he said, "everything appears to be fine, just fine." He handed her a slip of paper. "I want you to start taking prenatal vitamins right away. You don't smoke, do you? Good, good. He paused to thumb through the file on his desk. "I guess that's it. I'll want to see you once a month for the next few months, and then every week. Any questions?"

Susannah glanced at Black Wind. She wanted to ask the doctor if traveling through time would affect the baby, but couldn't bring herself to say the words out loud for fear of sounding like a lunatic. "No, I don't think so."

The doctor looked at Black Wind. "Do you have any questions?"

Black Wind shook his head, still somewhat stunned by the ride in the elevator. The building was larger than anything he had ever seen, filled with people who seemed to be in a hurry. He had sat in the waiting room while Susannah went in to see the *wasichu shaman*, conscious of the curious stares of the other people in the room. Even though he was dressed in jeans and a T-shirt, he knew he stood out from the others. And not just because of the color of his skin. There were people in the room with skin darker than his. He wondered if they knew, as he did, that he didn't belong there.

"Well, then." The doctor stood up and shook hands with Black Wind. "I'll see you next month, Susannah," he said, giving her a hug. "Give my regards to your family for me."

Susannah smiled at him. Jay Fries had been her mother's obstetrician, too. "I will. Thanks, Dr. Jay."

"Three months," she mused as they rode down in the elevator. "I didn't realize I was so far along." She glanced down at her stomach. "I hardly show at all," she remarked, and shook her head. It was amazing. She was three months pregnant, yet she'd been gone less than a month in her own time. She tried to figure out the time ratio between past and present, but it was impossible. She hadn't tried to keep track of time while in the past and had no idea how long she'd spent there. Did it really matter?

Black Wind's hand tightened around hers as the elevator lurched to a stop on the main floor.

"You okay?" Susannah asked, grinning up at him.

"Okay? What is okay?"

"It means all right. Are you all right?"

"I am all right," he replied, returning her grin. "Boxes that go up and down. Stairs that move. Has it always been so with the *wasichu*?"

"Not always."

He found that hard to believe. The *wasichu*, it seemed, could do anything. They made cars that went faster than a fleet pony and built buildings taller than the Devil's Tower. Susannah had placed his new leggings in one of her machines and they had come out soft and warm and dry.

Susannah fell suddenly silent on the drive home, making Black Wind wonder if there was something she wasn't telling him. He glanced at her several times, noting the worry lines on her brow, the way she chewed on her lower lip.

He followed her into the house, afraid the *wasichu shaman* had given her bad news that she didn't want to share.

"Su-san-nah?"

"Hmm?"

"What is wrong?"

"Wrong? Nothing."

He crossed the room and gathered her into his arms. "Something is bothering you. Can you not tell me what it is?"

"I was just thinking about my mother. She's going to be upset when she finds out I'm pregnant."

"Does she not like children?" he asked, astonished at the idea.

"It's not that. She's kind of old-fashioned." That was putting it mildly, Susannah mused. No doubt her mother would faint when she found out her only daughter was living with a man and was going to have a baby.

Susannah sighed. She loved her mother, she really did, but they hadn't gotten along since Susannah turned fifteen. Nothing Susannah had ever done had been right as far as her mother was concerned. She had hoped Susannah would become a doctor or a lawyer, something that would, in her mother's opinion "contribute something worthwhile to the world." She did *not* consider writing romance novels worthwhile.

"What is old-fashioned?"

"She thinks girls should get married before they get pregnant."

"We are married," Tate Sapa remarked. "You are my woman."

"I know."

Susannah wrapped her arms around Black Wind's waist and smiled up at him. She was a big girl now. She didn't need her mother's permission to fall in love; she no longer needed to earn her mother's approval.

And then Black Wind bent his head and kissed her. He might not feel at home in the twentieth century, Susannah mused, but he certainly knew his way around her heart. He deepened the kiss, stoking her desire, making her knees go weak.

She melted against him, everything else forgotten in the joy that engulfed her as he swept her into his arms and carried her to bed.

Chapter Twenty-five

Tate Sapa stood at the window in the living room, staring out into the darkness beyond.

With a sigh, he watched the cars pass by, marveling again at the wondrous machines the white man had created. He had learned much in the past few days. There seemed to be nothing the *wasichu* could not do. They had great ships that crossed the oceans, airplanes that soared through the skies, cars that traveled long distances faster than he had ever dreamed of going. The white man's weapons were far more deadly now than the rifles and cannons they had used to make war against his people. Susannah had told him of bombs that could destroy thousands of people in a matter of moments, missiles that could sow destruction in lands thousands of miles away. The *wasichu* were still trying to conquer the world, he thought bleakly, never content with what they had, where they had been born, always wanting more.

Black Wind lifted a hand to the window, feeling the smooth, cool glass beneath his palm. There was nothing in this time that was familiar to him, nothing save Susannah. He spoke her language, yet there were many words he heard that he did not understand, words that had meant one thing in his time and now conveyed a different meaning. Every fiber of his being yearned for home, for the vastness of the plains, for the sound of his native tongue, for the taste of food and drink that was familiar. He missed the scent of roasting buffalo meat, of sage and sweet grass. He longed for the freedom of riding across the vast sunlit prairie, for the stillness of the hills when snow lay heavy upon the ground.

Feeling as though the pale blue walls were closing in around him, he went into the bedroom, noting that his footsteps made no sound on the thick carpet. He plucked the prayer feather from the nail beside the bed and slipped the loop over his wrist. For a moment, he gazed down at Susannah, who was sleeping soundly, one hand tucked beneath her cheek. Resisting the urge to reach down and touch her, he left the house.

Outside, he drew in a deep breath, and then he began walking. The concrete was hard and cold beneath his moccasins, and Black Wind moved off the sidewalk onto the grass that grew along the edge of the cement, wondering why the *wasichu* avoided walking on Mother Earth.

A full moon hung low in the sky. Streetlamps made small pools of pale yellow light at intervals along the sidewalk. Walking briskly, he passed one house after another. Now and then, dogs barked at him. Occasionally, a car drove by, the growl of the engine breaking the silence of the night.

He walked faster and faster, until he was running, his footsteps muffled by the thick grass along the parkway. He ran for miles until he came to a large expanse of grass and trees. A few benches were scattered about. There was a small grassy mound beneath a weeping willow.

He made his way to the rise and sat down. Staring into the darkness, he wondered how he would ever fit into Susannah's world. There was nothing for him to do here, in Susannah's time. There was no need for a warrior; his skill with bow and arrow and lance were useless. Men did not hunt for game in this place; she had no enemies for him to fight, no need for his protection. How long would she love him, respect him, when he was no better than the coffee coolers who hung around at Fort Laramie, hoping the *wasichu* would give them whiskey?

He ran his fingers over the smooth spine of the eagle feather, felt it grow warm in his hand.

Only think of home, wish to be there, and I will take you back.

He heard the words clearly in his mind and knew that the power to go back to his own people, his own time, rested in his hands. He pictured the majestic beauty of the *Paha Sapa*. The Lakota called the sacred hills *Wamakaognaka*

E'cante, the heart of everything that is. It was the burying place of his ancestors, whose bodies turned to dust, returning to the earth from whence they came, making the ground holy. His people never lived in the hills, but camped on the plains. They cut their lodge poles from the trees that grew in abundance on the mountains, always leaving an offering to the gods in their place, never taking more than was needed.

In the hills to the south was a place called the Wind Cave. Sometimes, if a man listened carefully enough, he could hear the soft sound of Mother Earth breathing through the cave. An old Indian legend claimed that the first buffalo had been born within the womb of the cavern.

The *Paha Sapa* was the home of the Thunder Beings, who brought rain and thunder and lightning to make the earth green and fertile. He wondered if, in this time and place, his people still climbed the sacred mountains to pray.

To the north of the hills, standing apart from the *Paha Sapa* but still a part of them, was Bear Butte, another place that was sacred to the Lakota. Its rocks and pines rose high above the plains in lofty splendor. The leaders of his people had often gone there to seek the guidance of the Great Spirit.

But it was the memory of the *Paha Sapa* that symbolized all he was, all he had loved and lost, all that he yearned for. He thought of his people, of the young men who had been eager for war, of his father's wisdom, of Mato Mani's reverence and power. All were dead now, yet he knew if he returned to his own time, he would find them as he had left them, alive and on the brink of war with the *wasichu*.

And then, like a fox returning to its den, his thoughts turned to Susannah. He could not leave her now, not when she was carrying his child. The very thought of her bearing his son or daughter filled him with awe. There was nothing he could do to help his people. Their fate had already been determined. He would stay with Susannah until the child was born and then he would go back where he belonged. He only hoped Susannah would not hate him for his decision. It humbled him to know she was stronger than he was, that she had been able to adjust far better to his time than he could to hers. But he feared he would never belong here, in this place. He was a warrior in a time that had no need of warriors.

He felt the mystic power drain from the feather as he made his decision. Heavy hearted, he left the park and retraced his steps back to Susannah's lodge, wondering if, in deciding to remain in Susannah's world, he had forever lost the ability to return to his own.

He heard her voice as soon as he stepped into the living room.

"Black Wind, is that you?" She stood up and turned on the light beside the sofa. "I've been so worried."

"Su-san-nah, it is late. You should be sleeping."

"How could I sleep? I woke up and you were gone. Are you all right? Where have you been?"

"I could not sleep."

"Is something wrong?"

He shook his head, wondering how to explain it to her. The bed was too soft. The sounds of the night were unfamiliar. He missed the sighing of the wind through the cottonwood trees, the occasional bark of the camp dogs, the snuffling of the warhorse he had kept tied outside his lodge, the company of his father, the camaraderie of the young men.

"Can't you tell me?"

He shrugged. "The bed is too soft. The night is filled with strange sounds."

"Give yourself some time to get used to things. It's only been a few days."

She wrapped her arms around his waist, wishing she could think of a way to make him feel more at home in her time, thinking, again, how much easier it had been for her to go back in time than it had been for him to come forward. "I wish there was something I could do."

"Su-san-nah, are there no Lakota in your world?"

"Of course there are."

"Where are they?"

"Gee, I don't know. I suppose most of them are on reservations in South Dakota or Montana, I'm not sure which. Maybe when I get this book finished, we could take a trip there."

"I would like that."

"I've never seen a reservation," she replied slowly, "but I've been told they aren't very nice. There's a lot of poverty. . . . That is, most of the Indians don't have very much. A lot of them are alcoholics." Susannah frowned, knowing he wouldn't understand the word. "They drink too

375

much whiskey because they don't have a way to support their families. Do you understand what I'm trying to say?"

Tate Sapa nodded. In his time, there had been warriors who drank too much of the white man's firewater, men desperate for drink who had sold their women for whiskey, thereby bringing shame and disgrace to their families.

"I understand." He looked thoughtful a moment. "You said an old man gave you the prayer feather. I would like to meet him."

"I don't really know who he was. I met him at a powwow." She frowned. "I think I told you, he looked an awful lot like your father."

"Can we go there?"

"It's over now, but we might be able to find another powwow," she said, seeing his disappointment.

"I must find the man who gave you the feather."

"Why?"

He shrugged. "I do not know."

"Well, we might be able to find him. I still have the ad from the newspaper. Maybe I can find out where they were going next."

"Will you try?"

Susannah nodded, feeling a heaviness born of fear of what he might find. "I'll see what I can find out."

Chapter Twenty-six

As luck, or fate, would have it, there was a pow-wow at the Orange County Fairgrounds the following weekend.

Susannah felt a strong sense of foreboding as she parked the car. She glanced at Black Wind, who was wearing a pair of jeans, a white T-shirt, and his moccasins. The eagle feather was tied in his hair.

She felt a shiver of apprehension as they walked toward the fairgrounds. Did he feel it, too, or was it only her own unspoken fears making themselves known? In spite of his clothing, there was no mistaking the fact that Black Wind was a full-blooded Indian. Even now, surrounded by other Native Americans, he stood out from the rest like a mustang in a herd of draft horses. There was an arrogance about him, an inherent wildness, that set him apart.

"I guess we may as well start at this end," Susannah suggested. Several dozen booths stretched ahead of them, displaying the same types of crafts and souvenirs she had seen at the last powwow.

Tate Sapa nodded. It was exhilarating to be surrounded by Indians, to hear the sound of drums. Two men dressed in elaborate dance costumes walked by and he stared after them, astonished by the brilliant colors they wore and by the sound of his native tongue.

Following Susannah, he passed booths filled with Navajo baskets, another that held a variety of Hopi kachina dolls, some no taller than the length of his finger, others several times larger. There were eagle dancers and clowns and mud men. One booth displayed several bows and quivers of arrows, another had a half-dozen war shields, ceremonial pipes, and bear-claw necklaces.

He paused at a booth displaying a number of elaborately beaded vests, fringed leggings, belts, and several pairs of moccasins. He lifted one, recognizing it as belonging to the Cheyenne. Another was of Crow design. They were all old, faded, and worn.

"Can I help you?"

Tate Sapa looked at the man behind the counter, then glanced at Susannah.

"We're just looking," she said. "Thanks."

"Those are genuine Crow moccasins, circa 1881. I can let you have 'em for, oh, a hundred and fifty dollars."

"They're very nice," Susannah replied with a polite smile, "but we're just looking."

"Why would anyone want to buy old moccasins?" Tate Sapa asked as they turned away from the booth.

"Some people collect that kind of thing."

Tate Sapa glanced down at his own well-worn moccasins and shook his head.

Susannah grinned at him. "Native American stuff is very 'in' now. Very popular. Books, movies . . ." She shrugged. "Lots of people are becoming concerned with the condition of the earth and have begun to have an appreciation for the way the Indians took care of the land."

Tate Sapa grunted softly. Times had changed, indeed.

They passed several booths. He paused occasionally, his gaze lingering over familiar objects—a tortoiseshell rattle, a flute carved from cedar wood, a bone-handled knife, a buckskin medicine bag, a willow backrest. One booth displayed a buffalo robe. A wave of homesickness rose within him as he ran his hand over the shaggy hide.

Moving on, he saw other things that looked familiar yet different—dream catchers in brilliant shades of blue and red, orange and green, drums of all sizes, headdresses made of colorful feathers.

"Well, I don't see him anywhere," Susannah said. "Maybe he's not here. Do you want to go watch the dancing?"

Tate Sapa nodded. Hand in hand, they turned

away from the concession stands and made their way to the dance arena.

Tate Sapa stared in wonder at the dancers. Costumes from many tribes were represented, but he could not recall ever having seen bustles, feathers, and fans in such vibrant colors—brilliant reds and yellows, bright orange and green, vivid shades of blue, a clean pure white.

The sound of the drum seemed to penetrate deep within him, echoing the beat of his homesick heart. He heard the sweet welcome sound of his native tongue as the singer began to sing, and, for a moment, he was back in his own time.

He watched the women dance, their movements delicate and understated, the fringe on their long shawls swaying with the rhythm of their steps. Later, the men entered the circle, the tempo of the dance steps increasing with the beat of the drum. He was tempted to shake Susannah's hand from his arm and yield to the urge to join in the dancing, to feel the excitement flow through him as he executed the intricate steps, to feel the heartbeat of the earth beneath his moccasins.

The drumming built to a crescendo, then ceased, and the dancers left the circle, going to join their friends and families.

Tate Sapa glanced at the spectators, surprised to see so many whites and Indians intermingling, and then he remembered what Susannah had said about the *wasichu* and their interest in Native American crafts and customs—an interest that had come a hundred years too late to help his people, he thought ruefully.

He was about to suggest they leave when his gaze settled on a man he recognized.

"Is something wrong?" Susannah asked, frowning. "You look like you've seen a ghost."

Tate Sapa shook his head. "How is this possible?"

"How is what possible?"

"He disappeared five winters ago. He went on a vision quest and never returned. We thought he had been killed."

Susannah followed Black Wind's gaze, felt a cold chill slide down her spine when she saw the Indian who had given her the eagle feather. "You know him?"

"He is Hehaka Luta, my father's brother."

"That explains it, then," Susannah said. "I thought your father looked familiar when I met him. Now I know why. But how did he get here?"

"I do not know. There were some among our people who said *Wakan Tanka* had carried him away. Perhaps he is indeed a ghost."

"Well, there's only one way to find out," Susannah said pragmatically. "Come on."

Tate Sapa shook his head, his gaze fixed on the old man. Could this truly be Hehaka Luta's ghost? But no, he was speaking to a young girl, nodding to someone passing by. Surely a ghost could not be seen, especially by the *wasichu*.

"Are you coming?" Susannah asked, puzzled. He had been anxious to find the old man only minutes before. Why was he hesitating now?

Slowly, Tate Sapa made his way toward the old man. "*Hau, ate,*" he murmured.

"*Hau, tunska,*" the old man replied, an enormous smile spreading over his face as he clasped Tate Sapa's forearm, then embraced him. "So, *tunska*," the old man said jubilantly, "you are here at last." He released Black Wind and took a step back, his gaze running over the younger man from head to foot. "I had almost given up hope."

"You have been waiting for me?"

The old man nodded. He looked at Susannah, including her in his smile of welcome. "I knew the woman would bring you to me."

"Hello." Susannah came to stand beside Black Wind. She smiled tremulously at the old man.

"So, we meet again. Did you enjoy your visit to the past?"

"How do you know about that?" Susannah exclaimed.

"We must talk," the old man said, "but not here. Come, *tunska*, I have a trailer where we can speak in private."

Tate Sapa's mind was whirling as he followed Hehaka Luta across the fairgrounds to the parking lot and into a small trailer.

"Sit down," Hehaka Luta invited. "Are you hungry?"

Tate Sapa shook his head. "No." He sat down at the table, and Susannah sat down beside him.

Hehaka Luta pulled three cans of root beer from the fridge, then sat down across from Susannah and Black Wind.

"I have much to tell you," Hehaka Luta said. He handed them each a can of soda.

"We thought you were dead," Tate Sapa remarked. He looked at the can, then set it aside.

"I shall tell you my story, and then I will answer your questions. Shortly after the death of your mother and your sister, I went to the *Paha Sapa* to seek guidance. While I was there, *Wakan Tanka* spoke to me. He told me I must leave the people, that I would take a journey far into the future. He told me I was to prepare a place for the warrior who would follow me, a warrior who had been chosen to help our people, one who was brave and pure in heart, who would join me in the future. This man would learn the *wasichu* language so that he could record the history of our people while it was yet fresh within his mind. This man would go to the reservation and remind our young men what it meant to be a warrior. He would restore their pride in their heritage and teach them those things that have been lost."

Hehaka Luta paused, his dark eyes intent upon Black Wind's face. "You are that one."

Tate Sapa shook his head. "Why me?"

"You have always been a leader among our people. I have learned much since I have been here. There is tension between our people—contemporary Indians against those who hold to traditional ways, full-bloods against mixed-bloods. Thousands of our people live on reservations. More than half have no way to earn a living. They drink too much. Babies are born sickly. Many die. Only a few years ago, the white man's law would not allow us to practice our religion. Our children were forbidden to speak Lakota."

"What can I do? I am only one man. I cannot right the wrongs that have been done."

"You are young and strong and proud. If your

heart is good for our people, *Wakan Tanka* will show you what must be done."

Tate Sapa lifted a hand to the feather in his hair. "Was it my prayer feather that brought you here?"

"Yes. *Wakan Tanka* told me I must take the feather from the burial ground. He told me that a woman would come seeking *Wanbli*'s feather. He said I would know her when I saw her. He told me that her love for you would bring you here, where you are needed."

Hehaka Luta smiled at Susannah. "You love my nephew, do you not?"

"Yes, very much."

The old man looked at Tate Sapa. "And you love her?"

Tate Sapa nodded.

Hehaka Luta nodded, and then frowned. "But you are not happy here. You wish to go back."

"I have thought of it." At his words, he felt Susannah go suddenly still. He had never told her of the night in the park, when he had held the prayer feather in his hand, felt the power warm to his touch.

Hehaka Luta glanced at the eagle feather in Tate Sapa's hair. "You have the power to return to your own time," he said quietly. "But I warn you, *tunska*, should you choose to go back, you will not be able to return to this place."

"I understand, Uncle."

"I know what you are thinking, what you are feeling." Hehaka Luta took a drink of his soda, then smacked his lips. *"Waste,"* he remarked, grinning. "This is a strange place, nephew. Right now you think you will never belong here. But I tell you from my heart that you are needed here, that you can be happy here if you will let go of the past and learn to live in the white man's world."

"I will never be a white man. I am Lakota."

Hehaka Luta nodded. "That is why you are needed in this place. Your heart and soul are Lakota. You must help our people understand that they can live in the *wasichu* world without sacrificing their pride in their heritage. You must help our young men and women find their way back to the true path, the life path. Many have strayed from it."

"I will think on it, Uncle."

"I have a small ranch on the outskirts of Pine Ridge. It is in your name. Should you decide to stay, it is yours." The old man sighed. "I have done what *Wakan Tanka* asked of me, nephew. The rest is up to you. I know you will make the right decision, *tunska*. Our people have always depended on your loyalty and your wisdom. I know you will not fail them now."

Hehaka Luta stood up. "I must get back to my booth."

Tate Sapa stood up and embraced his uncle. *"Toksha ake wacinyuanktin ktelo, ate."*

The old man smiled. "And I will see you again." He winked at Susannah. "Both of you."

Tate Sapa stared after the old man. For five winters, they had thought Hehaka Luta dead, and all the time he had been here, waiting.

With a sigh, he faced Susannah. "Come," he said, holding out his hand. "I wish to leave."

He was silent on the drive home, his thoughts turned inward.

Susannah kept silent as well, knowing that this was a decision he had to make for himself. The thought that he might leave her, that he might return to his own time, left her feeling cold and hollow inside.

She parked the car and started for the front door, stopping when she realized Black Wind wasn't following her. "Are you coming?" she asked.

"I am going for a walk."

She waited, hoping he would ask her to go with him. When he didn't, she opened the door and went into the house. Kicking off her shoes, she went into her office and switched on her computer. One of the things she loved about writing was being able to lose herself in another world. Times when she was unhappy or blue, she could escape into her make-believe world where happiness was guaranteed and, sooner or later, there would be a happy ending.

But for once, the magic was gone. All she could think about was Black Wind. She knew he was considering what the old man had said, that he was deciding whether to stay in the present or return to the past. Had he been at home, in his own time, he would have gone up into the Black Hills to ask *Wakan Tanka* for guidance. Where would he go now?

Switching off the computer, Susannah went into the bedroom and stretched out on the bed. Feeling empty and alone, she stared up at the ceiling. If he wanted to go back, she wouldn't try to stop him. As much as she needed him, as much as she would miss him, she wanted his happiness more than her own, and if he could not be happy here, then she would let him go.

She couldn't stifle the sob that rose in her throat as she thought of what it would be like to live without him. Though he had been there but a short time, he was already woven into the fabric of her life. She fell asleep in his arms every night, woke to his kisses in the morning. His clothes hung beside hers in the closet, his toothbrush rested beside hers in the medicine cabinet. When she was working, she was ever aware of his presence in the other room. More than once, a quick lunch break had turned into an hour spent in his arms.

She felt her tears flow harder, faster. She liked having him there, liked cooking for him, caring for him. Sometimes, at night, they sat side by side on the sofa and he listened to what she had written during the day. Occasionally, he made suggestions, or corrected a misconception about Lakota customs or traditions. How could she let him go, knowing she would never see him again?

"Su-san-nah, why do you weep?"

Looking up, she saw Black Wind standing in the doorway. Her gaze moved over him lovingly, admiring the smooth copper color of his skin, the ebony fall of his hair, the width of his shoulders, his long, long legs. How could she face the future without him?

"I'm not crying." She sniffed, blinking back her tears. "I thought you were going for a walk."

Tate Sapa sat down on the edge of the bed and touched his forefinger to the tear slipping down her cheek. "Are these tears of joy, then?"

Susannah shook her head. "You're going to go back, aren't you?" She sat up, drying her eyes with a corner of the bedspread. "Aren't you?"

He shook his head, his long black hair moving like a dark cloud about his shoulders. And then he blew out a sigh that seemed to come from the depths of his being. "No."

"No?" Exhilaration spread through her like summer sunlight, chasing away the shadows of despair, filling her with warmth. "What changed your mind?"

"You." With infinite tenderness, he cupped her face in his hands, his thumbs caressing her cheeks. "I started to go for a walk, Su-san-nah, but I missed you at my side and when I turned back, I saw your house, with the light shining through the windows, and I knew that my future was here, with you. I could not live without my heart, Su-san-nah. I could not live without my soul. Both belong to you."

She couldn't speak past the lump in her throat, knew that never before had she loved him so much.

He smiled faintly as he lowered one hand and placed it over the gentle swell of her belly. "Our child will need a father. I will stay here and teach him what it means to be a warrior. With your help, I will learn to read and write and I will do as Hehaka Luta said. I will record the history of the Lakota nation as I know it. I must go to the reservation and try to help my people, as my uncle said. Perhaps he will come with me." He gathered Susannah into his arms. "With us."

He gazed into Susannah's eyes, thinking how beautiful she was, how very much he loved her, needed her.

"Will you come with me, Su-san-nah?" he asked quietly. "Will you teach me the things I must learn to help my people?"

"You know I will," she replied fervently. "I'll go anywhere you want to go, teach you anything I can." She smiled up at him. "And what I don't know, I'll find out."

"When I saw you in my vision, I knew you would change my life," he said, his heart swelling with tenderness. "Truly, *Wakan Tanka* has blessed me."

"And me. Do you know how much I love you?"

"Perhaps you should show me?"

"I will," she promised. "Every day of our lives together."

"Starting today?"

"Starting right now," she murmured, and lifted her face for his kiss. In that kiss was the promise of a lifetime.

Epilogue

Susannah sat in the shade of the front porch, her six-month-old daughter, Carrie Lynn, sleeping peacefully in her arms. She was an adorable child, with a wealth of curly black hair, dark brown eyes, and a dimple in her chin.

Rocking gently, Susannah sighed with soul-deep contentment. It was a beautiful day in early spring and life had never been better. Her children were happy and healthy, the ranch was prospering, and she had just signed a new four-book contract with her publisher that included a sizable advance.

A noise in the yard drew her attention. She smiled as her gaze met Black Wind's. She had never gotten used to calling him Daniel; to her, he would always be Black Wind. Dressed in a pair of faded blue jeans, a black T-shirt, scuffed black boots, and a black Stetson, he looked devilishly handsome.

He stood in the midst of at least a dozen boys who ranged in age from four to ten, teaching them how to fletch an arrow. Her oldest son, Daniel, stood beside his father. He wore jeans and a T-shirt and a Stetson hat, just like his daddy's. There was a look of pride on his handsome young face as he listened to every word his father said. Her two-year-old son, Jason, was perched on Hehaka Luta's shoulders, his chin resting on the older man's head. Both boys had their father's straight black hair, dark eyes, and copper-hued skin.

The last five years had brought Susannah more happiness than she had ever dreamed possible. Shortly after Black Wind decided to stay in the present, they had moved to Hehaka Luta's ranch in South Dakota. They had completely remodeled the old house, putting on a new roof, modernizing the kitchen, adding on a new master bedroom with a built-in fireplace and a walk-in closet, and a new bathroom. They had built a new barn and replaced the old corrals, planted trees and flowers. Young Daniel and his friends often spent the night in the Lakota lodge in the backyard. A favorite game was cowboys and Indians; of course, it was hard to find someone willing to play the part of the cowboys. It went without saying that the Indians always won.

Susannah smoothed back a wisp of her daughter's hair. Somehow, amidst all the confusion of the move and the remodeling and childbirth, she had managed to write three historical romances; the last one, loosely based on her adventures in the past, had made *The New York Times* best-seller list.

Between them, Black Wind and Hehaka Luta had managed to bring hope and a small measure of prosperity to some of the families on the reservation. With the help of men from Pine Ridge, they raised cattle and horses, as well as a few head of buffalo for old times' sake. The cattle provided a steady supply of beef for the reservation; the horses were sold, with the profits being equally divided amongst the ranch hands. Susannah loved to watch Black Wind work with the wild ones, watch him gentle them with his hands and his voice. He rode with an innate grace and skill that was beautiful to watch, never breaking a colt's spirit, never losing his temper, never rushing a horse into something it wasn't ready for.

Every Saturday morning, boys and girls from the reservation came out to the ranch to spend the day. In the summer, Black Wind and Hehaka Luta often took the kids fishing or backpacking. Sometimes they put on a rodeo, or went for picnics in the meadow.

Black Wind had become a surrogate father to several fatherless boys who usually spent their summers and weekends at the ranch. They were in the process of adopting a three-year-old girl whose parents had been killed in a drunk-driving accident. They had taken in a teenage runaway who had sought shelter at the ranch for a night and never went home.

Once Black Wind had decided to stay in the future, he had adapted to the twentieth century with astonishing speed. They had been married in a private ceremony before they left L.A. so there would be no question later about Daniel's parentage or legitimacy. Susannah had taught Black Wind to read and write, and in his spare time, he was writing the history of his people as it had been told to him. He had picked up on local slang; she had learned to speak Lakota. Their oldest son spoke both languages fluently.

Black Wind had learned to drive a car, although he much preferred driving the big black four-by-four she had bought for him last Christmas. He could whip up a gourmet meal in the microwave, change a diaper, and, if necessary, do a load or two of wash when she had a deadline to meet.

Susannah felt a familiar tingle of happiness bubble up within her as Black Wind left the group and walked toward her. He was still the most handsome man she had ever seen. More than one teenage girl on the reservation thought herself madly in love with him. Susannah couldn't blame them. Impossible as it seemed, she loved him more deeply with every passing day. He was a loving husband and a wonderful father, ever patient with her, with their children, never too tired or too busy to answer their questions.

He worked tirelessly to make things better for his people, never turning anyone away, never refusing to give aid when it was asked. The young men looked to him for guidance. He counseled them about everything from schoolwork to their love lives and had helped more than one rebellious teenager get his life straightened out.

Susannah lifted her face for her husband's kiss, felt her heart swell with love as he caressed their daughter's cheek with infinite tenderness.

"Hehaka Luta is going to take the boys down to the river to swim," Black Wind remarked.

He leaned back against the porch rail, his ankles crossed, his arms folded over his chest, and she thought again how handsome he was with his black hat pulled low and a smile hovering over his lips.

"You keep an eye on our boys," Susannah said. Young Daniel could swim like a fish, but she still worried about Jason.

Black Wind raised one brow, silently rebuking her for thinking he would let anything happen to his sons. "Do you think you could put together about twenty sandwiches for us?"

"Oh, I'm sure that can be arranged. It'll cost you, though."

Black Wind nodded. It was an old and familiar game they played. "How much?"

"Oh, I don't know. I'll think of something. You can give me another kiss now, sort of like a down payment, and I'll figure out the rest later."

Grinning, Black Wind dropped to one knee in front of her. Cupping Susannah's face in his hands, he kissed her long and hard, his tongue sliding over her lower lip. Heat spiraled through her, hotter and brighter than the South Dakota sun.

"Think you could throw in some apples and chocolate chip cookies?" he asked, his eyes glinting with merriment.

"I think so," Susannah replied, breathless from his kiss, "but it's gonna cost you something extra."

"Another kiss?" Black Wind asked with a roguish grin.

"I was thinking of something a little more intimate," Susannah said, struggling to keep from laughing out loud. "Like a candlelit bubble bath after the kids are in bed and the lights are out."

"I'm willing to pay the price," Black Wind said with mock resignation. "No sacrifice is too great to make my boys happy."

"My hero," Susannah murmured. And knew that no truer words had ever been spoken.

MIDNIGHT FIRE

MADELINE BAKER

"Lovers of Indian Romance have a special place on their bookshelves for Madeline Baker!"
—*Romantic Times*

A half-breed who has no use for a frightened girl fleeing an unwanted wedding, Morgan thinks he wants only the money Carolyn Chandler offers him to guide her across the plains, but halfway between Galveston and Ogallala, where the burning prairie meets the endless night sky, he makes her his woman. There in the vast wilderness, Morgan swears to change his life path, to fulfill the challenge of his vision quest—anything to keep Carolyn's love.

_4056-5 $5.99 US/$6.99 CAN